Praise for
Ann Major

"Engaging characters, stories that thrill and delight,
shivering suspense and captivating romance.
Want it all? Read Ann Major."
—Nora Roberts,
New York Times bestselling author

"Compelling characters, intense,
fast-moving plots and snappy dialogue have made
Ann Major's name synonymous with the best
in contemporary romantic fiction."
—*Rendezvous*

Praise for
Marilyn Pappano

"Marilyn Pappano has been supplying tightly
written, visually satisfying action thrillers for a
decade now, and she just gets better and better.
A Pappano book is an automatic guarantee
of spiraling excitement and tension."
—*Romance Communications*

"Intense emotion and riveting drama
are hallmarks of Marilyn Pappano's work."
—*Romantic Times Magazine*

ANN MAJOR

has written forty novels for Silhouette Books, many of which have placed on national bestseller lists. She is a founding board member of the Romance Writers of America. She loves to write and considers her ability to do so a gift. Her hobbies include hiking in the mountains, sailing, reading, playing the piano, but most of all enjoying her family. She lives in Texas with her husband of many years and is the mother of three grown children. She has a master's degree from Texas A&M at Kingsville, Texas.

MARILYN PAPPANO

brings impeccable credentials to her writing career— a lifelong habit of gazing out windows, not paying attention in class, daydreaming and spinning tales for her own entertainment. The sale of her first book brought great relief to her family, proving that she wasn't crazy but was, instead, creative. Since that first book, she's sold more than forty others to various publishers and even a film production company, and she's come to love almost everything about writing, except that she would like a more reasonable boss to work for, which is pretty sad, since she works for herself. She writes in an office nestled among the oaks that surround her country home. In winter she stays inside with her husband and their four dogs, and in summer she spends her free time mowing the yard that never stops growing and daydreams about grass that never gets taller than two inches. You can write to her at P.O. Box 643, Sapulpa, OK, 74067-0643.

ANN MAJOR

MARILYN PAPPANO

FORGET ME NOT

Published by Silhouette Books

America's Publisher of Contemporary Romance

 SILHOUETTE BOOKS

ISBN 0-373-21716-1

by Request

FORGET ME NOT

Copyright © 2001 by Harlequin Books S.A.

The publisher acknowledges the copyright holders of the individual works as follows:

THE ACCIDENTAL BODYGUARD
Copyright © 1996 by Ann Major

MEMORIES OF LAURA
Copyright © 1993 by Marilyn Pappano

Visit Silhouette at www.eHarlequin.com

Printed in U.S.A.

CONTENTS

THE ACCIDENTAL BODYGUARD
by Ann Major   9

MEMORIES OF LAURA
by Marilyn Pappano   167

Dear Reader,

I am thrilled to be in *Forget Me Not* with
Marilyn Pappano, who is one of my favorite authors.

I believe in love and magic, in romance and wonder.
I believe there is more to life than meets the eye.

Why do we sometimes feel we know a person instantly?
Why do strange lands sometimes feel so familiar? Why
do some souls seem so much wiser than others? How
can we fall in love instantly? I once met a woman at a
conference and within a minute we were in tears. She
has been a dear friend ever since.

In my story I explore life and death and the boundaries
of love.

Enjoy,

Ann Major

The Accidental Bodyguard
by Ann Major

Prologue

"**C**handra is a conniving little do-goody bitch!" Holly said.

The rest of the family, which included, among others, Holly's parents, Ned and Sandra Moran, as well as her husband, Stinky Brown, and his brother, Hal, nodded in silent unison.

Lucas Broderick stopped scribbling on his legal pad and lifted his head to observe the young woman who spoke so vehemently against the cousin who was to gain control of the Moran fortune.

Holly Moran had chocolate-dark curls, an hourglass figure and a flare for drama a trial lawyer such as Lucas couldn't help but envy. She still had on the black sheath and the rope of pearls she had worn to her grandmother's funeral. But the dark eyes that locked with Lucas's were clear and lovely, unmarred by any trace of grief as she let him know that even though she was married, she was hot and...available.

A billion dollars was one hell of a turn-on. Well, almost a billion, give or take a hundred million or two.

Holly was as drop-dead gorgeous and just as drop-dead mean as his ex-wife, Joan, had been. Holly had that too-bright glow of a woman who hadn't yet settled comfortably into marriage. For half a second, Lucas, who was lonely for the kind of pleasure a woman like Holly could provide, was tempted.

Then his rational mind clicked in.

Been there. Done that.

His steel-gray eyes glittered as he gave her an ironic smile. *Been taken in by that act before, pretty lady.*

The last thing he needed was another Joan. His ex-wife had given him the shaft and taken him to the cleaners as nobody had since he'd been a green kid. As no woman ever would again.

He'd given his heart to Joan, and she'd ripped it out while it was still beating. She had taken most of his money, and she'd done a number on their sons.

His enemies said he had no heart. Who needed one?

Holly's silky voice grew more vicious, not that she was addressing anybody in particular. "I tell you her do-goody act was all fake. How could Gram have left everything to her?"

"Not quite everything," Uncle Henry dared to object. "Gertie did leave each of us two—"

Of the four voices that shouted him down, Holly's was the softest, and the angriest.

"She might as well have! You may be able to get by on a lousy million or two since you're content to live in that miserable unair-conditioned shack on your godforsaken farm like a hermit."

For three hours the Morans had been ranting about Gertrude Moran's will in the ranch house's richly paneled library while Lucas, their legal hired gun, had reposed in a deep leather armchair, listening impassively as he watched the clouds move in and thicken against the distant horizon. Occasionally he wrote down a note or two on his yellow pad, which he would probably never so much as glance at again.

Much had been written about the rugged, legendary lawyer who was now sprawled in the library's most comfortable chair in scuffed boots, faded jeans and a crisp white shirt. But the majority of the press coverage was false.

Lucas could have told the Morans a thing or two about poverty, more than they wanted to know, more than he wanted to remember. For he had been born in India to an impoverished missionary. His father, a zealot and an idealist, had forced his family to live in the same dangerous, squalid slums as the people he helped. Then the old man had given all his love and attention to the impoverished Indians.

Left alone to fend for himself in dangerous neighborhoods, Lucas had been beaten by jeering gangs of bullies more times than he could count, his meager possessions stolen, his emerging male self-confidence shattered. His father's response had been to feel sorry for the young criminals and to tell Lucas to turn the other cheek. Lucas had sworn that when he grew up he would be the fighter and the taker. He would hit hard. Others could turn the other cheek.

But Lucas's real roots were something he worked very hard to conceal. He didn't want anybody to know that he harbored a deep-rooted feeling of abandonment and poor self-esteem. He wanted people to think he was tough and cruel—a winner. So he manipulated his public image as ruthlessly as he manipulated the minds of jurors when he made them believe the most preposterous arguments, or as easily as he convinced clients like the Morans they couldn't possibly get what they wanted without him. His profession was a high-stakes game, which he always played to win.

Texas journalists loved to quote him. "God may have created the world, but the Devil put the spin on it." "Ten thousand times more crimes have been committed in the name of love than in the name of hate." "No good deed goes unpunished." These cynical if less than original statements, which seemed to sum up his philosophy about life, had appeared in dozens of profiles of him in Texas magazines and newspapers.

He was widely hated and only grudgingly admired. Flamboyant quotes were hardly Lucas's only talent. He was a superb athlete, and he excelled in mathematics. He automatically converted everything into numbers—especially his time, that being to him the most valuable of all commodities because, once it was gone, it was gone forever.

Since all Lucas's clients bombarded him with tales of woe, he usually found these long preliminary consultations tiresome, especially if he was expected to fake compassion. But the Morans' tale was too bizarre and their threatened fortune too huge for their story not to compel his full attention. He was struggling to pretend sympathy. What the hell? He'd sold himself before for a lot less than a billion.

While Holly attacked Stinky for always taking Beth's side and not seeing her as a threat before today, Lucas reviewed his notes.

The family's do-goody dark horse, a Miss Bethany Ann—he'd made a scribble that she wanted to be called Chandra—had come from out of nowhere and galloped away with the family fortune.

Both the girl and her story intrigued him. He furrowed his black brows as he tried to read his nearly illegible scrawl.

Bulk of fortune goes into charitable foundation. Complete control given to Miss Bethany Ann.

Weird little girl. Prematurely born in Calcutta when her mother and father were on a round-the-world tour.

India—so he and she had been born in the same hellhole.

An oddball from birth, she was claustrophobic. She was also a vegetarian who refused to eat beef. Never fit into the family. When she was two and had begun to talk, she'd told her family that her name was Chandra, not Beth. She had babbled frantically of memories of another life and of belonging to another, poorer family. When she grew older she said her enraged older sister, in an effort to save the family from shame, had shut her inside a box and buried her alive beneath a house when she found out Chandra had gotten pregnant by the town's local bad boy whom she loved instead of her betrothed.

Under hypnosis Chandra had spoken in a foreign language that a language expert at the University of Texas had identified as an obscure dialect of Hindi. Upon investigation, a family in a remote area of India where this dialect was spoken had been found. Names, dates and facts of this family's history exactly fit Chandra's story.

Gertrude and all the Morans had flown to India. A seven-year-old Chandra had led everybody to a ruined house and insisted they dig up a brick floor. Chandra's former sister, a woman by then in her mid-fifties, had burst into guilty tears when a crumbling box with the bones of a young girl and those of her unborn child had been discovered, and Chandra had accused her of burying her alive. The grave of the dead girl's bad-boy lover was visited next. Apparently he had stepped in front of a train and had been sliced to death shortly after he'd been told that the dead girl had run away.

Weird. Lucas, who knew more than he wanted to about India and reincarnation, had underlined the word three times. This girl, Bethany, Chandra, whatever, had ~~wanted~~ to share the Moran money with those less fortu~~nate~~

derstandably alarmed, the entire Moran clan had been determined to erase the inappropriate "memories" and eradicate such inappropriate attitudes. They had taken the little girl to countless doctors, psychologists, and finally to a hypnotist who was no help at all, since he had said this looked like a genuine case of reincarnation if ever there was one. He pointed out that Chandra's claustrophobia was perfectly natural under such circumstances.

Gertrude Moran had fired the hypnotist on the spot and refused to take the child to any more "charlatans." After Bethany's parents had been killed in a car accident, the old lady had done everything in her power to make the girl forget her "former life" and mold her into a true Moran. But the impossible child had been kicked out of every fancy boarding school she'd been sent to, and the old lady had had to take charge of the girl's education herself. Gertrude had taken the child everywhere and taught her about investments, real estate, bonds, ranching and stocks.

But apparently the shape of Bethany's personality had been as difficult as the old lady's. Not that the girl hadn't appeared gentle and loving and generous and biddable. But no matter how intelligent and receptive she had seemed on the surface, her character had been as true to its own shape as the most uncarvable stone. She continued to sympathize with those less fortunate than she. At the age of twelve she had her name legally changed to Chandra. As she grew older she had a tendency to date bad boys—because she said she was looking for the man she had loved in her former life. When she was eighteen and on the brink of marriage to Stinky Brown, a slick charmer Gertrude Moran had considered totally unsuitable, she and her grandmother had had a disastrous quarrel. Chandra had broken off with Stinky and run away without a dime, never to be seen or spoken of or to again.

Until now.

For a fleeting moment Lucas felt an unwanted respect for a girl who could stand up to Gertrude Moran and walk away from such a huge fortune. Then he reminded himself there was no such thing as selfless good, that somebody always paid.

Lucas's last words on the yellow page were Holly's. "The conniving little do-goody bitch. I tell you her do-goody act was all fake."

Could be, pretty lady. Fortune hunters and con artists damn sure came in all sorts of interesting shapes and varieties. But this kid with the innocent face and the freckles and the masses of golden hair was damn good.

Lucas lifted a picture of a seven-year-old girl standing before a hut in India with her "other family." Next he looked at a grainy black-and-white newspaper picture of her standing beside some look-alike heiress buddy named Cathy Calderon. They both wore ragged jeans, steel-toed work boots and hard hats as they posed in front of a concrete blockhouse one of her church groups had recently completed for a Mexican family.

Couldn't tell much other than the fact that Bethany Chandra damn sure had long legs and a cute butt.

Been there. Long legs and a cute butt had cost him big time. Joan had *started* by taking half of his estate. She'd won child support, lots of it. Then she'd dumped the boys back on him.

His housekeeper had quit the first day, shaking both fists and screaming, "Your sons are savages, Mr. Broderick. If you don't pack them off to a military school, and soon, you'll be sorry."

No housekeeper he'd hired since had lasted more than a week, and his once elegant house was a shambles.

Forget Joan and the housekeeper problem.

The intriguing fortune hunter with the intriguing backside was living in an impoverished barrio and running a huge, privately endowed, highly successful, nonprofit organization called Casas de Cristo, which built houses for the poor all over northern Mexico. She had tribes of wealthy philanthropists who trusted her enough to donate their millions. She had church groups and college kids from all over the United States providing money and free labor.

Missionaries were a tiresome, impractical breed. He should know. His father had played at saving the world. What the hell? The more starving Indians he'd fed, the more babies they'd produced with more mouths to be fed. One thing was sure. The old man had damn sure failed to provide for his own sons. Lucas had had to work his tail off to get a start at the good life.

Thus, Lucas was mildly surprised that he felt such distaste at the thought of defaming this girl when such an immense fortune and therefore his own lucrative fee were at stake. All he had to do was drum up a few witnesses to say that Bethany was cheating her benefactors by building her houses for less than she said or that she was taking bribes from the poor families selected to have houses built for them.

He loathed do-gooders. Why should it bother him that there wasn't a shred of evidence that she was anything other than what she appeared to be—that rare and highly bizarre individual like his father who actually wanted to help other people?

Odd that he didn't particularly relish having to prove that Gertrude Moran had been senile when she'd drawn up her new will, either.

But that last part would be easier.

A flash of movement flickered across the golden urn that sat in the center of a library table. The urn, conspicuously located but now forgotten, was surrounded by stacks of legal documents, coffee cups, wineglasses, beer bottles and half-eaten sandwiches. Lucas glanced from it out the window, where he got a double surprise.

The sky was now an eerie green. A dark man in a black Stetson sat in a blue van parked beside his Lincoln. After studying the storm clouds and the newcomer for a tense moment, Lucas relaxed, dismissing them both as of no immediate importance.

Not that the Morans had noticed either the clouds or the van. And they had quit all pretense of interest in the urn that contained Gertrude Moran's ashes immediately after the reading of her will, at which point they'd started hunting their lawyer.

Fortunately Lucas had been close by in San Antonio visiting Pete, his older brother, who was a doctor.

Lucas leaned forward in his chair and lifted the urn with his left hand. Whatever he had seen there had vanished. All he saw now was his own brooding dark face and his thick tumble of unruly black hair. Turning the urn carelessly with his other hand, he glanced at the portrait of the woman whose ashes he held.

Gertrude Moran's sharp, painted eyes glinted at him with an expression of don't-you-dare-try-to-mess-with-me-you-young-upstart. In old age with her soft snowy hair, she had remained a handsome woman. Holly had told Lucas that the portrait had been finished less than a month ago. Lucas found it hard to imagine someone who looked so forceful and intelligent not knowing exactly what she was doing when she'd drawn up her will.

Gertrude Moran had been shrewd all her life. The original Moran fortune had been in land and oil. She'd diversified, doubling her fortune while other oil people went broke. In an age when most rich people were stuffy and dull, she had been a hoot. The newspapers had been full of her stunts.

Lucas lowered his gaze. Well, she'd damn sure stirred

the family brew by secretly changing all the ingredients in her will and leaving only a few million to these spoiled bastards.

"Well, Mr. Broderick, can you get us our money back or not?" Holly leaned forward and issued another invitation with her dark, glowing eyes and a display of cleavage.

Been there, he reminded himself, but he dropped the urn with a clang.

Stinky jumped as if he was afraid Gertrude's spirit would spring out of the urn like a bad genie. A hush fell over the room, and for a long moment it did seem, even to Lucas, that those keen, painted eyes brightened with mischief and that some bold, alien presence had invaded the room.

He almost felt like clanging the urn again to break the spell.

His hard face tensed. "Can I get the money?" He leafed through the will. "It's a crapshoot. It's not too difficult to break a will that involves leaving one family member an entire fortune at the expense of the others. But charitable foundations with iron-clad, carefully thought out legal documents such as these are tricky, especially when the foundation will contribute substantially to several powerhouse charities who have teams of lawyers on their payroll."

"But Beth bamboozled Gram into giving her everything—"

"Not quite everything. Your grandmother did adequately provide for you. At least most judges would see it that way. Technically your cousin won't actually be inheriting the fortune, Ms. Moran. She would merely be managing the foundation."

"For a huge salary?"

"A six-figure annual salary for overseeing such a vast enterprise would hardly be out of line."

"Beth is a thief and a criminal."

Lucas felt an insane urge to defend the absent heiress.

"Those are serious charges that might not be so easily proven. From the picture you've drawn of Beth—a goody-two-shoes Samaritan building houses for the poor in Mexico—it might be difficult and unpleasant to convince twelve disinterested people she wouldn't sincerely honor your grandmother's last wishes. If she's a fake, we've got a chance. But if she's not—" He paused. "Unfortunately juries and judges have a tendency to favor do-gooders. I suggest that you talk to your cousin. Try to persuade her it would be in her best interests to divide the money between all of you."

"You have no idea how stubborn she is."

"Maybe one of you will come up with a better idea."

A pair of black-lashed, olive-bright eyes set in a gorgeous face met his, and Lucas was chilled when he sensed a terrible hatred and an implacable will.

The black clouds were rolling in from the west. The mood in the library had darkened, as well. Other faces turned toward him, and they were equally hard.

Lucas almost shuddered. No wonder the saint had run.

Strangely, his feelings of empathy for the girl intensified. He tried to fight the softening inside him, but it was almost as though he was on her side instead of the Morans'.

Ridiculous. He couldn't afford such misplaced sympathies.

"If you take the case, how much will you charge?" Holly demanded.

"If I lose—nothing."

"And—if you win?"

"I would be working on a contingency basis, of course—"

"How much?"

"Forty percent. Plus expenses."

"Of nearly a billion dollars! What? Are you mad? Why, that's highway robbery."

"No, Ms. Moran, it's my fee. I play for keeps—all or nothing. If you want me, and if I agree to take the case, I swear to you that if there is any way to destroy your cousin's name and her claim to your fortune, I'll find it. I am very thorough and utterly merciless when it comes to matters of this nature. I'll study these documents and send my P.I. to Mexico to investigate Casas de Cristo and see what dirt I can dig up on her down there. She's bound to have enemies. All we have to do is find people who'll talk about her and get them talking. Fan the flames, so to speak."

Lucas began gathering documents and stuffing them into his briefcase. "Just so you can reach me anytime—" He scribbled his unlisted home phone number and handed it to Stinky. "I'll let myself out."

Lightning streaked to the ground. Almost immediately a sharp cracking sound shook the house. Wind and torrents of rain began to batter the windows.

The drought was over.

But none of the ranchers who had prayed for rain rejoiced. They were watching Lucas's large brown hands violently snap the locks on his briefcase as he prepared to go.

The mood in the library had grown as ugly and dangerous as the storm outside. The Morans were in that no-win situation so many people involved in litigation find themselves. They were wondering whom they disliked the most—their adversary, the family saint, or their own utterly ruthless but highly reputed attorney.

One minute Lucas was bursting out of the library doors into the foyer, intent on nothing except driving to San Antonio as fast as possible. In the next minute, Lucas felt as if he'd been sucked blindly into a cyclone and hurled into an entirely new reality in which an incredibly powerful force gripped him, body and soul. In which all his dark bitternesses miraculously dissolved. Even his fierce ambition to work solely for money was gone.

Unsuperstitious by nature, Lucas did not believe in psychic powers or ghosts. But this otherworldly experience was a very pleasurable feeling.

Dangerously pleasurable. Almost sexual, and dangerously familiar somehow.

All his life he'd been driven by anger and greed or by the quest for power.

And suddenly those drives were gone. What he really wanted was in this room.

He stopped in midstride. His huge body whirled; his searing gray eyes searched every niche and darkened corner of the hall.

The mysterious presence was very near. As he stood there, he continued to feel the weird, overpowering connection.

She was as afraid of this thing as he was.

She?

For no reason at all Lucas was reminded of the times he and his brother, Pete, had hidden together as children from the Indian slum bullies, not speaking to one another but each profoundly aware of the other.

"Hello?" Lucas's deep querying drawl held a baffled note.

He held his breath. For the first time he noted how eerily quiet the foyer was. How the presence of death seemed to linger like an unwanted guest.

How the hall with its pale green wallpaper was heavy with the odor of roses past their prime. How these swollen blossoms, no doubt leftovers from Gertrude Moran's memorial service, were massed everywhere—in vases, in Meissen bowls. How several white petals had fallen onto the polished tabletops and floors. Holly had shown him the old lady's rose garden and had told him she had loved roses.

Lucas's senses were strangely heightened as he stood frozen outside the library doors, struggling to figure out what was happening to him. He inhaled the sickly-sweet, funereal scent of the dying roses. He listened to each insistent tick of the vermeil clock.

The summer sunlight was fading. Much of the white and gilt furniture was cast in shadow. The threadbare Aubusson rug at his feet had a forest green border.

When he saw the closet with its door standing partially ajar, he felt strangely drawn to it. Oddly enough, when he stepped toward it, the connection was instantly broken. He was free.

All his old bitterness and cynicism immediately regained him.

He bolted out of the Moran mansion faster than before.

One

"Kill!"

Sweet P.'s earsplitting voice blasted inside Lucas's black Lincoln as he raced toward the hospital. The shrieks seemed to slice open his skull and shred the tender tissues of his inner ear as handily as a meat cleaver.

There should be a law against a three-year-old screaming in an automobile speeding sixty miles per hour on a freeway.

Just as there should be a law against a kid being up at five in the morning experimenting with her older cousin's handcuffs.

Just as there should be a law against Peppin owning a pair of the damn things in the first place.

"You get off here," Pete suddenly said as they were about to pass the exit ramp.

Tires screamed as Lucas swerved across two lanes onto the down ramp.

"Mommy! Carol!" Patti yelled between sobs.

Too bad Mommy was out of town and Carol, her sitter, had called in sick.

Patti shook her hands violently, rattling the handcuffs.

Lucas's temples thudded with equal violence.

It was Monday morning. Six o'clock to be exact. Lucas felt like hell. Usually he never dreamed, but last night a weird nightmare about a girl in trouble had kept him up most of the night. In the dream, he had loved the girl, and they'd been happy for a while. Then she'd been abducted, and he'd found himself alone in a misty landscape of death and stillness and ruin. At first he'd been terrified she was dead. Then she'd made a low moan, and he had known that if he didn't save her, he would lose everything that mattered to him in the world. He'd tracked her through a maze of ruined slums only to find her and have her utter a final low-throated cry and die as he lifted her into his arms. He'd bolted out of his bed, his body drenched in sweat, his heart racing, his sense of tragic loss so overwhelmingly profound he couldn't sleep again.

The girl's ethereally lovely face and voluptuous body had seemed branded into his soul. He'd gotten up and tried to sketch her on his legal notepad. Sleek and slim, she had that classy, rich-girl look magazine editors pay so dearly for. She had high cheekbones, a careless smile, yellow hair and sparkling blue eyes. He'd torn the sheet from the pad and thrown it away, only to sketch another.

Due in court at ten, Lucas had intended to be halfway to Corpus Christi by now. Instead Pete, Sweet P., the boys and he were rushing to the emergency room, where Pete was on call. Some girl had overdosed, and a doctor was needed STAT, medical jargon for fast. Gus, an emergency-room security guard, had volunteered to remove the handcuffs if Pete brought Sweet P. when he came.

Disaster had struck right after Lucas had loaded the luggage and boys into the Lincoln and Pete and Sweet P. had gotten into Pete's Porsche. The Porsche wouldn't start because *someone* had left an interior light on all night.

Someone had also removed Lucas's jumper cables from his trunk. And that same mysterious *someone* had also lost the key to Peppin's handcuffs. Thus, Lucas and the boys had to drive Pete and Sweet P. to the ER before they could head for home.

Why was Lucas even surprised? His personal life had been chaos ever since the boys had moved in. For starters, they must have dialed every nine-hundred number in America, because his phone bill had run into the thousands of dollars the first month they'd lived with him.

Lucas put on his right turn signal when he saw the blue neon sign for San Antonio City Memorial and swerved into the covered parking lot for the hospital's emergency room. With a swoosh of tires and a squeal of brakes, Lucas stopped the big car too suddenly, startling Sweet P. into silence. Her watery blue eyes looked addled as she took in the blazing lights of the three ambulances and the squad car.

Lucas's expression was grim as he lowered the automobile windows, cut the motor and gently gathered Sweet P. into his arms so Pete would be free to check his patient.

As he got out of the Lincoln with the squirming toddler, Lucas gave Peppin and Montague a steely glance. "You two be good."

"No problem." Peppin's sassy grin was all braces. Huge mirrored sunglasses hid his mischievous eyes.

As always Montague, who resented authority, pretended to ignore him and kept his nose in a book entitled *Psychic Vampires*.

The emergency room was such a madhouse, Lucas forgot the boys. Apparently there'd been a fight at the jail. Three prisoners lay on stretchers. A man with hairy armpits and a potbelly wearing only gray Jockey shorts with worn-out elastic was standing outside a treatment room screaming drunkenly that doctors made too much money and he was going to get his lawyer if he didn't get treated at once. In another room an obese woman was pointing to her right side, saying she hurt and that her doctor had spent a fortune on tests and that she was deathly allergic to some kind of pink medicine and that her medical records were in Tyler on microfilm if anybody cared about them. Six telephones buzzed constantly. Doctors were dictating orders to exhausted nurses.

In the confusion it took Lucas a while to find Gus. Meanwhile Sweet P. was so fascinated by the drunk and the fat lady, she stopped crying. Enthroned on the counter of the nurses' station, she was having the time of her life. A plump redheaded nurse was feeding her pizza and candy and cola, which she gobbled greedily while Gus rummaged in a toolbox for the correct pair of bolt cutters.

"Now you hold still, little princess," Gus said.

Suddenly Pete's frantic voice erupted from an examining room down the hall.

"She's gone!"

Lucas left Sweet P. with Gus and raced to the examining room, where an IV dangled over an empty gurney with blood-streaked sheets. Bloody footprints drunkenly crisscrossed the white-tiled floor.

"She has little feet," Lucas whispered inanely, lifting a foot when he realized he was standing squarely on top of two toe prints.

Pete yelled, "Nurse!"

A plump nurse in a blue scrub suit, wearing a plastic ID, ambled inside.

"Oh, my God!"

Pete thumbed hurriedly through the missing patient's chart, reading aloud.

"No name. A Jane Doe. Brought in by a truck driver who found her hitchhiking on the highway. Tested positive for a multitude of legal and illegal drugs. Head injury. Stitches put in by plastic surgeon. Contusions on wrists and ankles. Disruptive. Belligerent. Very confused. Amnesia. Possible subdural hematoma. Refused CAT scan because she went insane when we put her face inside the machine. Claustrophobic."

"What does all that mean?" Lucas demanded.

"Not good. She's high as a kite, badly confused."

"Doctor—" The nurse's whisper was anxious. "A while ago someone called about her. Said he was family. Sounded very concerned. Described a girl who could have been this girl. Sammy's new, and I'm afraid she told him we'd admitted a girl matching her description. The caller said he was coming right over. But when Sammy told the patient that a family member was on his way, she became very agitated."

"Get security on this immediately," Pete ordered. "This young woman is in no condition to be out of bed. Check the entrances. The parking lots. In her condition she couldn't have gone far."

Fire and ice.

Chilled to the bone, burning up at the same time, the barefoot girl shivered convulsively in the parking lot. Her thoughts kept slipping and losing direction like a sailboat in rough waves.

She didn't know who she was.

Or where she was.

Or who wanted to kill her.

When that freckled nurse had asked her her name, terrible images had rolled through her tired brain.

A name? Something as specific as a name?

"Oh, dear God," had been all she could whisper brokenly.

She could remember the van rolling, catching fire. She kept seeing a gray face, its hideous vacant eyes peering at her through plastic.

Pain and terror shuddered through the injured girl.

They knew who she was, and they were coming after her.

Her head throbbed. When she tried to walk, her gait was wide. Her feet felt like they didn't quite touch the ground, and she had the sensation she was about to topple backward.

Crouching low outside the entrance, the girl had tracked blood down the concrete steps because slivers of glass were still embedded in her heels. Her torn, blood-encrusted jeans and hospital gown clung to her perspiring body like a wet shroud.

Vaguely she remembered someone cutting her red T-shirt and her bra off. Patches of yellow hair were glued to her skull. Dark shadows ringed her blue eyes. She kept swallowing against a dry metallic taste in her mouth. She kept pushing at the loose bandage that hid the row of stitches that were yellow with antiseptic. What was left of a heparin lock oozed blood down her arm.

She had to get out of here.

But how? When ambulances and cops were everywhere? When those two curious boys in the black Lincoln kept jumping up and down and staring restlessly out of the car.

Feeling muddled, she shut her eyes. Her entire life consisted of a few hours and less than half a dozen foggy memories that made no sense. It was as if she was a child again, and there were monsters in the dark.

Only the monsters were real.

She remembered huge headlights blinding her as she'd thrown herself in front of them. She remembered the frightened trucker, lifting her and demanding angrily, "Girlie, what were you trying to do?'' Next she remembered the hospital.

The two boys in the Lincoln must've grown bored with leaning out the windows because all of a sudden they slithered into the front seat like a pair of eels. They leaned over the dashboard, fighting for control of the radio, holding the seek button down through several stations until they came to rap music. Gleefully they slapped their right hands together, turned the volume up and settled back to listen.

''Boys! That's way too loud!''

A stout security officer edged between the girl and the Lincoln. The boy with the slicked-back ponytail and the shark-tooth necklace quirked his head out the window again. When his huge mirrored glasses glinted her way, she was afraid he'd spot her.

''Sure, Officer,'' he said, clumsily faking a respectful attitude as he thumped the dash with his hand in time to the beat.

The officer lingered a minute or two till the volume was low enough. Only then did he stride away. When he had gone the boy leaned out of the car again, hand still thumping the side of the car as he stared fiercely in the direction of her shadowy hiding place. Twelve, thirteen maybe, he had the surly good looks of a wannabe bad-boy.

The fingers stopped thumping. He yanked off his mirrored glasses and wiggled so far out of the car, he nearly fell.

She heard more sirens in the distance as his gray eyes zeroed in on her.

Dear God.

His sulkily smirking lips mouthed, ''Hi.'' He started to wave.

She put a finger to her lips in warning as two more squad cars, sirens blaring, rushed into the lot. A dozen officers with hand-held radios jumped out.

She shrank more deeply into the shadows, her pleading eyes clutching the smiling boy's as a fat cop shuffled over to the Lincoln.

"You been here awhile, kid?"

The sassy smile faded. He gave the cop a sullen nod.

"You seen anything suspicious?"

Sulky silence. Then slowly the black ponytail bobbed. "Yeah." He pointed toward the alley at the opposite end of the parking lot. "I saw…a girl with a—a bandage on her head. Way over there."

The cops shouted to the others and they took off in a dead gallop. When they had disappeared, the boys slapped their right hands together.

Then, ever so cautiously, they eased a door open and scuttled toward her. Hovering over her, their dark narrow faces seemed to waver in and out of focus.

They were so alike they could have passed for twins. Not that they were trying to pass. The taller and skinnier of the two had shorter hair, wire-rimmed glasses and pressed jeans. The huskier kid with the ponytail and the gold earring wore rumpled black clothes. A vicious shark tooth dangled from his necklace.

When they leaned down, their hands, shaking, a whirring sound beat inside her ears and made her feel so dizzy and sick, she almost passed out.

She barely felt their hands as they gently circled her. Or heard their frightened whispers.

"We have to help her."

"But she's hurt. Look at all those bruises, and her eyes—"

"And her feet! We should take her into the hospital so Uncle Pete—"

"No!" She grabbed their arms, her broken nails digging into their skin, her huge eyes pleading.

"Can't you see how scared she is?" a young voice

croaked hoarsely. "Somebody bad might be after her. We gotta save her."

"What'll Dad do?"

The whirring inside her head got louder. Half-carrying, half-dragging her, they crawled with her to the car and made a bed of lumpy pillows and blankets for her on the floorboard of the back seat. The boys unfolded a blanket and covered her, whispering that if she was quiet they could smuggle her home and hide her in their room until she got well.

The girl lay there, trembling uncontrollably, terrified of the claustrophobic feeling she had because the blanket was over her face.

Only vaguely was she aware of footsteps hurrying, of car doors slamming, of men's voices talking low in the front seat, of a little girl's excited shouting. "See there! Got 'em off!"

"Oh—big deal."

But the girl in the back seat instantly registered a man's beautiful, gravelly drawl. "Peppin, the officer told me you helped them."

There was something so familiar about the sound of his voice. Something so warm. It seemed to resonate in her soul.

She knew him. She had loved him. Somewhere. Some time.

"Yeah, Dad. Peppin really helped 'em," the older boy said.

"Shut up, Monty!" Peppin slugged his brother.

"Hey!"

"Who are all the cops looking for anyway, Dad?"

"Some young girl got high on drugs and had a wreck. It's a very serious situation. She could die without proper medical attention."

The girl felt hot all over. Tears pooled in her eyes.

"Die?" Peppin croaked as a key turned in the ignition. His young face bleached a sickly white, he stared at his tearful hideaway.

She shook her head at him, tears escaping under her eyelids.

Peppin sucked in a long, nervous breath. "So—Uncle Pete, what sort of treatment would she need?"

"Hmm?"

"Your patient?"

Peppin bombarded his uncle with questions, demanding specific details.

Once again Peppin's father praised his son in that deep melodious drawl of his—this time for his intellectual curiosity.

The man's low voice was husky and somehow devastatingly familiar, and yet at the same time it lulled her. She wanted to go on listening to it, for nothing seemed left in the whole world but that voice wrapping around her.

Who was he? Why did she feel she knew him?

She was too tired for thought, and her eyelids grew heavy again, fluttering down and then rising as she fought to stay awake.

She slept soundly for the first time since the van had rolled and the driver had chased her into those blinding headlights.

She slept, knowing she was safe, because the man with the beautiful voice was near.

Two

Bluish flashes ricocheted in the boys' bedroom.

It had rained like this the night the blue van had rolled and burned.

What van? Where? Why?

The girl lay rigidly awake, longing for Lucas as she listened to the surf and to the sharp cracking sounds of thunder. Torrents of rain beat a savage tattoo against the bedroom window.

He was two doors down from her. Peacefully asleep in his huge bed, no doubt. Unafraid of the storm and blissfully unaware of the strange woman sleeping in his sons' bedroom closet.

He might as well have been on the moon.

She stretched restlessly, almost wishing she was as happily unconscious of him as he was of her. But she needed him because he made her feel safe.

Why did her demons always come alive when she closed her eyes in the dark?

She hated feeling shut in and alone, and she felt she was—even though the closet door was louvered and her darling boys were just outside, snugly tucked beneath quilts in their bunk beds, oblivious to the storm and her fears. She lay stiffly on her hidden pallet in their huge closet and stared at the ceiling, watching the lightning that flashed through the louvers and caused irregular patterns of blue light to dance across the walls and hanging clothes.

Her strength had returned rapidly, but, so far, not her memory. Vague illusive images from her past seemed to flicker at the edges of her mind like the lightning, their brief flares so brilliant they blinded her before they vanished into pitch blackness.

Her entire world had become Lucas Broderick's coldly modern mansion perched on its bluff above Corpus Christi Bay. But more than the mansion's high white walls and polished marble floors; more than its winding corridors and spiral staircases intrigued her. With every day that passed, she had become more fascinated by Lucas Broderick himself.

From almost that first moment when she had awakened in his sons' closet to their rush of adolescent chatter, they had made her aware of *him*.

"What if Dad finds her?"

An audible gasp and then terrified silence as if that prospect was too awful to contemplate.

"You'd better not let him—stupid."

She had opened her eyes and found their fearful, curious faces peering eagerly at her. She'd had no memory of who they were or how she'd gotten here.

But she'd quickly learned that they were Lucas's adorable sons, and that they looked endearingly like him.

"She's awake."

"Told you she'd live."

"We've got to feed her something or she'll starve like your gerbil."

"What's your name?"

Her name? Blue lights flickered, and she shook her head and made a low moan.

"Pete said she had amnesia, dummy."

Pete? Who was Pete?

"You hungry?"

"Maybe...some broth," she whispered.

Their heads swiveled and they stared at each other in round-eyed consternation as if they'd never heard the word. "Broth?"

"Then water," she managed weakly.

That started a quarrel over who got to fetch it, each of them wanting to.

For ten long days and longer nights those two wonderful boys had fought many battles over the privilege of nursing her. They had checked medical books out of the library. They had cleaned her wounds and doctored them with medicine from Lucas's huge marble bathroom. They had painstakingly picked the slivers of glass from the soles of her feet with tweezers, plunking the jagged bits into a metal bowl. They had soaked her feet in pails of hot water, and she could almost walk without limping.

They took turns pretending to be sick themselves so that one of them could stay home from school with her. They had given her the antibiotics they tricked their uncle into prescribing for them. For the first few nights they'd coaxed their father into buying and cooking the few foods she could keep down—chicken broth, Jell-O and boiled vegetables, which they'd smuggled up to her.

At first she'd been too weak and ill to worry about the way her presence in their home had forced them to deceive their father. But as she'd grown stronger and more attached to her lively, affectionate nurses, she blamed herself for their burgeoning talent at duplicity. Nursing her wasn't the worst of it. They were hard at work on a covert project they called Operation Nanny.

The boys didn't want Lucas to hire a new nanny. "Because," as Peppin explained, "we couldn't fool one of those nosy old bags so easy as Dad. A nanny'd be up here all the time—she'd probably find you the first day."

Thus, every time Lucas informed the boys of a home interview for a prospective nanny, Peppin, who could mimic Lucas's voice to a T, phoned the woman and told her the job had been filled.

At first the girl had been too ill and too grateful and too terrified of being thrown out of the house to care, but now she felt stricken that she had become a corrupting influence on their characters.

Although Peppin and Montague bickered incessantly, they could be an incredible team. During the day, when Lucas was at work, the boys gave her the run of his huge house, with its soaring ceilings and skylights and views of Corpus Christi Bay. One wall of his bedroom was made entirely of glass. Sometimes she would step out onto his balcony and let the tangy sea air ruffle her hair.

Sometimes she showered in his pink marble bathroom that had both an immense enclosed shower and a bathtub as big as a small swimming pool. Sometimes she spent a languid hour buried beneath mountains of foamy bubbles in his tub. Sometimes she would pick out old clothes from his abundant closets to wear. Always she would linger in his room, studying his things, running his slim black comb through her hair and brushing her teeth with his yellow toothbrush. She would open his drawers and run her fingertips over his undershirts and cuff links, marveling that one man could have so much of everything. But what she loved best was lying in his bed and hugging his pillow to her stomach and imagining him there beside her, holding her. She gathered flowers from his gardens and arranged them in crystal vases everywhere, taking special pains with those that she left on the white table beside his bed. It pleased her when he picked a pale yellow rose from that vase and pinned it to the black lapel of his three-piece suit one morning before he rushed to his office.

She tried to think of ways to repay him for all that his boys had done for her. The endless stark hallways of his beautiful house had been strewn with everything from rumpled clothes, baseball bats, soccer gear and Rollerblades to newspapers when she'd arrived. Dirty dishes had overflowed from the white-tiled kitchen counters onto the ebony dining room table.

When she'd gotten better, she'd convinced the boys that maybe their father wouldn't be so anxious to hire a nanny or a housekeeper if he didn't feel the need for one so strongly. She had made a game of cleaning the house.

While they picked up, she would lie on a couch or a chair, perusing the tattered album that contained black-and-white pictures of Lucas's childhood in India, wondering why he'd looked so unhappy as a boy. Wondering why the pictures of India especially fascinated her even as she prodded the boys to pick up.

Every time Peppin or Monty touched something, the rule was that they had to put it where it belonged. She began talking them through the preparation of simple meals, using the cans in the pantry and the frozen dinners in the refrigerator, so that Lucas always came home to a hot meal. At first they complained bitterly, but she just laughed and tried to motivate them by telling them they were learning basic survival skills.

Mostly they went along with her projects because she lavished attention on them. She walked with them on the beach, threw horseshoes with them and played games. The only thing she refused to do was to let them lead her into the tunnel that wound from the garage under the house down to the beach. When they had unlocked the doors to that weird, underground passage, and she had smelled the mustiness of the place, she had felt as if the black gloom was pressing in on her and she was being suffocated.

Ghastly minutes had crawled by before the feeling of claustrophobia subsided.

"I can't go in," she had whispered, clutching her throat, not understanding her terror as she wrenched her hand free of theirs.

"Why?" they asked excitedly, the beams of their flashlights dancing along the wall.

Suddenly she had some memory of being trapped in a box and knowing she was being buried alive. She remembered coughing as dirt sifted through the cracks of her coffin. She remembered kicking and clawing and screaming when the narrow box was black and silent.

"What's wrong?" the boys demanded.

Blue lights flickered, and the memory was gone.

"I—I don't know." She edged away from them toward the open garage doors and brilliant sunlight. "Let's go inside the house...and watch a video or something."

How she ached for them when once more they were safely inside and they showed her their home videos and photograph albums with photos that had been taken of their family before the divorce. There were very few pictures of them. The boys told her that their parents had never had time for them, even when they'd been married. It was worse now, though, since their mother had run off and their father kept threatening to send them to military school.

She began to understand that maybe the reason they doted on her was that she was the first adult who ever enjoyed them and made them feel needed.

She encouraged them to go to their father and talk to him. Foolishly she had caused one quarrel between the father and sons by giving some of Lucas's and the boys' clothes to their yardman and his family. After Lucas had caught the poor man in a pair of slacks from one of his custom-made suits from London, he had yelled at the boys for an hour. She had wept for causing all three of them so much pain. But the incident had blown over, and Lucas had bought the slacks back from the man.

She had taken two pictures of Lucas from his albums to keep when she was in the boys' room alone. One was a photograph of him as a man, the other of him as a boy unhappily perched on top of a huge elephant in India.

Lucas kept a box full of articles about himself in the den. She read them all. Apparently Lucas had a professional reputation for toughness and greed. She read that he never made a move unless it was to his financial advantage, that even the women he dated were always rich—as Joan, his first wife, had been. One reporter had likened his predatory nature to that of a barracuda.

The nights when Lucas was at home were difficult because she felt lonely and isolated in the boys' closet, clutching the photographs of Lucas. But the worst hours were those when all the lights in the house were off and she fell asleep, only to have nightmares.

Most nights she would slip into an old chambray shirt of Lucas's. After Peppin shut the louvered closet door for her, she would lie there while either Peppin or Montague read aloud. This week they had been reading a book called *Psychic Voyages* because she had found *Psychic Vampires,* their favorite, too terrifying. She would lie half-listening to the weird and yet compelling stories of people who believed they had lived other lives.

Eventually she would fall asleep, and it was never long before the dreams came—vivid, full-color visions that seemed so real and loomed larger than life.

Tonight was worse, maybe because it had stormed.

She was a little girl again, playing in a sun-splashed rose garden beside a vast white mansion with a dark-haired girl. At first they carefully gathered the roses, filling huge baskets with them. Then her dream changed. The sky filled with dark clouds, and the house was a blackened ruin. There was nothing in the baskets but stems and thorns. She was older, and her companion was gone. Suddenly a fanged monster with olive-black eyes sprang into the ruined rose garden and began chasing her. She knew if he caught her, he would lock her in a box and bury her alive. But as she ran, her speed slowed, and his accelerated, until she felt his hot breath on her neck and his hands clawing into her waist and dragging her into a dark cave. At first she was afraid she'd been buried alive. Then suddenly fire was all around her and she was struggling through the thick suffocating smoke, trying to find her way out. The last thing she saw was a dead man's gray face.

She screamed, a piercing, ear-shattering cry that dragged her back to the lumpy pallet. The louvered door was thrown open instantly, and Peppin's small compact body crouched over hers. His fingers, which smelled of peanut butter and grape jelly and of other flavors best not identified, pressed her lips.

His eyes were big and bright. His thin whisper was colored with excitement. "It's okay. Go back to sleep."

A door down the hall banged open.

Montague whistled from his bed. "Psst! Dad's coming!"

The louvered doors that were yanked together didn't quite close. Peppin scampered to his bed, diving under his covers a second before their door opened.

"Another nightmare, Peppin?"

She lay huddled beneath her blanket, her trembling easing ever so slightly when she heard *his* beautiful voice.

Every night for ten nights her screams had brought him to this room.

The storm had abated, and the night, though still, was held in a humid pall. The worst of the rain had moved out to the gulf, but she could hear the occasional drip of moisture from the eaves.

Even as part of her mind was stampeding in panic, she lifted her head and put her eye to the thread of light that sifted through the slats. The screen saver of the kids' computer gave off a flickering bluish glow. In the charcoal gray shadows of the moonlit room, she could just make out Lucas's tall, broad form silhouetted in the open doorway.

Tonight he was shirtless, and she found herself staring at his bare chest and corded muscles, and at the long white scars that crisscrossed his torso.

Already accustomed to the lack of light, she could see the drowsiness in his silver eyes and the rumpled waves of his inky dark hair that he wore too long for a lawyer. His face was leather-dark and starkly arrogant, yet she sensed he had known pain. He seemed huge and dangerous, uncompromisingly tough and masculine. And yet she felt astonishingly safe with him in the bedroom.

"Yes, Daddy, a really bad nightmare," Peppin said in a breathless, thready voice.

Lucas padded silently across the room, and the mattress groaned as he sat on the edge of his younger son's bed.

"What was the monster like tonight?"

Lucas's drawl had the power to hold her spellbound.

"Oh—he was just awful. He had huge purple eyes just popping out of their sockets. And a tail with green spikes."

"Green spikes?"

She watched Lucas's large pale hand stroke Peppin's hair, and it was almost as if he soothed her with those long, callused fingers.

"You know, Peppin, I've had a few weird dreams lately, too."

"About monsters?"

"No." Lucas's voice softened. "About a girl."

The girl in the closet lay very still. But her breathing accelerated, as did her heartbeats. His words seemed to linger inside her, registering almost hypnotically in that sweet, secret place in her soul.

"The first dream was a nightmare. It was about this girl who was terrified. I wanted to save her but I couldn't. She kept screaming, but when I reached her, it was too late." His voice broke. "She died in my arms. I woke up in a cold sweat. The dream was so vivid. She was so real. I still can't seem to get her out of my mind."

"I'd rather dream about a pretty girl than about a monster with big teeth any night, Dad."

"Big teeth, huh?" Lucas murmured.

Lucas's voice resonated pleasantly along the girl's nerve endings.

"Pointy teeth with silver tips. I was afraid he was going to eat me alive. Or...or maybe suck my blood like a giant vampire." Peppin punctuated this last with a hideous slurping sound.

Lucas's hand continued its gentle strokes. "I'm here, and I'm not going to let anything or anyone into this room."

She closed her eyes, feeling as though Lucas was caressing her and speaking to her, feeling some undeniable powerful attraction to him.

She sighed, wishing she could remember her own nightmare, yet thankful she couldn't.

She ran her fingertips over *his* chambray shirt, hugging the cotton fabric to her skin, liking the way his masculine scent clung to his shirt, and therefore to her.

Lucas.

He didn't even know she existed.

Her chest swelled with some unnamed emotion for him that was more potent than any she'd ever known.

The idea of him obsessed her, consumed her.

The boys thought that if they kept him from hiring a nanny they could keep her existence a secret. But she knew differently. Time was their enemy. Lucas was too smart not to discover her, and when he did, he would probably despise her. Still, she thrilled to the fantasy of their first encounter with every fiber of her being. Even as she dreaded it.

A long time later, Lucas's melodious voice trailed into silence. When he was sure his sons were both asleep, he got up and left.

And later, when she dreamed of the monsters again and of the face with the olive-bright eyes, Lucas was there. Moving with the speed of lightning and scooping her up against his muscled chest, he carried her to safety. And there, far away from danger, he kissed her, his mouth fastening upon hers with greedy, all-consuming passion.

This time when she awoke, she was hot and breathless and so filled with longing for him that she could not suppress the urge to get up and tiptoe quietly down the hall to his room.

His bedroom door was ajar, and his large bed where she had lain and daydreamed about him was awash in moonlight.

Silently she made her way to him.

She gasped when she saw how beautiful he was, sleep having washed the worry from his harsh face. His bronze skin appeared amazingly smooth, unmarred except for the long white scars that ran across his chest. Where had he gotten scars like that?

She had come to ease her longing, but one glance at the sheets molding the tanned sprawl of his huge body only increased her longing for him a hundredfold.

She had been alone so long. *Without him for so long.*

Without him? What made her think she had been with him before? But strangely, she did.

Would he recognize her? Would he be able to tell her who she was?

All she knew was that he did not seem like a barracuda to her. No. To her he was very, very dear.

Her mouth went dry. Her heart ached. Her knees trembled.

Hugging her waist, she sank to the floor beside him, swallowing against the tight constriction in her throat.

She clenched her hands. Never had she wanted anything so much as she wanted to run her fingertips through the thick tumble of black hair on that snowy pillow or let them glide over his wide shoulders.

A great tenderness welled inside her as she studied his bluntly carved features and hard mouth. She remembered her dream and his kiss, and fresh desire raced through her veins. She wanted to taste him, to know him. To belong to him.

And suddenly her loneliness made her hunger for him too much to resist.

Even though she knew it was crazy and an invasion of his privacy, she crawled closer to his bed. There she swept the masses of her yellow hair back with one hand and leaning toward him, carefully brushed her lips against his hair that fell across his brow, next to the dark skin at his temple.

He was as hot as if he had a fever.

And suddenly so was she.

Two kisses. Only two. He was so warm. Instantly her breathing was shallower, raspier. So was his. Instantly she was driven by a nearly overpowering need to trace the shape of his lips with her mouth, to deepen her kisses until he awakened and knew she was there.

He stirred suddenly and groaned. His mouth curved in a sensual white smile, as if he was having a wanton, lascivious dream.

She felt a blinding current of emotion, unlike anything

she had ever known, leap from him to her as she jerked away from him.

She had to leave.

But the tantalizing taste of him remained on her lips.

For one long second she closed her eyes and imagined him waking up and finding her. Would he know her? Would he accept her or reject her? She imagined him reaching for her, accepting her into his bed, into his life, telling her that he had always loved her.

Dear God. What was she doing to herself?

Then, terrified he would sense her presence, she stifled a low moan and ran down the hall to the boys' closet, where she lay sleepless on her pallet, feeling dissatisfied, aching with new needs and desires.

She couldn't bear to stay in his house another day.

She couldn't bear the thought of ever leaving him.

Three

When his Lincoln slewed overfast onto Ocean Drive, radials whining, Lucas jammed the accelerator down hard. His X-rated dream last night was living proof he'd gone too damn long without a woman. He'd awakened in a sweat again, only this time the gorgeous blonde who'd decided to haunt his dreams of late had climbed into his bed and run her mouth and tongue all over him.

· He'd awakened so steamed up he'd driven to his gym to work out before going into his office.

Now he felt hot and sticky and irritable. He'd forgotten the notice in the locker room yesterday about the water being turned off today for plumbing tests.

"What? My fault? How the hell do you mean?" Lucas growled into his cellular phone as he jerked the steering wheel to the right. Palm trees, hot-pink oleander and sparkling views of the bay spurted past in a blur.

Lucas was quickly coming to dislike this Mrs. Peters, the nanny who'd been a no-show yesterday.

His fault? Until she'd said that, he'd been only half listening. He was late, and his mind had been vacillating between the girl who'd tormented his dreams and his nine o'clock appointment with the ever-uptight Stinky Brown.

Stinky was proving to be an impossible client. He had been happy enough when Gertrude's doctor had agreed to testify that the old lady was senile. But Stinky had been going crazy ever since he'd found out about the blackened body in Bethany Ann's burned van. Apparently the girl had told her friends in Mexico that her grandmother had written her about changing the will. She'd also informed them of her grandmother's sudden death and her plan to return to the ranch for her grandmother's memorial service.

Lucas had sent an investigator to Mexico. Ugly gossip was rife about the heiress. Wanted for questioning by the police, Bethany had vanished. Which meant she was probably guilty as sin.

Stinky should have been thrilled. Instead he seemed terrified that the media would get wind of the scandal and blow it all out of proportion. Stinky wanted the girl found and the rumors silenced—fast.

"But Mr. Broderick," came Mrs. Peters's penetrating, dry voice over his phone, "while I am sorry that you came home early expecting to meet me there, you yourself called me yesterday afternoon and told me you'd already hired someone. That is the only reason I didn't show up."

Lucas forced his mind from the missing heiress. An image of a pale Peppin peering at him in the foyer flashed in Lucas's mind. Peppin's voice had been grave. "Mrs. Peters? Why, er, no, Dad. We waited by the phone just like you said. She didn't even call."

"What time did I call you, Mrs. Peters?" Lucas demanded, his stern tone almost convulsing with anger.

"Really, Mr. Broderick, you should know that better—"

Lucas exploded. "What time?"

Stubborn silence from the woman.

Then she said in an exasperated tone, "A little after two. I remember because—"

Lucas didn't give a damn why the blasted woman remembered.

"I didn't call you, Mrs. Peters. I know that because I was in a conference all afternoon."

"Oh. Then who—"

"Never mind."

"Do you want to reschedule the interview?"

When hell freezes over, lady. Lucas said a clipped good-bye and hung up.

"Damn!" Lucas was coldly furious with himself for not figuring out before now that Peppin and Montague had had something to do with the six nannies who'd stood him up.

For eleven miraculous days the boys had been so good he'd been tempted to check their shoulder blades to see if they'd sprouted wings.

Why hadn't he been more suspicious of that eerie feeling that some unseen angel had moved into his home and was making his life with his sons magically better?

His mind flashed back, struggling to interpret the bizarre events of late. First, he remembered that odd experience in the Moran foyer when he'd felt—there was no other word—haunted.

No, he had told himself to forget that. With great effort he forced the intriguing episode from his mind and thought instead about the changes in the household since he'd returned to Corpus Christi.

The boys had been pleasant, companionable, thoughtful and neat. They'd fixed several meals for him. In fact, ever since San Antonio, Lucas's home life had been downright idyllic. Aside from his concern over his sons' fevers, queasy stomachs, nightmares and absences from school, aside from that act of bizarre generosity when they'd given the yardman two of his best suits, this was the one week since Peppin's birth that being with his sons had been almost a joy.

Lucas grew increasingly puzzled as he remembered them asking him to show them how to boil broth and vegetables—even broccoli. Other than French fries and onion rings, they'd never eaten a damned vegetable in their lives. Why, they'd never touched broccoli with so much as the tip of a fork.

And all those medical questions. All those calls to Pete. Damn it. Why?

Lucas wasn't the only person they'd duped. Pete had prescribed a light diet, antibiotics and bed rest.

What had the brats really done with those pills and vegetables and bowls of soup they'd pretended to gobble down? Lucas frowned as he remembered how they'd tracked back and forth to their room with those endless bowls of broth and vegetables.

And then it hit him.

They were feeding something up there. Something large and ravenous that was either badly injured or diseased.

Vegetables ruled out anything as remotely attractive as a large dog.

It had to be something so repulsive they were sure he would never let them keep it. And why had Peppin awakened him every night screaming? Had the creature gotten loose in the house? Were they scared of it?

Damn it! *What were they hiding up there?*

Lucas switched on the radio, only to turn it off instantly when the newscaster began an update on the serial murders of several Texas lawyers. Some maniac was shooting lawyers in their homes in an execution-style manner. The story was making headlines all over the state, and his partners and staff attorneys hadn't been able to talk of anything else since a Houston associate had been found shot in the head in his backyard.

Hot-pink oleander blossoms waved airily above the high white wall that hid all but the top story of Lucas's mansion from the boulevard. Lucas swerved through the gigantic gates past the Realtor's For Sale sign, which had been erected shortly after the divorce.

Lucas had little liking for his three-story, ultra-modern, glass-tiled monstrosity with its elaborate security system, tennis courts, pool, Jacuzzi, boathouse, docks, fishing pier and servants' quarters, all of which were Joan's exorbitantly priced creations.

Lucas had grown up in small houses and felt lost in the large, overdecorated rooms. The place had become an albatross around his neck. The Realtor kept giving him lists of necessary repairs, and the first item on every list was to seal the ancient tunnel beneath his house that led to the bay. The tunnel was a curious relic from the turn-of-the-century mansion Joan had bought at great expense and torn down to build their home.

The Lincoln jerked to a stop at the massive house, and Lucas jumped out. Even before he opened the front doors, he could hear rap music pouring from his boys' room in a tidal wave of jivy drumbeats.

Good. The little savages were home. For once their music served some purpose other than to drive him crazy. He could use the pounding beat as a cover to sneak up on them.

He raced up the winding staircase and down the hall, past his bedroom, noting that his shower was on. How many times had he told them to use their own?

When he reached their closed door, he listened outside for a moment. Then, without knocking, he flung it open and charged inside.

Rap music pulsed from two immense speakers.

"We're all going to be stone deaf," he yelled as he

rushed toward the amplifier and jerked three plugs from the wall.

The sound of the running tap from his bathroom could be heard in the deafening silence that followed, which was odd, because both boys were already dressed for school. Peppin, who was patting pale powder all over his face and smudging eyeshadow under his eyes with a Kleenex, jumped guiltily.

"D-Dad? How come you're— You're home!" he squeaked, his eyes darting to Montague.

Lucas picked up the boxes of powder and eye shadow and pitched them in the trash in disgust. "So—you're not really sick!" He paused. "I talked to Mrs. Peters."

Montague, who was sprawled on the floor reading a booklet entitled *Step by Step: How To Make Awesome IDs* while he laced up his combat boots, wisely kept his eyes glued to a page that dealt with the many uses of laser copiers.

"I want to know what the hell you two have been up to!"

"N-nothing, Dad."

Lucas's hard gaze flicked away from Peppin's chalk-white face. Today, as of late, their room was abnormally tidy, and there was no sign of their large, repulsive pet. No stale scent of droppings, urine or old food. Not so much as a paper or a book on the floor. Only one stray horseshoe.

A bouquet of plump pink roses adorned Montague's desk. Now that was odd, because Lucas couldn't remember either of his sons ever so much as looking at flowers, let alone picking them and arranging them in a vase. Suddenly Lucas was remembering that roses were all over the house. In fact, there was a vase of white roses beside his bed.

Did the pet give off some peculiar odor the flowers masked?

Lucas stalked to the closet and threw open the doors, but

he saw nothing other than a rumpled sheet, two photographs of himself, a blanket and the favorite old chambray shirt he'd been looking for.

The animal's bedding? He snatched up his shirt.

Furious, Lucas turned to them. "Where is it?"

"What, Dad?" Montague's voice was calm, but his hands had frozen on the tangled laces of his second boot.

"Damn it. Your new pet."

Peppin made a low choking sound. "P-pet?"

"Where is whatever you've been feeding all that chicken soup to? *What is going on?* You've played sick, behaved yourselves, cleaned house, cooked supper—all to put me off my guard."

In the silence, he heard his shower, really heard it.

"Dad, we're going to be late for school. Could you give us a ride—"

Late was a buzz word. Lucas glanced at his watch and remembered Stinky Brown.

Through gritted teeth, he said, "I'm going to shower. We'll talk on the way to school."

The boys stared at him white-faced. "D-Dad. No. We can explain—everything. Right now."

"I've run out of time—now. It'll have to wait."

He was vaguely pleased that the boys looked so cowed. If he couldn't resolve the issue in the car, with any luck at all, they would talk to their friends and find a new home for whatever it was, and the problem would have solved itself by the time he got home tonight.

"You two had better be ready when I am." Lucas began stripping as he stalked away from them toward his bedroom.

Peppin raced after him. "But, Dad—"

Lucas whirled. "Yeah? What's with this sudden willingness to confess?"

"Dad, I—I was going to take a shower—"

"Use your own bathroom."

For once Montague, whose black-booted feet looked amazingly large, had come after him, too. "Hey, Dad, maybe you could use our shower—"

"Suddenly everybody wants to talk and keep me out of my shower." Lucas yanked his running shorts off. "Well, too bad. I'm stark naked and I've run out of time and patience with your games."

As he strode through his bedroom into his steamy bathroom, he thought he heard Peppin say rather uneasily, "Cool it, Monty. Didn't he say he wanted to meet our new pet?"

"So?"

"Chill out. This could work."

What could work?

"Maybe they'll dig each other."

"You're stupid."

"It *could* happen."

Clouds of steam were pouring out of his overlarge shower as Lucas yanked the door open and stepped onto the pink marble that was slippery with soap.

Lucas shut his eyes as the warm water hit his face full force. Automatically he grabbed for the bar of soap in his soap dish, but it wasn't there.

Then soft warm fingers placed a bar that smelled of roses in his right hand.

"Thanks," he said as he began to soap the nape of his neck.

It took him a second to get it.

He wasn't alone.

His hand stopped scrubbing.

His eyes snapped open, and she was there—stepping out of the pink mists behind him like a naked goddess from the wildest adolescent fantasy he'd ever had, like Venus rising from that shell in the sea in that painting he'd seen in Florence.

He knew her.

Her blue eyes flashed with recognition, too.

High cheekbones. Yellow hair. Model-slim. Gorgeous. Skin as creamy as alabaster.

She was an exact replica of the girl who had come to him in his dreams. She was the girl of his nightmare, as well as the girl who'd gotten friendlier and friendlier in every dream since until the one last night when she'd crawled on top of him and teased him until he was insane with desire.

Was he dreaming now? Or was she for real?

For no particular reason he allowed himself to remember the spooky feeling he'd gotten when he'd walked out of the Moran library and he'd felt so positive that someone was watching him. Only there hadn't been anybody there. And yet he had felt as if some alien spirit who was very powerful and very sweet had connected to his soul. For a few blissful seconds he'd felt unleashed, set free from all his cynicism and bitterness. Torrents of blocked and longed-for feelings had flowed out of him. He still was at a loss to explain it.

Then there were the dreams about the blonde. And suddenly here she was. In the flesh.

This was crazy. Too crazy to believe.

"Hello?" came her velvet voice beneath his ear.

She was real.

He blinked once, twice, and she was still there. Her eyes sparkled. She was lovelier than ever—and as naked as the day she was born. He inhaled the scent of roses.

For a week he had been haunted by that scent. And now he knew why. It was her scent.

He felt like Adam finding his Eve.

He felt that every moment in his life had been leading to this one.

Funny—even as his eyes locked with hers, even as he carefully forced himself not to lower them, even as he forced himself to concentrate on the way her black lashes were clumped together with dewdrops of moisture around her incredibly blue eyes, he still saw everything.

Shampoo suds spilled from her throat and clung in foamy white mounds to her nipples.

She was built, really built, with high, shapely breasts, a gently rounded belly, a narrow waist and smooth legs that went on forever. Her lips parted in a tender half smile, and he saw that she had a slight gap between her two front teeth. And Lucas, who had been an English major in college, remembered Chaucer saying that was an indication of a sensual nature.

Did she give off a glow? Was that why he felt so dazzled?

As if in a daze, he remembered Peppin's cryptic remark. *Didn't he say he wanted to meet our new pet?*

Maybe they'll dig each other.

Thus far, she hadn't cried out or made any sound at all— maybe she was as stunned as he.

Or maybe—how did he know this?—she'd been expecting this moment, too.

Slowly Lucas raised his hands above his head, as if in mock surrender—to show her he wouldn't touch her or hurt her or molest her in any way.

But it wasn't necessary—because, amazingly, she really wasn't afraid of him. She was the first to let her eyes travel boldly from his face down his bronze flexing chest muscles, which were matted with dark, crinkly hair, down the length of his flat, tapering stomach and the rest of his lean body. Then she looked at him where his tan line stopped with the same intense curiosity and lack of modesty. It was as if they were already lovers and she had a right to do so. Her eyes continued to touch him intimately. Pulsations of liquid heat raged through him.

He flushed at her saucy impudence and then hastily pushed the shower door open, cursing as he stumbled backward so fast he stubbed his big toe on the shower door. In between grunts of pain, he hopped toward the rack and grabbed a towel.

Where the hell had Peppin and Montague found her?

"Boys!" he shouted as he bunched the thick white terry cloth around his waist. Then, louder, "Boys!"

They were far too clever to answer.

She turned off the faucets and said quietly, "I'm sorry if you hurt your toe." And then, "It's not their fault, you know."

"Don't defend them." A pause. "Who the hell are you?" Lucas whispered, hotly aware of her lithe golden body. "How long have you been living—"

But he already knew. "Eleven days?" he croaked, his answer sounding choppy and thick-tongued.

Her face turned crimson. She nodded. "I wanted to meet you, but I was afraid—"

She was the pet. She was the mysterious angelic presence he'd sensed in the house who'd magically improved his life with his sons. Her spell was so powerful she'd even managed to insert herself into his dreams.

No wonder the boys had been determined to fire all those nannies and stay home and tend her.

The girl stepped out of the stall, her blue eyes shining through the mists, her wet hair glued in tangles to her shoulders.

Lucas observed a neatly stitched pink line along her hairline as he roughly pitched her a towel. For no reason at all he remembered Peppin bombarding Pete with all those medical questions. He had felt such fatherly pride at the seductive dream that maybe, after all, Peppin might really amount to something and become a doctor.

His aim was off, and the towel fell to the floor. He leaned down and picked it up, and as he held it out to her, his hands accidentally touched hers. He felt the silken heat of her soft skin, and his heart beat faster.

Her reaction to him was equally intense, although she, too, attempted to hide it, not that she was any better at it than he. For he saw that her hands trembled as she wrapped the towel around herself, and that once it was snugly secured above her breasts, he saw that they trembled, too, as if she was breathing irregularly.

What the hell was going on here?

Never in his entire life had he felt so powerfully drawn to another human being.

Never before had he met a stranger and felt he already knew her.

She hadn't bothered to dry herself properly, and heated rivulets of water and soap oozed down her skin and pooled beside her bare feet.

She kept staring at him, the pupils of her eyes so drastically dilated that only a ring of blue fire seemed to encircle them. "I wish I knew who I was," she replied honestly in a small, frightened voice that undid him. "If I knew, maybe I'd know where I belonged and I'd have already gone. I—I thought maybe you could tell me."

"Me? How the hell would I know?"

"But you looked at me as if you know me."

He stared at her feet because it seemed the safest thing about her to look at. There were ugly scratches on her slim ankles.

She had tiny feet.

He lifted his gaze and studied that fresh pink scar at her hairline. There were tiny scratches on her cheek. For no reason at all he remembered tiny bloody footprints across a white tile floor. Next he remembered Peppin's first medical question had been in that hospital parking lot.

And then Lucas knew.

Again he saw the dangling IV above those blood-spattered sheets in the examining room.

This girl was Pete's patient.

This glorious angel with the soapsuds in her hair who had invaded his house and made him a happy man was the escaped dope addict. She could be anybody.

There was only one thing to do.

He had to call Pete.

"Get dressed," he said curtly. "Then we'll talk."

"Yes, Lucas."

Lucas.

His name. Just his name. So familiar and yet so... erotically alien. Her husky velvet voice had made it into something indescribably precious.

The adoring quality in her voice did strange things to him. He felt ten years younger and all the logical, self-serving rules he had lived by were shattered.

He felt her silent plea. *Tell me who I am.*

Damn, people couldn't talk to each other without words.

He felt turned on by her. And ridiculously safe. As if he'd come home from a long journey to the one person in the entire universe he wanted to spend all eternity with.

Which was absolutely absurd.

He had no bond with her. She didn't give a damn about anything except using him. She was just some troublesome stranger, a runaway, a doper, maybe. She had invaded his house, tricked his sons into betraying him—

The house sparkled. She had cooked meals for him. Brought roses to him. Roses that he had worn all day, the scent of which had haunted him.

He remembered how badly the boys had taken his finding a new home for their pet Doberman pinscher who'd bitten the postman and chased all the neighbor kids. They liked this girl a whole lot more than they'd liked Kaiser.

So did he.

Lucas reminded himself that she was a worse liability than Kaiser could have been, that he had to get rid of her as soon as possible.

"Get dressed," he repeated, but in a gentler tone to put her off guard.

Her smile died.

As she stared into his eyes, he had the unsettling sensation that she had zapped into his brain and read every single dark intention and suspicion he had concerning her.

"Please don't send me away," she said.

"You can't stay here."

Her warm, frightened eyes met his again. "If you throw me out, they'll find me and kill me."

Two heartbeats. His and hers. As a grander emotion flared into being.

"Who will kill you?"

"I—I don't know."

No way could he let anything happen to her.

"I want to stay here with you," she said, her gaze and voice warm.

This time it was he who read her mind.

She wanted him to seize her, to wrap her in his arms and pull her down to the marble floor, to make swift violent love to her, while they were still flushed and steaming from the shower.

She wanted him to love her. Forever.

This whole damn thing was too much. Way too much. Crazy, in fact.

"Hold me," she whispered in a barely audible voice. "Just hold me."

"Later."

"No."

Maybe he could have walked away from her if she hadn't smiled so sheepishly and charmingly. If the towel above her breasts hadn't shifted that fraction of an inch lower.

If they hadn't both reached to keep it from falling.

If their fingertips hadn't touched.

If they both hadn't laughed nervously.

If her laughter hadn't died in that breathless hush. "You want this as much as I do."

"What?"

She smiled sexily and reached up and stroked his wet hair.

"This," she said huskily, winding a black strand around a fingertip. "And... And everything."

If her innocent glances and caresses stung him like flame, what would the full tide be?

Strange, how he felt he already knew.

Her warm knowing gaze locked with his and drew him inside her, fusing all that was holy and all that was not to her shining spirit.

He was a hardened man who had had many women.

He had been badly burned by the one woman he had loved and married.

But this was different.

Utterly and completely different.

And ten thousand times more dangerous.

He could no more resist her than a swimmer could resist the force of a dangerous tidal current.

As he drew her into his arms, wanting her soul as well as her body, he felt a thunderstorm of unreasoning, inexplicable emotions.

For a long moment he savored the sweetness of pressing her resplendent soft damp flesh against himself.

Very slowly, very gently he lowered his mouth to hers.

His kiss was neither hard nor long, but it vibrated inside

them both with deep, underlying tenderness and awakened them to shattering, never-felt-before needs.

He would never have believed that a single kiss could hold the power to change him—forever.

"Who are you?" he whispered again, frantic at the speed of this thing, even as he gave her the gentlest smile he had ever given any woman. "Where did you come from? Why?"

"I—I don't know. I just know that I feel I've known you before."

"I've never set eyes on you till today. Believe me. You're not somebody I could forget." He wasn't ready to admit to her that he had dreamed about her.

She gave him an uncertain look that said she didn't quite believe him.

Amnesia, he reminded himself. She had amnesia. She could be anybody. She could be married. What if there was—

Suddenly he was terrified of all the horrendous possibilities.

God. No. He couldn't bear the thought of another man possessing her, touching her. Or of her loving someone else.

His grip tightened around her waist.

He would cross those bridges later—if it came to that.

Now she was his. Totally and completely his.

He kissed her again, harder, in a fury to stake his right of possession.

But it wasn't necessary. With every answering kiss, she told him that she was already his and would always be his.

He panicked, afraid of where this was taking him, but he couldn't stop kissing her even when tears spilled from her lashes as she kissed him back just as fearfully.

Four

Lucas's spacious L-shaped office—done in dramatic marble and pale parquet floors and furnished with Oriental rugs and antique porcelains—exuded understated wealth and power.

Stinky stared at Lucas hard. His voice was measured and deliberate. "Frankly, I expected more from someone with your ruthless, hard-boiled reputation. You haven't done a damn thing."

Lucas's jaw tightened at the slur, but his gaze didn't waver. "Because what you want isn't in your best interests. You say the cops have a murder weapon and they've found drugs in the burned van and more drugs in one of her partially built houses in Mexico. An eyewitness says she was at the wheel of the van when it hit that other car and rolled. The police think she was trying to find a place to dump Miguel Santos's body. He was her driver. You ought to like the way this thing is heating up. The longer Bethany's on the run, the worse it will be for her."

"Exactly. That's why you have to find her."

"But—"

"Chandra couldn't be involved in drug-running or murder."

"I'm not talking about innocence or guilt."

Stinky's bloodshot black eyes narrowed as he leaned forward. The heavy scent of cologne wafted with him, as did the fainter odor of booze.

It was early yet, but Stinky had already had a drink or two. Maybe more.

Stinky had plenty of surface charm. Most women probably found his rugged body and his classically handsome face perfect. He had reddish-brown hair with a widow's peak and a chin with a deep cleft in it. In his dark, custom-made suit, he had the sleek, pampered look of a movie star playing a rich businessman. But neither acting nor business was his trade. Lucas had researched the man. One way or another, Stinky had always made his living off wealthy women.

"No, counselor. We're talking about life or death—Chandra's."

"You're trying to tell me your only concern here is for her welfare?"

Lucas's dark brows arched cynically as Stinky sank back into his leather chair and began rummaging in his briefcase. His trembling tanned hand closed around a file folder, pulled it out and thumbed through it. With a tight smile, Stinky tossed it onto Lucas's desk.

"What—" As Lucas opened the folder, three eight-by-ten glossy photographs of a beautiful blonde fell out.

Stinky grabbed them and spread them face up on top of Lucas's papers. "I ask you—is this the face of a killer?"

Lucas was about to argue that that was hardly the point, but as he lifted a photograph, he found himself staring into a pair of vivacious blue eyes that drank too deeply of his soul.

Oh, my God—

His tongue thickened. Had his life depended upon it, he couldn't have uttered a word.

He was stunned that even a mere picture of *her* generated that strange, awesome power over him.

Panic began to rise in Lucas as he studied the scintillatingly luxuriant yellow hair, the inviting lips that were parted in laughter, the flawless, full-bosomed, slender-hipped figure.

Chandra Moran was the girl he'd met naked in his shower less than an hour ago. The girl whose lips he'd kissed. The girl who'd haunted his every waking thought and had even haunted his dreams for days.

So—this was what she looked like in full glory when she was happy and unafraid and completely healthy. When her skin was golden from the sun.

She was really something. Hell, as if he didn't already know that.

In another shot her hands were splayed open on her hips as she stood halfway up the gray steps of a Mayan pyramid. In tight jeans and a halter top, with her golden hair streaming in the wind, laughing at her photographer, she looked younger and more carefree than she had looked in his shower. In another photo she had laid her head on a sacrificial stone chopping block and was sticking out her tongue at the camera as if she was taunting her executioner.

Fully clothed, she was every bit as sexy as she was naked.

Cute butt. Long legs. The three pictures were all it took to make Lucas's desire for her well up. Only now she had a name, a very dangerous name. Now his desire for her was laced with fear and danger because he had a head full of questions that he was suddenly afraid to ask.

His hands clenched, wrinkling the edges of the photos before he dropped them on his desk. He knew he was behaving stupidly, that he had to say something fast. Somehow he managed a hoarse whisper.

"This is... Bethany Ann Moran?"

Stinky's hard, bright eyes locked with his. "I'll grant you, she's a looker."

Reluctantly Lucas forced a disinterested nod. "I imagined her differently. More like a straight-laced nun or a schoolteacher type."

"Not our Chandra. She's had dozens of wild boyfriends."

Lucas flushed, angry at the mention of other men.

"I was her first." Stinky reddened, too. "She dumped me."

"Why?"

"None of your damned business. You just find her, counselor, before the wrong guy does."

"You mean—the cops?"

"Not necessarily."

The only ethical response was to admit he already had her. But as he watched Stinky rise from his chair, some raw, gut-level instinct stopped Lucas.

The silence between the two men lengthened and grew strangely uncomfortable, at least for Lucas.

"You okay, counselor? You seem kind of nervous all of a sudden."

Lucas finger-combed his inky hair and tried to act casual. "Worked late. Big new project. Very big."

"Hope it won't distract you from Bethany."

"Oh, er, no chance of that."

"Good."

Stinky's black eyes fastened on Lucas as Lucas hastily jumped up and ushered him to the door.

The minute Stinky was gone, Lucas canceled the rest of his morning's appointments to consider this new information.

Bethany Ann Moran was living in *his* house. She had been in a car wreck. She had been brought to the hospital with head injuries; she'd also been high on drugs. She was wanted by the police. His own kids had played savior and doctor.

The legal ramifications of not giving her up were horrendous. If anything happened to her, her family could sue him for every dime he had. He didn't want to think about the police. Then there were the financial aspects. He would lose his shot at the Moran will.

So be it.

Was she or wasn't she innocent? Was someone trying to kill her? Until he knew more, Lucas had to protect her.

What the hell had really happened in that accident? Lucas couldn't believe Chandra had murdered Santos, her driver, and had planned to dump his body somewhere.

So, damn it, what had happened?

He got up and went to a window. His office was on the seventeenth floor and commanded a view of the bay. In no way did the brilliant sunshine and clear blue sky reflect the growing darkness of his mood.

He went back to his desk and ran his hands through his hair. Suddenly he remembered something that had seemed insignificant at the time.

There had been a van at the Moran ranch. A blue van with a dark man in a Stetson waiting patiently in it while the sky turned black. The van had still been there when he'd driven away from the mansion.

But not the driver.

Lucas's mind raced.

He remembered that he'd felt a strange empathy for Chandra even when he'd been in the library. Then, when he'd stepped into the foyer, he'd sensed that weird connection to some powerful otherworldly presence.

He had felt Chandra.

Chandra had been there.

He knew it in his bones.

That night in San Antonio he had that nightmare about her that had kept him up till dawn.

God.

Had she been in trouble, crying out for help? Had he somehow sensed it? This whole thing kept getting weirder and weirder.

Lucas phoned his top private investigator, Tom Robard, and told him to come over. When Robard got there, Lucas spit out rapid-fire demands. He wanted to know everything about Chandra Moran. Everything about every other Moran, too. Everything about anyone living on the Moran ranch or on the Moran payroll, as well. Everything about Casas de Cristo and the people who ran it. And the investigation had to be kept hush-hush. Lucas had Robard send two bodyguards out to his own house to make sure nobody could get to Bethany, and to make sure she couldn't wander away, either.

Lucas was about to go home when he remembered he still hadn't called Pete.

The answering service said Pete was tied up in surgery.

Damn.

Later.

As Lucas hung up, a woman with a cap of shiny dark hair, a nervous young staff attorney in a black suit, stopped by his office.

"I was wondering if you'd heard, Mr. Broderick?"

Lucas looked up and saw that she was pale and had a dazed look in her eyes. Which meant trouble.

Wearily he shook his head.

"A guy claiming to be the serial killer phoned our office and said you're next."

"Good God. Just what I need."

Five

Lucas froze as he got out of his car and heard his sons' excited shouts, quickly followed by peals of warm, feminine laughter. He heard the clang of a heavy iron horseshoe against an iron stake. And Peppin's triumphant cry as he pitched another horseshoe.

His sons.

Her laughter.

She even sounded beautiful.

The three of them seemed so happy together as they played behind the house somewhere near the pool.

Lucas caught his breath. Drugs? Murder? Could such a gorgeous, innocent-looking woman be capable of such heinous—

Then he remembered Joan. Joan, who had lied to him with a smile. Joan, who had neglected and abandoned her own sons. Joan, who had been so undeniably beautiful and passionate in his bed but in so many others, as well—even that of his best friend.

Bitterly, Lucas wished he was wrong about Chandra, and if she was truly evil, that he could exorcise her from his fevered brain and heart before it was too late.

She emitted another silvery peal of laughter that tugged at his heart.

It was already too late.

He loved her.

And so did his sons.

The foundations of his logical life were crumbling. He could feel everything he'd worked so long and so hard for going down the tubes, even his career, and there wasn't a damn thing he could do about it. If Joan had gutted him and left him for dead, this girl might be about to deliver the coup de grace.

Warily he prowled around to the back of his white mansion where he found Peppin, his outstretched hand still in the air as he watched the horseshoe he'd flung arc high against the darkening opalescent sky before falling, ringing the iron stake with an awesome clatter. Chandra clapped as the boys ran to gather up their horseshoes.

"Hello—again." Lucas's deep cynical drawl sounded lazy, but he felt as tightly strung as piano wire.

Chandra, who was standing against a mass of fuchsia-colored bougainvillea, whirled, her face flushing with delight when she saw him. Tiny blue flames began to blaze in her eyes as hotly as bonfires. A similar answering excitement coiled warmly around his heart.

She was so beautiful. He held his breath, his eyes unable to leave her face. He stood motionless, as one enchanted. She dominated his field of vision with her yellow hair gleaming as brightly as pure gold.

In that sparkling moment all his doubts melted away, and she was everything to him. He had missed her acutely in the brief hours they'd been apart.

He was too cold and too cynical and too smart to feel this way.

He was inflamed by her beauty and caught by the sweetness of her fragile smile and radiant face as she looked at him.

With that bright hair falling softly around her shoulders, she was a vision in his old chambray shirt and Peppin's too-tight jeans. He was heartened that the shadows beneath her eyes were lighter and that her cheeks were rosier. One look was enough to tell him that no matter how he fought it, he would never be released from the hold she had on him.

Still, he raged against it inwardly.

She stiffened and grew shy of him, too, somehow sensing the exact moment he started to recoil from her.

Two sea gulls swooped down, fighting for a tidbit of fish, circling, squawking. Distracted by the birds, she laughed nervously.

Peppin picked up one of four huge, bulging plastic garbage bags. "Hey, Dad, look what we did!" Peppin dropped the bag and pointed toward three other overflowing bags lined neatly in front of the pool house.

"She hid a treasure on the beach under a piece of driftwood. She said we were pirates who couldn't remember where we'd buried our treasure and we had to pick up trash while we looked for it," Montague explained.

The beach was constantly littered with bottles, foam cups, plastic bags, boards with rusty nails, pieces of fishing equipment—every imaginable sort of debris that could be thrown overboard from fishing boats or swept from the city streets via the storm sewers.

"That's great. Just great," Lucas said grumpily. Usually the boys threw tantrums at the prospect of picking up so much as a single bottle cap. Lucas resented having still another fresh reason to admire her.

"I have supper waiting," she said, her slanting eyes having grown warily hurt.

"Let's go inside, then," he said. It was all he could manage.

It was a first—the four of them eating together—and she had worked hard to make it special. Dinner was a warm, golden, candlelit affair in his normally white, sterile dining room. She'd had the boys set the table with a melon-colored cloth and matching napkins. Roses scented the room from a crystal vase. Romantic piano music tinkled faintly— Schubert. She had cooked a roast and mashed potatoes and green beans. She'd even made flan— Peppin's favorite.

His, too.

How had she known?

Why was he even surprised? She seemed to know everything about him.

He watched her avoid the beef and pick at her vegetables, while he ate lustily. The roast, which she had flavored with garlic and delicate spices, seemed to melt in his mouth.

The boys chattered about some redheaded friend named Jeremiah who had been sent to the principal's office three times that day. The adults nodded, speaking only when necessary and only to the boys, although each was acutely conscious of the other.

Lucas's tension grew as he sensed the boys watching the two of them, especially him. Finally Peppin, who could never be quiet for long if he was bothered by something, blurted out the question foremost on everybody's mind. "Are you going to be mean to her like you were to Mom and make her go away?"

Like you were to Mom? Was that how they saw it?

"Or can she stay?"

All three of them peered at him in the flickering candlelight. Even in the golden light Chandra was ashen, her gaze wide and frightened, like a doe at bay, not wanting to pressure him and yet pressuring him more than the boys' dark avid faces.

"I hadn't thought much about it."

Liar.

Lucas cut off a piece of roast, inserted it into his mouth and began to chew methodically.

"We like her, Dad," Montague asserted.

"You don't know one damn thing about her." Lucas kept his gaze on his potatoes, but he felt the betrayal she felt when he uttered that lie.

Damn it. He didn't believe in extrasensory perception or whatever this weird bond was between them.

"We know all we need to know, Dad," Peppin said. "She's pretty and nice...and patient. She fits in. And she says she likes you a lot."

"Thank you, Peppin." She flushed. "But I really don't think—"

"And," Peppin continued, "she listens when we talk. She doesn't raise her voice when she gets mad. She doesn't just shout orders and treat us like children. She makes us mind, too. She senses what we want or need to do even before we do."

Incredibly, it was all too true. She had woven her spell on them all. Lucas speared another piece of roast and jammed it defiantly into his mouth. Again it melted on his tongue.

"So—how long do you expect this cozy arrangement to last?" he asked Peppin between succulent bites.

"She's already done a better job and lasted longer than any of the nannies or housekeepers *you* hired," Montague said.

"That might not be so true if you two hadn't sabotaged—"

"We want to keep her, Dad."

She said nothing, but he felt her soul-to-soul plea even more powerfully than either of his sons'.

Please, Lucas, just for a little while.

Okay. Okay, he shot back at her, using ESP just to see if she was tuned into his frequency, too.

Bingo.

Cheeks glowing, her bright gaze lifted to his, and she smiled in astonishment and pleasure as she read his mind.

Her pleasure filled him, saturated him, thrilled him.

This was weird, he thought vaguely, right before he thundered, ''All right! You win! She can stay!'' He shoved his chair back, stunned. ''But that's only because I can't fight everybody.''

He got up, furious at himself, at her, at all of them, and stalked to his liquor cabinet, where he made a martini. He tossed it down and made another. With a grimace he tossed that one down, as well, and poured and stirred still another.

''Lucas—''

He turned, his face harshly intense. ''You got what you wanted.''

''But did you?'' she asked in a concerned voice.

She really did sound as if she cared about his happiness more than her own.

He contemplated her beautiful upturned face, and despised himself for the ridiculous, crazy, youthful elation he felt at the mere sight of her. The bitterness and the anger that were always in his heart had all but vanished.

''Yes and no.''

''I want to thank you,'' she said very softly.

When she reached out and put a hand on his sleeve, he jerked convulsively from even that slight touch, mostly because it pleased him almost beyond bearing.

''Don't,'' he growled as his hands began to shake.

''Don't what?''

''You can stay, but I want you to leave me alone.''

"Why? I—I thought—"

"Because I don't understand this thing between you and me. Because I don't like feeling compelled every time I look at you or hear your voice. Because I don't like feeling like a teenager—driven, not myself. Because…just because this whole crazy thing is happening too damn fast. I'm not myself when you're around. Nothing like this has ever happened to me before. I don't trust it. I feel like we're getting in too deep."

"Okay. I guess it isn't fair to expect— I mean, I've had eleven days to get used to you," she said simply, reasonably. "To get used to the idea of loving you."

"Don't even say that stupid word. Love doesn't happen this fast."

"I didn't know there were rules."

"Well, there damn well should be."

"I think I've felt this way forever."

"Do you know how ridiculous you sound?" He whirled on her, hating himself when the color drained from her face. "How do you know what you feel when you don't even know who you are?"

"Because I know what I feel in my heart," she said brokenly.

"Damn it. No—"

"Lucas, I do. I had a dream about us last night. I had to leave you, and you were terrified I was abandoning you. You didn't believe me when I said I'd come back."

Odd, her dreaming that. His big fear about love always had to do with the fear of losing it. He felt that way now about her.

Silently, moodily, he mixed another martini, disbelieving her. Disbelieving this whole damn situation.

"Haven't you had enough to drink for one night?" she asked in a wifely tone, which he didn't like.

"Way too much," he agreed pleasantly as he downed

the martini. "And way too much of this impossible conversation."

"I'm sorry—"

"This is a big place. You keep to your part of the house. I'll keep to mine." With that he stormed outside.

After he talked to the bodyguards, he went down the narrow path on the bluff to the beach. He stomped mindlessly across the wet sand, not caring that his good Italian dress shoes sank deeply into the stuff. He hurled a few flat shells, sending them skimming across the dark water before he felt her watching him and glanced at the house.

Every window was ablaze. She was standing in one, staring out at him as he'd known she'd be. Her voluptuous beauty drew him like a beacon. More than anything, he wanted to quit fighting her and go to her.

He began to walk fast, his long strides carrying him away from the tall white house and the woman with the golden hair, but not from the confusion burning in his heart.

Impossible relationships were his special talent. It had been love at first sight with Joan, he remembered bitterly.

But he hadn't ever felt like this, a tiny voice that he didn't care to listen to said. He hadn't even slept with this girl, but she had an intuitive grip on his heart and soul that Joan had never achieved even after years of marriage.

An hour later, when he returned, his dark hair ruffled from the wind, his mood only marginally lighter, Chandra was listening to a musical and singing about raindrops on roses while she washed dishes. Her golden hair was tousled, loose tendrils falling around her rosy, flushed cheeks. The sight of her at his sink and the sound of her happy, lilting voice filled him with more of that strange, intense emotion.

Shakily he forced himself to stay safely on the opposite side of the kitchen from her.

She made easy idle conversation, telling him what was

on television that he might like, telling him that his kids were upstairs doing their homework.

"Amazing," he muttered, opening the refrigerator and taking out a cola. "I—I think I'll go check on them."

Anything to avoid her.

"Lucas—" Her husky voice and luminous eyes begged him to stay just a little while longer.

He tore his briefcase from the counter and dashed upstairs.

The kids' computer was off. Monty really was rechecking Peppin's math. They were working together—productively, happily.

Another first.

"She's a good cook, isn't she, Dad?" Peppin asked.

"The best," Monty concurred, glancing up slyly from the math textbook.

Lucas had come upstairs to forget her. In a hard voice, he said, "Guys, you won."

"But you're being mean to her, Dad. She was crying in the kitchen a while ago."

Lucas winced, remembering the haunted vagueness in her eyes when he'd told her he was leaving her to go upstairs.

Unsteadily he said good-night to the boys. Then he forced himself to walk past the guest bedroom he'd assigned Chandra and down the hall to his own bedroom. He changed his mind and went to her room and opened the door. The trailing silk and lace nightgown and bed jacket he had picked up at a fancy shop on the way home lay across her empty bed, which was gilded by moonlight. He had hung several dresses in her closet and placed a shirt and a pair of jeans in her drawers, which she would no doubt discover in the morning.

He had made another stop before he'd come home—the drugstore, where he'd bought a package of condoms. Just in case he weakened and wasn't strong enough to resist her.

The drugstore cashier had recognized him and had given him an odd look as he'd rung up the purchase. Lucas had felt so hot under the collar he'd yanked his tie loose. The teenage cashier had chuckled and said, "Have a good one, Mr. Broderick."

Lucas went to his room. Slamming his briefcase on top of his desk beside his computer, he picked up the phone and hurriedly dialed his brother.

For once Pete answered on the first ring. Lucas could hear Sweet P. yelling in the background.

"Pete! Finally. I've been trying to get you all day. I've talked to your service, receptionists, machines—"

"Sorry. Two of my partners are on vacation, and the office and surgery schedule are jammed. How're the boys? They over their bout of flu yet?"

"You'd never guess they'd been sick."

"For a while there they really had me going with all those strange symptoms."

"You and me, brother."

"I couldn't figure out whether they were a pair of hypochondriacs or budding doctors," Pete said.

Lucas hesitated, not wanting to admit the truth. "I—I was wondering about that overdose patient with the head injuries who ran out on you at the ER."

Pete's voice tensed. "Now that's a strange situation."

"How?"

"Well, for one thing, we never found her. Then her records disappeared that same night. Everything, her chart, her medical history—it's even out of the computer. Which you, as a lawyer, would probably say is a lucky break for me because there's no record she was ever here. Which means I'm not liable. You know, even the red T-shirt we cut off her vanished.'' Pete hesitated. ''Then yesterday, this guy called me about her and got really nasty.''

''What?''

''He demanded to know the exact nature of her head injuries—how lucid she was, what she'd said, who she'd talked to. I told him several times that the doctor-patient relationship was privileged. He asked me if she'd talked to the police.''

''So who was he?''

''The creep hung up before I could ask him. But you want to know something else really strange? His last question was about you. He asked me if you and I were related.''

''And?''

''I told him it wasn't any of his business.''

Worriedly, Lucas changed the subject and hung up a few minutes later. He opened his briefcase and took out the Moran will. A billion dollars was a hell of a motive.

But killing Chandra wouldn't change anything. The money would still go to the foundation.

Maybe somebody just wanted revenge.

Lucas found it difficult to concentrate as he read through the complicated document. He kept feeling alarmed that the caller had connected him to Pete.

Chandra was vulnerable and alone, perhaps running for her life. If some killer really was after her, Lucas should be comforting her and protecting her. Instead he had pulled that macho, I-have-to-have-my-space crap on her. Now he wanted her in this room where he could see her and know she was safe. He wanted to apologize. And yet he was afraid if he got near her again, he wouldn't be able to keep his hands off her.

No, this lonely hell was smarter than getting more deeply involved. He had to keep his distance—at least till he got some answers.

Still, it got harder and harder for Lucas to concentrate on the will. He couldn't stop wondering where she was or what she was doing or when she'd come upstairs to bed.

He thought of a dozen excuses to go downstairs—he was hungry for leftovers, he was thirsty for a soft drink, he needed to put the garbage out.

She'd already gotten the boys to put the garbage out.

He wanted only one thing—to be near her, to watch her, to listen to her. To get high on the buzz she gave him.

A dozen times he prowled across the room to the door and a dozen times he forced himself to return to his desk.

Finally he heard a faint sound on the bottom stair. A light switch was flicked off. Next he heard hushed footsteps in the hall and her soft voice as she said good-night to the boys. Last of all came the sound of her door easing open and softly closing.

She was next door—stripping, getting ready to shower and go to bed.

The memory of her in his shower that had teased and tortured him all day hit him again full force. He remembered her breasts, the way the soapsuds had clung to their hardened pink tips. He remembered her bare skin had felt as soft as warm, living silk beneath his hands. He remembered the hot taste of her sweet mouth and the wondrous glory of her curved lips. She'd been as light as a hummingbird when he'd molded her to his body. He wanted to hold her again. To kiss her again.

No. He wanted way more. He wanted her naked, their bodies glued together, her legs and arms wrapped around him, her mouth opening endlessly to his.

The mere memory of her coupled with his fantasy made his blood run so hot, he felt drenched with desire. Finally he burst from his chair and paced restlessly to the door.

When he touched the doorknob, he felt it move ever so slightly.

She was there.

He felt exactly as he had in the Moran foyer when all the bitterness had left him and her gentler soul had commingled with his.

Sensing her nearness, he stood stock-still, his heart drumming. Had she felt his need for her and come to him?

Desperately he swallowed and wiped his sweating brow with the back of his hand. She must not come in and find him lurking at the door ready to pounce on her like some sex-starved maniac. Then the doorknob turned, and he realized it was already too late.

When the door opened, he shoved it closed, leaning against it heavily to keep her and the desire he didn't want to feel for her at bay.

But she knocked gently.

He closed his eyes and clenched his fists as the rhythm of her knocks thudded inside him at the same mad pace as his heart.

He thought of the long, celibate months since Joan, when he'd buried himself in his work to avoid women. Was it any wonder that ever since that tantalizing episode in the shower, he couldn't stop thinking about Chandra? About her slender pale body or her dazzling sapphire eyes or her silken hair? He caught the scent from the roses on his bedside table. Even her scent was all around him. The entire house reeked of the damned flowers. The gardens outside brimmed with them. He had worn a rose she had given him to work.

Damn her! What was she trying to do to him?

Suddenly he couldn't stand knowing she was out there a second longer. Flinging the door open, he blocked her way into his bedroom like a hostile giant. With his legs thrust widely apart, his heart pounding faster, his whole body taut and perspiring, he demanded, "What do you want?"

He saw his own stark longing mirrored in her eyes. He saw her fear and sad confusion, too.

"I can't live like this. I want us to be friends," she whispered. "I want to make you happy."

Friends? Why did women always say crazy things like that? But the sound of her velvet-soft voice made his blood run like fire in his veins. "Impossible," he growled.

"Lucas," she began softly, "if my presence in your home is making things difficult for you, I'll leave."

"No!" God, no.

"But—"

Her face was deathly pale. Anxiety and exhaustion had darkened the bluish smudges beneath her eyes. She was barely out of the hospital. She didn't know who she was. She was fragile. What if the bastard who was trying to kill her got her?

She was wanted for murder. The cops would eat him alive. So would the media.

"And just where in the hell do you think you'd go?" he demanded roughly.

"I don't know."

"There. You see. You're safe here. That is *the* top priority. You have no choice but to stay."

"But if you don't want me here—"

"Did I say that?" he rasped. His heart thundered in agony.

"Then what is it? Talk to me."

He ran a shaky hand through his hair. "I can't. Not yet. This whole thing is—" He shrugged. "Hopeless. Just go back to bed."

She peered at him. "I'm begging you—talk to me. Why is that so hard?"

He caught the dizzying smell of her. He longed to touch the luscious skin of her bare arms again, and her throat, her cheek—knowing that every part of her would be as soft as roses. He longed to drag her into his arms and pull her close.

"Damn it, it just is."

Her sad eyes grew huge. "Lucas, I want to thank you for the clothes."

"You're welcome—so go," he ordered gruffly. The way she kept looking at him with her very soul lighting up her eyes got to him. "Look, you don't know who you are, and ever since I met you, I don't know who I am, either. This whole damn thing has me pretty rattled."

"Then you don't hate me?" she whispered, sounding pitiful and lost.

He fought the urge to grab her and comfort her and caress her. "Hate you?" He laughed mirthlessly even as her desperate eyes clung to his. "Good Lord, no. You want the truth, girl? I wish to hell I did hate you."

She kept her eyes fastened on the wall. Her voice was quiet. "I'm so sorry for causing you all this trouble."

"Just go to bed," he whispered raggedly. "Before I—"

Before I do something we might both regret in the morning.

"Okay." But her voice was unsteady, and she lingered a dangerous moment longer.

"What the hell are you waiting for?"

"For this." Impulsively she stretched onto her tiptoes and kissed his cheek. He shuddered at the unexpected fire of her lips. With her mouth on his and her breasts accidentally grazing his bare arms, his need for her racked through him.

Without thinking, his arms went around her and he dragged her to him and kissed her long and deeply, his lips playing greedily across hers, opening them.

Oh, God. She tasted like honey. Her sweetness invaded

every pore of his body. She felt so good. His arms tightened around her.

Suddenly he pushed her away, his heart pounding. "Damn it. Go to bed, girl!"

Her eyes pleaded with him, invited him.

He felt almost a physical pain deep in his belly. He was about to seize her when she turned away shyly and ran.

The minute she was gone, he wanted her back.

He knotted his hands, scared he'd lose control again.

She wanted him, too, and turned, her blue eyes molten as she hesitated at her door.

She smiled and then grew very still.

He stared at her grimly, feeling awkward, unsure, as conflicting emotions surged inside him.

More than anything, he wanted to go after her.

"Good night," he croaked.

When her door shut behind her, he strode onto his balcony. His hands gripped the railing like talons as he leaned forward, staring sightlessly at the glistening bay and the waxing moon. Navy helicopters pulsed against the black sky as they buzzed across the bay on training missions. The waves sucked against wet sand. A bodyguard ambled lazily near the pool.

But all Lucas heard was *her* voice. All he saw was *her* face. Her body. All he tasted was her mouth. The memory of her shy smile haunted him, as did the wanton invitation in her eyes.

He wanted her badly.

He let the salt-scented breeze caress his perspiring body till it cooled him, and he gradually calmed down.

With iron control he undressed and crawled between the icy sheets of his bed.

But he couldn't sleep.

He lay in the dark as tense as a cat, wondering what he'd do if she screamed, as she'd done every night since she'd lived in his house. If he went to her room— If he so much as touched her velvet cheek, if he held her, he would have to taste her. Then he'd be lost for sure.

Lying in the dark, he thought of her lips and hair and breasts. He remembered her nipples growing hard when he'd stroked them.

God. He was driving himself crazy.

He jumped a foot when the telephone rang.

Usually he let the machine answer.

But he picked it up, glad for the distraction.

Six

Hesitantly Chandra leaned closer to the mirror, and as she did so, her image grew huge. Her lovely, enlarged face looked back at her sadly, questioning, as she raised a shaky fingertip and traced the shape of her mouth, still swollen from Lucas's kiss.

She lingered a second longer, and then, moistening her lips with her tongue, she pursed them and brushed them teasingly against the mirror.

The glass was cold.

Lucas's mouth had been hot and fierce and demanding, his arms crushing her.

So why had he rejected her?

Alone and miserable in her blue-tiled bathroom, her breath misting the glass, Chandra began to twist and untwist her yellow hair as she surveyed her pale features in the steam-clouded mirror, trying to find some fault in them. She rubbed the mirror with a towel.

A lone, glistening tear trickled from the corner of her eye down her pale cheek. She let her yellow hair fall to her shoulders. Always she was examining herself, trying new hairdos, new expressions, different postures, hoping for some tiny clue of recognition as to who she might be, hoping for a memory, a name, an image—anything other than those scary blue flashes.

Even before Lucas's rejection, she had felt erased. Formless. Shapeless. As if she was nobody.

But his rejection had left her too dispirited to even try to fight the amnesia. She was wondering why Lucas had returned from his office so dead-set against her. In that first instant when he'd seen her in his shower, his eyes had recognized her and adored her.

She couldn't be mistaken about that.

Yet after his passionate kisses and incredible kindness that morning, he had returned from his office determined to reject her.

Something had happened to him after he'd left her. Something that made him warier of her. And she hated that. For she wanted only to please him. All afternoon she had worked to make his homecoming special, to offer her thanks with a home-cooked meal and scented candles and friendship. But he had been hostile and rude and had gone out of his way to avoid her and reject her offerings.

Why?

If the argumentative exchanges with Lucas had left her feeling tired and very drained, that final rejection had finished her. She had been getting stronger every day. But now she felt almost as weak and depressed as she had the first day.

Wearily she leaned down and ran her bath. Then she pulled off her shirt and jeans and slipped into the tub. The warm water and foamy bubbles both soothed her and sapped what little remaining strength she had. She bathed quickly, then toweled herself off and put on the white diaphanous nightgown and the bed jacket Lucas had laid out on her bed.

She was so exhausted when she crawled into bed that she fell asleep the moment her head sank into the downy pillow, only to be jarred awake minutes later by the telephone on her nightstand. Impulsively she answered it at the exact moment Lucas did.

"Broderick here."

Without preliminaries a man said, "Damn it, Broderick. Have you found her?"

Chandra shot bolt upright in her bed, her knuckles whitening as she gripped the receiver. She knew without knowing *how* she knew that they were talking about her.

The other man's familiar voice made her shiver with horror.

"Damn it, no!" Lucas replied with a note of exasperation. "And don't call me at home. It's too dangerous."

Lucas's receiver clicked, but the other man stayed on the line a few tense seconds longer, breathing heavily, as if he sensed she was there. Then he hung up, and so did she.

Did Lucas know who she was? He had seemed familiar to her all along, and she'd registered that look of instant recognition when he'd first met her.

Yet he'd sworn he'd never met her before.

Nothing made sense.

But then lies never did.

Could this mean his sons—

No. She would never believe Montague or Peppin were involved in anything other than helping her.

She got out of bed and went to her balcony. The lights in the aqua pool were on, so the rectangle gleamed like a jewel. The lawn was dark as it sloped down to the bay. In the moonlight, she saw two heavily built armed men, keeping to the shadows as they prowled the grounds. One of them stopped, his hand automatically going to his shoulder holster as he turned to stare at her.

And then she knew.

Her heart began to pound as she backed slowly into her bedroom and shut and locked the glass doors.

Lucas *had* lied.

Not only that. He had made her his prisoner.

Knowing she would never be able to sleep, she raced to his bedroom. She pushed the door open and rushed inside before she lost her nerve.

He flushed with guilt and angry surprise as he glanced at her from his desk and found her staring at him, wide-eyed, with her white gown floating around her hips because she had stopped so abruptly.

He wore pajama bottoms only. The sight of his dark bare chest with those odd scars and his muscular arms sent a shiver through her.

She seemed to have a similar effect on him. The moment he saw what she was wearing, his dark expression grew charged with desire. His heated gaze ran from her face down her body, which was clearly revealed by her nearly transparent nightgown. And as he looked at her, again she felt as if he were already her lover, as if he'd made love to her hundreds of times, as if they belonged together always.

She tried to remind herself how cold he'd been all evening. But he excited her. Underneath her doubt, some truer part of herself believed he was the one man who would never hurt her.

Vaguely she noted that his computer was on and that his briefcase lay open. Dozens of documents and files spilled from the briefcase all over his keyboard and cramped work space. When she walked toward him, her gown swirling seductively about her hips, he jammed several papers into his briefcase and snapped it shut before he jumped up. Suddenly she was curious not only about his mysterious caller and the strange men prowling outside, but about the contents of that briefcase.

"What were you working on?" she asked, surprising herself with the calm in her voice.

"Nothing." His voice was too crisp, too sharp. "I thought we already said good-night."

"Lucas, who are those armed men outside? Are you keeping me...prisoner?"

His turbulent gray eyes grew hard. "Damn it. I hired them to make sure no one bothers you while you're here."

"I've been here for days without guards."

"I hired them to protect you."

"Why now? I don't understand."

"Why now?" His eyes fastened on her face. "Because I didn't know about you till this morning. My kids rescued you out of a public hospital parking lot. You were doped up and badly injured. You say somebody tried to kill you. You say you're scared they'll try again. And you ask me why? My reasons should be perfectly obvious. Anybody could have seen you get in my car. I don't know a damn thing about you or who might be after you. All I know is that you or my kids might be in danger.

"Also," he continued, "there's a guy making a name for himself killing Texas lawyers. In fact, he just blew an associate of mine away in Houston."

"I—I'm sorry about your friend, Lucas," she murmured.

"I received a death threat from the bastard—or from a crazy prankster pretending to be him—today."

She stared at him in mute horror.

Just for an instant his voice softened. "Now do you understand why I hired the bodyguards?"

The faint tilt of her head was barely perceptible.

"Good," he whispered. "I'm glad that's settled."

"Lucas, if you knew who I was...would you tell me?"

The merest fraction of a second passed before he answered. ''Of course.'' His voice was smooth, easy, and yet there was another element in it. ''Why do you ask?''

''Who called a while ago?''

This time there was no hesitation.

''It was a wrong number.'' His eyes burned into her, daring her to challenge the lie.

When she didn't he said, ''Now would you go to bed?''

Later, in her bedroom, Chandra was dreaming she and Lucas were in a strange land and about to be married. Their silken costumes were exotic. A curtain of brightly colored beads hung in a doorway. All the women wore long gowns and veils. She wore a golden veil and golden bracelets, and Lucas was smiling at her, his gaze filled with warmth and love. But just as he was about to place the ring on her finger, his face changed and he was someone else. Someone with fierce black eyes and hate in his heart.

Then she was in another place and another time. It was almost as if she was another person. She was hiding from Lucas in a closet. He was in a room with tall ceilings. Dozens of vases and bowls held dying roses. People in black with long faces filed conspiratorially out of a library as Lucas dragged her out of a closet. The black-robed people nodded as he carried her away and locked her inside a dark, airless space. She began to scream as she realized he was going to bury her alive.

She cried Lucas's name again and again and woke to find herself in his beautifully appointed guest bedroom, its lilac colors bleached silver in the moonlight. She got up and, feeling cold, ran swiftly to open the doors. She stood in the draft of warm air, staring out at the bodyguard on the beach.

The night air was heavy with humidity. The tide had come in and the surf was rushing across the sand all the way to the rocks. She watched the water for a long time, but it did little to calm her. Her forehead and upper lip were beaded with perspiration as she shivered in terror from the residual horror of her nightmare.

"Hey, hey" came Lucas's gentle rasp from her doorway.

She had turned even before he spoke, because she had sensed he was there.

Their gazes met. In the silver light his harsh face was as unreadable as stone. Still, she felt that shock of recognition, and the electric excitement he aroused so easily rushed through her and mingled with her dread of him.

"It's only me," he murmured.

Again he was shirtless, and she stared at the brown chest covered with thick black hair. Still shaking with fright, she was struck by how strong and unyielding he was, and by how much she wanted to be held in his dangerous arms.

"Lucas—" Her mind swirled with all the fearful questions in her heart.

Again she felt that they had a past together, that they were more deeply involved than he was willing to let on.

"What's wrong?" he demanded.

"You were there," she whispered. "In my nightmare. You are one of them."

"No," he began hoarsely. "I'm not."

But she backed away from him, shivering, even as she longed to run to him and beg him to kiss her.

She forced herself to say, "You were plotting with them to kill me."

"No, oh, God," he whispered, reaching for her and cradling her body against his.

The sea breeze was ruffling her hair, sending long strands of the stuff against his cheek and throat. He smiled at her, his eyes kind as he stroked her cheek and smoothed her blowing hair. As he continued to hold her, she gradually relaxed. All night she had wanted this. Forever she had wanted it. If he knew who she was and wouldn't tell her, so be it. If she had to die, his arms were where she wanted to be.

With a helpless sigh she circled his neck with her trembling hands and whispered brokenly, "Not you. Please not you, too."

"I wasn't there."

She looked at him and saw that he burned with desire. The darker image of him looking hard and ruthless in that rose-filled foyer in her nightmare flashed into her mind.

"You were in a room filled with dying flowers."

He whitened, and she sensed there was more than an element of truth in her dream. And yet— *His eyes were kind.*

"Hold me," she whispered. "Just hold me."

At first his arms were gentle, but gradually they wound around her tightly until their bodies seemed to flow into one another and become one.

He had held her before. Many times.

She reached up and pressed a warm kiss against the hot skin of his neck. She felt his savage indrawn breath as male need raged through him. He buried his fevered lips in her hair with a hungry kiss that set her entire being aflame.

Without a word she began to explore his neck and throat with her mouth.

"Kiss me. Love me," she begged.

Unable to stand, they collapsed to the floor, their pulses beating together. She lay on the carpet, staring up at him as he silently tore off her clothes and then his own. When she was naked, his callused hands roamed from her breasts to her waist to her thighs, exploring, caressing, already knowing exactly what would most please her as if he was very experienced with her particular body. And she had that same instinctively accurate knowledge about him.

Soon she forgot everything except the pleasure of his

delicately flicking tongue and his fingers moving urgently between her legs.

Her hands trailed over his hair-roughened chest, sensuously stroking ever lower down the length of his flat belly. She felt too aroused to ask him about the long scar on his torso. And as her fingers closed shamelessly around him, he swore, then groaned as he caught her waist and flipped her over onto her back.

Then he was on top of her, straddling her, his great dark body hot and hard and pulsating. His fingertips again stroked her inner thighs. She felt his thumbs skimming the satin folds between her legs, opening her like the petals of a rose.

As surprised as he, she cried out when he encountered the unexpected painful barrier.

"I'll stop," he offered hoarsely, desperately, "if you want me to."

"No." Her voice sounded as fractured as his. "Don't stop."

"But you're a virgin," he whispered. "I don't want to hurt you."

"It doesn't matter."

"To me it does." He pressed his lips to hers.

Arching her body to his, she cried out when he lowered his head to her breasts before sliding down the length of her until his open mouth was pressing against her most heated flesh. Then he began making love to her slowly while she moaned and twisted beneath him. Only when her knees clamped around his head did he quit kissing her and haul her underneath him again.

"Oh, God," he said, looking into her eyes. "You're beautiful."

She locked her arms around his neck. When he drove into her, her cry was filled with both rapture and pain. He whispered passionate endearments. After a while he slowly sank deeper. Then he began rocking harder and faster in a dreamlike, frictionless rhythm that was as old as time.

A rogue wave exploded on the beach below the white mansion, foam and spray shattering against the sand and racing up the beach to the bluff.

She felt carried away on a similar dark tide. The journey was like that great wave, swelling and swelling and then bursting into thousands of geysers before dying. And afterward, when she lay spent in a sated stupor of delirium and ecstasy, with his warm perspiring body sprawled heavily across hers, she clung weakly to his waist, tracing her trembling fingertips through his damp hair, never wanting him to let her go, never wanting the wondrous feelings she had for him to end.

When he recovered, he lifted her into his arms and carried her into his bedroom.

They did it in his marble shower because he had been fantasizing, ever since he'd met her there. This time he used a condom. With the warm water streaming down upon them, he braced her against the wall, entered her and then commanded her to wrap her legs tightly around him. His hands cupped her buttocks as he forcefully took her a second time.

"This is what I wanted the first instant I saw you," he growled.

Without a single reservation she urged him deeper. "Me, too."

Chandra felt as if she was in the middle of a swirling kaleidoscope of sunlight and brilliant hot colors as once again she was filled with him and felt the same building joy. And when it was over she was filled, as well, with the same unbearable and utterly illogical knowledge that tonight was not the first night they had made love.

But how could that be when she'd been a virgin?

Exhausted, they slept, their bodies intimately tangled beneath the sheets. In the middle of the night, he teased her awake by stroking her earlobe with his tongue, by trailing more kisses from her delicately arched feet up the curve of her thighs. But this time his lovemaking was softer and slower, and the pleasure she found in him indescribably spiritual. And again, he remembered to protect her.

When she awoke, a rosy light was sifting through his windows. How strange she felt, wrapped in his arms. She didn't care if she'd forgotten her life, as long as she'd found him. She felt so gloriously alive. Even though she was shamelessly naked beside him, she was not at all embarrassed.

She traced the gold design of his heavy cotton bedspread with a fingertip. Then she turned on her side and savored his nearness. His dark face seemed relaxed, almost content. With a sigh she melted against the heat of his long body.

She remembered how he had looked last night, with his silver eyes on fire for her, with his mouth heavy with sensuality. Slowly the bizarre realities of their situation returned. Her knowledge of him ran too deeply for them to have been strangers. And yet he swore he hadn't known her before.

He had posted armed bodyguards outside his house. He had talked cryptically about her to a man whose familiar voice terrified her.

Very carefully, so as not to awaken him, she untangled herself from his arms and legs and got out of bed. The room was shadowy as she glided to his closet and removed his terry robe. She had intended nothing more than to return to her room, but when she stumbled in the darkness, she bumped the corner of his black lacquered desk and saw his half-open briefcase. She stared at it, suddenly too curious to leave.

Her gaze flicked across the room when Lucas stirred. He had not opened his eyes.

Queasily she opened his briefcase.

And then she could only gape as she lifted a color blow-up of herself. In the picture her head lay across a stone block as she made a face at the camera.

Where? When?

Nothing clicked. Not even a blue flash. Absolutely nothing.

The photograph could have been that of a stranger. She lifted the paper under the photograph.

It was a pencil sketch. Again she recognized herself.

She dropped the photograph and the sketch as Lucas kicked his sheets off. She whirled and saw that he was watching her now from the shadows, his silver eyes predatory in the hot dawn light.

"What are you doing?"

She jumped at the steely sound of his low voice and slammed his briefcase. "I—I thought you were asleep," she whispered guiltily, her low voice betraying only the slightest trace of her fear.

"So you decided to spy."

"I was on my way to my room so the boys won't find us together."

"Leave my stuff alone and go," he commanded harshly, crawling out of bed.

"Who am I, Lucas?"

He hesitated and then said forcefully, "I don't know, damn it."

"Don't you?"

Before he could answer she turned and ran, too shaken by his dark look and rough tone to admit she'd seen the photograph of herself taken in another time and place and the sketch of herself as well.

Angrily he bunched the black embroidered spread at his waist and chased after her, catching her just inside her door.

''The boys,'' she whispered in a hurt, baffled voice. ''I don't want them to hear us.''

''I don't give a damn about the boys.''

''You're angry, then?''

''No,'' he said softly, surprising her. ''I'm sorry for the way I treated you. You caught me by surprise, that's all.''

Very slowly he lifted her hands to his shoulders and then grasped her waist, drawing her stiff, reluctant body against his.

The bedspread fell to the floor.

She felt like she was melting in his heat.

''Marry me,'' he whispered.

''What?''

As always with her body plastered warmly against his, she found it impossible to think. But she knew that a proposal from him was no light, impulsive matter. And it scared her even more than the photograph.

''Forget your questions and doubts about me,'' he begged, ''and I swear I'll forget mine about you.''

''What if I can't?'' she whispered, even though she was thrilled by his nearness as well as by the prospect of becoming his wife.

''We belong together. No matter what you've done or what I've done. No matter who you are. No matter how crazy and fast all this seems.''

''I can't. Not till you tell me everything.''

''Damn it, we met in my shower for the first time yesterday!''

''The truth is more complicated than that. My body held no secrets for you.''

''Damn it. I can't explain my feelings. But you were a virgin. I swear I never made love to you before.''

''Maybe we did everything else except for—'' she blushed ''—except the sex act itself.''

''We didn't. I swear it. I never saw you. I never touched

you. I never kissed you—before yesterday.'' He stared at her, his dark face intense and baffled. ''But I can't blame you for thinking that. I don't have amnesia, but every time I'm with you I have the feeling I know you, too. You don't even have to talk, and I know what you're thinking and feeling. When you came to my door earlier, I knew you were out there even before I opened it. I'm confused, too. And a little scared. All I can think of to do is to give it time.'' A slow smile played around the corners of his mouth. ''Maybe we should just enjoy it till we figure it out.'' He lowered his lips to hers.

''Are we going to make love again?''

His voice grew husky. ''Is that an invitation?''

When she was silent, he lifted her into his arms and carried her inside, kicking the door shut behind them.

He wasn't telling her everything.

But his body radiated heat and his touch was tender as he laid her beneath him on the bed.

She didn't know whether his kisses were taking her to heaven or hell. His hard body rasped silently against her soft breasts and stomach and thighs. His mouth and hands explored her hungrily, leaving no part of her unclaimed. When he pushed her legs apart and drove inside her, she cried out because the indescribable pleasure he gave her made her whole.

In that final heated moment of melting release, she didn't care who he was. Or who she was.

Or even if he was her worst enemy.

She put a hand on either side of his hot cheeks, and with utmost deliberation, kissed him on the mouth.

The act was a pledge.

No matter who he was, she belonged to him.

She always had and she always would.

Seven

Billion-Dollar Moran Heiress Wanted For Murder.

The two-inch-high newspaper headline slammed into Lucas's gut as hard as a balled fist.

If Chandra read that headline, she might get her memory back in a hell of a hurry. But what would such an unpleasant shock do to her?

His hand jerked, causing him to splash hot coffee all over himself. On the front page was a full-color photograph of Chandra and a lurid shot of the coffin that contained what was left of Miguel Santos. There was a small story about Gertrude Moran's new will and rumors that the notorious Lucas Broderick had been hired by the family to break the will.

Damn.

A feeling of profound dread filled Lucas.

Chandra had looked so pale and fragile this morning when he'd left her asleep in her bed. Too fragile to deal with this.

Any minute she'd be down for breakfast. If some slimy bastard really was after her, he could have leaked the stories to the press to flush her out. If she turned herself in to the law and didn't get her memory back, the cops would crucify her.

Lucas decided he couldn't let her see this yet. She didn't need any additional trauma. But that wasn't what scared him the most. To tell her the truth now might be a further risk to her life. If she felt compelled to talk to the cops or to reporters, the killer would know exactly where she was.

Grabbing a towel, Lucas sopped up the spilled coffee and then raced to the den, where he punched his television remote. News stories about the Moran scandal blared from every channel. One showed Santos's weeping widow in a black shawl with her five weeping children slumped together on rickety folding chairs in a small adobe chapel for the funeral service. Another showed shots of officers pulling sacks of drugs out of the burned van. In still another a cop was saying that they had the red T-shirt Chandra was last seen wearing, and that Santos's blood was all over it. There was only one positive story. It was about Casas de Cristo and the houses Chandra had built for barrio families. Lucas listened closely to the interviews with Mexican officials and several poor families who touchingly defended her, saying that Chandra could not possibly be involved in anything illegal.

When his phone rang, Lucas grabbed it, and a drunken Stinky roared obscenities into his ear.

"I'm as upset about this as you are, Brown. But if you call me at home again, we're through." Lucas slammed the phone down.

The heat to solve the mystery was on. Only it was even worse than Stinky had predicted. The press was going to town with the scandal. Chandra was so hot, she had even upstaged the serial killer who'd threatened Lucas.

Suddenly Lucas heard his boys' stampeding footsteps and rough shouts as they raced downstairs. As he switched off the television set, Montague and Peppin burst in upon him.

"We know who she is, Dad," Peppin exclaimed in a breathless rush. "Her name's Bethany Ann Moran and she's real real rich and—"

"I know," Lucas said quietly.

"They're framing her, Dad!" This from Montague. "She didn't kill anybody. We gotta make the cops see that."

"Look, guys, I've been thinking. Maybe it's not such a hot idea to turn her over to the cops—I mean, right now, when some goon is after her and before she gets her memory back. We need to be able to prove she's innocent. Otherwise the cops might slap her in jail. It's a good idea to come clean, but we can always do it later. I want you to get every television set and radio out of the house and put them in my car."

"But, Dad, maybe if we tell her who she is, she'll get her memory back. Maybe she can tell the cops exactly what happened. Who the real killer is. And then she could live here always."

"No, dumbo. She's rich. Do you think she'd still want to stay with us after she found that out? She'd leave."

Both boys grew silent at that possibility.

"I don't think we should decide anything without medical advice," Lucas said. "I'm driving her to San Antonio to see Pete today. And I'm not even going to try to find a sitter for you guys—so I want you two to come straight home from school and intercept and destroy every newspaper or magazine that carries this story."

"Dad, how come you're trying to help her when those guys on TV say you've been hired to break the Moran will—"

"Shut up, Peppin. We gotta start uplugging stuff fast," Monty ordered tersely. "Dad's on her side the same as we are."

"Holy cow! She's rich and the bad guys are after her. Maybe after us, too. This is way better than a movie," Peppin crawed. "I'm gonna get my baseball bat out of my closet and hide it under my pillow along with my knife."

"What good will that do?"

"Stupid! What if *he* gets in here?"

"Boys, not now."

Electrified into action that appealed to them immensely, they raced up and down the stairs, whispering and arguing about strategies a mile a minute while they filled Lucas's trunk and back seat with every electronic gadget in the house.

Lucas went to Chandra's bedroom to distract her. When he entered the lilac room, Chandra was dressed in the new yellow dress with the tight bodice and full skirt he'd bought her. She was leaning across her bed, so that he got a marvelous view of her slim waist, shapely hips and long legs as she straightened the spread.

He closed the door with a click, and she stopped tucking the pillow under the lilac silk spread and smiled spontaneously.

Enraptured, he could only stare at her speechlessly.

"So, there you are," she said, rushing to him. "I just couldn't seem to wake up after—"

A wanton image rose in both their minds of their bodies writhing together. Blushing, she tossed her mane of hair and laughed. Her blue eyes glowed. The shadows beneath them were very faint.

"You look wonderful in that dress."

"Thank you. You have excellent taste."

"Not usually."

She could not seem to stop looking at him any more than

he could stop looking at her. Again he was stunned that the foundations of his life had shifted so swiftly and so irrevocably.

"I was afraid you might have already gone to your office," she said hesitantly.

"Without kissing you goodbye?" he murmured.

As she stretched on her tiptoes to offer him her lips, he caught her fiercely against his immense frame and held her for an endless moment. And as he did, a lifetime of bitter emotion flowed out of him.

He had known her a mere twenty-four hours, and already she was the single thread of his life, the one thing that, if severed, would destroy everything. No matter what he had to do, no matter what lie he had to tell or what secret he had to keep, he couldn't lose her.

"I am going downtown, but not for long," he murmured. "I've decided to spend as much time as I can with you—until I'm sure you're completely recovered."

"But, Lucas, that's not necessary. The last thing I want is to be a burden to you."

"You're not. I'm linked by modem, telephone and fax to my office. I can work here almost as easily as there. But I'm taking off today to drive you to San Antonio."

"Why?"

"My brother is a doctor. I want him to check you and to make sure that you're really okay."

"That's not necessary."

"Just say you'll go."

"But—"

"I thought you wanted to make me happy."

"I do."

"So, will you go?"

"Yes. Yes. Yes."

He grinned at her. "Why can't you say that when I ask you to marry me?"

"I will...soon. I'm sure of it. Only—"

Her voice trailed off. Her blue eyes were troubled, her white face fragile.

Lucas's heart filled with panic. He was used to getting what he wanted when he wanted it. If she didn't marry him now, maybe she never would.

He analyzed the situation with his cold lawyer's intelligence that not even the fire of his new passion could altogether extinguish. Once she knew who she was and who he was, once the media and the police and her family started in on her, anything could happen.

He needed time to win her.

Time to figure this mess out.

And he was running out of time.

Lucas strode hurriedly across the plush Oriental rugs and unlocked the cabinet that contained his private fax machine. There were two curled pieces of shiny paper in the tray. He picked them up and began to read.

TIGER ONE SECURITY AGENCY
1414 Shoreline Boulevard
Corpus Christi, Texas

Fax to: Lucas Broderick
Fax from: Tiger Security

Dear Lucas:

Subject held in high esteem in northern Mexico by Rafe and Cathy Steele.

The Steeles temporarily in charge of Casas de Cristo since subject's disappearance. Steele very suspicious and belligerent to our questions.

Subject regarded highly by her benefactors and employees. Friends swear drugs were planted in her houses.

Truck driver who picked subject up on highway night van burned has positively identified her photograph.

Unable to contact witness who says subject was driving burned vehicle.

Subject's fingerprints all over the unregistered Colt .45 police claim killed Santos.

Police determined to build a case against subject.

Media camped outside Moran ranch.

Holly Moran pretended to be reluctant about giving evidence, but she told police that Chandra had said she was on her way to ranch. She also gave damning evidence about subject's mental state.

Everybody at ranch denies seeing subject or van at the ranch the day of memorial service.

Henry Moran illegally sold guns to Central American freedom fighters.

Stinky Brown's parents died in bizarre boating accident. Stinky did jail time in the eighties for beating up and nearly killing a rich debutante who jilted him right before he dated Chandra.

Unable to confirm Brown's claim that his brother Hal has gone east to visit relatives.

No criminal record on any of the Morans or Hal Brown.

More details to follow.

Sincerely,
Tom Robard

The second fax was a long list of Chandra's unsavory boyfriends.

Lucas wadded it up and burned it in his ashtray.

As he watched the names go up in flames, he felt a raging jealousy. Until he remembered that she'd been a virgin.

Feeling calmer, Lucas locked Robard's fax in a drawer

filled with other confidential reports in the same cabinet that contained his private fax machine.

Lucas felt more restless and dissatisfied than ever. Other than her friends' belief in Chandra, there was nothing to exonerate her.

Damn it. She was innocent.

But he had to prove it.

Lucas sat down at his desk and dialed Stinky.

"Have you found her?" Stinky's slurred voice was like ice.

"No."

"Then you're fired, counselor."

Both men slammed down their phones.

Lucas sighed ruefully. If only the rest of this mess could be solved so easily.

His intercom buzzed, and Lula's brisk voice informed him that a police detective, a Lieutenant Sheldon, was outside.

"And there's a reporter from the *Caller* who wants to talk to you when the lieutenant is finished."

Black-gloved hands clenched the steering wheel. "Gotcha!" A poisonous hammering began inside the watcher's skull.

From the driver's seat of a nondescript gray car that was parked four houses down from Lucas's opulent white wall, the watcher smiled as Lucas Broderick's Lincoln swept out into the bustle of traffic on Ocean Drive.

The watcher's eyes went glassy with delight when they fastened on the girl in her late twenties with the showy blond hair. *Beth!*

Broderick's arm was draped over the seat, his hand casually resting on her bare shoulder. She was thinner, but she looked almost well again. Maybe not completely. But no longer was she the battered, bleeding, vacant-eyed zom-

bie who had emerged from the burning van and dashed
suicidally in front of that truck.

She leaned closer to Broderick, and the watcher realized
she was in love.

Big damn surprise.

So, the sickening hunch had been dead on the money.
All the waiting and careful plotting worth it.

Broderick was a liar and a thief and a gold digger. He'd
had her the whole damn time.

When the bastard had seen a way to do better than his
forty-percent fee, he'd sure as hell gone for it.

Broderick had lied to the family as well as to all the
authorities.

Which meant the bastard had to die, too.

The beast inside the watcher smiled grimly.

The gray car slid into traffic and, lagging a safe distance,
followed the Lincoln all the way to San Antonio.

All the way to Dr. Pete Broderick's discreet brick mansion in the woody hills on the fashionable northwest side
of San Antonio.

Bastards. All of them.

But they'd be sorry.

The beast was free and on the rampage.

At long last.

For Lucas the next few days were wonderful and terrible
and desperately crucial. He had to win Chandra so completely that when she knew the truth, she would forgive
him everything. At the same time he had to protect her and
solve the mystery.

Somehow Lucas had convinced the police and the press
he knew next to nothing about the Moran case, and they
turned their attentions elsewhere.

Lucas had warned Pete not to reveal anything he knew
about Chandra's true identity before he'd taken her to San

Antonio. Pete said that Chandra's injuries hadn't been as severe as the emergency room doctors had led him to believe. He also confirmed her belief that she couldn't have done better with teams of surgeons and nurses caring for her. But when Pete got Lucas alone, he said Lucas was correct to fear her mental state was still very fragile, that she needed to be nurtured and protected and that she should not be told who she was and especially not that she was wanted for murder until she was a good bit stronger.

"She is blocking the truth because it's too horrible to accept."

"So, when can I tell her?" Lucas had demanded tensely.

"Give her a week. Till Friday, at the very earliest. Say, what is she to you anyway?" Pete smiled. "I've never seen you so—"

Lucas frowned, unwilling to say. "She's...good with the boys."

"I'll bet!" Pete flashed him a grin. "The family's going to love her."

"Oh, yeah. For sure. She'll fit right in. Another missionary. Just what we need."

"She's just what *you* need. And you know it."

Pete changed her medicine and gave Lucas a sheet of instructions and joked that Peppin and Montague might indeed make good doctors. When Lucas and Chandra drove away from his house with Pete's glowing report, Lucas's spirit rocketed sky-high. He hugged her close for a very long time, feeling immensely relieved that she was over the worst of her injuries and that her amnesia wouldn't be permanent. In fact, he was so thrilled by the prognosis that he decided to celebrate. For the next few hours he forced himself to set aside his fears for her and the sensation that danger was thickening all around them, and he simply enjoyed being with her.

Lucas found an out-of-the-way restaurant and ordered a

seafood dinner to go. Then he took her to a state park in the hill country where the warm air was sweet with the scent of cedar and a clear green river ran between tall limestone cliffs. They ate beneath the spreading branches of a live oak tree. Then they slow-danced beside his car to the music from a tape in the car player. They drove home in the star-spangled darkness, roaring along the straight interstate with the windows of the Lincoln partially down so that wisps of her hair blew against his cheek. He drove at a speed that made his blood rush with excitement, or maybe it wasn't the speed that made his blood heat but the fact that she was nestled in his arms.

It was two in the morning when the big car nosed its way through the white walls and up the drive to his house. They went inside and made sure the boys were safely asleep. Then he took her down to the beach where they walked hand in hand, barefoot along the water's edge.

He felt like he was in a dream as he led her running through the warm salt water and then across the sand up to the doors to the tunnel in the bluff.

He started to unlock the heavy steel doors, but she turned white and said no, that she wanted to take the path up the cliff to the house.

"But this is the shortcut," he whispered, "and soon it'll be sealed up for good."

She trembled and forced herself to take slow deep breaths. "The sooner the better. The very idea of it gives me the creeps."

He grinned. "You and my Realtor. I need to call a contractor."

She smiled at him. Then she turned and raced up the cliff path. He dropped the lock, and it banged against the metal door as he chased after her.

Before they let themselves in through the patio doors that opened onto the deck, he sprayed the sand off their feet and ankles with the hose. Together they raced along the dimly lit corridors and stairways to his room, where they closed the door and she lit candles. Then they fell upon his bed and made love to each other greedily, desperately, as if they could never get enough of each other.

And this time he didn't practice safe sex because he selfishly knew that he wanted a baby from her. She was wonderful with his boys. And the image of her holding a baby, his baby, maybe a little girl with blue eyes and golden hair like hers, branded itself into his soul.

But it wasn't only the child he wanted. It was Chandra who was the ultimate prize. She had to be his, and he knew if he got her pregnant that would be still another bond that might make her want to stay with him forever.

Even in love that ruthless quality in his nature that had driven him to excel in law drove him to conquer, obtain, acquire whatever he wanted. There was an insatiable, selfish completeness about his feelings for her that made him know he *had* to win her.

For better or for worse, he was head over heels in love with her. He *had* to marry her.

But when he told her so and asked her to marry him again, she held him very close and kissed him. Then she said no.

Almost imperceptibly the tensions between Lucas and Chandra built during that week. The police talked to him again, as did the press. He told the reporters that he was no longer representing the Morans.

Determined to be with Chandra every possible minute, Lucas worked at home as much as he could. But spending more time with her taught him how vastly different were their personalities and characters. She was cut of finer, nobler cloth than the base stuff he was made of.

After reading dozens of Robard's reports about her missionary work, Lucas couldn't help but compare her inner purity to his own selfishness. He was unworthy, shallow, materialistic. He had lived solely for himself before he met her, seizing what he wanted with no thought of the consequences to others. He had charged to the max for his services, his only restraints being—can I get away with it without breaking the law?

Ruthlessly he had gone after only the cases that could make him rich or famous. He had sacrificed idealism at the twin altar of his ego and ambition. He had sacrificed friendships, his first marriage, his integrity, even his sons.

And though his love for Chandra had changed him to some degree, he knew that he would never be a white knight. Even though he felt ashamed and was determined to change, he could not totally remake himself. Thus he, who had always been so brashly self-confident, was afraid that she wouldn't love him when she really knew him.

He forced himself to back out of juicy cases, but signed on to defend a group of immigrants whose landlords refused to provide indoor plumbing.

Less than pleased with the new Lucas Broderick, his law partners began grilling him about some of his decisions. They were furious that he'd lost the Moran case. He told them he'd quit the firm and go out on his own if they didn't let him do as he pleased.

More than anything, he was working to find some shred of evidence to prove Chandra's innocence. Her memory didn't return, but she was so intuitive about him that she sensed the darkening in his mood every time he returned from his office knowing Robard had found nothing to clear her, only more that incriminated her.

The media coverage grew more shocking by the day, the rumors about her more vicious. The federal government decided to investigate her. What disturbed Lucas most was that the most damning stories about Chandra's supposedly shady operation in Mexico were his own idea. Only he hadn't ordered his men to spread those rumors. Someone who had been in the Moran library had.

But who?

According to Robard, every single person in that library had an airtight alibi the night of Santos's murder.

Lucas used some of his time at home to take care of mundane chores around the house that he never had time for. He met with the contractor and set Saturday as the day to seal the tunnel.

The images in Chandra's nightmares were becoming clearer. The memory of Lucas in a room with gilt furniture and dying roses was becoming sharper. She said she remembered being locked in a dark room and repeatedly drugged with syringes. She remembered a man with black eyes.

Practically all the Morans and everybody on the ranch had black eyes. Stinky's were the darkest. But Stinky and Holly had been entertaining mourners at the ranch the entire evening of the murder. So had Hal. At least according to Stinky.

Every night, after one of Chandra's nightmares, Lucas would hold her close and comfort her until her face lost its chalky pallor and she could breathe and talk normally. Last night she had dreamed she'd crawled out of a van right before it caught fire.

Every day that passed, his tensions and fears coiled around Lucas more tightly. He felt trapped in a spider's web.

Only he couldn't see the spider.

Their quarrel started with a phone call.

Lucas and the boys were out by the pool, so Chandra, who had just gotten up from her afternoon nap, answered the phone. When Lucas came running inside to catch it, he found her leaning against the kitchen counter looking numb, her white face as frozen as if she'd just awakened from a nightmare.

"Who is it?"

"I don't know. He won't say anything."

Lucas tore the phone from her. "Who the hell is this?" The line was dead.

Lucas slammed the phone down. "How many times do I have to tell you not to answer the damn phone?"

"Well, excuse me for living," she whispered tightly, rushing past him up the stairs. "I was tired. I didn't think."

He raced after her, feeling fury, remorse, love—the whole impossible gamut.

"I want you to tell me what is going on," she demanded when he followed her inside her bedroom.

"No. I need you to trust me."

She sat in front of her bureau and stared anxiously at her reflection in the mirror. With a tentative fingertip she pushed her hair and touched the fading zipperlike scar at her hairline. The scratches on her cheek were almost gone. She was growing stronger by the day. She spent less and less time taking naps.

"Trust you? There's nothing I want more. But that's very hard when I have no memory. I feel so empty and yet I keep having these terrible flashbacks. I love you and yet I know that you're keeping secrets from me."

"I told you. Pete said you need a week or so more to recover—"

She whirled. "I'm sick and tired of being treated like a baby."

"You nearly died. You need to get well. I'll tell you everything Friday."

"Friday? That's three whole days away. I don't know if I can wait."

Gently he tucked a stray strand of gold behind her ear. "Friday, I swear," he pleaded softly. "Maybe it won't even be that long. Maybe you'll get your memory back before then. Maybe the guys who are after you will make a wrong move."

"But this waiting, feeling like we're being stalked is hell. If I knew everything you know, maybe I could help you."

"Maybe. But right now your most important job is to rest and get well. If I don't have all the answers by Friday, I don't see that we have any choice but to do as you ask. Trust me…just a little longer."

She stared at him gloomily, moodily—hesitating.

"I know it's hard," he said reaching for her.

"Do you? You're always so in control!" She spun away from him. "I can't stand the way I feel—like we're living under siege."

"Look, some bastard tried to kill you. I'm afraid he'll try again."

"Why can't I at least watch television? Or listen to the radio?"

He shifted slightly, so that even if she wouldn't let him touch her, he was near enough to feel the warmth of her body.

"Because it might upset you too much. We agreed…Friday. If you don't get your memory back or I don't solve this thing, I'll do it your way."

Again she moved away from him. "I—I feel so trapped and isolated—so afraid."

"That's why I stay home as much as I can."

Her wide luminous eyes said, *But I'm afraid of you, too.* Aloud she whispered, "Lucas, you're in all my nightmares now, and you're always against me."

"No! I'm on your side. I swear it. You belong to me. I belong to you. I love you. I would lay down my life for you."

She didn't answer.

He got down on his knees in a posture of supplication. "Look into my eyes. What do you see?"

She knelt, too, and cupped his jaw with her fingertips. As she stared at him, the flame in her eyes lit an answering spark of emotion inside him.

"I do see love. Pure love," she whispered at last, "but I'm not sure if I can trust that."

"What else is there to believe in? What else is worth dying for?"

The late-afternoon sunlight was streaming through the windows. She looked wan and very vulnerable and so tired he could almost feel her exhaustion. He felt the same ache he always felt when he watched her sleep in the afternoons or at night when he comforted her after one of her nightmares.

Her luminous blue eyes continued to search his, distrusting him even though he knew she saw all the way into his heart. "I would die for you, too," she said.

He nodded, although he wasn't satisfied, and pressed his lips together tightly. "Let's hope it doesn't come to that."

"Lucas, last night I dreamed about that man's gray face again. It caught fire. His skin melted. But I saw a mustache this time, and the color of his dead eyes. They're brown—almost black. Who is he? Why does he haunt me? Why do I feel so guilty every time I see him staring at me with open-eyed horror?"

Santos.

Oh, God.

Tell her.

Lucas's hand closed around hers and gave it a nervous squeeze. "Friday."

Eight

"**G**otcha!"

The good-for-nothing lardy bodyguard never saw the horseshoe aimed at the back of his skull.

One minute the oaf was staring at the placid brown bay. The next he was crumpling heavily forward into the grass. Then the bloody horseshoe was picked up by a black-gloved hand and pitched onto the grass with the others. Slowly the watcher leaned down and grabbed the guard's ankles. The limp body was dragged, feet first, head bouncing along the stone path past the rose garden and into the garage. The doors were opened and the inert body was dragged inside the tunnel.

The beast felt excited as he heaved the bloated guard beside the other unconscious guard, who was gagged and bound. This was almost as good as shooting Santos and setting his body on fire.

Murder was the best of all highs.

Especially when it meant you didn't have to share what was rightfully yours with someone you hated.

The beast, who had stalked Lucas Broderick and Chandra Moran for the past week, should know. For the beast, the real person, had killed four times. And loved it.

The first murder had been the hardest.

The second had been Gertrude Moran.

The third—Miguel Santos.

The fourth had been that other self that had dared to inhabit the same body and had tried to cage the beast.

The false person had been pleasant and likable and had had lots of false friends. The false person had not cared that the beast seethed with rage and hurt and hatred every time the false person was nice to the false friends.

But the beast had vanquished the false person forever. There would be no more smiles that made the shared lips feel stiff or twitchy, no more lies that nauseated the real person.

While he thought, the beast methodically stripped the bodyguard and tied and gagged him. Next the beast put on the bulky uniform, the badge, the gun.

Then the beast felt powerful. All powerful—like a god.

The beast locked the brass padlock to the tunnel and strutted out of the garage into the brilliant, late-afternoon sunshine.

The oversize uniform was hot and scratchy.

So the hell what?

It would be dark soon, and cooler.

From the edge of the lawn, standing in a thicket of mesquite and tallow trees, the beast watched Lucas's Lincoln sweep into the drive. The black eyes narrowed as Lucas got out of the car with an armload of roses. The eyes became slits when Beth rushed out of the house and laughingly blushed as she took them. Her showy golden hair swirled about her shoulders as the lying bastard lifted her and made love to her first with his gaze and then with his lips.

Damn the bitch.

How the hell had she gotten out of that van? She should have fried.

Anger suffused every cell. Damn the lying betraying bastard lawyer for hiding her.

Obscene gurgling sounds came from the back of the beast's throat as Beth kissed Broderick deeply and passionately.

Fingers itched along the smooth trigger.

A silent voice cautioned, "*Wait till it's time.*"

A station wagon filled with six or seven boys rolled up. Both back doors were kicked open. Broderick's two brats spilled out of the house and raced toward the wagon.

After a parental lecture from Broderick and hugs from Beth, the little devils got in the wagon with their duffel bags to be driven away.

But the nosy kid with the ponytail lowered his silver sunglasses and stared long and hard at the beast until the wagon rolled out of the drive.

Melting into each others' arms, Beth and Lucas obviously thought they had the house to themselves and were looking forward to a romantic evening.

Little did they know.

The beast couldn't wait to sneak up on them and whisper, "Gotcha!"

Nine

Lucas sped home by way of Ocean Drive. There was a sailboard regatta on the bay. Not that he paid the slightest attention to the brightly colored sails rounding the final mark before skimming downwind toward the finish line as gracefully as butterflies. Nor did he note the landscaped mansions with their sculptured green lawns, palm trees, scarlet bougainvillea and pink oleander.

The traffic was heavy. But he didn't pay much attention to the steady stream of red taillights in front of him.

His mind was on Chandra.

It was Friday. Chandra had given Lucas till midnight to level with her. Even though he'd sworn he'd tell her everything, the week had gotten no better as it had worn on. If anything, the tension between Chandra and him had worsened. She had grown stronger and more restless by the day. She never napped now, and had more time to fret. She said she felt like a prisoner, that the suspense of not knowing her identity was killing her. Lucas had repeated Pete's advice so many times it had become a refrain. "Baby, Pete says it'll be better if you recover your memory on your own."

"I just keep thinking you'd tell me unless I—I'm some terrible sort of person—"

"It's complicated. You're not a terrible person."

"Then why are you so afraid to tell me?"

He always changed the subject at that point.

Lucas felt worried as he drove up to his house. Neither he nor Robard was a damn bit closer to solving the mystery of Miguel Santos's murder or to proving Chandra's innocence. And Lucas, who had built and won so many cases, Lucas who had written so many closing arguments to convince juries, couldn't seem to figure out the right words or the right way to tell Chandra something as straightforward as the simple truth.

Your family hired me to break the Moran will and defame you. I was tempted. God, how I was tempted. Until I found out who you were. Oh, and, by the way, you're wanted for murder, and the media are roasting you alive. They're saying you're a liar and a thief and that you've been taking bribes down in Mexico. They say you've run drugs. And, oh, I gave the lying bastard who's spreading this garbage the idea to slander you.

Lucas hadn't lived like a saint. Making her believe in his innocence and his love for her wouldn't be easy.

He had been boxed into tougher corners than this one.

But he had to win this one.

She'd been in his home less than three weeks, but already he depended on her quiet efficiency around the house. Already he delighted in the wonderful meals she took such pains to prepare for him. Already he admired her wonderful rapport with his sons and loved the way she made it possible for him to enjoy them, too. Peppin had even been bringing home a few As on his report card.

Most of all, of course, Lucas simply wanted Chandra for himself. In his bed. By his side. All the time. He wanted to bask in the loving glow he felt whenever he was around her. Forever. She made him happy. She made even the duller moments in his life meaningful and joyful. Just knowing she was in his house made the darkness lift from his soul.

Romantic gestures were alien to him.

But he'd bought flowers for this occasion. And a good sparkling California wine from a château he'd once visited in Sonoma.

Before he told her the truth, he wanted to set the mood.

The boys were scheduled to go on a beach camp out at a neighbor's house with several friends. He and Chandra would have the house to themselves.

Lucas had bought a steak for himself as well as roses. And lots of vegetables, everything from zucchini to spinach.

After dinner he planned to woo her and make love to her.

Afterward he would tell her. Maybe she'd even let him put it off until the morning.

And just in case she understood and forgave him, he had bought an engagement ring.

He would broach the shocking truth with infinite gentleness and patience. He would go down on his knees when he confessed he had been hired to steal her inheritance and defame her. He would tell her about the incident in the foyer, when he hadn't even seen her but had been so shaken by her presence. About all the dreams he'd had before he'd met her, especially the nightmare he'd had the night she'd been injured.

Somehow he had to make her believe what he himself

did not understand—that the two of them had a special bond that went far beyond the ordinary.

He had to make her see that even though he had considered the Moran case and worked for the Morans briefly, he had never deliberately done anything to hurt her.

Except to show some slimy bastard how to slur her good name and thereby ruin her reputation.

He only hoped that the truth would change things for the better between Chandra and himself, instead of for the worse.

Tonight. Tomorrow at the latest. No matter what, he would tell her the whole, unvarnished truth. Who she was. Who he was. And then he'd show her the newspapers that he'd been keeping in his trunk and beg her to forgive him.

They would face this thing together.

As he got out of the Lincoln he noted the bodyguard in a baggy uniform, slouching against a palm at the far edge of his property.

A new man. That was odd. Lucas thought he knew all Robard's men.

The guard sensed his interest, and when Lucas waved to him, the guy's hand went to his gun for a second before he lifted his hand and waved back. Then he skulked behind the palm tree.

Damned odd fellow. Gave off negative vibes. Worth investigating.

Lucas was about to go over and introduce himself when Chandra came running out of the house to greet him.

She hesitated on the last step, and he saw the fear and uncertainty in her eyes as well as the radiance of her love.

She was just as afraid of tonight as he was.

Concerned only for her, he forgot the bodyguard. This thing was hard on her. She'd been through a lot.

But maybe not the worst of it.

She was wearing the aqua dress with tiny pearl buttons

down the front he had bought for her the first day. Strands of fine gold hair were blowing in the faint breeze. There was a private smile, just for him, on her lips.

He grinned and held up the roses. And felt a little foolish. Four dozen red, pink, white and yellow blossoms spilled from his arms.

When she flashed him an even brighter smile and began to blush, walking shyly toward him, his chest swelled with the passionate emotion he felt for her, which was growing more incredibly potent with the passing of every day.

Her eyes were ablaze when he gently gave her the flowers.

Their fingertips brushed, and as always there was magic and warmth even in her lightest touch.

Then she buried her nose in the fragrant petals and said softly, "I love roses. Why do you suppose I love them so much?" She looked at him. "But not nearly as much as I love you. Now why do I feel—" Her blue eyes flashed and she broke off shyly.

Her face was flushed. Her entire being seemed aglow. And her warmth filled him.

Nobody had ever cared about him as she did. Not when he was a child. Not when he was a man. He had been lonely all his life.

Till her.

He had had success—wealth, fame. Everything and nothing—till her.

He hadn't believed in love.

Because he hadn't had the slightest idea what love was.

Till he'd stepped into his shower and her dazzling blue eyes had seared his soul the same way they were doing now.

For far too long he had wanted all the wrong things for all the wrong reasons—to make up for the emptiness inside him.

But they never had.

She alone could make him happy.

He was too old not to know that this sort of feeling wouldn't come twice in his lifetime.

He had to make her stay with him forever.

Lucas had wanted the evening to be perfect, and it was. She seemed to understand the ephemeral quality of everything they did together, that when she knew the truth, everything they had come to count on and cherish might be lost.

So for this brief shimmering space of time, they both wanted nothing except each other.

The sky darkened to opalescent purples and lavenders and indigos. Lucas and Chandra were easier with each other than they had been all week, their words and glances accompanied by frequent quiet laughter.

He warmed dinner and then they swam while the food was heating up. She lay in a lounge chair, content to admire his long brown body sliding through the water. The blue heron she sometimes fed on the patio flew up from the beach and joined her.

"Beggar," she whispered when he cocked his long beak and shyly regarded her. Laughing, she held out her empty hands to the tall bird that seemed to be so awkwardly perched on his stiltlike legs.

She laughed as a flock of brown pelicans soared and dove into the bay. When Lucas climbed out of the pool, he told her that pesticides in the fifties had almost obliterated brown pelicans in south Texas, but that they were making a comeback. She forgot her joy in the birds and came up to him and wrapped a towel around his broad shoulders. With another towel she dried his hair.

When she was done, she ran her hands through the damp

strands and then blushed. "Thank you for tonight. For this week."

He put a fingertip under her chin and guided her sweet face to his and gave her a long kiss, which held both fire and ice. Instantly he felt that intense hunger for her that ran so very deeply in him.

What he felt for her was both spiritual and physical. It was timeless. She was everything.

With her mouth she began to explore the sensitive hollow at the base of his throat. He kissed her, and as always the delicate taste of her acted upon him like an aphrodisiac.

"Let's forget supper and go inside," he said hoarsely.

Slowly she slid her hands across his wide bare chest, down the length of each of his scars.

"How did this happen?" she asked, thinking the jagged marks were scars, as everyone did.

"They are nothing. I was born with them."

"Birthmarks?" she said in a low voice. "How odd. They look more like scars."

Her gaze grew very bright, very serious when he laughed and told her about the Indian nurse who had infuriated his Christian father when she'd said his baby son had acquired the strange marks in another life, that they were marks left from scars—probably when he had died. "She said I was slashed to death by something big and heavy—maybe a machine." He paused. "My father ranted that what she said was a ridiculous, idiotic, stupid, superstitious lie. She told him that sometimes when the air is too heavy for a dying soul to rise, it enters the body of a newborn."

"Oh." Tenderly her fingers traced the white lines and came to rest instinctively upon his heart. When he tried to circle her with his arms again, she smiled and broke away.

"Not yet," she whispered. "I'm hungry."

"So am I. But for—"

"No. Please, Lucas. Let's wait."

They had supper by the pool, and afterward they pitched horseshoes, but they gave the game up quickly, deciding it wasn't the same without the boys.

The moon rose, brightening the sky. The strange bodyguard was nowhere to be seen. But Lucas had forgotten all about him when he seized Chandra and led her inside.

He threw open the glass doors to the balcony of his bedroom so they could hear the surf and smell the tangy salt air. A faint breeze stirred the sheers, causing them to fan out in eerie silver swirls. Moonlight streamed across the bed.

For a time the lovers stayed in the shadows. She edged closer, smiling, but when he reached for her, she whispered so faintly he almost didn't hear her, "No. Wait."

Raising both her hands, she began unbuttoning each tiny pearl button of her dress. She had beautiful hands, and in the moonlight, they were the color of ivory as they gracefully skimmed up and down those glimmering buttons on her bodice.

The aqua fabric parted gradually, and she eased the silky stuff over the graceful waves of her shoulders, letting it fall slowly away into a shadowy pool at her feet. She undid her black bra, and it slid to the floor with her dress.

He tried to say more but a vast silence enveloped them, and as always they spoke without words. Then her mouth was seeking his again, no longer teasing but in deadly earnest. Every muscle in his strong arms and legs flexed. Their sexes met. Teased. And clung. Suddenly he thrust, and as she launched her hips upward to meet him halfway, he knew a wild thrill that was more powerful than any he'd ever known as he sank inside her deeply.

With her thighs, she gloved him.

When she began to move, he clasped her to him, staring into her eyes for a long moment, telling her with his mind and heart that he loved her. Only when she silently communicated the same emotions did he begin to move inside her, steadily, without stopping, as she clasped him ever tighter. He grew hot, burning hot as she drew him deeper and deeper into that swirling black flame that was soft and yet an all-encompassing velvet darkness.

As he brought her to climax after climax, a corresponding firestorm built inside him.

His arms wrapped around her like steel bands.

He was burning up.

And then exploding and soaring on long hot waves of ecstasy.

Dying. And then bursting again and again every time she cried out.

He caught her to him, filling her completely as he held her tightly beneath him. Then he heaved one final time, shuddering against her, finding his own sublime release.

For a moment they were two beings alone in their own time and space, sharing a paradise of the senses. Then he mindlessly buried his lips against her silken throat and whispered her name.

"Chandra."

Lucas had fallen asleep instantly. Not she.

For a long time Chandra lay beneath Lucas's heavy body, unmoving, as utterly spent as he, even as the electrifying name he had spoken with such passionate ardor echoed inside her.

Chandra?

Yes, she *was* Chandra. An entire lifetime had come back to her. She was Chandra Moran, who had been officially christened Bethany Ann Moran.

And Lucas?

Lucas Broderick was that awful lawyer.

Why had he made her love him?

She knew why.

The warmth that had raced through her lush body moments before chilled, and she began to feel strange, not herself, and yet really herself for the first time since the accident, as painful images and traumatic emotions and memories, some of them only half-formed and poorly understood, bombarded her.

She knew the exact moment when Lucas's heavy breathing grew more regular and he fell asleep. Then, very carefully she wriggled free. Slowly she got up and, moving as soundlessly as a sleepwalker, glided into the bathroom. Numbly she showered and put on a pair of white jeans and a white embroidered blouse.

For a long moment she studied her face in the steamy mirror, as she had so many days and nights before. Only tonight the triangular face with the high cheekbones and vivid blue eyes was no longer that of a stranger.

She was Chandra Moran—heiress.

No wonder Lucas hadn't told her who she was.

Lucas Broderick was a slick, ambitious lawyer who had a reputation for playing dirty—and winning, if his defendant was rich and able to pay. More than a few of her benefactors had had bad dealings with him. With an eye to her fortune, he had romanced her and played her for a fool.

Exactly as Stinky Brown had so many years before. Gram had wisely had Stinky investigated, and when Gram had confronted Chandra with the unsavory stories about the other rich girls Stinky had courted and then Chandra had caught him in bed with Holly, Chandra had run away from them all.

Lucas Broderick *was* her enemy. Ugly phrases echoed in the dark places in her mind.

Lucas's deep husky drawl, heard for the first time, beloved even then as she'd hidden in the foyer closet, had made hideous promises to her family.

Utterly merciless. Destroy your cousin's name and her claim—

None of them had known she had arrived at the ranch and had been eavesdropping outside the library when Lucas had sworn to her family that he would break the will and destroy her.

More memories deluged her.

She was a child again in India, holding tightly to her stern grandmother's hand as a dark-skinned man with a white turban wrapped around his head dug up the floor of a crumbling house. Again she stared in horror at the gaping eye sockets in that tiny skull, at the dusty bones and rotten fabric in the box under the ancient rotting flooring. She had wept hysterically over that poor murdered girl because she had known, somehow she had known that some physical part of her former self was buried in that shallow grave.

Chandra had lived before, but nobody in her present family had ever believed her—not even Gram. Not even when she'd led them to her grave.

Her family had brought her back to Texas more determined than ever to erase all her memories of that other life.

Next Chandra saw a rose garden and a dark-haired girl snatching the roses Chandra had painstakingly gathered from a basket. The girl was shouting and crushing them under her cowboy boots, and Chandra said, "Don't, Holly—"

Holly, her beautiful cousin who had been so jealous of her, and the way Gram and she had loved each other. In the end Holly had taken Stinky because she always had to have everything that was Chandra's.

Next Chandra was in a closet in the Moran foyer. She'd come home after an estrangement of twelve years because Gram had written her a letter, begging her forgiveness and telling her that she was going to leave her in control of the Moran fortune. But when Chandra had called Gram from

Mexico, she had been told by Stinky that Gram had died suddenly and that there was no reason for her to return.

Chandra had gone home the day of the memorial service only to discover Holly and the others in the library plotting to break Gram's will. Chandra had hidden in a closet after she had heard Lucas's voice and realized he was leaving and would catch her eavesdropping if she didn't run or hide.

She remembered the dying roses in the foyer, the lonely strangeness of the house that day without Gram. But most of all she remembered the strange way Lucas's voice had held her spellbound. It had been gravelly and rough-edged and musical as he had promised her family he would break the will and spread rumors that Chandra had used payoffs and bribery in Mexico. Even though he'd been hired to ruin her, his words had lingered and resonated almost hypnotically in some sweet secret place in Chandra's soul.

Again his cruel words and phrases came to her in horrible fits and starts.

"Utterly merciless. Destroy your cousin's name and her claim."

In freeze-framed images Chandra saw him as she'd seen him from the partially opened closet door where she'd hidden that day. She had been drawn to him even though he had given off an aura of rage and arrogance.

His brilliant gray eyes had reminded her of angry smoke from a smoldering fire. His face had seemed stark and bold. Even so, fool that she was, she'd imagined she'd sensed some inner pain behind his cruel, self-serving exterior. She'd imagined herself nurturing and easing that pain.

Worst of all, she'd felt a blinding current of emotion drawing her soul to his. Even though he hadn't seen her, he'd seemed to feel it, too. He had stopped in mid-stride, his searing gaze searching every niche and darkened corner of the hall. He had called out to her, and she'd had to bite her tongue not to reply. When he'd started toward the closet, she'd desperately begun counting backward to break the connection.

Miraculously the ploy had worked.

But when he'd stalked out of the house, she'd wanted to run after him.

Because, insane though it would seem to everybody else, she'd known why that dangerous man had the mysterious power to attract her. She had known with an unfathomable certainty what no other woman in her right mind would have believed—*that she'd known him before.*

Just as she had known that he was the one person she had been searching for all *this* life without even realizing it. Every bad-boy boyfriend her family and friends had objected to, even Stinky, had been an attempt to find *him.*

Their love had been forbidden in her former life. She had been murdered because of it. And he had died horribly, too—he'd been run over by a train—when he'd been told by her sister she'd abandoned him.

Somehow she had sensed his presence in the world and had struggled to find him.

But her new family, who except for Gram had never understood her and who had always been against her, had unwittingly hired him as a tool to destroy her.

She remembered how she had stayed in that closet feeling drained and hopeless after he had gone. How she had wanted to race after him but hadn't let herself.

And then someone had opened the door.

For some reason she still couldn't see the face. But the voice that had greeted her had been familiar. "Welcome home, Bethany. I've been waiting for you. Just like I waited for Gram the day…she died."

Gram…murdered?

She had tried to run, but strong hands had seized her.

"Gotcha!"

Chandra remembered the blinding flash of the syringe, the warm, dizzying sensation of the drug flowing into her veins as the world went bright white and the realization struck her that she was going to die.

But—somehow—she had escaped death.

Who had opened that closet door?

What had happened next?

Who had tried to kill her?

Was it Lucas?

Why couldn't she remember?

Instead she saw a man's body wrapped in plastic.

And this time she saw the corpse's face. This time she remembered his name and shuddered.

Miguel Santos.

Her foreman in Mexico.

Poor, dear Miguel.

Next she was on a highway, barefooted and limping, her clothes covered with blood. Santos's or her own? She was holding a gun and running straight into blinding white headlights.

She remembered a horn honking right before she crumpled in the middle of the highway.

But no more memories came.

Dear God.

Had she done murder?

Trembling, more terrified than ever before, she got in bed, careful to stay as far from Lucas as possible.

Who was he? The tender lover of the past week?

Or an unscrupulous gold digger? The lawyer her family had hired to destroy her?

Gram had said she would always be a fool about men.

Chandra stared at Lucas. His dark face looked so young, so completely relaxed and guileless, like his sons' did when they slept. In no way did he appear to be the treacherous monster she told herself he must surely be.

A tear welled in the corner of her eye. Then another. Until she was sobbing helplessly.

What explanation would he give her in the morning?

He had pretended to love her so deeply, so passionately, and she felt that she could not live a single hour without his love.

And yet she would have to.

Not knowing what to fear the most—the truth or his lies—she pulled the sheets over her shivering body and lay awake in the darkness, dread and terror filling her heart. She wept and tried to make sense of her new knowledge as she waited for the dawn.

Ten

"**G**otcha!" The whisper was soft, triumphant.

The next three sounds resonated like a rattlesnake's hiss. Click. Snap. Spin.

Chandra's drowsy mind snapped awake.

One minute she'd been lying with her head cozily nestled against Lucas's shoulder, having been lulled by his body heat into sleep despite herself. Still caught in that hazy twilight zone between dream and reality, she was about to snuggle closer to him.

The next minute she felt the cold barrel of a revolver nudge her temple.

"It's loaded, bitch."

She opened her eyes and stared, too shocked to move or make a single sound.

The monster with the dead black eyes from her nightmares loomed over her.

Only he was real.

She recognized him.

He had an innocent boyish face, dark eyes and curly auburn hair.

He had opened the closet door. He had drugged her and shot Santos and tried to shoot her, too, on that lonely stretch of highway near the border.

He had found her again. Somehow, even during those weeks of amnesia, she had sensed him tracking her.

Feeling her stiffen, Lucas opened his eyes.

"Stinky?" Lucas jerked upward, registering only a shadowy hulk holding a gun to her face.

"Move, and I'll splatter her brains all over your face, counselor."

"No, Lucas. Not Stinky." Chandra's voice fell. "It's Hal."

Sweet, gentle, baby-faced Hal. The younger brother who for whatever reason couldn't make it on his own, so Stinky had felt responsible for him. Hal was the brother Stinky had sworn to take care of after a boating accident had claimed their parents' lives and left them with only each other.

"You don't look too good, Hal," she murmured, remembering for the first time that he had been badly injured when the van had crashed.

His sallow, unshaven face was haggard. The skin around his eyes was yellowish purple. An infected cut ran jaggedly down the middle of his brow. He had unhealed scratches all over his hands. He reeked of sweat.

A silent scream rose in Chandra's throat.

"You need a doctor," she said.

"Shut up. I'm not going to fall for that sympathetic crap you spout ever again. You don't care about me. You never did."

"That's not true! You were like a brother to me."

He laughed and scowled at the same time, and she realized how little he resembled the courteous young man she'd once adored.

"You shot Miguel. You tried to shoot me, too," she said. "Why?"

"Bitch! Thief! Because I was angry about the will! You walked away twelve years ago—so high and mighty—like you didn't give a damn for the old lady's money or how you hurt Stinky."

"He slept with my cousin."

"I had to stay and help him get over you. I had to take crap from your grandmother. While you—"

"I didn't have it so easy, Hal. I worked very hard."

"Well, you won't get away from me this time. Neither will you, counselor."

As Chandra stared from Hal to Lucas, she was remembering everything that had happened. Gram had sent her that first letter about the foundation in which she explained her late-in-life change of heart about what she wanted to do with her money. Apparently she'd had some sort of mystical experience at Skippy Hendrix's funeral when she'd watched a crop-duster pal of his scatter Skippy's ashes near a favorite windmill. She had decided that the money wasn't fun for the family anymore. Stinky had married Holly for it, and now everybody was just sitting around making each other miserable while they waited for the old lady to die. Gram had decided that Chandra had had the right idea all along—that the money should be given to people who really needed it. Chandra had called to talk to her grandmother, only to learn she was dead.

Chandra remembered Miguel driving her to Texas. They'd arrived too late for the memorial service, but just in time to discover her family plotting against her with their lawyer. She'd heard Lucas's voice and recognized him as her other half. Then Hal had opened that dark closet and drugged her.

Hours later she had awakened bound and gagged in a fetal position in the cellar. Then Hal had carried her out to the van and locked her inside, beside Miguel's bloody corpse. Hal had laughed when he'd told her he would burn the van with her inside. He'd said he hadn't liked sucking up to the Morans all those years and that he wasn't about to let all the Moran money go to Mexico.

More terrible than all the rest had been the claustrophobic feeling that had overwhelmed her in that darkened, locked van as her drugged brain had pondered her impending doom. That's when she had suddenly recalled how she had been murdered before.

Vividly she remembered dirt sifting through the top of a box as her own sister had buried her alive. Chandra had clawed at the boards until her fingers were raw long after her sister had left her to die, long after she'd known she had no recourse other than to surrender to that final darkness.

As Hal had started the van with murder in his heart, she had gone mad with the fierce will to destroy him. So mad that her passion had obliterated the drug's lethal power as she'd lain there and calculated a means of escape.

Groping in the darkness, she had somehow freed her bound hands and untied her feet. Then she had dug through the compartment until she found the jack. Crawling woozily over Santos's bloody body, she had crept behind Hal and slammed the jack into his head. When he'd whirled to counterattack, the speeding van had weaved crazily. She had grabbed the wheel, sideswiping a car before the van careened off an embankment and rolled.

There had been an explosion of glass and crumpling metal. When she woke up, she was lying beside Hal. The front of his forehead was split wide open. Blood was all over his face, matting his hair, drenching her clothes and his. When she had tried to help him, he had grabbed her by the hair and picked up his gun and a gasoline can.

"Gotcha," he'd whispered, right before he'd started laughing.

But as he had uncapped the gasoline can and cocked the hammer of the revolver, a fat woman from the car they'd hit had yelled at them. "Lady, do you have a car phone? My little boy's bleeding something awful."

When Hal had stared toward her distractedly, Chandra had grabbed his gun and pointed it at him.

"You haven't got the guts, Beth!" Hal had taunted, charging her.

She pulled the trigger. But her hand shook so much, she hit the van, which caught fire. When Hal rushed her, Chandra ran straight into the path of an oncoming truck.

Hal's contemptuous voice jolted her to the present.

"You won't get away this time, bitch, and neither will your lover."

"You're the one who won't get away with this," Lucas warned.

For the first time Chandra remembered Lucas. "Let him go, Hal. He doesn't really have anything to do with this."

"Oh, doesn't he? You little fool! Who do you think convinced me that we shouldn't try to talk you into a compromise about the will? Who convinced me I had to destroy your good name and kill you? Everything I did was his idea!"

"No—" Lucas broke off. "I know what you're thinking, but, Chandra—"

"Do you?" she whispered. "Do you really? I don't think so. You're a very good actor. But are you even human? I read all those articles about you, and I wouldn't let myself believe you were as cruel and predatory and greedy as everybody said you were. But now… You slept with me when

I was sick and ill and too confused to know what I was doing. You used me. You took advantage of me. Why?''

"I love you."

"Don't lie to me now. Don't you ever lie to me again. I—I mistakenly thought I was someone special to you."

"You are."

"Well, you aren't to me." She fought to ignore the sharp glimmer of silent pain in his eyes. "Not anymore."

"Hear that, counselor?" Hal whispered. "She's got you figured for the no-good scum you are."

"Tell her the truth!" Lucas snarled.

Hal laughed. "You're damned good, counselor. I'd almost believe you if I didn't know better. Framing her was your idea. You told Stinky not to interfere with the bad publicity about her because it was good for our case."

"What publicity?" Chandra whispered.

"You're wanted for murder, sweetheart," Hal said. "Counselor Broderick here was damned smart to recognize you at the hospital and take you home and keep you all to himself, and now everybody thinks you did murder Santos 'cause you ran. Yes, sir. You've been very helpful, counselor."

"Chandra—" When Lucas reached for her, Chandra shrank away from him.

"Is that true, too, Lucas?"

"Damn it, no!" He hesitated. She continued to stare at him. "Well, not exactly. I mean—"

"Stinky *did* call you," she whispered, remembering the familiar voice she hadn't recognized until now even though it had terrified her.

Hal pulled a wadded front page from a recent newspaper out of his back pocket and pitched it to her.

Chandra straightened the crumpled newspaper and began to read. Her throat went dry. Black print began to blur.

Every sentence made the hollowness inside her breast expand.

She was wanted for Miguel's murder. For a hit-and-run accident in which a woman's little boy had been badly injured.

"You shot Santos," Chandra croaked. "You were driving the van. Not me."

"But, thanks to Stinky, I have an airtight alibi. And thanks to Counselor Broderick everybody thinks it was you."

Her gaze fell to the newspaper again. There was a second article, full of vicious rumors about her. She'd heard Lucas promise to spread such rumors that day in the library. There were stories about payoffs and bribes and a corrupt system for selecting the families for which her houses would be built. An investigation into her charitable organization had been launched.

Sickened by the filth and the blatant lies, she dropped the paper without bothering to read every word. She looked at Lucas in stricken bewilderment.

"You kept me a virtual prisoner in your house while you...while you and Stinky and Hal spread these lies. You didn't want me to read newspapers or look at television because you were afraid I would learn the truth about you before you totally destroyed my good name."

"No." To Hal, he said, "Damn it. Tell her the truth."

"I already have, counselor. Everything you think is true, Beth, except that part about Stinky. He was trying to find you because he was afraid of what I might do to you if I got to you first. You see, Stinky suspected the truth about our parents' deaths. And the truth was that I murdered them. I took the plug out of their boat because they were so worried about me they were going to put me in a special school. When they got out into deep water, their boat filled and sank. I had taken the life jackets off the boat, hoping they would drown. Their bodies washed onto the beach a week later.''

"That's horrible," she whispered.

"Stinky loved me anyway. See, he understood that I couldn't be locked up. He as much as told me so at their funeral. He said he'd always take care of me. And he has. I'd die for Stinky, same as he'd die for me. It was me and him—way before you or Holly ever entered the picture. He always had this knack of making himself irresistible to women. We decided that if he married a rich enough woman, there would be a living in it for the two of us. Only thing is, Stinky tends to get too involved with his women. He forgets our mission and lets them run over him. Like you did when you ran out on him twelve years ago. Like Debra before you. Like Holly now.''

"Who's Debra?" she asked even though she was afraid she already knew.

"The girl Stinky was engaged to before he met you."

"The one he beat up?"

"Stinky never laid a hand on any woman."

"But—"

"Oh, he went to jail for beating her after she jilted him. Only he didn't beat her. I did. That's how come Stinky has been so all-fired determined to find you before I did. He has a way of sensing my true feelings even when I try to hide them. He went to jail for me that one time even though he was mad at me for hitting Debra. I don't want to make him mad by hurting nobody again, but I can't let you take all the money.''

"Hal, if I die, the money will still go into the foundation.''

"You think you're real smart, Beth. You think I don't know that?" Hal pulled the hammer back. "At least you won't get to be the one to enjoy it.''

Some strange new element, a total finality, in his hard voice and eyes made her more afraid.

"Chandra, be quiet," Lucas warned. "He's gone completely crazy."

"I'm not crazy!" With an evil smile he shifted the gun to Lucas.

Even though Hal was shaking violently and his finger was on the trigger, Chandra never really thought he'd do it.

The sudden blast was loud and obscene.

There was a blaze of fire, and Lucas fell back against the pillows, a black hole gaping in his brown shoulder, a stain of red seeping from beneath his body.

With a cry, Chandra knelt over him, her eyes glazed and tearful.

Hal yanked her away by the hair.

"Forget him!"

"But—"

His fist slammed into her jaw.

Someone was stuffing something that tasted of sour sweat and dust into her mouth, and she was strangling on the wretchedly thick cloth.

As Chandra tried to turn her head she realized she was lying on hard, clammy concrete in some dank, dark place that smelled of mildew and mold. Her hands were bound so tightly behind her, the muscles in her arms were cramping.

But it wasn't her discomfort that brought her sharply to consciousness. It was Lucas's low-pitched whisper near her ear.

"Chandra."

She opened her eyes.

Lucas's dear, white, strained face hovered inches over

hers. At first she thought she was dreaming. Then she saw the blood all over his chest.

He was alive.

He finished gagging her and eased her head gently against the concrete.

"Nice work, counselor. As always."

Lucas's gray eyes were cold and dark and utterly soulless as he slowly got up.

Hal giggled. "May you rest in peace, dear Bethany." He turned off the light.

And Chandra realized she was in the tunnel under the house that would be permanently sealed with concrete tomorrow.

And Lucas was walking away.

With Hal.

They were going to bury her alive.

Something small and awful with lots of disgusting legs scuttled across her lips. She tried to scream, but the gag choked off all sound.

Dear God.

Suddenly the darkness was a living thing, a suffocating force pressing down upon her. She began to writhe and twist so hard and fast that soon she couldn't breathe.

She lay back, exhausted, her heart hammering, as she forced herself to take slow, measured breaths.

Lucas was one of them.

She had dreamed it. She had known it all along.

Only she hadn't wanted to believe it.

Until now.

Nameless, paralyzing horror swelled inside her when she heard Hal chuckle again. Then he shut the big door with a ringing clang that echoed endlessly in that hollow chasm.

But the silence afterward was far more chilling.

Eleven

Lucas stumbled out of the garage.

The breeze had died to a whisper. The night sky was steamy purple and so hotly aglow it seemed to burn with a fever.

Or was it just Lucas who was burning up because a bullet had passed through him? Because he had helped lock Chandra in a hellish place that terrified her?

"Move it, counselor. You may be half dead already, but I want to do you over by the pool."

The searing pain in his right shoulder blocked all feeling in his other nerves. Lucas couldn't feel his legs as he moved slowly forward, holding the blood-soaked towel against the bullet wound to staunch the flow. He walked with the listless gait of a zombie. Maybe it was the loss of blood that made him feel so numb, but he didn't think so.

What had really gotten him was the look of utter despair in Chandra's eyes when she'd become convinced that he was a brute and a killer.

''Get down on your knees, counselor. I'll let you say a prayer before you die.''

Lucas's eyes narrowed. His heart convulsed with hate.

''I'm gonna do you like that crazy serial killer said he would, so everybody will think he shot you. Then I'll wait up for your kids and do them, too.''

The boys.

Fresh hatred flooded Lucas. All his fear was gone. He had to save Chandra. He would die or he would kill.

''I said kneel, counselor.''

Lucas sagged weakly beside a wrought-iron lawn chair.

''Put your head down on the ground and your hands on the back of your head.''

Lucas felt his life slow to a beat as he lowered his head to the damp grass. Another beat.

He was going to die.

If he didn't do something fast.

Now.

But even before his left hand closed like a vise around the leg of the lawn chair and he slung the heavy piece of furniture straight at Hal, Hal had screamed in pain. The gun jumped a fraction of a second before it went off, causing the bullet to plow into the grass an inch away from Lucas's face.

The bastard was rubbing his hand and moaning in pain. He had missed.

The revolver and a horseshoe clattered onto the concrete apron by the pool.

Peppin had flung the horseshoe with deadly precision. He raced forward and kicked the gun and horseshoe into the pool.

Hal was lunging for the gun like a madman when Lucas tackled him and hurled him hard against the concrete.

Hal's skull cracked. Too stunned to move for a second or two, he just lay there. When he finally opened his eyes,

Lucas attacked him like a demon, his balled fists pounding his jaw and stomach relentlessly.

Both boys dived into the pool for the gun.

Peppin burst to the surface with the gun and Montague with the horseshoe. Lucas had his hands around Hal's throat and was squeezing the life out of him.

"Go ahead. Kill him, Dad!"

"Yeah! Go for it!"

Peppin's and Montague's blood lust and cheering penetrated Lucas's crazed brain, and he suddenly realized that the large brown hands on that thick throat were his own.

In a daze Lucas jerked them away and stared at the unconscious Hal like a man awakening from a dream.

Then Montague said, "Dad, you're bleeding."

"He shot me."

Then Peppin asked, "Where's Chandra?"

Oh, God. "The tunnel!" Lucas whispered.

She was lying as still and rigid as a corpse when she heard the first muffled sounds.

Then the door banged open, and she heard Peppin and Montague fighting over who got to go in first.

Lucas's deep, husky voice boomed inside the tunnel.

"Chandra, we've come back!"

The light was turned on.

"I get to untie her."

"No, I do."

"I threw the horseshoe."

"Metal mouth! Stupid!"

"Nerd!"

And the boys were there, hovering over her, squabbling exactly as they had when she'd regained consciousness in their closet.

They loosened her gag and eased it away from her mouth.

"My two darling angels."

The boys beamed.

She hugged them and tried to smile. But she wept instead.

When Lucas hesitantly knelt beside her, her beautiful face whitened and became filled with distress. She flinched and began to tremble. "Please! Please! Don't let him touch me!"

"But I love you," Lucas whispered, frantic to make her understand. "I would never hurt you. Never."

"Liar," she whispered, clutching the boys. "You already have." She began to weep again. "Get him away from me!" That was the last thing he heard, because he fainted.

Nobody believed her.

Not the boys.

Not the police.

Even after she was out of the tunnel, Chandra was still scared.

Within minutes after Peppin called the police, Lucas's house was part madhouse, part war zone. Ambulances and police cars littered his driveway, their colored lights twisting and blinking as the boys raced excitedly from one cop to the next, bragging more each time they retold the night's adventure.

Chandra and Lucas and the two bodyguards and Hal were all lying on gurneys, about to be put in separate ambulances. The boys, with Lucas's and Chandra's help, were trying to explain everything.

A surge of fear flowed through Chandra every time Lucas came near her or tried again to tell her he loved her. She would beg the police to keep him away from her.

"No," she kept saying to him, forcing herself to ignore

the silent agony in his eyes. "Stay away from me." And to anyone in a uniform who would listen, she said, "Why won't you believe me? I tell you, he was one of them."

Twelve

Lucas's firm occupied the top two floors of a downtown office building and commanded the city's finest views of the sparkling bay. Despite the oppressive heat, the office felt as crisply cool as an alpine summer day.

Usually the elegant suite was as quiet as a bank vault or a hallowed sanctuary. Usually legal aids and lawyers and their clients spoke between these marble walls in the same hushed, reverent voices they might use at a funeral.

Not today.

Excited adolescent shouts from the aluminum-walled elevator could be heard even before the chrome doors burst open and the Broderick boys exploded into the huge reception area like a matched pair of rowdy volcanoes, each zooming straight for Lucas's office.

Not that Lucas's legal secretary, who knew how cranky Lucas had been of late, didn't try to halt them.

"You can't go in there!" she snapped primly in that no-

nonsense tone most people wisely obeyed. "He's with a—"

They brushed past her and kicked his door open. Lucas's dark face looked thin and worn as his head snapped up. Not that he hadn't heard them coming.

He still felt a little weak. He hadn't fully recovered from the bullet wound.

His silver eyes narrowed explosively.

"Dad!" Peppin waved a torn piece of paper like a tattered banner. "Chandra finally wrote to us. She invited us to Mexico."

"That's nice," Lucas said in a dull, lost tone. "I'm very happy for you. She won't give me the time of day."

"You've gotta quit being so sulky and stubborn just because she sent a few of your old letters back."

"Me—sulky and stubborn? She sent *all* my letters back! And all my flowers! She won't take my calls! She had me stopped at the border and arrested when I tried— I spent a night in jail with half a dozen drunks. Do you remember that? Do you? A guy punched me. And I started hemorrhaging again."

No woman, not even Joan, had ever made him feel so low. So unwanted. So abandoned. So utterly bereft and alone.

"You've gotta go down there again and be nice and bring her back. We'll help you," Peppin said.

A big leather chair swiveled. Then a man's sharp boom of laughter from the depths of the chair made both boys jump. "Chandra had you thrown into jail? Why the hell didn't you tell me?"

For the first time the boys grew aware of the dangerous and powerful-looking man with the jet black hair seated in the big leather chair in front of their father's desk.

"Don't tell anybody. I'm not especially proud of that

night," Lucas grumbled. "It would be the last straw with my partners."

The boys stood stock-still and went mute as they registered the charismatic stranger's presence.

"Hello, guys," the man said, eyeing them, and then Lucas, expectantly.

"Boys, this is Mr. Rafe Steele." Lucas introduced everybody grumpily.

Peppin let out a war whoop.

Montague whispered in awe, "Chandra's friend! You're the bodyguard. Do you really know Jo Jo and his heavy metal band?"

Rafe nodded and flashed them a warm smile. "I was his personal bodyguard till I got smart and walked off the job. He's a jerk. Hey—but it sounds like the three of you were accidental bodyguards...for Chandra. I owe you."

"We love her. We've gotta get her back, Mr. Steele. Will you help us?"

"Funny, I was just telling your father the same thing. But he wouldn't listen, even though I can vouch for the fact that this past month Chandra's been miserable without the three of you."

The boys rushed closer, no longer afraid of the big, tough-looking stranger in their father's chair.

"Dad, you've gotta let Rafe do something. And fast. Before we lose her forever."

"No! And that's final! Consider her lost. She left." He hesitated. "Look, I don't like it any better than you do, but she's made up her mind. I was a bastard to her. And she hates me."

But Rafe countered, "No, she doesn't. She's made peace with her family—even Holly. If she can forgive them and compromise with them, she can damn sure forgive you."

"I said no." Lucas's low voice was lethal.

"What if I told you she was pregnant?"

Lucas's gray eyes lit up as if a match had been struck.

Watching those eyes blaze and his face whiten as the news sank in, the boys smiled at each other and then slapped their right hands together.

Lucas's lips thinned at their burst of unwelcome applause, but he neither lashed out at them nor objected when Rafe said, "Hear me out, guys. I have a plan."

Chandra hadn't found a suitable replacement for her driver, dear, sweet, Miguel Santos, and never had she missed anybody more than she missed him. She had some sort of stomach virus, which lowered her energy level to zero, and she was doing his job and hers, as well.

Which was good, in a way. Because she was too tired and too overworked and too ill to think or to mourn—

No. She wouldn't let herself think of them.

For an instant she saw Lucas's fierce beloved dark face. She saw his gray eyes, which had been glazed with pain in the hospital when she'd told him goodbye. He had looked so downcast. So utterly rejected, with his chest bandaged and his right arm in a sling.

No. She wouldn't let herself think of him. Because the agony of that loss and betrayal was still so keen and raw it scared her.

Sweat streamed from under Chandra's Stetson as she turned the steering wheel of the huge truck, which was heavily loaded with roof panels. She shifted, panting as she ground the gears inexpertly, and the heavy vehicle clumsily weaved into the barrio where two of her church groups had houses under construction.

Hal was being held in jail without bond. He had confessed to planting drugs in her van and then later in one of her houses. He had stolen her bloody T-shirt from the hospital and mailed it to the police. Stinky had admitted that he had lied when he'd said Hal had been with them the night of the wreck. The government had halted its investigation of her operation. She had been completely exonerated, and all her backers had regained their confidence in her. And the serial killer who had threatened Lucas had been caught and was behind bars, as well.

Even so, ever since she'd returned to Mexico, she'd had too much to do. She was depressed and stressed to the max.

For one thing, it was hot. A sweltering one hundred and fifteen degrees in the scant shade of a mesquite tree, to be exact. Today the cab felt like an oven.

Maybe that was the reason for the trouble at site four.

Rafe had said that three of the volunteers were real troublemakers.

Which was odd. Usually people who signed on to help with their church group were willing to endure great physical hardship for the single week it took to build a house. Trouble-prone teenagers often worked even harder than their adult chaperones. Rafe and Cathy had said they were at their wits' end with this particular trio, and they'd asked her to personally drop by and try to say a few words to inspire them.

The barrio street was unpaved and deeply rutted, and brown dust churned from behind the truck's big black wheels. Dozens of small children in dirty, ragged clothes raced from their hovels into the street, braving the dust and the flies to grin brightly and wave at her, for she was a much-beloved figure in this neighborhood. She smiled and waved back. But not for long. With only one hand on the wheel, the truck lurched sharply to the right, rattling violently and nearly hitting a cactus plant.

The truck didn't have power steering, and since the seat couldn't be moved, she could barely reach the worn clutch pedal even when she sat as far forward as possible. So it took all her strength and all her concentration just to drive.

Except for the summer heat and the constant oppression

of poverty, worse now because of the long drought and recent political corruption in Mexico City, Piedras Negras was a nice town—as Mexican border towns go. Flat, pale ranchland, parched bone-white by the drought, and the sluggish brown Rio Grande girded the city. But the blue sky was roomy, and the desolate location made for less prostitution and crime, so the town seemed more like the rural towns in the interior.

Thick dust coated the vine growing on the barbed wire fence surrounding the building site. The walls of site three were ten feet high, which was why Chandra was bringing that group roof panels.

She frowned when she saw site four, where the walls had only two layers of concrete blocks, and they seemed to already be slanting inward.

Oh, dear.

This was trouble.

If the church group didn't finish by Saturday, and there was no way they could short of a miracle, Chandra would fall behind schedule and build one less house. Which meant one of the deserving families in the barrio who had won her lottery would not have a house until next year.

Chandra pulled the emergency brake up, then banged on her door and cried out to the job foreman that she needed a strong man to open the door or she couldn't get out. She'd bought the truck used. It was so old and battered the doors could only be opened from the outside, and only by a very husky individual.

When two men who had been laying a third row of cinder blocks set their forty-pound blocks down and rushed toward her, the foreman grabbed them by their shoulders and ordered them to keep working.

Chandra felt confusion and irritation.

Until the foreman sent a skinny, familiar-looking boy who had been mixing thick white mortar in a tub over to the far corner of the building site. With dawning horror she watched the lanky messenger pull off his surgical mask and lean over a tall man who was reclining as lazily as a Spanish conquistador in the hammock.

The tall man's face was covered by a cowboy hat, his lean, line-backer's frame stretched full length under the shade of a fluttering tarp. Chandra couldn't help but feel disgust when she noted the dozen or so church women with their sunburned cheeks and noses slaving under the blazing mid-morning sun.

The man shot up, his gray eyes instantly piercingly alert as he tipped his wide-brimmed hat toward her. When he recognized her, he grinned in startled surprise and pleasure. He shot upright. Then his long strides carried him swiftly toward Chandra.

Lucas.

The lanky messenger was Montague.

"No!"

Rafe had tricked her. She lunged at the door to escape.

But it wouldn't budge.

She was trapped.

Until somebody released her.

"Somebody—let me out!" she screamed frantically, searching for her site foreman, who had mysteriously disappeared. As had most of the other workers.

Lucas opened the truck door, and she practically fell into his arms.

Her hands grabbed at him for support, one hand closing around his denim-clad thigh, the other his waist. Clumsily she levered herself up his body.

"Hey, that was kind of fun," he whispered, so jauntily she longed to slap him. Of course she couldn't do that. Not in front of the big-eyed church women.

"Well, what are you looking at?" she yelled at the women.

"Hey, don't get so riled," Lucas whispered. "It's not their fault."

"No! It's yours! I hate you!"

"Are you sure about that?" He clasped her tighter.

He was hot, and so was she. But he felt good, so incredibly good, so good she felt another touch of vertigo. Suddenly she was breathless.

For four long, agonizing weeks she had slept alone and tried to forget him.

She was still sure she could, in time, so she pushed frantically at his chest. But it was like trying to budge a steel wall with her puny strength.

"I love you," he whispered, pressing her closer. "I love you."

"No."

"Forgive me," he begged hoarsely, his low voice so strangely choked she thought he might be about to cry.

The broken sound caught at her heart, and she couldn't resist glancing at him.

Their eyes locked. His rugged face was fierce. He wasn't weeping, but the all-powerful emotion she read in his eyes was more profound than tears.

I love you. Believe me. Because I'll die if you don't.

I forgive you.

It took them a moment to realize that neither of them had spoken. At least not with words.

And yet they had.

In their own special way.

Then his face softened, and he enfolded her in a crushing embrace.

She couldn't fight him any more than she could fight herself. All her life she had been looking for him. At last she had found him. And she knew that no matter what he had done, no matter who he was, she wanted to be with him always.

Quiet tears of joy slid down her cheeks. "Thank you for coming," she whispered. "I was such a fool. Of course, I forgive you. For that is the nature and power of true love."

"I tried to come before. I spent a night cooling my heels in one sorry Mexican jail cell with some pretty disgusting individuals."

"I know. I'm sorry."

Chandra clung to him, aware of a thrilling happiness as she surrendered her lips to his hard mouth in giddy delirium.

As he kissed her, only vaguely was she aware of two hands slapping each other triumphantly in the background, of two excited adolescent voices that were belovedly familiar.

"So, is she or isn't she going to have a baby sister?"

"Or a baby brother."

"When's he gonna ask her and give her the ring?"

"Shh! Let 'im kiss her first, stupid."

"Not stupid."

"At times you are. Girls like kisses."

"Boys, too."

"Just sissies."

Slowly the quick, pulsating phrases and words became recognizable as the voices of her darling boys. Her angels. *Her sons.*

They wanted to know if she was going to have a baby sister.

A baby?

The thought electrified her.

Never once had she considered that wonderful possibility. She had just thought her stomach was upset from nerves or from something in the border food. She remembered how oddly Rafe had looked at her every time she had insisted that was all it was, how solicitous he'd been, how determined he'd been in his search for a new driver.

Rafe was a father himself. He must know the signs.

Her mind raced backward. She always felt sickest in the morning. Suddenly she was nearly positive that she was, indeed, going to have Lucas's baby. How could she have been so blind?

"Marry me," Lucas said when at last he withdrew his lips.

"Yes. Oh, yes. Yes. Yes," she whispered, right before she reached up and kissed him again.

A long time later she thought she heard two hands come together in another loud slap.

"See, I told you, stupid."

"Not stupid!"

It was she who had been stupid. She who had carelessly thrown away the three people in the whole world she cared most about.

She would have to spend the rest of her life making it up to them.

The breathless kiss she gave Lucas was only the beginning.

Epilogue

———

Below their charming hotel, Posada la Ermita, which was perched loftily on a hill, the colonial Mexican town with its cobblestone streets, jacaranda trees and many churches dozed quietly in the hazy, pink and lavender light.

"I told you San Miguel de Allende was the perfect place for our honeymoon," Chandra said to Lucas as she came out onto the tiled balcony of their suite just as a white-coated waiter arrived to set the table so they could enjoy a private dinner with the boys after they finished swimming.

The air was refreshingly crisp and cool after the summer heat of Texas. The sound of water splashing in the nearby fountain and the plaintive notes of a Spanish guitar in a cantina could be heard.

Lucas set his beer down and got up to help her to a chair.

Her face was glowing in the rosy sunlight. The last rays burnished her golden hair, making it look like flame. Her blue eyes were radiant. He had paid the boys a fortune to stay away all day and had spent the afternoon making love to her while the boys had explored the village and cavorted down at the pool.

"Aren't the views and the sunlight wonderful?" she asked, staring at the lime green jacaranda trees and a trellis brimming with purple bougainvillea.

"Wonderful," he agreed, squeezing her hand, but he was looking at her.

"That's why it's been an artist colony for years," she continued. "Except for the church bells, it's very quiet."

There were dozens of bell towers, and the bells started ringing before dawn and didn't stop until well after midnight.

"It's damned hard for the ordinary tourist to get to."

They had come in a friend's private plane.

"You're spoiled, my love," she said.

Furious shouts drifted up from the pool. The boys, who had been told to watch for the waiter and their dinner and to come up as soon as they saw him, had forgotten that parental order and were fighting over a pair of flippers and a float.

Lucas smiled at her. "The boys are as noisy as the church bells."

"I don't mind their noise," she whispered.

"I guess you'd better get used to it, since we're well on our way to a house full of kids."

The waiter left them.

"Oh, Chandra," Lucas said, pulling her close and burying his face in her golden hair. "All this happiness is going to take some getting used to."

She clung to him just as tightly. "I feel the same way. I still can't believe—"

"What?"

"That I finally found you."

"That again?"

"I know you don't believe in reincarnation—"

"That's right. One lifetime of happiness is definitely all I would ever ask for," he stared, kissing her so she couldn't reply.

Dinner was over.

"So, Dad, if those birthmarks on your chest were really scars and you two knew each other in another life, were we there, too?" Peppin asked his father.

"Look, one lifetime is enough of a challenge for me," Lucas said. "Like I keep saying, I'm not at all sure I can buy into this reincarnation theory. I don't remember anything about any other life in India."

"That's 'cause you weren't murdered, Dad!" Montague inserted in a sage tone.

"What does being murdered have to do with anything?"

"Just everything! I'll loan you my favorite book, *Psychic Vampires,* and then you'll understand. Murdered people are more likely to remember their past lives."

"Thanks. But I'll pass." Lucas chuckled. "Loving Chandra now, in this lifetime, on this side of the world, is miracle enough for me."

Chandra was standing naked in the mists of their hotel bedroom's shower when Lucas stepped in and joined her.

Their eyes met.

As they had before.

Without speaking, she picked up the bar of soap and began running it over his thighs and abdomen in electrifying circles that made his brown skin heat.

He grabbed her wrist and shoved her gently against the wall. The bar of soap fell and slid to the drain. Lucas stepped over it.

In a wild outpouring of sexual exultation, he picked up

his wife and fitted her snugly against his hips, driving inside her.

Their sexes joined, their souls, as well. She wrapped her legs around him and let her swanlike neck fall back as gracefully as a ballerina so that warm water streamed over her face and hair and swirled around their naked forms.

She had never felt so hot or so good. As if he and she were made of some molten liquid that flowed together and became one.

Without realizing it, he began to move.

She said his name, over and over, and her low, soft, staccato voice made it so incredibly erotic he came.

She exploded, too.

For a long time he clasped her hips to his, wanting to stay inside her forever.

It had never been this sublime with anyone. It never would.

What he felt for her was beyond love. Beyond time.

Beyond this world and all eternity.

He picked her up and carried her to the bed, where he patted her naked body dry with a towel.

She crawled on top of him, and kissed the new bullet wound. With her tongue she traced the long white birthmarks that crisscrossed his torso.

She looked into his eyes and smiled that dazzling smile that he felt he had always known.

And he wondered. In spite of himself, he wondered.

And he knew he always would.

*   *   *   *   *

Dear Reader,

I've always loved amnesia stories, but I held off writing one of my own until I had an idea with a few more twists than usual. Of course, having extra twists meant more plot questions to work out, so the story stayed in my head for a good long while.

Fortunately, my husband's a retired federal agent who also has an extensive background in psychology. He helped me figure out all the twists and tangles that make Carly's past such a mystery. I hope you enjoy figuring them out, too.

Best wishes,

Marilyn Pappano

Memories of Laura
by Marilyn Pappano

For Bob,
who knows something about everything
and everything about some things.
You truly do astound me.
I couldn't do this without you.

Chapter 1

The pain came swiftly, blinding and sharp, and brought with it a wave of nausea and the uncomfortable dampness of a sudden sweat. Carly Johnson immediately moved her foot to the brake and steered the car to the shoulder of the road. As soon as she shifted into park, she leaned forward and rested her head on the steering wheel.

She'd had the headaches for three years, but they occurred less frequently now. The doctor had told her that one day they would eventually go away, and every time she prayed that this one would be the last.

So far her prayers had gone unanswered.

When the agonizing pain receded to a steady throb, she opened her eyes, instinctively squinting against the bright sun in spite of the dark glasses she wore. There was a road sign only a few hundred yards ahead, but she could barely make out its legend. Nowhere, next exit. She didn't know if Nowhere, Montana, was big enough to merit a hotel, but with every pain-sharpened nerve in her body, she hoped so.

Otherwise, she would have to find a place to park and crawl into the back seat until this episode passed.

Carefully she shifted into gear and pulled back onto the interstate. The pain affected her vision, making it harder to bring things into focus, and the bright afternoon sunshine didn't help. She compensated on the two miles into town by being overly cautious, an added stress that made her head ache even more.

There *was* a hotel, she saw with relief. Located right in the heart of Nowhere, it reminded her of the old westerns she liked to watch on Saturday afternoons. The sidewalk outside was wood, and the steps leading to the double doors—swinging double doors, she noticed—were broad and unpainted. Wide plate-glass windows stretched across the front showed a registration desk on the left, a dining room on the right.

Her ears were starting to ring, making everything sound distant and slurred, and the nausea threatened to empty her stomach of its contents. She didn't take the time to get her suitcase from the trunk, but went inside and straight to the desk. Right now she needed only two things: a glass of water so she could take the pain medication her doctor had prescribed for her and a bed to collapse in when the medication took effect.

The clerk behind the counter was on the phone and had her back to Carly. "Excuse me," she said, her voice sounding feeble in her own ears. She knew from past experience that she looked ghastly—that in spite of the sweat that beaded on her forehead, her face was pale, that her eyes were dark and shadowed with pain, that her knees were weak and her hands trembling. The poor clerk would probably think there was something terribly wrong with her.

Right now, there was.

The woman finished her call and hung up the phone, then

turned around. "Hi, can I help—" Immediately she became motionless, her mouth gaping open, and she simply stared.

Carly started to remove her sunglasses, but stopped herself. The lights in here were too bright, her eyes already too sensitized by pain. She couldn't bear any more. "I need a room, please."

The woman slowly approached the counter. "My God...*Laura*. I didn't think you would ever come back. Have you been to see Maureen yet?"

The aroma of spices—chili powder, garlic and pepper—drifted out from the restaurant across the lobby. Carly had to swallow rapidly, and she resorted to breathing through her mouth to avoid the overpowering smells. "Please," she whispered through dry lips. "My name is Carly Johnson, and I need a room for tonight."

After staring at her a moment longer, the clerk slowly slid a three-by-five card across the counter. "Whatever you say. You can have room three, top of the stairs, turn right. That always was your lucky number, wasn't it?"

Carly scribbled in the required information, realizing as she squinted at the card that her handwriting was barely legible. She paid in cash, gratefully accepted the key and started up the stairs.

"What about your luggage, Laura?" the clerk called.

Carly gripped the rail tighter and continued her slow climb. "I'll get it later," she said, summoning up a sickly smile for the woman below. Later, when the icy-hot pain had faded. Later, when she could stand without swaying, breathe without retching, see without squinting.

Clutching the room key, she trudged down the hall, passing rooms nine, seven and five. At the next door she stopped and, before she fitted the key into the lock, simply leaned there for a moment, steadying herself against a new wave of pain so intense that she vibrated with it.

Finally she got the door unlocked and went inside. Stopping beside the dresser, she removed her sunglasses and dumped the contents of her purse, searching for the small pill bottle. When she found it, she twisted the cap off on the third try and with trembling hands shook out two fat round tablets. Then she filled a plastic cup with water from the bathroom sink, and she drank it down with the pills.

For a moment all she felt was the roiling of her stomach. She clenched her fingers tightly around the pill bottle as she struggled against the sickness. This headache had come too quickly, and she'd waited too long to take the medication. If she couldn't keep the pills down, she would have to wait this one out—not a pleasant prospect.

But slowly her stomach settled. With a sigh of relief, she staggered back into the bedroom. She would remove her shoes, her sweater and her jeans in a minute, she decided as she lay down. In just one more minute…

Her eyes drifted shut, and the bright, vivid, dancing colors of pain began to fade. Her heartbeat slowed, and her breathing became less labored, and finally she gave herself up to the blessedly oblivious peace of sleep.

Buck Logan sat down at his desk and began sorting through the mail one of his deputies had opened for him. There wasn't much interesting, other than a flier from the Butte Police Department bearing the photograph of an unidentified body they'd found. He studied the photo for a moment, assured himself that he didn't know the man, then laid it aside. It would go up on the bulletin board so that all his officers could see it; then it would be filed away and forgotten. Chances were good that no one who saw the flier would know the man. He would wind up just another John Doe, his body unclaimed, and his family, if he had any, would never find out what had happened to him.

He was preparing to file the rest of the mail when the phone rang. Janssen—his newest and youngest deputy, and the nephew of Nowhere's mayor—was supposed to be answering while the dispatcher was at lunch, but he was involved in the sports magazine he was reading. Swearing beneath his breath, Buck reached for the phone. "Sheriff's office."

It was Hazel over at the hotel, and she was talking so fast that the words fell over one another. But he understood enough. After promising to come right over, he hung up and reached for the silvery-gray Stetson on the rack behind his desk. When he stepped out of his small, cramped office, he called, "Harvey, I'll be over at the hotel."

The deputy manning the radio looked up and nodded before returning to his game of solitaire.

The hotel was across the street and down one block. Like everything else in Nowhere, it was old. There hadn't been any new construction in town since about 1940, Buck guessed. Before he was born. Nowhere hadn't done any growing. It had, in fact, steadily lost its residents over the last fifty years, shrinking from a high of some twelve thousand citizens to its current population of less than three thousand. But if what Hazel had told him was true, that number had just gone up by one. Nowhere had just regained one lost resident.

She was driving a blue Chevy, Hazel had said, and he saw the car as he crossed the street. It wasn't anything flashy, not like the red Corvette she'd driven away from Nowhere. It was just a plain, efficient means of transportation. Its Washington tags, he noted, would expire next month. Of course. Next month it would be three years since she'd disappeared.

Pausing beside the car, he glanced in the windows. There was a box of tissues on the passenger seat, along with a half-dozen cassettes. A road atlas was stuck between the bucket seats, and a jacket had been tossed into the back. There was nothing in the car that gave him any clues about its owner. Even the tapes were a mix of easy listening, classic rock and country music—something to please everyone.

Hazel was waiting for him at the door. He climbed the steps to the wide veranda, setting one of the rockers there in motion as he passed, and went inside.

"It's the strangest thing, Buck," she began before the doors swung shut behind him. "I've known Laura all her life—heavens, I've even changed her diapers a time or two. But she acted like she'd never seen me before, and she insisted her name was Carly. Carly Johnson. Can you imagine that? After all this time away, she comes back and lies about who she is? As if we won't *know*?"

He'd known Laura all her life, too, Buck thought grimly, but he had long since passed the point where anything she did could surprise him—demands, tantrums, disappearing acts. *Re*appearing acts. "Can I see the registration card?"

She pulled it from her pocket and handed it to him. He studied it in silence. Carly Johnson. The address was in Seattle, and he recognized the Washington area code. The tag number she'd written down matched the blue Chevrolet outside, and payment for the room, according to Hazel's note, had been made in cash.

He handed the card back, then, with just a hint of hesitance, he asked, "How did she look?"

The clerk's face brightened as if she'd been reminded of a juicy bit of gossip. "*Awful,* Buck! The poor girl must be sick—maybe she has that flu that's going around. Maybe that's why she acted so strange. Oh, but she's still pretty. Still the prettiest girl in Nowhere." She leaned closer and, even though there was no one else around, lowered her voice. "What do you think's going on? Why is she lying about who she is? And where has she been all these years?"

"Maybe it's not Laura," he suggested more calmly than he felt. "Maybe Carly Johnson just looks a lot like her."

Hazel didn't accept his suggestion at all calmly. "I didn't mistake a total stranger for someone I've known more than thirty years, Buck. That *is* Laura Phelps upstairs. There's not a doubt in my mind. You just go on up there and see for yourself."

Buck smiled thinly. "That's just what I intend to do. What room is she in?"

"Three."

He climbed the long staircase and automatically turned right. Number three was at the end of the hall, a big corner room that looked down on Main Street. He knocked, waited a moment, then knocked again.

There was no sound from within the room—no television or radio, no running water, no creaking floor or squeaking bedsprings. Maybe the mystery woman had gone out again, he thought, but immediately discounted that possibility. There was no way she could have gotten past Hazel downstairs.

Then he remembered the clerk's words. Laura looking awful? Not as long as there was breath in her body. He knew her more intimately than anyone else in town, but he couldn't remember ever seeing her at less than her best. Even early in the morning or just out of the shower—even in bed after making mad, passionate love—she had always looked damned near perfect.

The poor girl must be sick, Hazel had said. Sick enough that she couldn't answer the door? Sick enough to need help? Sick enough to justify him entering her room uninvited?

What he was doing was wrong, he admitted as he tried the doorknob and felt it turn. But if it was Laura inside, she wouldn't care. And if it wasn't…well, he would just make sure the woman was all right, then leave again.

Silently he entered the dimly lit room, closing the door behind him. For a moment he simply stood there, watching the woman lying on the bed ten feet in front of him. She was atop the covers and fully dressed. Her back was to him, so he couldn't see her face, but her hair… How long had it been since he'd seen hair that pure, delicate shade of gold?

More than three years ago. Closer to four. Laura had liked her golden blond hair for one reason: because it was so easy to turn into something else. She'd colored her hair red and platinum blond and a half-dozen shades of brown, and the last time he'd seen her—the last time before she had left town, the time she had warned him that she would make him sorry—it had been shocking black.

And now she was blond again. Beautiful golden blond.

He delayed circling the bed so he could see her face, putting off that moment when he would know for certain if Laura had finally come back or if this was some freak coincidence. Drawing out the moment, he looked instead around the room. Her purse had been emptied on the dresser, as if she'd been in a hurry to find something. Her room key was there, too, along with her car keys, but there was no sign of any luggage. She must have left it in the car out front.

Finally he forced himself to walk around the bed, to stand quietly on the opposite side and look at her. He knew instantly, from the shock that hit him like a fist, from the clenching in his gut, from the sudden surge of emotion from deep within, that Hazel hadn't been mistaken.

It *was* Laura.

Dear God, she'd come home.

He stared at her a long time, trying to sort through what he felt. Relief that she was all right, that she had survived the last three years. Curiosity about why she'd come home now instead of a year ago, or two. Remorse for all that had happened because, in spite of himself, he had almost loved her. Resentment because, again in spite of himself, he had always needed her.

And anger. White-hot, blistering anger that she'd left the way she had—running out on her family, on people who cared about her, on *him*. Fury that she had left him to wonder and worry over what might have happened to her, to finally realize that knowing she was dead would be better than knowing nothing at all. Rage that she had been right, always right, about what he would do and how he would feel, because she *had* made him sorry, God help him, sorrier over losing her than he ever could have imagined.

The last three years had brought few changes to her. Her nose, once straight and perfect and one of her vanities, had been broken and bore a small bump near the bridge. There was a scar, thin and curving, disappearing across her forehead into her hair. Knowing Laura, she took great pains when she was awake to style her hair to cover the minor imperfection. And, of course, she had aged, as they all had.

But she was still achingly beautiful.

Still angelic.

Still Laura.

Realizing that he'd clenched both hands into fists, he forced the muscles to relax. Such tension wasn't unusual where Laura was concerned. Their time together had been sheer pleasure...and pure hell. So unutterably beautiful, so wickedly manipulative, so unfailingly selfish, she had been his one weakness, his one...

Obsession. He shied away from the word, uneasy with its implications, disliking its connotations. Sometimes he had almost loved her. Sometimes he had definitely hated her. But always he had needed her, had needed whatever she had that no one else could give. The need had been more than lust, much more, something powerful and dark and intense, a hunger that he could no more have turned away from than he could have willingly stopped breathing.

He had survived three years without her—three years of running his own life, of doing what *he* wanted, of answering to no one. Three years of being in control again, of choosing his lovers instead of being chosen, of seducing instead of being seduced.

And now she was back.

Breathing unevenly, he took a step forward, and the floor creaked in protest. She sighed softly, but gave no sign of waking. She was sleeping pretty deeply, Buck thought. Odd, since Hazel had called right after she'd checked in.

Then he saw the pill bottle she clutched even in her sleep.

Bracing his hand on the metal bedstead, he leaned over and carefully unfolded her fingers, flinching at their warmth and softness, then removed the bottle from her grip. He recognized the medication as a pretty strong painkiller, one that he'd taken himself after the football injury that had ended his college career. Why did Laura need it?

He scanned the label again. It was issued to Carly Johnson, and it came from a Seattle pharmacy. Why was Laura getting prescription medication under a false name? And why had she chosen to settle in Seattle? Why was she calling herself Carly? What was she hiding?

Pocketing the pill bottle, he walked back around the bed, stopping this time beside the dresser. The contents of her purse were spilled across the worn wood surface. They were typical, he supposed, of the contents of any woman's purse: a billfold, a checkbook, a package of tissues. A small, flat pillbox. Two pens, a small notebook, a lipstick and a compact. Three grocery receipts, two breath mints and a gum wrapper.

He touched her wallet, then drew his hand back. He wanted to know how far she was carrying this charade, whether her driver's license was issued under the false name, whether she had obtained credit cards as Carly Johnson. But he had no authority to search through her wallet, and as much as he wanted answers, he wasn't likely to find them there.

His answers, he acknowledged grimly, would have to come from *her*.

The hours passed slowly. Buck left the room only twice: once to warn Hazel not to tell anyone about Laura's return, and the second time to use the pay phone in the hallway. He called his office and asked Harvey to run Carly Johnson through the computer. Since they had no computers of their own—the county budget wouldn't stretch that far—a check meant waiting while the deputy used their second line to call Sheriff Crowder over in the next county and have one of his men run the information. He waited while his deputy obeyed him, and only a few moments later Harvey came back: no outstanding warrants.

Next he called Doc Thomas in the next block to ask him about the medication. He hadn't been mistaken. It was a painkiller, and a powerful one. It wasn't something he would prescribe to anyone on a regular basis, the doctor said.

So why was Laura taking it?

Returning to the room, he watched her sleep for a while. Tiring of the dim lighting, he raised the vinyl shade that blocked the afternoon sunlight, but when the rays touched her face, she shifted restlessly, making a soft, helpless sound and covering her closed eyes with her hand. Immediately he pulled the shade down again, and she slowly relaxed.

Most of the time she slept peacefully, deeply, but occasionally she murmured and tossed from side to side. She'd never been a restless sleeper—*he* had been the restless one in bed, because he hadn't wanted to be there almost as much as he'd needed to. He wondered if it was pain that caused her distress, or perhaps an unpleasant dream.

She deserved more than a few of those for leaving the way she had. She had certainly caused him a few nightmares of his own. For a long time her disappearance had haunted him. All he'd been able to think of was the good times, few though they were, and then the bad times, when she had asked for—no, demanded—more than he could give her. They had argued, and she had threatened, and then she had left. Disappeared. Vanished.

And here she was, back again. Alive and well. Three years ago she had walked away. Today she'd walked right back, tossing whatever peace he'd found right out the window. And damn it, he wanted to know why. She owed him that much, at least.

He settled into the rocking chair in the corner. It was after five o'clock, past time for him to call it a day and go on home. He could have one of his deputies come over and keep an eye on her, but he didn't want to do that. He didn't want to leave just yet. He didn't want to go until she was awake, until she looked him in the eye and told him everything he wanted to know.

As the sun began to set, he turned on one of the bedside lamps, carefully tilting its shade away from her; then he returned to the rocker and waited. Once Hazel came to the door with a quiet knock. She was carrying a tray with a pot of coffee, two cups and two pieces of her cook's famous cherry pie. Buck deliberately blocked her view of the room, took the tray and thanked her, then closed the door before she could catch even a glimpse of Laura.

Back in the rocker once more, he ate one of the pieces of pie. Three cups of coffee later, he ate the second piece, too. And he waited.

He was good at waiting, he thought with a humorless

smile. She had always kept him waiting—for her attention, for a respite away from her, for her tantrums, for her demands. He had waited three years for her to quit pouting and come home. Now he waited for her to wake up, waited to see not just the golden blond hair and the fragile lines of her face, but to see her eyes—her cool blue eyes—and to hear her voice.

He waited to see if she still wanted him.

He waited to see if he still needed her.

And he waited to find out if he still hated her.

Carly awoke completely alert. After two weeks of vacation, she had grown used to awaking in strange rooms. Awaking in the evening was a little disorienting, though, as was awaking fully dressed, but the first movement she made explained both. While the medication had taken the raw edge off her headache, the throb was still there, sharp and powerful.

The lamp on the bedside table glowed softly in the dark room. Had she turned it on before she'd fallen asleep? She couldn't remember. But then she couldn't remember removing her shoes, either, or covering herself with the quilt that had been folded at the foot of the bed, but apparently she had, for her feet were bare and the cover was tucked around her now.

She wet her lips. They were dry, and so was her mouth, too dry to swallow. But she was hungry. That was a good sign. That meant she would survive this headache, just as she had survived all those in the past.

Carefully she sat up. She knew how quickly the nausea could return, how easily the pain could overwhelm her. When nothing happened, she just as carefully swung her feet to the floor and slid them into the shoes that waited there. She was finally standing when a voice spoke from the shadows.

"Hello, Laura."

She started, and the sudden movement made her feel queasy. Covering her mouth with one hand, she reached for the iron headboard with the other to steady herself.

Slowly the figure who'd spoken detached itself from the shadows. It was a man, more than six feet tall, broad-shouldered and dark as the night. In spite of the softness of his greeting, there was something threatening, menacing, about him. Something angry.

The rapid beat of her heart began to slow when he came into the light enough for her to see the uniform he wore. The name tag on his shirt identified him as Logan, the badge as Sheriff Logan. The desk clerk had acted strangely when she'd checked in, she remembered vaguely. Had the woman for some reason called the sheriff on her?

He came a few steps closer. "Nothing to say? No 'Hello, Sheriff'? No 'It's been a long time, Buck'? No 'I've missed you, sweetheart'?"

Carly forced herself to breathe slowly, deeply. With all her other troubles this evening, the last thing she needed was to hyperventilate. That had happened once before, when the pain from the headaches had been so intense that she'd thought she would die from it. Then, as the old joke went, she'd been afraid that she *wouldn't*.

"Hello, Sheriff," she said evenly, striving to sound cool and composed, but the words came out merely strained.

Now he was standing less than a foot in front of her. She wanted to flinch, to shrink away, but she didn't allow herself to show any emotion whatsoever. If she was patient, he would say what he wanted—*git outta town, stranger, before the sun goes down,* she thought giddily—and then he would leave. Then she could take two more pills, get some dinner and go to bed for the rest that she still desperately needed.

What had he said his name was? she wondered fuzzily.

Buck. Buck Logan. It sounded like some Wild West cowboy. He could trade the uniform for a pair of dusty jeans and a chambray shirt, the gleaming boots for a pair of work-roughened ones and the immaculate Stetson on the dresser for a sweat-stained, battered version, and he would fit the name perfectly.

Come to think of it, she decided, rubbing the pain between her eyes, he fit the name just fine in his sheriff's uniform. Macho. Masculine. Manly.

When one minute passed into the next and he still said nothing, she gave in. "What do you want, Sheriff?"

"Come on now, Laura, you always knew what I wanted." He paused, then grinned slyly and added, "You always knew what I liked, too."

Laura. The clerk had called her that, too, hadn't she? Or had that been part of a bad dream? Maybe this was all a bad dream. Sometimes she had them—some just minor disturbances that left her with a vague discomfort when she awoke, others full-fledged nightmares. When they came, it was her own screams that awoke her to a pillow soaked with tears and bedclothes drenched with sweat. But she never knew what they were about, neither the disturbances nor the terrors. She didn't *want* to know.

"My name is Carly Johnson," she said flatly. "Not Laura."

"Uh-huh." He gave her a long look, from head to toes and back again, and grinned in a manner that could only be described as wicked. "Right."

How had it happened, she wondered in despair, that she'd chosen to spend the night in the one town in Montana with a sheriff who'd been involved with a woman who must look a great deal like her? A *great* deal, she emphasized, because she couldn't quite imagine Sheriff Buck Logan getting his women mixed up.

And why did the sheriff have to be so good-looking that

if she weren't so sick, she would probably feel a moment's regret that she *wasn't* the mysterious Laura? she wondered crankily. With his dark hair, dark eyes, dark skin and wicked grin, he was by far the handsomest man she'd seen in a long time.

The handsomest…and the most dangerous. In spite of the almost friendly, conversational tone of his voice, there was an edge of malevolence to his words, an antagonism that made her grateful that she wasn't the woman who had caused it. Now she only had to convince *him* of that.

"You've made a mistake, Sheriff," she said. "My name is Carly Johnson, and I'm from Seattle. I was just passing through Montana on my way home. I'm not this Laura person." That said, she stepped around him, careful not to brush against him, and went to the dresser. Had she dumped her purse here, or had he? She couldn't remember, although she supposed she had. She'd been in such a hurry to find her pills when she had gotten to the room. Besides, she assumed a sheriff would be more careful when he went through some unsuspecting—make that unconscious— woman's purse.

She sorted through the contents as she replaced them in the handbag, but there was no pill bottle. For just a moment she stood there thinking; then she went to the bathroom. The glass she'd drunk from earlier sat there on the counter, but there was no pill bottle there, either. It wasn't on the nightstand or on the rumpled covers or—

"Looking for this?"

The sheriff was holding the bottle. She hadn't noticed it earlier because the bottle was so small and his hand was so big. When he folded his fingers around it, it completely disappeared.

With a sigh, she dragged her fingers through her hair. "Is that why you're here? Because you think you've caught someone with illegal drugs?" She sighed again. "I assure you, Sheriff, the prescription is perfectly legal. If you'll wait until morning, you can call my doctor and ask him.''

''What are they for?''

''Headaches.''

''I took this stuff once back in college. One of these could knock an elephant flat on his—'' When he saw the tightening of her jaw, he broke off, then went on. ''Those must be some powerful headaches.''

''I wouldn't be here right now if they weren't.'' Her patience was wearing thin, and she was feeling worse with every minute that passed. ''I was on my way home,'' she repeated, her voice as taut and trembly as the muscles in her neck. ''I got sick, and this was the closest town, so I stopped here for the night. I haven't done anything wrong, Sheriff—and certainly nothing that entitles you to force your way in here, go through my belongings and question me.''

''I didn't 'force' my way in. You left the door un-locked.''

She noticed he didn't deny going through her things. How thorough a search had he done? she wondered, think-ing of the sixty-seven dollars in her purse that had to get her home to Seattle. Then she remembered the quilt and her shoes and regretted her suspicions. This man—this *sheriff*—wasn't going to steal a few dollars from her purse, then remove her shoes and tuck her in so that she slept more comfortably.

''Obviously you've made a mistake, Sheriff. I'm *not* this Laura. So if you'll return my property and leave my room, I'd like to see about getting some dinner before this town closes up for the night.''

''The restaurant downstairs is open until ten, Laura. You know that.'' Instead of placing the medicine bottle in her outstretched hand as she expected, he grabbed her arm and started pulling her toward the door. ''I missed dinner while waiting for you to wake up, so I'll just join you down-stairs.''

''No!'' Carly jerked away from him as if burned, then concentrated for a moment on regaining control. She was breathing hard and trembling again. She hated the weakness that accompanied these headaches. It left her totally inca-pable of dealing with a man as forceful as Sheriff Buck Logan.

Struggling to deepen her breathing, she combed her fin-gers through her hair, then picked up her purse and her keys. When she turned to face the sheriff again, she pre-tended to herself that she was in control, even though he obviously didn't think so. Hell, she couldn't even convince herself. ''You have no right to harass me, Sheriff. I haven't done anything wrong. Now I'm going downstairs to eat— *alone*. I don't care what you do as long as you don't do it anywhere near me. All right?''

Without waiting for his agreement, she opened the door and waited pointedly for him to leave. When he did, she followed him out and locked the door, then slid the key into her purse. For a moment she simply stood there, using the door for support. She felt so badly that if she got any-where near food, she might get sick…but she was so hun-gry that if she didn't try to eat, she would definitely be ill.

Moving carefully, she pushed herself away from the door and turned toward the stairs—only to find the sheriff wait-ing. She should have known that getting rid of him wouldn't be so easy. After all, he was the law in a nothing-special little town. It probably gave him an exaggerated sense of importance.

It also gave him plenty of opportunities to abuse his au-thority, and there would be no one around to stop him. He could dog her all night, question her relentlessly, accuse her of whatever he wanted, and no one could make him back off—at least until she was able to bring a lawyer into it. Please, she wearily prayed, don't let that happen. Not tonight.

She ignored him as she made her way along the brightly lit hallway. At the stairs, she clutched the railing in one hand and tried not to notice the clunk of his boots that echoed her every step. When she paused in the restaurant door, she pretended that he hadn't stopped beside her.

The dining room was large, with about twenty tables in the center and another ten booths along the walls. About half the tables were filled with diners, but she didn't even glance at them as she started toward the booth in the far corner. A waitress scurried over and set the table with napkin-wrapped silverware, coffee cups and menus, then went to stand at the nearest occupied table.

All of the tables back here were empty, Carly thought as she reached the booth. How had the waitress known she was coming to this particular one? And why did she have the eerie feeling that everyone was staring at her and that all conversation had come to a standstill when she'd entered the room?

Because they were and it had, she saw when she turned to sit down. At least thirty pairs of eyes were focused on her, and for a moment she stared back, her wary gaze moving from one strange face to another. Slowly she started to slide into the booth; then suddenly she changed her mind and switched to the other side. Now, thanks to the high back, they couldn't see her, but she could still see their reflections in the plate glass. She could still hear their silence.

The sheriff hung his hat on the brass hook at the end of the booth, then sat across from her. He didn't bother to pick up the menu the way she did. He simply folded his hands together and watched her.

"What's the deal, Sheriff? Is your social life so pathetic

that the mere sight of you with a woman is enough to stun your neighbors into shocked silence?'' she asked dryly.

"I've had my share of women since you left, Laura." He was grinning when he answered, but it didn't reach his eyes. They were dark, hostile, challenging. Maybe his Laura was a jealous woman, Carly thought, but she was too damned tired to work up any response to his challenge.

Scowling, she concentrated on the menu, searching for something her stomach could tolerate. Instinctively she knew the chili would be too hot and that even the beef stew would be too spicy for the shape she was in tonight. And the fried chicken was greasy, the chicken-fried steak tough, the french fries were frozen and the onion rings were home-made. Maybe the turkey platter would be her best bet, followed by a piece of the pie she'd seen on the counter, coconut cream topped with mile-high meringue.

"Why do you bother looking at the menu?" the sheriff asked. "You always order the same thing—the turkey dinner and cream pie."

She looked up sharply, her eyes narrowing on him. How had he known? she wondered, a chill dancing down her spine. Then she gave a shake of her head. So this woman who looked a lot like her had the same taste in foods. It didn't mean a thing. Simple coincidence.

What a shame they didn't have the same taste in men. As handsome as he was, Carly didn't like cocky, arrogant, bossy men—and she'd never met anyone who fit that description as perfectly as Buck Logan.

He gestured to the waitress, and she hurried over, coffee-pot in one hand and order pad in the other. She filled the sheriff's cup first, then turned to Carly's. Deliberately she turned the mug over. "I'd like iced tea, please," she requested. "And I'd like the deluxe hamburger and fries."

Logan grinned as if he knew she'd changed her order to spite him. For himself he ordered a double deluxe cheeseburger and a double order of onion rings. Carly had seen the two empty dessert dishes upstairs in her room, holding nothing but a few crumbs from a pie crust and a dribble of cherry glaze. How could he eat like that and remain so lean? Of course, even if through exercise or some miracle of metabolism the calories did his outside no harm, on the inside there had to be plenty of damage from all that fat and choles—

"No cholesterol warning?" he asked. "No lectures on the dangers of a diet high in fat and sugar?"

The chill returned, and she shivered with it. How had he known what she was thinking? Coincidence again? A lucky guess? Maybe. Probably, she assured herself. After all, most people were diet-conscious these days. Although she preferred exercise over diet to stay in shape, she was aware enough of the risks that an order like the one he'd given the waitress could spark only two thoughts: how delicious and how unhealthy.

"Where have you been the last three years?"

The look she gave him was decidedly bland. "You've been through my purse, Sheriff. You know where I live."

Suddenly his good humor disappeared, and the anger she had sensed when she'd first seen him returned. "My name is Buck."

"And my name is Carly. Not Laura. *Carly.*"

He stared at her, and she stared back, unblinking, unyielding. She was surprised when he backed down first. She didn't think he often did that. "Okay. Fine. Have it your way, *Carly*. Now let me hear you make that same little speech to her." He gestured toward someone approaching them, and Carly leaned around the edge of the booth to see.

Almost instantly she was enveloped in an embrace that pulled her out of the booth and onto her feet. For one panicky moment she felt as if she were drowning in the overpoweringly sweet fragrance worn by the woman who held her trapped, and she tried to pull away, but the woman was stronger.

"Laura! My God, Laura, it *is* you!" The woman was sobbing. "I couldn't believe it when I got home from Helena and heard that you were back! I prayed every night that you were safe, that you would come back to us, and thank God, you have! Oh, sweetheart, why didn't you let us know you were coming? Why didn't you keep in touch with us?" Then her voice broke, and she asked plaintively, "Oh, Laura, why did you leave the way you did?"

Stop it! Carly was silently shouting. It took all her will-power not to shove the old lady back, then run away screaming until she found safety. She hated this embrace, hated the fragrance, hated the suffocating closeness. Her head ached and her skin crawled, and she didn't want to be rude, but finally she had to wrench free of the woman and back away.

"You've made a mistake," she insisted, her voice shaking as badly as her body was. "I'm *not* Laura. My name is Carly—Carly Johnson. I'm from Seattle. I'm just passing through Montana on my way home. I'm sorry your Laura's gone, but I'm not her. I'm *not*."

"Why, Laura…" The old lady looked hurt. "Buck, why is she saying these things? What is she talking about? Of course she's Laura. Anyone who ever knew her can see that. Heaven's sake, girl, I raised you myself, just like you were my own, just like Trina. How can you stand there and pretend you're someone else? How can you be so cruel?"

The woman reached for her again, and Carly shrank back. Now there was no place left to go. She was caught in the corner between the booth and the window, the old lady was crying pitifully, and everyone in the room was staring at her, including a young woman standing in the doorway. For an instant the malice in her glare penetrated Carly's confused panic. Trina, she thought numbly. That was Trina. Whatever everyone else's feelings about the missing Laura were, Trina's were clear. She hated her.

"Please come home, Laura," the woman pleaded, reaching for her again. "Come to the house and we'll work this out. We'll make everything all right, I swear we will. Please, Laura…"

"For God's sake, Sheriff, tell her!" Carly insisted. "Tell her I'm not Laura! Tell them all!"

There was movement beside her, and then he was on his feet. "Maureen, calm down. Go over there and sit down and get hold of yourself. Trina?"

The younger woman jumped when Logan called her name and came hurrying over. She escorted the now-sobbing Maureen to a nearby table, giving Carly a look of pure hatred as she did so.

Caught up in Trina's resentment, Carly was taken by surprise when Logan took her arm in a firm grip and started steering her across the dining room. She endured it as long as possible—less than a minute—before trying to free herself, but just as the old lady had been stronger, so was the angry man.

He didn't release her until they were shut away in the privacy of her room, and even then he remained close, too close, forcing her against the dresser and using his body to block her escape. "You've got ten seconds," he said through clenched teeth, his face only inches from hers, "to come up with a suitable explanation. What the hell's going on, Laura?"

Suddenly it was all too much—the pain, the sickness, the anger, the frustration. Carly did the only thing her body was physically capable of at that time.

She fainted.

Chapter 2

Rolling onto her side, Carly snuggled deeper under the covers, eyes still closed, and smiled smugly. The doctors had advised her to take it easy for a day or two following one of these headaches, and in the beginning they had been so crippling in intensity that she'd had no choice but to follow orders. But this morning, except for an uncomfortable emptiness in her stomach, she felt fine. Better than fine. She felt as if she could make the five-hundred-mile drive from this nowhere Montana town home to Seattle and still have enough energy to unpack, do her laundry and shop for groceries, and maybe even run a few miles on top of that.

What she *didn't* have the energy for, she admitted a grim moment later, was the man who was watching her from the foot of the bed. Spending the night in a rocking chair hadn't done much for Sheriff Logan's disposition, which hadn't been too sparkling to start with. He was watching her with a scowl that she knew instinctively had put fear into men braver than her. Between that look and the night's beard that darkened his jaw, he resembled some demon from below. Her very own personal demon, sent to make her brief stay in Montana an unpleasant one.

Her very own personal and disgustingly handsome demon, she amended. Trust her hormones to remind her of that. But that was only natural, she supposed, considering that the closest she had come to intimacy with a man in she didn't know how long was the myriad examinations her doctors had put her through. She wondered briefly, wistfully, what it had been like—to feel a man's arms around her, to be touched by hands as big and strong as the sheriff's, to shelter a man's body within her own, to share something so special, so important...

Abruptly she stopped herself, as she always did when she considered the past she had lost—the memories, the personality, the *life,* that the accident had taken from her three years ago—and turned her attention to a more immediate question. How had she gotten to bed? Her memory of last night ended with the sheriff's terse, angry demand that she explain what the hell was going on. Had she fainted? Had the sheriff been left with the task of getting her into bed?

Her face burned with embarrassment because she hated the weakness that fainting implied, because she hated the idea of being carried to bed by a stranger—by an arrogant, dangerous, hostile stranger. And maybe, she admitted with unflinching honesty, she hated the idea just a little that her first close encounter—in memory, at least—with a handsome man had taken place while she was unconscious.

After checking to make sure that she was decent under the covers—she still wore her jeans and sweater—she sat up, drawing her feet close, resting her arms on her knees. "Isn't it more common to place a guard *outside* a room?"

Her voice was husky, the throaty, just-enjoyed-some-wonderfully-hot-sex voice that Laura had used so well, Buck thought, glowering a little harder. There had been times when she had used no more than that to make him want, to make him plead. Well, by God, he was *not* going to respond to it now.

"I brought your luggage in," he said stiffly. "Take a shower, change clothes, do whatever you need to do. Then we're going over to the office to talk."

She slid to the edge of the bed and stood up, then leveled an even, cool gaze on him. "After I take a shower and change clothes, *I'm* going to get some breakfast," she said with a mildness that was deceptive. *Everything* about her, he knew from experience, was deceptive. "Then I'm going home."

He deliberately misunderstood her. "Good. Maureen will be happy to see you."

Ignoring him, she lifted the smaller of the two bags onto the bed and began removing toiletries: shampoo, conditioner, cologne, makeup. For two years her things had filled his bathroom—items with rich scents and richer price tags—but none of these brands had ever been included. The cologne, he could see from the rocker, was just that—cologne, and not the obscenely expensive perfume she had always preferred—and the makeup could be found in any grocery or drugstore. It wasn't the top quality, guaranteed-to-keep-her-beautiful-forever stuff she had used in the past.

Not that she needed such products. Even without makeup, even with her hair tousled and tangled, even with the scar that he could see from here, she was still beautiful. Damn her for it.

Damn her to hell.

She took the items into the bathroom, then returned to open the suitcase. He watched her remove a pair of gray trousers and a slightly wrinkled white shirt. She reached into the bag for something else, then hesitated, glancing uncertainly at him. Rising from the chair, he saw what had given her pause: a bra, small and gauzy and palest yellow. Whatever else had changed, Laura hadn't lost her liking for sexy lingerie, he thought with a humorless smile.

Taking his smile as a challenge, she picked up the bra, then a froth of matching lace panties. Then she faced him, watching. Waiting.

"You plan to shower sometime this morning?" he asked irritably.

"Do you plan to leave my room?"

"Come on, Laura—"

She stiffened at that. "My name," she said coldly, deliberately, "is Carly."

Had he considered her fragile last night? he wondered. Because there certainly wasn't anything fragile about the woman in front of him now. She looked annoyed enough— and determined enough—to take on anyone who got in her way. That was a change. The Laura he had known and sometimes hated had never confronted anyone face-to-face. She had gotten her way through manipulation and seduction, through teasing and tormenting.

He walked past her, careful not to get too close, not to touch her, not to feel her warmth, not to smell her scent. "I'll be waiting in the restaurant," he said ungraciously. "And don't try to sneak out. You'll get caught."

Downstairs, the dining room was nearly empty. Buck ignored the few customers and went to the back booth where they had sat last night, where they had always sat whenever they'd eaten in the restaurant. When the waitress filled his coffee cup, he placed an order for steak and eggs, then went back to his brooding.

What was Laura's game this time? What could she possibly have to gain by pretending to be someone else? And how could she possibly be stupid enough to think her charade would succeed?

Laura Phelps was many things, but stupid wasn't one of them. Maybe she was just feeling particularly cruel. Maybe this was her idea, no matter how sick, of a joke.

Or maybe the woman upstairs in room 3 truly wasn't Laura.

He considered the possibility with all the objectivity he was able to muster under the circumstances—which, he had to admit with a deeper scowl, was precious little. Maybe Carly Johnson simply bore an incredible resemblance to Laura. Unlikely as it seemed, it happened. Maybe Carly really was a tourist on her way home to Seattle who'd had the bad luck to stop in Nowhere for the night. Maybe it really was just coincidence.

But he couldn't buy it. Every instinct he had told him that this was Laura. This was the woman he had argued and made love with for two long years. This was the woman he had tried desperately to stay away from. This was the woman who had blithely informed him one day that they would become lovers, the woman he had distrusted and disliked, the woman he had fought so damned hard to avoid. This was the woman who had laughed when he had finally given in, when desire had overpowered dislike, when need had overcome pride and self-control.

This was Laura.

There was a sudden murmur from the customers at the other end of the dining room, and he looked up to see Laura standing in the doorway. Selfish, wicked, beautiful Laura. His weakness.

His obsession.

Funny. She didn't look selfish or wicked or any of the other things he knew her to be. She looked wary. A little lost. An awful lot alone.

Sympathy for Laura, he thought with a derisive chuckle as she started toward him. Sympathy for the devil.

She stood for a moment beside the booth. Waiting for

an invitation? Laura had always simply invited herself wherever she'd wanted to be. But he could play along for a moment, and he did so, offering her a sarcastic invitation to join him.

"You said you wanted to talk." The huskiness was gone from her voice now, leaving it soft and feminine and normal. "I have a long drive ahead of me. If we can talk now—"

"We'll go to the office after we eat."

She accepted coffee from the waitress, then scanned the menu and ordered pancakes, fried potatoes, biscuits and gravy. It was a hell of a breakfast for someone who rarely had more than coffee before lunch, especially for someone who had always watched her weight. Buck was watching her moodily, trying to figure her out, when she looked across and met his gaze. Looking embarrassed, she explained, "I missed dinner last night. That makes it all right to splurge today."

Missing meals was nothing new for her, he thought, annoyed by her behavior. Her appearance had always been of the utmost importance to her. Being thin was far more desirable in her eyes than being well nourished.

"Am I under arrest?"

He shifted his attention back to her. "No."

"Am I suspected of some crime?"

He shrugged lazily. "Lying isn't illegal—most of the time, at least. Assuming a new identity isn't illegal, either, unless it's done for the purpose of committing or avoiding punishment for a crime."

At his mention of identity, her mouth tightened and narrow lines appeared across her forehead, distorting the faint curve of the scar there. She hadn't covered it with makeup, he realized with a jolt. In fact, she wore damned little makeup at all—lipstick, eyeshadow, a touch of mascara.

Laura Phelps in public with next to no makeup. Would wonders never cease.

"If I'm not under arrest or a suspect, then you can't force me to stay here, can you?" she was asking, her words thoughtful, her tone polite, her expression determined. "You can't make me go to your office or answer your questions or respond to your accusations, either, can you?"

"No. But if you insist, I imagine an arrest could be arranged." Smiling sardonically, he leaned toward her. "You want to go the whole route? Rights, handcuffs, strip search? It's kind of kinky, but, hey, you always were a little… unconventional."

That made twice today that he'd seen her blush. But Laura had never blushed, not once in all the years he'd known her. She'd been too bold, too brash, too immodest. So maybe this *was* all a mistake. Maybe this woman really wasn't…

No. No one but Laura had ever made him feel this way— both unwillingly attracted and undeniably violent. No other woman had ever brought his antagonism so effortlessly to the surface. No other woman had made him both want and loathe at the same time.

No other woman had ever frightened him the way Laura did.

The way *this* one did.

"I'll answer your questions, Sheriff," she said with quiet dignity. "Then I'm going home. I'm going home to Seattle, and I'm never coming back here again."

And no one, he thought morosely, *no one* would be happier about that than him.

Nowhere was a pretty little town, Carly thought as they walked along the main street. She could easily see it as the set for a western movie—trade the cars for horses, remove the two stoplights and turn off the neon sign that proclaimed Bar, and turn back the clock a hundred years. Dress Buck Logan in jeans and a leather vest and replace his sheriff's badge with a marshal's star, and he would fit right in, too.

Nowhere was also, she acknowledged with a shiver of unease, a familiar little town. Maybe it *had* been used for a movie. Maybe she had seen pictures of it in the tourism brochures she had used to plan her vacation. Maybe she had visited it sometime before the accident. But whatever the reason, it felt vaguely comfortable. Like a distant memory that wasn't exactly a memory.

Déjà vu.

As pretty as the town was—as pretty as the sheriff was— she was anxious to see the last of it. She wanted to go home, wanted to forget the confusion and bewilderment of the past eighteen hours. She wanted to get back to life as she knew it, where no one mistook her for their long-lost lover, niece or friend.

It was ironic, after she'd finally gotten reacquainted with herself, after she'd learned to accept the sketchy version of her past that had been pieced together following the accident, that she'd wound up in a place where everyone insisted that she was someone else. She wondered if Laura, wherever she was, realized how much she was missed.

She wondered why she'd gone away.

If she was coming back.

And exactly what her relationship with the sheriff had been.

He hadn't spoken to her since leaving the hotel. He had simply turned toward the small wooden-frame building that served as the sheriff's department and expected her to tag along. The building stood off by itself, a parking lot separating it from the stone courthouse on one side, a vacant lot setting off the cemetery on the other.

He'd made no secret of the fact that he and the missing

Laura had been lovers. What kind of lover was he? Carly wondered as they crossed the street. Passionate? Certainly. Creative? A sure bet, judging from that wicked grin of his. Tender?

Maybe it was just her—maybe she brought out his bad side—but she didn't see much tenderness in him. He was hard. Intense. *Dark.*

He held the door for her, then, ignoring the staring deputies, led the way to the small office at the back. It wasn't as easy for Carly to ignore them. Like everyone else she'd seen, they seemed startled, almost unnerved, by her resemblance to their friend. She was grateful when they reached his office and he drew the blinds on the large window that hid them from the deputies' view.

The office was exactly what she had somehow expected—neat, organized and tidy. Everything was dusted, the corkboard that hung on one wall was covered with neatly posted bulletins, the desk was cleared of everything but a small pile of mail and a telephone, and two ivies—why had she expected plants? Logan certainly didn't look like a green thumb sort of person—flourished on the windowsill.

He sat down behind the desk, folded his hands across his stomach and gave her a long, sour look. "Where do you want to start?"

She seated herself in the only chair, a straight-backed chair of oak with a wide, scooped seat and thick slats across the back. "You're the one asking questions. You decide."

He decided too quickly, and he went in a direction she hadn't expected. His first question wasn't "Why are you lying about your name?" or "Where have you been?" or "Why have you come back?" It was "How did you get that scar?"

Instinctively she raised her hand to her forehead, fluffing her bangs across the pale, thin line. It wasn't the only scar she had, not by any means. Some had come from the accident; others had been there before, sources unknown. For the most part, she ignored them. No one ever saw the rest except her doctors, and the one on her face—well, her friends and co-workers knew about the wreck, and everyone else was too polite to mention it.

Except Sheriff Logan.

She wished she had used a heavier hand with the makeup this morning. She wished she hadn't had her bangs trimmed the first day of her vacation. She wished she wasn't vain enough to care that the sheriff had noticed it.

Most of all, she wished she had never had the damned wreck in the first place, because then she never would have suffered the head injuries that had left her in a coma and had contributed to the post-traumatic syndrome, of which the headaches were a symptom. If she didn't have the headaches, she never would have stopped in Nowhere, and she never would have met Buck Logan or heard of Laura Phelps.

She had done a lot of wishing in the last three years, for all the good it had done her. Like now.

The sheriff was waiting, watching her with that narrow, dark scowl. She scowled right back at him. "I was in an accident."

"What happened?"

The question came quickly again, demanding an answer, and she gave him the one that had been given her by the doctors. "A drunk driver ran a red light and collided head-on with my car."

"Where?"

"In Seattle."

"When?"

"Three years from this November." The first year had been filled with anniversaries: the date her life had almost ended; the day she had awakened from the coma; the days

she'd been released from the hospital and cleared to return
to work. The second year she had marked only the date of
the accident. It had been a day of mourning. On that date
her life had changed forever. She might someday get parts
of it back, but the longer she went without regaining any
memories, the doctors had warned her, the less likely the
chances that she would.

This year, two months from now, she intended to ignore
the anniversary. Just as she ignored her scars. Just as she
had ignored the other diners in the restaurant this morning
and the deputies outside this room.

"Were you hurt badly?"

There was an odd tone to his voice this time—compassion, she thought, in a man who didn't want to feel it.
Maybe there was some small bit of tenderness inside him,
after all. "A few broken bones," she replied, looking at
the bulletin board instead of him. "And I banged my
head."

That sounded so much better—so much less pitiable—
than the truth: broken bones, bruises and lacerations, a
coma of nearly two months' duration and—the kicker—
amnesia. Her entire life wiped clean. No childhood, no ad-
olescence, no nothing. For all *she* knew, she very well
might be his Laura. If not for her identification, her neighbors and co-workers and her personal belongings, she
would have had no idea that she was Carly Johnson.

But she *was* Carly.

She was.

"How long were you in the hospital?"

Was that information protected by patient confidential-
ity? she wondered. If she lied to him, if she shaved the
length of her stay by, oh, a few months or so to make her
tale sound more plausible, could he find out?

Her hesitation made him suspicious. "How badly did
you bang your head, Laura?"

She looked at him then, her gaze sharp. "My name—"

"All right," he harshly interrupted. "I'll play your damned game. How badly were you hurt, *Carly*? What did you get besides that scar? A concussion? A skull fracture? Were you knocked unconscious? Were you in a coma—"

He broke off, seeing the answer she was trying to hide. For a long moment he simply stared at her as if she were some sort of oddity—which, she acknowledged, she was, medically, at least. She was one of that small number of patients to awaken from a protracted coma relatively unharmed—unharmed if you didn't count the memory blanks. She'd had to relearn a few skills, but all in all, she had survived the experience in good shape.

"You were, weren't you?" Logan asked softly. "You were in a coma. For how long?"

"Nearly two months." Her mouth barely moved. She didn't want to talk about this, didn't want to give him ammunition to support his argument that she was Laura Phelps.

"And when you woke up? You didn't remember anything, did you? You didn't even know your own name, did you?"

She leaned forward and reached one hand toward him, subconsciously pleading with him to see his mistake. "I know what you're thinking, but you're wrong. I'm not your friend. I didn't go off and have an accident and forget my name. I didn't decide to be Carly Johnson when I woke up. That's who I *am*!"

"That's who you *think* you are. But you don't really know, do you?"

With a soft rustle her purse slid from her lap and onto the floor, landing with a thump. For a moment she simply stared at it, then she jerked it up and pulled her wallet out. "Look, here's my driver's license," she said, making an effort to remain calm. "Here's my social security card, my credit cards, my bank card. That's *me*. That's my name. That's who I am.''

She laid the evidence out before him, but he barely glanced at the objects. All those little plastic cards were her life, but to him they meant nothing. His chilling dark gaze locked on her, he said softly, ''You don't know who you are.''

''I *do!*'' she snapped, losing her battle for control. ''I have friends, people who knew me before the accident! The people I work with, my neighbors—*they* know who I am!''

''When did you move to Seattle?''

The sudden switch to a new line of questioning left her numb for a moment. ''About a month before the accident.''

''The middle of October. Almost three years ago.'' He smiled thinly. ''Funny, you left here—sorry, *Laura* left here the beginning of October. Almost three years ago.'' Scooping up her license and cards, he looked at each one, then tossed them all onto the desk top as he spoke. ''Every one of these was issued right after you—right after Laura left Nowhere. They don't prove anything—except that for some strange reason Carly Johnson needed all new identification and credit cards three years ago.''

She sank back in her seat. She could understand his confusion—hell, she even shared it. It was an amazing coincidence—her resemblance to Laura, the other woman's disappearance about the same time Carly had settled in her new home, her amnesia, her decision to stop for the night in this particular town.

What if it was more than coincidence?

No! It couldn't be. She might not have any memories to support it, but she *knew* who she was. That knowledge was just about the *only* thing she was certain of, and she wouldn't let Buck Logan take it from her.

But what about the resemblance? The timing between Laura's disappearance and her move to Seattle?

What about the waitress knowing last night which booth she was going to sit in? The sheriff knowing what she was going to order from the menu, right down to the dessert?

What about the sheriff's knowing, last night, that she was about to comment on his unhealthy diet? Her certainty that the missing Laura was definitely not missed by cousin Trina? Or the nagging familiarity of the town as they'd walked from the hotel this morning?

Coincidence? Lucky guesses? Déjà vu? Any of those was easier to accept than the alternative.

Looking away from his probing eyes, her gaze fell once more on her wallet. Other than her last sixty-seven dollars, it was pretty empty now, except for a few credit-card receipts and two small photographs. Her only real link to the past, she carried them with her everywhere.

Of course, the pictures! Carefully sliding each one from its plastic sleeve, she set them in front of the sheriff. ''Do you know those people?''

He looked at the first one, then the other, studying the grainy faces, the dated clothing, the sixties hairstyles. Then he turned them over, reading the spidery writing there. Carly didn't need to see them; she had memorized the inscriptions by heart. *Mark and Helene with Carly (3 mos.) Dallas, Texas* the first one read. The second, the one of the gap-toothed little girl in a navy-blue cardigan and white blouse, was inscribed, *Carly Ann, six years old, first grade.*

Looking unconvinced, he added the photos to the small pile of identification. ''That little girl could be any of a thousand women. You want to put up photographs as proof? Try this one.'' He reached into the bottom desk drawer, withdrew a frame and tossed it between them.

It landed faceup. Carly didn't reach for it right away. She didn't want to see it, didn't want to look at Laura Phelps and doubt herself. But she forced herself to pick it up, forced herself to reach out and curl her fingers around the engraved wooden frame and draw it across the desk. She forced herself to focus her gaze on the image underneath the dusty glass.

"Oh, my God."

She looked as if she had seen a ghost, Buck thought. Maybe, in a sense, she had. The woman she had become after the accident had come face-to-face with the woman she had been before. A ghost from the past—from a past that she couldn't remember.

If she was telling the truth. Laura had never been above lying when it suited her, but he couldn't imagine her pulling off a lie as complex as this. No, the bewilderment, the confusion and the fear seemed genuine. She wasn't playing a cruel game or acting out a malicious joke. She really didn't know who she was.

She didn't want, he thought grimly, to be who she was.

Very carefully she returned the frame to the desk and got up to pace the room. There wasn't much space to move—a few strides across, double that back. She stopped at the window behind him and stared out.

When she finally spoke, her voice was soft. "You believe I *am* her."

He swiveled his chair around so he could see her, but he didn't answer. She didn't need his answer.

"You think I ran away from here and somehow created a new identity for myself, and then I had the accident and forgot everything. And when I regained consciousness, the lies were all I had, and I believed them." She turned to look at him then. The sun was shining through the window, touching her hair, making it gleam, forming a halo behind her that hurt his eyes. "Would she have known how to do that?"

"She?" he echoed.

"Your Laura. Would she have known how to create a new identity?"

Your Laura. She had that part wrong. Laura had never been his or anyone else's. She had always done the possessing. She had never been possessed by anything, except selfishness. Greed. Evil.

His smile felt bitter. It was difficult to associate those qualities with the woman standing in front of him now. Evil? This slender, beautiful woman with an angel's face? Vulnerable was a much more suitable description.

He steeled himself against that small weakening. Laura had always sensed his weaknesses and had used them against him, had used them to get what she'd wanted. And what she had wanted then, five years ago, had been *him*. She had wanted to control him. She had wanted to break him, to make him need what he had so desperately not wanted. She had wanted to prove that she was stronger, more powerful, and she had succeeded.

He had never known why she had chosen to torment him in particular. There had been other men, men who would have willingly given her everything she had asked for, men who would have been grateful for whatever she gave in return. Men who didn't dislike her, men who didn't soon learn to hate her. Maybe it was because he hadn't been one of those men. Maybe she had liked the challenge he'd represented. Maybe she had simply wanted to disprove the old saying that you can't always have what you want.

Laura had always wanted, and she had always gotten.

Until the end.

"Sheriff?"

Her voice startled him from his thoughts. It had changed in the last three years. Except for this morning when she had first awakened, she didn't sound like Laura. Maybe it was because she was speaking normally, for no purpose other than to communicate. In the past she had used her voice in much the same way she'd used her body—as a tool, as one more weapon to seduce and torture and taunt.

Would she have known how to create a new identity for herself? "I don't know," he replied thoughtfully. "Maybe. You were—she was smart. If she didn't know, she could have found out."

"Maybe from you."

He scowled at her. "I would have remembered such a conversation. *I'm* not the one with amnesia." It was the first time either of them had used the word, and he saw her flinch. He could almost feel sorry for her if it weren't for who she was. If he didn't almost envy her. His two years with her had been ugly enough that losing his identity and his memories seemed at times a reasonable price to pay for forgetting.

For a moment she fingered the leaves of the ivy beside her; then, with a sigh, she moved away from the window and settled in the chair again. "I'm not her."

She spoke quietly and with such certainty. Was she really so sure of her identity? Buck wondered. Or was she merely so certain that she didn't *want* to be Laura? Maybe the ugliness had been too much for her, too. Maybe she had wanted to forget. Maybe being Carly Johnson was easier than being herself.

"We look a lot alike—I'll admit that," she said, gesturing toward the photograph. "But that's not so unusual. Everyone's seen those celebrity look-alikes. Normal people can have them, too. Laura and I could be twins—that's all it is. This picture—" She picked up her old school photo. "*This* one is me. You just don't want to see the resemblance, plus you didn't know me before the wreck, before the scar and the broken nose—"

He interrupted her to make a chillingly quiet point. "You didn't know yourself before the wreck."

Her determination wavered for a moment, then she continued, "I suppose it's possible that I could be your friend, only because *anything* is possible. But I'm not her."

"How do you know you're Carly Johnson? Because of these?" He scooped up the ID and credit cards, holding them in the air before clenching his fingers around them. "Because some people you'd known a few weeks told you so? And who *is* Carly Johnson? Where did she come from? Doesn't she have any family who miss her? Didn't she have any friends before she showed up in Seattle? Didn't she have a *life* before she showed up in Seattle?"

"I moved to Seattle from Texas. My parents are dead. I was an only child. I know I must have relatives somewhere, but I assume that we weren't close, since I had no record of them in my personal things."

"How do you know you came from Texas?" he demanded. "How do you know your parents are dead? How do you know this isn't all part of some elaborate lie?"

She was losing patience with him, but he was used to that. Laura had little patience with anyone who stood in her way, who didn't automatically acquiesce to her wishes, agree to her demands and accept her opinions. "The company I work for in Seattle still has my job application on file. That's where I got some of the background information. The rest came from friends."

"And you prefer to accept their version of your past over the truth."

"I prefer to accept the past that makes sense, that has some facts to support it, over *your* wishful thinking," she said stiffly. "Now, if you'll excuse me, Sheriff, I think I've given you enough of my time. I've got to get home."

She stood up, pushing the chair back with a scrape, and held out her hand. He flexed his fingers around the sharp plastic edges of the cards, reluctant to give them up, aware that he had no right to refuse. Slowly he got to his feet, walked around the desk and laid the cards in her palm. "What about Maureen?"

Buck noticed that the momentarily blank look in her eyes

was replaced by a flicker of guilt. Maureen had always been her only soft spot. She had been grateful to her aunt for taking her in after her mother's death, for making a home for her, for believing only the best of her. Even though her cousin Trina had simply been one more of her victims, Laura had always treated Maureen as well as she was capable of.

"The old lady from last night," she murmured.

"You can't just leave without a word. She thinks you've come back. She believes God has finally answered her prayers. You owe her an explanation."

"I don't owe her anything, Sheriff. I never saw her before last night." She finished replacing everything in her wallet, zipped her purse, then faced him. "Tell her it was all a mistake. Tell her that I'm not her niece. Tell her the truth."

"Which truth? Yours or mine? Because I don't think she's going to like mine very much. I don't think, after a lifetime of loving you better than you deserved, that she's going to be happy to hear that you're too damned selfish to give her even a few minutes of your precious time."

She closed her eyes, squeezing them tightly, then rubbed the tense spot between them. It was a simple gesture, but it made her look so damned defenseless. It made him remember how sick she had been yesterday, how unsteady she'd been when she had first awakened, how insubstantial she had felt when he had carried her to bed.

It made him feel sorry for her.

It made him *feel*.

For *her*.

Then she looked at him again, and the weakness, the fragility, was gone. She had drawn new strength from somewhere inside, and he in turn drew it from her, hardening himself against her, against these strangely unfamiliar emotions he was discovering.

"I don't care what you tell the old lady, Sheriff," she said calmly, evenly. "I'm going back to the hotel to pack, and then I'm going home."

He recognized the emotion surging inside as she walked out of his office and through the squad room. Panic. He had watched her walk away before with the same panicky fear that she might never come back. It had been matched by an equal fear that she would. Sometimes he had followed her.

The last time he hadn't.

Today he did. She was walking along the sidewalk, halfway to the courthouse, when he stepped outside. He called her name and saw by the way her shoulders stiffened that she'd heard, but she didn't look back.

"Laura!" He reached the curb a moment after she'd stepped off, and he stopped there, trying one last time. "Carly."

She came to a halt in the middle of the empty street and slowly turned around.

He closed the distance between them one foot at a time. "Doesn't any of this seem familiar to you? The hotel? My office? The salon over there? Don't you remember?"

As if in a daze, she looked around, then back at him. "I haven't been here before," she insisted in a soft voice. But was she trying to convince him or herself?

"Do you remember where you lived? Where I lived? Do you remember the school? The lake? The old movie theater?"

A pickup rumbled by in the other lane, passing only a few feet from them, but she didn't notice. She was staring at him, her eyes wide, her face ashen. She whispered something so softly that he couldn't hear anything but the *k* at the end of the word; then her gaze shifted to the left, following the street to the east. A mile out, the road disappeared around a curve as it began its climb out of the valley. It ran exactly five miles from the sheriff's office before it dead-ended.

At the lake.

He took a step back, then another. For a moment the loathing was so great that he thought he would be sick with it; then it subsided. The woman standing in front of him wasn't the Laura he hated. She was one he would probably never forgive and would definitely never like, but she was no longer the woman he despised. She was no longer the woman who had made him despise himself.

"You remember, don't you?" He spoke almost as softly as she had, not certain he wanted to hear the words out loud. "You remember the lake."

There were tears in her eyes—not tears of joy or relief, but of distress, of an awful kind of grief. "The lake," she repeated. "At the end of this road. Where you..."

She couldn't bring herself to finish, so he did it for her in the easiest terms he could. "Where you and I made love."

Flinching, she turned away and practically walked into the side of a passing car. The sound of the horn startled her, and she stopped abruptly, then turned back to face him. "Maybe I've been here before. Maybe I stopped here on a trip."

There was an edge to her voice of desperation, of damn near hysteria. She didn't want to believe this, and hell, he didn't blame her. She'd had her identity taken from her once already; here it was happening again. But even if it frightened her, even if it hurt her, he had to let it happen again. He had to *help* it happen again.

"Looking the way you do?" he demanded harshly. "You think you could have just waltzed into town and no one would have noticed you? You think *I* wouldn't have noticed you?"

"Maybe—maybe I saw the lake on the map. I looked at

so many—so many maps when I was planning my trip. Maybe—''

He shook his head, silencing her. "It's not on any maps. It's not even big enough to really be a lake. Laura—'' He reached out, but she backed away.

"Don't call me that! My name is Carly, damn it, I know it is!''

A car came to a slow stop beside them, and the driver, an old friend of Buck's family, gave him a curious raised-brows look through the bug-spattered windshield. Buck acknowledged him with a grim nod, then reached for her again, this time taking her arm firmly and leading her out of the street.

"Maybe... Listen to me,'' he demanded when she jerked away. "Maybe this is just a bizarre coincidence. Maybe you aren't Laura. Maybe you really are Carly Johnson, with no family, no history and no past. But don't you want to *know*? Don't you want to know if you belong here, if your family is here? Don't you want to know if all those memories you lost were created here? If you go back to Seattle today, won't those questions bother you?''

When she replied, she sounded weary and drained. She looked that way, too, thanks to him. "I can live with questions, Sheriff. I've had a million of them ever since I woke up in the hospital.''

She turned away and found herself in front of a plate-glass window with the words Lenore's Hair Designs emblazoned across the top. Buck saw her tremble, then saw the women inside, one with her hair dripping, two in rollers, and Lenore herself, watching them with ardent interest. It used to be that Laura had thrived on such attention. Now she moved to the side, out of their sight, and leaned tiredly against the granite-block wall.

"I have some vacation time left,'' she said dully. "I was planning to paint my apartment.'' She fell silent for a mo-

ment, then gave a sigh that seemed to come from way down
in her soul.

"I'll stay a few days."

Chapter 3

Shades of the past.

He should have let her leave, Buck thought as he walked into his bedroom. He should have escorted her back to the hotel and watched her get into her car and drive off, and then he should have gotten down on his knees and thanked God for sending her away again, for saving him from her once more.

But, no, he was too damn much of a fool for that. Instead of looking out for himself, instead of protecting himself, he had convinced her to stay. He had asked—had argued with—Laura to stay.

He must be mad. If he fell under her spell again, she would destroy him for certain. He wouldn't be lucky enough to escape her a second time. And the fact that she had changed, that she was gentler, softer, more human, wouldn't protect him. It just made her all the more dangerous.

He was certifiably insane.

Tossing his hat on the bed, he removed his gun belt, then loosened the narrow leather belt beneath it. He'd been in this uniform for close to thirty hours, and he felt dirty, unclean—although there was a good chance that feeling came from the woman down the hall rather than from rumpled clothes and no shower. Being around her could do that to him.

He removed his shirt, boots and socks and started to unzip his trousers, then stopped long enough to close and lock the door. Maybe he was being overcautious, but he wouldn't put it past her to invite herself right into the bathroom while he was in the shower.

Stepping into the tub, he closed his eyes and let the hot water stream over his head. For the first time since they'd left the sheriff's department in his Bronco, he voiced aloud the litany of curses burning inside him.

Damn her for coming back.

Damn her for not remembering.

Damn her for being different.

Damn, damn, *damn!*

He wasn't going to accept her story at face value—he knew better than that. No matter how real it sounded, no matter how genuine her frustration and confusion, he wanted more proof than a scar on her forehead that she wasn't lying. First, he decided, he would call Dr. Fredericks and ask about Laura's dental records. He didn't have much hope for help there, though; when the dentist had given up his full-time practice in favor of semiretirement a few years back, a lot of records had been destroyed, lost or somehow misplaced. With his luck, Laura's was one of them.

So the next step would be to run her fingerprints. Maybe Carly Johnson was wanted somewhere, which would suit him fine, because she sure as hell wasn't wanted here. Next he would talk to Doc Thomas and find out more about head injuries and amnesia.

Then he would have to talk to Maureen.

And through it all he would pray.

He didn't want her back in his life, even if she was different, even if she didn't remember what she had done to him. He didn't want to see her around town, didn't want that constant reminder of the two worst years of his life. He didn't want to live with the fear that someday she might remember their affair, that someday she might want to resume it.

Dear God, he would rather see her dead than back in his life.

Hot water soon gave way to warm. Bathing quickly, he dried off and shaved, then got dressed in the bedroom. In the room where he had often brought Laura. How many dozens of nights had she spent in that bed? Enough so that the nights without her had been curiously peaceful and, at the same time, painful. Waking up without her had been unsettling, but waking up with her had been worse. The mornings after had always been the worst, when his disgust at his weakness had been strongest, when he'd feared that he would spend the rest of his life that way—needing her and hating her. Unwilling to live with her and unable to live without her.

If she hadn't left when she had, she would have destroyed him. He'd known that then, but he had never been able to find the strength to walk away. He had developed a need for her, a raw, consuming need that had eaten away at him, killing him a little at a time. It had been as powerful as any addiction, and as harmful. He couldn't walk away from it.

But she could. She had.

And now she was back, twenty feet down the hall in his living room. Back and different. Still beautiful. Still alluring. Still seductive.

But innocent.

Now she was deadlier than ever.

He had delayed as long as he could, though not nearly long enough. Picking up clean socks and his boots, he walked down the hall to the living room. He stopped there in the doorway, his defenses slipping a bit as he watched her.

She was standing in front of the bookshelves that flanked the fireplace, a framed portrait in her hands. The photo was nothing special—just his younger sister and her four kids—but she seemed intrigued by it. The look on her face was one of absolute yearning. Of longing and just a bit of envy.

What kind of photographs did she have in her apartment? he wondered. Were there pictures of people she didn't know, people she claimed as family, like those in her wallet? Were there strangers looking down on her every day, or did she settle for scenic pictures, wall hangings or nothing at all?

With a soft sigh, she returned the frame to the shelf. The whisper of sound reminded him of her appearance in the hotel dining room this morning, when she had looked so lost, so out of place. Was that how she felt? Had her sense of belonging disappeared along with her identity?

He came further into the room, deliberately making her aware of him. Even though she didn't look at him, he saw it in the stiff lines of her body and heard it in the strained tones of her voice as she asked, "Is this your family?"

His gaze shifted from her to the photograph. "My sister and her kids. The one at the other end is my grandmother."

Carly's first impulse was to look up at him, but she indulged it with only a quick, sidelong glance. That was enough to see that he wore a pair of dark green uniform trousers and a khaki shirt, that his shirt wasn't buttoned all the way, that his feet were bare and his hair was wet and slicked back. That was more than she wanted to see.

She continued to study the items on the shelves—a

crudely carved bird, a pine cone with edges dipped in gold paint and, above, too high for her to read the inscription, a trophy of some sort. There were the photographs—his sister and her children and his white-haired grandmother—and there were books, dozens of books, and all apparently well-read. Technothrillers shared one shelf with westerns, and all the rest were mysteries. Natural enough for a cop, she supposed.

At last she took a seat on the hearth in front of the cold stone fireplace, folded her hands tightly together and asked, "What do we do now?"

He went to the phone and dialed a number. She watched and waited, listening to his end of the conversation. No doubt Fredericks was the local dentist, and there was no doubt, from the sheriff's grim look, that Laura had no dental records available for comparison.

After hanging up, he sat down in the rocker and began putting on his socks, then his boots. Without looking at her, without softening the antagonism in his voice, he asked, "Do you know if you've ever been fingerprinted?"

She shook her head.

"Then we'll start there."

The absence of dental records had discouraged her. Now she felt a sudden sense of relief. "You mean it's that simple? You'll take my fingerprints and compare them to hers and—"

He silenced her with a shake of his head. "Laura was never printed."

So much for hope. "Then what's the use?" she asked dejectedly.

"Maybe Carly was printed prior to three years ago. If so, that would prove that you aren't Laura."

Carly rested her arms on her knees, her chin on her arms. "You're saying that I might be a criminal." Dejection was quickly turning to dismay. Someone had told her once that if her memory returned, she might not like the person she had been or the life she had lived, but she had insisted that any memories had to be better than none at all.

Maybe, just maybe, she had been wrong.

"There are a lot of reasons to be fingerprinted—besides the obvious one of having been arrested. If you were in the military. If you were a cop. If you had security clearance. If you had a gun permit."

"And what if the fingerprints don't prove anything?"

Her questions seemed to annoy him—she could see his struggle for patience, could feel it in the electricity in the air. "Then maybe you'll remember something. Maybe being around Maureen and Trina will help."

And *him*. If anything helped jog loose a memory or two, it should be him, she thought privately. If she was Laura, then she'd had an affair with him. She had made love with him up at the lake and probably here in this house, too. She had known all the most intimate details about him— how he looked naked, how he kissed, where he liked to be touched, how he liked to be stroked. She had known if he'd liked his loving gentle or rough, tender or wild. She had known his fantasies—and had hopefully fulfilled a few of them, because he could certainly make a few of hers come true.

If she was Laura, she had probably been in love with him.

The mere suggestion had a powerful effect on her. She had to clear her throat—and her mind—before she could continue. "And what if I don't remember anything? What happens then?"

He looked as if he didn't want to consider that possibility. Was he so anxious to have his Laura back that he wouldn't consider that it might not be true? Was he desperate enough to settle for her even if she wasn't the real thing?

"I don't know," he replied grimly.

I don't know. The story of her life.

"You don't want to believe it, do you?"

The accusing tone in his voice made her smile. Did it offend him that she wasn't thrilled at the idea of being his lover? If so, she could soothe his ego. If she discovered with absolute certainty that she was Laura, then she would be happy to get back together with him, and more than happy to resume their affair. But letting herself believe without proof, letting herself hope—and probably fall in love with him all over again—only to find out that it was all a mistake...

That would destroy her.

"Think about all the memories you have, Sheriff—of growing up with your sister, of your parents and grandparents, of summers and vacations, Christmases and birthdays. Do you remember your first day of school? Your first best friend? Do you remember watching fireworks on the Fourth of July, eating homemade ice cream and swimming in a lake? Do you remember riding a bike for the first time? Getting your driver's license? Going out on your first date?" She paused for breath, then quietly added, "Do you remember the first time you made love?"

A flush turned his dark cheeks bronze and made his reply gruff. "Of course I do."

"Well, I don't. I don't remember any of those things. It's as if I didn't exist until three years ago. I don't know if I liked school or if I had a best friend. I don't know when I started dating, or *if* I started dating. I don't know if I had a lover. I don't know if I ever loved someone, or if anyone ever loved me." Again she paused, breathing deeply to ease the pain inside. "You have a lifetime's worth of memories, Sheriff. Changing your name wouldn't change who you are because of those memories. But all *I* have, Sheriff, is a name. Take that away from me, and I have nothing. *Nothing.*"

"You would have a new name. A home. A family," he argued. "That's hardly 'nothing.'"

"Prove it to me. Prove it first, and then I'll accept it. But you can't ask me to give up my only identity on the chance that you *might* be able to supply me with a new one. You can't do that, Sheriff. *I* can't do it."

In the silence that followed they stared at each other for a long time. He looked away first as he rose from the chair and finished buttoning his shirt. "Let's get going," he muttered. "We've got a lot to do."

Their first stop was the sheriff's department, where he turned her over to a deputy named Harvey to be fingerprinted. Carly had expected the sheriff to do it himself, then decided that it was better that he hadn't. Middle-aged, quiet and polite, Harvey was all business. His impersonal, efficient manner reminded her of the doctors at home in Seattle, and that allowed her to view this as just one more of the numerous procedures she had undergone in the last three years.

Still, it would have been nice to have a little contact with the sheriff, she had thought with a twinge of regret as she'd washed her hands in the bathroom. There was nothing the slightest bit impersonal about *his* touch, and after three years of impersonality, of professional interest and detachment, she could benefit from a personal touch.

A visit with the doctor was next on their agenda. His office was two blocks from the sheriff's, on the first floor of a building that also contained Dr. Frederick's dental office and a part-time lawyer's office. The waiting room was empty and the receptionist's desk unmanned, but that didn't deter the sheriff. He headed straight for the door behind the desk, and opened it, calling out the doctor's name.

"Come on back to my office," came a distant reply.

They passed three examining rooms, a file room and a supply room before finally reaching the private office. The door was open, and an elderly man stood waiting inside. "Hello, Buck. Good to see you," he greeted the sheriff, but he never took his eyes off Carly. He walked right up to her, stopping only inches away, and studied her face, left and right, as if he could find proof of her identity there.

She stood still for his scrutiny. After all, she was used to being scrutinized by doctors. She could endure it. But when he reached out to touch her, she involuntarily stepped back. The old man only smiled, then brushed her bangs aside to examine the scar they partially covered. "Nice job" was all he said before he turned away and went to sit behind his desk.

Carly looked at the sheriff, who simply shrugged, then gestured to the nearby chair. She slid into it while he brought another from the corner to join her.

"So...which name do you prefer?" the doctor asked.

"Carly."

"Carly it is. Now, Carly, Buck tells me you were in an accident nearly three years ago and have had amnesia ever since."

She gave the sheriff beside her a long, chastening look. "Checking out my story?" she asked softly.

The familiar scowl was back as he answered just as softly, "Every last detail."

Who was it he didn't trust? she wondered. Her? Or Laura?

The doctor looked from one to the other, then continued in an even, soothing voice. "Of course, I can't see your records or even talk to your doctors without your permission, Carly. If you don't want to give it—"

She smiled tautly. "My medical records and I have been examined by more doctors, nurses, interns and residents than you can imagine. One more won't make any difference. My primary physician is Jim Parker. Would you like him to mail you a copy of my records, or will talking with him on the phone be sufficient?''

''A phone call will be fine.''

Buck watched as she accepted the telephone from Doc Thomas. She dialed the number from memory, spoke first to a receptionist, then to a nurse and finally to the doctor himself. After a moment, she handed the phone back to Dr. Thomas, then wandered over to the window. The sheriff joined her there.

''Any more surprises?'' she asked softly as she traced a pattern in the dust on the windowsill.

''We're going to see Maureen this afternoon.''

She looked at him over her shoulder, her eyes dismayed, her mouth open to argue.

''She's waited long enough,'' he said accusingly. ''You've got to see her.''

''But she's so...overwhelming.''

''I'll talk to her first. I'll explain....''

''Provided, of course, that the doctor backs up my claims.'' She sighed. Like before, it was very soft. Very forlorn. ''I'd rather not sit in on this. I'll be in the waiting room.''

She seemed almost insulted, he thought as he watched her slip away and out of the room. Had she expected him to accept her story on faith? He knew how easily she could make a lie sound more believable than the truth, and the old Laura knew that he knew. Of course she would have forgotten that, along with everything else.

Or maybe she hadn't forgotten it. Maybe she had never known it, because maybe she wasn't Laura.

Dr. Thomas brought his call to an end, then waited for Buck to return to the desk. ''She's lucky to be alive,'' he said without preamble. ''She had some serious injuries— head trauma, lacerations, chest wall and pericardial contusions, a broken nose, left arm, right wrist and four ribs. She was in a coma for more than seven weeks.''

Buck thought back to this morning in his office when he had asked Carly how badly she'd been hurt. A few broken bones and a bump on the head, she had replied. That was a hell of a difference from the list the doctor had just read off. It wasn't like Laura to minimize her injuries. In her telling, a common cold had always become life-threatening pneumonia, a sprained ankle *had* to be fractured, and a headache was never anything less than a migraine.

''Could she be faking the amnesia?''

''Anything's possible, but her doctors in Seattle don't think so. This was a serious accident, Buck. She was hit head-on. There was so much damage to her car that it was barely recognizable. As sheriff, you understand better than most what that can do to a body. She was truly lucky to survive it.''

The doctor was right. He had seen more than his share of traffic accidents, far more than his share of fatalities. He knew the damage two tons of steel could do to a person. It was easy enough to imagine the scene that November day in Seattle—the twisted metal, the shattered glass, the broken body.

Laura's broken body.

How many times had he wished her dead? Countless—and once more just today. She had come damned close to making those wishes come true for him, and she had paid for it with pain and sorrow and with the loss of her identity.

''You've known Laura all her life, and you've met Carly,'' he began, reluctant to ask the question, not sure what answer he wanted to hear. ''Could the injuries—the head trauma—be responsible for the changes in her personality?''

''You want to know if a good hard thump on the head could turn Laura into a decent human being?'' Dr. Thomas

chuckled. "It's possible. Personality changes aren't un-
heard of following severe head injury and/or coma. The
brain is such an intricate piece of machinery. Who's to
say—if this is Laura—exactly which portions of her brain
were damaged and exactly which aspects of her personality
they controlled?"

Who, indeed?

Buck got to his feet and shook hands with the doctor.
"Thanks a lot, Doc." But at the door, he stopped and
turned back. "This personality change...is it permanent?
Will she always be like this, or could she go back to the
way she was before?"

"Your guess is as good as mine, son."

That wasn't encouraging. When it came to Laura, he
needed more than guesses. He needed promises. Foolproof
guarantees.

Guesses just weren't enough.

She was waiting for him in the lobby, flipping through
a Montana sportsman magazine. Rising from the chair, she
simply looked at him, her head high, her gaze steady and
cool. She was waiting for him to say he was sorry, that she
had told the truth, that he had been wrong to doubt her.
She was waiting for an apology, and she would get it.

On a cold day in hell.

"I had to check," he said flatly. "I wouldn't be much
of a cop if I didn't."

She didn't say a thing, but turned and walked out the
door. He followed her, clamping his Stetson on as he
stepped into the afternoon sun.

"Now where?"

Buck looked down at her. There were stress lines brack-
eting her mouth—he could feel a matching set in his own
frown—and at the corners of her eyes, and her color didn't
look so great out here. Maybe it was tension or ruffled
feathers, or maybe she wasn't fully recovered from last

GET 2

HOW TO GET YOUR
2 FREE BOOKS AND FREE GIFT!

1. Peel off the MIRA sticker on the front cover. Place it in the space provided at right. This automatically entitles you to receive two free books and an exciting mystery gift.

2. Send back this card and you'll get 2 "The Best of the Best™" novels. These books have a combined cover price of $11.00 or more in the U.S. and $13.00 or more in Canada, but they are yours to keep absolutely FREE!

3. There's no catch. You're under no obligation to buy anything. We charge nothing – ZERO – for your first shipment. And you don't have to make any minimum number of purchases – not even one!

4. We call this line "The Best of the Best" because each month you'll receive the best books by some of today's hottest authors. These authors show up time and time again on all the major bestseller lists and their books sell out as soon as they hit the stores. You'll like the convenience of getting them delivered to your home at our special discount prices . . . and you'll love your *Heart to Heart* subscriber newsletter featuring author news, horoscopes, recipes, book reviews and much more!

5. We hope that after receiving your free books you'll want to remain a subscriber. But the choice is yours – to continue or cancel, anytime at all! So why not take us up on our invitation, with no risk of any kind. You'll be glad you did!

6. And remember...we'll send you a mystery gift ABSOLUTELY FREE just for giving "The Best of the Best" a try.

SPECIAL FREE GIFT!

We'll send you a fabulous surprise gift, absolutely FREE, simply for accepting our no-risk offer!

Visit us online at
www.mirabooks.com

BOOKS FREE!

The Best of the Best™ — Here's How it Works:

Accepting your 2 free books and gift places you under no obligation to buy anything. You may keep the books and gift and return the shipping statement marked "cancel." If you do not cancel, about a month later we will send you 4 additional novels and bill you just $4.24 each in the U.S., or $4.74 each in Canada, plus 25¢ shipping & handling per book and applicable taxes if any.* That's the complete price and — compared to cover prices of $5.50 or more each in the U.S. and $6.50 or more each in Canada — it's quite a bargain! You may cancel at any time, but if you choose to continue, every month we'll send you 4 more books, which you may either purchase at the discount price or return to us and cancel your subscription.

*Terms and prices subject to change without notice. Sales applicable in N.Y. Canadian residents will be charged applicable provincial taxes and GST.

If offer card is missing write to: The Best of the Best, 3010 Walden Ave., P.O. Box 1867, Buffalo, NY 14240-1867

BUSINESS REPLY MAIL

FIRST-CLASS MAIL   PERMIT NO. 717   BUFFALO, NY

POSTAGE WILL BE PAID BY ADDRESSEE

THE BEST OF THE BEST
3010 WALDEN AVE
PO BOX 1867
BUFFALO NY 14240-9952

NO POSTAGE
NECESSARY
IF MAILED
IN THE
UNITED STATES

night's headache, but she looked as if she needed nothing so much as a hot meal and a warm bed.

She had automatically turned toward his office, where they had left his Bronco, but he stopped her. "Let's get some lunch."

The mention of food seemed to cheer her. The idea of returning to the hotel restaurant didn't. "Could we go someplace where everybody doesn't stare?" She sounded both wistful and hopeful—and younger and more innocent than she had, in reality, ever been.

Innocent Laura. The words simply didn't belong together. But innocent Carly. Yeah, they fit.

"Don't men stare at you in Seattle?" he asked, disliking the idea even as it formed, disliking the fact that he cared even more.

"Of course not. Why should they?"

"Because you're too damn beautiful." Gesturing down the street, he said in the same matter-of-fact voice, "Pete Wilson's barbecue place is a couple of blocks that way. Want to go there?"

More than a little bemused by his careless compliment, Carly agreed. As they walked past store windows, she tried with limited success to catch a glimpse of herself. *Too damn beautiful? Her?* Granted, she wasn't as familiar with her face as she should have been, but she rarely saw anything so impressive in it. Ego decreed that it was attractive enough, even better than average, but beautiful? She was flattered.

Pete's BBQ shared a long, narrow building with Mary's Fashions next door. The restaurant was smoky and was furnished with redwood-stained picnic tables and benches and checkered vinyl tablecloths. The silverware was plastic, the plates paper, and the painted concrete block walls were decorated with calendars from the local hardware store.

Carly saw one for practically each year of her life as she accompanied Buck to the counter at the back.

The young woman working the cash register—identified by her name tag as Cheryl—was more polite than anyone else Carly had met. Cheryl stared, but furtively. She didn't make Carly feel like a specimen under a microscope. After taking the sheriff's order, she then turned to Carly, who was studying the menu board overhead.

"I'll have the rib platter," she finally decided, lowering her gaze to find both of them watching her.

"Ribs?" Cheryl echoed. "Pork ribs?" She looked at the sheriff for verification, and he only shrugged and pulled out his wallet to pay the tab. As soon as she counted out his change, he steered Carly to the most distant table.

"I take it Laura didn't eat pork," she remarked, settling herself on the bench against the wall.

"No, she didn't."

"Was it a religious thing?"

"It had to do with looking good." He considered it for a moment, then almost smiled. For a moment he had forgotten to be cold and distant and hostile, and she had almost seen a true, genuine smile touch his lips. "Actually, yeah, that could have qualified as a religion with Laura."

"Well, *I* like pork chops and ribs and ham, and I *love* bacon. I could live on bacon, lettuce and tomato sandwiches."

He looked at her for a moment, then, with a baffled look, simply shook his head. "Sometimes I feel like I don't know you at all."

A somber mood settled over her so quickly that she could actually feel its weight on her shoulders. "You *don't* know me, Sheriff. Even if I used to be Laura, for the last three years, I've been someone else. You don't know *this* me at all."

The bemusement was gone, the ill temper back. "I know

you well enough to call you by your name,'' he said irritably. ''When are you going to get past calling me 'Sheriff'?''

She tried his name silently and found herself pulling away. She could think of him that way, but saying it out loud would give her too great a sense of familiarity, too comfortable a sense of intimacy. She preferred the distance, however small, that ''Sheriff'' provided. ''What is your first name?''

''Buck.''

''I mean your real name.''

This time when he scowled, it wasn't so fierce or so real. What it was, she admitted, was appealing. Too damn appealing. ''That's the name on my birth certificate.''

''Oh. I thought it was a nickname, like Buddy or Duke.'' She watched as Cheryl approached them, two steaming plates on the tray she carried. After she had served them, then returned to the counter, Carly said quietly, ''So…tell me about Laura.''

Her request made Buck uncomfortable. Why? He had been open enough last night—but then again, last night he'd been convinced beyond a doubt that she was his missing lover. This morning, at least he had admitted the slim chance that she wasn't.

''What do you want to know?'' he asked at last.

''What kind of person was she?''

''She was beautiful.''

She rolled her eyes. Typical male. The most important thing about the woman he'd been involved with was her looks. ''How old is she now?''

''Your age.'' At her frown he relented. ''Thirty-four.''

''I'm thirty-two.''

''So your driver's license says.'' But the discrepancy didn't bother him. ''If Laura was going to go to the trouble to create a new identity, she would knock at least a few years off her age.''

''So she was vain.'' The more she learned about Laura, the more she suspected that she wouldn't like the woman. She was beautiful—and made a religion out of remaining so. She was vain. She had inspired a tremendous amount of hostility in her lover and a tremendous amount of hatred in her cousin. Even the other people Carly had seen—there was more than simply shock in their reactions. There was...discomfort. Dislike.

Fear?

She hastily retreated from that idea. She didn't want to be someone whom others were afraid of. She didn't want to be capable of the kind of behavior that would create fear.

But Laura must have had some good qualities to balance the bad. After all, she had an aunt who loved her. She'd had Buck who, even after three years apart, still harbored strong feelings for her.

Although his feelings weren't exactly positive. Was it because Laura had been a bad person? Or was he angry with her for leaving him, for staying away so long? She preferred to believe the latter—that he had cared very much for Laura, that he was hurt because of the way their relationship had ended, that he hadn't yet forgiven her for the pain she'd caused him. Carly wanted to ask what had happened between him and Laura, whether they had argued, why she had left, if he wanted her back. But those questions were too personal. Even though they might tell her something about her own life, they were entirely too personal to ask right now.

They finished their meal in silence; then Buck announced that it was time to visit Laura's aunt. Carly had a queasy feeling in the pit of her stomach. She'd meant what she had said in the doctor's office. The woman was too overwhelming. She didn't want to see her again, didn't want to smell that fragrance, didn't want to be drawn into that over-powering embrace again.

She was about to offer him a bargain—give me the rest of today off, and I promise to go and see her tomorrow—but one look at his hard face told her the answer. She could make it easy on herself—relatively speaking—by meekly going along, or she could make it harder than it needed to be, but he was taking her to the Phelps home now whether she wanted to go or not.

She opted for easy.

Relatively speaking.

They walked back to the sheriff's department and picked up his Bronco, then headed toward the interstate. Carly watched the scenery, wondering if any of this was familiar, if she had once known this road as well as Buck, if she had known that they would have to turn onto the narrow gravel road around the last curve. Had she picked up the mail from the battered aluminum box at the edge of the highway? Had she roamed these hills when she was a child? Had Buck brought her home here after a date? Had they necked at the end of the tree-shaded driveway?

I don't know. She could save herself a lot of time and frustration and just tattoo the words on her forehead. She had hundreds, probably thousands, of questions, but she had only one answer. *I don't know.*

The driveway ended in a clearing some fifty feet from the house. The clearing had been cut out of the hillside, leaving the lawn and the house towering overhead. A set of stone steps were cut into the hill, and the same stone formed a retaining wall that dwindled away to single stones and weeds in each direction.

Carly climbed out of the Bronco and closed the door, then leaned against it to study the house above. It was three stories tall, and, looking at it from here, it seemed to lean toward her, to tilt at an awkward top-heavy angle toward the ground far below. It was Victorian in style—sort of a warped Victorian, she amended. The builder had taken a style known for its lush excesses and had carried it even further. Every available roof space had been towered, turreted and gabled, and it was covered in pink fish-scale shingles. Rails, porches and balconies extended everywhere, their spindlework elaborate and overdone, their colors ranging from pale green to salmon to bright red. Ornate gingerbread hung from every corner, every rail, every gable—scrolls upon curls upon extravagant lace.

Victoriana run wild.

Buck joined her while she took in the house where Laura—where *she* might have lived. She might have slept in one of those grotesque towers. She might have entertained friends beneath the lacy arches, might have kissed Buck good-night in front of the cherry red front door.

The idea made her shudder.

"Wait here," Buck said at last. "I'll talk to Maureen."

She nodded, then watched him start toward the stone steps. When she looked back at the house, towering overhead in all its garish glory, she shook her head in dismay. "That is absolutely," she muttered to herself, "the most god-awful, ugly house this—"

On the steps, Buck came to a sudden halt, then turned around. The look on his face was pinched and hard, and his eyes were blazing with anger. "What did you say?"

"Just—" She shifted uncomfortably. "Just that the house is ugly."

"The most god-awful ugly house this side..."

He was waiting, his presence—even though he hadn't moved a muscle—somehow threatening. Hugging her arms to her chest, Carly swallowed hard and finished. "This side of creation." It wasn't a phrase she ordinarily used, none of it was. It had simply seemed to fit this monstrosity of a house.

Judging from Buck's expression, Laura must have shared her opinion.

Right down to the phrasing.

The hair on the back of her neck was standing on end, and once again she experienced the panicky urge to run away screaming, to find a safe place and hide herself away from this town, these people, these questions. But there was nowhere to go and no way to get there, not with the sheriff glowering at her from ten feet away.

He came to her then, came so close that she was pinned between the truck and his body. He didn't physically touch her, but she felt the contact, anyway—the heat and the anger, the tension and the pure malevolence. In the restaurant a while ago, she had decided that Buck was hurt and angry with Laura, that he simply hadn't yet forgiven her for leaving. Now, shrinking away from the look in his eyes, she wondered frantically if that was truly the case. Was he merely angry with Laura?

Or did he hate her?

"You stay right here," he commanded in a low, unsteady voice. "Don't even think about running away again, because if you do, I'll find you. I'll be back in ten minutes."

She was trembling when he walked away, and she wasn't even certain why. Because he had frightened her? Because she had apparently remembered something from her past?

Or because Sheriff Logan seemed to hate her?

It took a little more than ten minutes, but she was standing in exactly the same spot when Buck returned. Maybe he had been too harsh—maybe? he echoed. No doubt about it. He had scared her. Odd. Laura had never known fear before. She had always been too wrapped up in herself to let anyone's threats touch her. Even when their arguments had turned vicious, even when he had been left sick and trembling from the emotion, she had merely laughed and gone on her way.

This time, for the first time, he had frightened her. After all the times she had made him afraid, it seemed only fitting that finally the tables were turned.

So why did he feel like such a bastard for it?

"I talked to Maureen," he said, his voice flat, his expression blank—an effective camouflage for all the tension churning inside him. "She's ready to see you now." He moved off the bottom step and waited for her to join him.

She wanted to say no. He knew that. She wanted to avoid this meeting, wanted to go away and continue pretending that she wasn't Laura. And that was only natural. Her aunt was the only person who had ever loved her unconditionally. She was the only person Laura had tried not to hurt. She was the only one Laura had never used, then somehow abused. Maybe Carly didn't know that, the way he did, but she sensed it.

She must also sense that this meeting was going to be difficult for Maureen. After three years of praying for her niece's safe return, her prayers had been answered—but with a cruel twist. Laura was back, but she wasn't. She was Maureen's niece, but she was a stranger. The face was the same, the body was the same, but the person inside was different.

After a long moment, Carly moved away from the Bronco and began climbing the steps. He was right behind her. They passed yellowing grass and trees and shrubs pruned into fanciful shapes, finally reaching the broad porch. As they approached the door, Maureen's face appeared in the lace-curtained window, and she abruptly pulled the door open.

In spite of their discussion, in spite of his warnings, the first thing she did was reach for Carly. Just as she'd done with Doc Thomas, the first thing Carly did was back away, bumping into him. Even when the old lady dropped her arms to her sides, Carly remained close. If she considered him the lesser of two evils, he thought grimly, giving her a little push into the house, she was mistaken. He could do her far more harm than Maureen ever could. Maureen could only frighten. He could hurt.

And Carly could destroy.

"Come on in and sit down," Maureen invited, her voice trembly, her gaze constantly shifting from one to the other. She had never played formal hostess to her own family, and she wasn't sure how to do it. Finally turning away, she led them into the living room.

Carly chose an uncomfortable chair, leaving the sofa for Maureen, the love seat for Buck. She *really* didn't want to be here, he thought, noticing how she sat on the edge of the chair, how her hands were knotted in her lap, how she looked around with only the most furtive of gazes. She reminded him of a frightened little rabbit ready to bolt at the slightest provocation.

"Buck says I should call you Carly," the old lady began. "That's a lovely name."

"Thank you. I'm sure my mother thought so."

"Your mother— Oh. Yes, I'm sure she did. Would you like something to drink, dear?"

Carly stiffened at the endearment. "No, thank you."

"Would you like to look around? Maybe see your— Laura's room?"

Buck expected her to curtly refuse that, too, but he surprised him. With a taut smile that was meant to be polite but in reality was merely painful, she rose from the chair and replied with some measure of relief, "Yes, I would like that."

Maureen seemed relieved, too, and nervously led the way upstairs. He brought up the rear.

Laura's room was in the front tower. Back when the

house had been built, the towers, with their perfectly rounded rooms and curved windows, had been something of an architectural wonder in these parts. Even the door curved outward to fit perfectly into the wall.

This was one of the few places associated with Laura where Buck didn't feel uncomfortable. Until her disappearance, he had never set foot inside this room. She had slept here, but he never had. They had never indulged in anything more than a good-night grope in her aunt's house.

He closed the door, then leaned against it and watched Carly. If any of them had hoped she would experience some sudden return of memory, they were disappointed. She was interested in the room, more so than an average guest, but there was no hint of recognition on her face. She walked around the bed, gazed at the photos on the dresser and the walls, ran her fingers across the stacks of cassettes atop the stereo and glanced inside the closet at the clothes still hanging there.

But there was no remembrance. No recognition. No familiarity.

Stopping in front of the desk underneath one window, Carly picked up a photo there. From the brief glimpse he'd gotten of it, Buck knew immediately what it was—Laura and him—and when it had been taken—in the middle of their two-year affair, before he'd started to hate her. She looked at it for a long time, in much the same way she had studied the picture of herself in his office and the photos of his family at home. Photographs seemed to intrigue her, not so much for what was in them but for what they were: a moment frozen in time. A tangible memory. Something she could hold in her hands even if she couldn't find it in her head.

"Would you like to keep that?" Maureen offered, and Carly hastily returned it to the desk.

"No. No, thanks." She finished her slow circuit around

the room, rejoining them at the door. "I'm sorry, Mrs. Phelps. I thought... I just don't know...."

Maureen smiled patiently. "It's all right, dear. Listen, I bought a coconut cream pie from the hotel restaurant. I know that was— Well, that was Laura's only weakness when it came to sweets. Why don't we go down to the kitchen and have some?" She started to reach out, then caught herself with a rueful look and broadened her smile instead. "We'll forget the calories and eat and just talk— maybe get to know a little about each other. All right?"

The old lady was trying so hard, Buck thought, that if Carly didn't agree, he would make her damned sorry. But she offered a smile of her own, a bewildered little gesture, and said, "That sounds nice, Mrs. Phelps."

He could have left them alone in the kitchen. They each understood the unwritten rules: Maureen wouldn't call her Laura or indulge in her usual touches, hugs and pats, and Carly would make an effort to be friendly, to pretend that this wasn't the last place on earth she wanted to be. They would get along fine without him.

But he didn't leave them. He didn't sit at the table with them, but he stayed, and he listened. Maureen asked questions that he hadn't gotten around to—about Carly's apartment, her job, her life in Seattle—and she asked in such a friendly, interested manner that Carly couldn't help but answer. A lesson to a cop, he thought grimly as he stared out the kitchen window. Carly gave the old lady far more information than she ever would have volunteered to him.

He learned that she was a secretary in a large insurance firm—not *just* a secretary, as some would say, but a secretary who liked her job and the people she worked with. She lived alone, and her closest friend was the single mother next door, whose daughter she sometimes cared for. She liked seafood and the water and spent occasional Saturdays over in Victoria, British Columbia. She read and went out with her friends and saw at least one movie a week, and her favorite way to spend a sunny afternoon was outdoors or at a craft show.

Secretarial work? Baby-sitting and friends and crafts? *Laura?*

"And what about your social life?" Maureen asked.

"That *is* my social life," Carly replied with a soft laugh.

"Don't you date? Aren't there any men in your life?"

Buck wished he hadn't stiffened at the question. He wished he didn't care about the answer. He wished...Damn it, he wished Carly would quit stalling and respond.

But before she said anything, the back door opened and Trina walked into the kitchen. She saw Buck first and smiled that simpery little smile that she seemed to reserve just for him. Then she saw Carly, and everything pleasant disappeared from her face. Everything pleasant disappeared from the room, leaving an uneasy tension in its place, the same sort of quiet, the same sense of foreboding that accompanied a thunderstorm, that spread across the countryside ahead of the storm, warning of the violence to come.

Trina laid her purse on the counter and slowly entered the room, circling the table in the center, her gaze never wavering from Carly. Buck moved, too, away from the window and closer to Carly, close enough to step in if it became necessary. Trina didn't have a history of violence—in all her countless battles with Laura, she had never gotten physical—but she looked furious enough now to take someone as delicate as Carly apart limb by limb.

She finished the circle and rested one hand on the table, the other on the back of Carly's chair. Bending close, she asked in a low hiss, "What the hell is *she* doing here?"

"That's enough of that language, Trina," Maureen said evenly, rising from her seat and carrying the dirty dishes to the sink. "We're having a little visit. Would you like to join us?"

Buck grimaced at the casual invitation. Maureen had lived with Trina and Laura's squabbles for nearly twenty years and was used to them. She didn't see that this time was different. She didn't consider that Carly was different. That Trina was threatening.

"You can't come back here like this," Trina said, still bent close to Carly, right up in her face, every slow and steady breath sour with enmity. "After the way you left, after the things you put Mother through, you can't just walk back into our lives. You can't come back as if you *belong* here. You can't just worm your way back in. I won't let you. Do you understand? *I* won't let you."

Buck saw that Carly knew. She sensed what Maureen didn't—that this wasn't a mere cousinly quarrel. That Trina was a danger to her. That whatever Trina had felt for Laura before—jealousy or resentment or dislike—now it was hatred, pure, hot and unreasoning. Carly felt it, and she was afraid.

He closed the distance between them, pulling Carly from the chair and behind him at the same time he laid his hand over Trina's on the chair back. He offered her a reassuring smile and softly said, "It's all right, Trina. We're leaving now."

She slowly straightened and looked up at him. For a moment her hostility was transferred to him, and she twisted, trying to free her hand. Then, as if a plug had been pulled, the anger and malice drained away. Her hand went limp beneath his, and that strange little smile of hers returned. "I'm sorry, Buck. This is no way to treat a guest." She took a deep breath, smoothed her hair with her free hand, then asked, "Do you have to be going? It's not often we see you out this way anymore."

She sounded wistful and pitiable, Carly thought from her safe position behind the sheriff. She had seen the woman's smile when she had spotted him in the kitchen, before the venom for *her* had destroyed everything else, and now this pathetic little note in her voice…

Trina Phelps had it bad for the sheriff. No wonder she hated her cousin.

No wonder she hated Carly.

"I've got to get back to work, Trina," Buck was saying. "Maybe next time… Maureen, thanks for the pie. Carly?"

He moved aside, waiting for her to lead the way, and she was suddenly face-to-face with Trina again. There was only a flicker of antagonism this time, not the all-consuming contempt of earlier. "Carly?" she echoed, loathing evident in her voice. "Is that what you call yourself now?"

"I'll explain it all to you, dear," Maureen said. "Buck, Carly, thanks for stopping by. I'll see you again soon."

Both women saw them to the front door. When Carly paused at the top of the stone steps and looked back, only one was watching. The lace curtains, so delicate and lovely and inviting, made an unseemly frame for Trina's plain, hate-distorted face. They simply stared, each at the other, and for a moment Carly felt sympathy for the other woman. She was beginning to understand what it was like to dislike Laura, to be jealous of her, to want what she had.

But the moment passed quickly, and the sympathy faded, and all she felt was dismay.

Revulsion.

Fear.

Chapter 4

"So, Sheriff, what's the story?" Janssen asked before Buck even got out of his jacket Friday morning. "Why is Laura pretending to be somebody else?"

He gave the deputy and everyone else in the room a cross look. His first instinct was to tell the young man to mind his own business, but in a sense, Carly *was* department business. He was using department time to unravel her mysteries, department resources to verify her identity. And he couldn't blame his men for being interested—he would have been disappointed in them if they weren't. They had all known Laura, either from growing up here in Nowhere or through his own association with her. He couldn't blame them for their curiosity.

But how much should he tell them? Knowing that she was already the main topic of conversation all over town, exactly what was he supposed to say? Going into detail about her accident wouldn't be fair to her. She was already being treated like some sort of freak—a feeling he suspected wasn't totally new to her. What had she told Doc Thomas yesterday—that she had already been examined by more people than he could imagine? Considering how few people recovered so completely from a deep coma, she must have been of major interest to all sorts of doctors— not as a woman, not even as a patient, but as a specimen. As an object of study, something to poke and prod.

And here she was, under the microscope again.

"The woman you're talking about, Janssen, may not be Laura Phelps," he said, speaking loudly enough for all the deputies to hear. "Her name is Carly Johnson, and she has amnesia. We have reason to believe that she *is* Laura, but we don't have any proof yet." He turned toward his office, then stopped, looking at each of his men in turn. "I don't want to hear any gossip about her, not in this office and not from any of you. Anyone who passes along information we turn up here is fired. Understood?"

There was a nod of heads, a few murmured replies. He went into his office and closed the door, then sank into his chair. When Harvey arrived a moment later with a cup of coffee, he accepted it gratefully, washing down three tablets from the aspirin bottle in his drawer.

Carly had been in town two nights, and he'd already lost two nights' sleep over her. Just like old times. She was under his skin again, tempting him, taunting him. Even after he'd dropped her off at the hotel yesterday, she had remained with him, only a thought, a memory, an ache away.

It was funny how some things had changed. She was so different—so much more real, so much more human. *So much more likable.* And other things hadn't changed at all. He still wanted her, and he still didn't *want* to want her. He still didn't trust her. She was still dangerous.

He had gone home alone last night and eaten dinner in front of the television. He couldn't remember what shows he had seen, what commercials he had watched, what news he had heard. All he could remember was sitting in that same chair hours earlier and watching Carly with his sister's picture. Hearing her talk about all the memories she didn't have.

He had no shortage of memories. When he'd given up and gone to bed, they had followed him there. All those nights she had spent in his bed…all those nights that had been erased from her memory. All the times they'd had sex there, all the times they'd argued, all the mornings he had awakened there and had sworn on his life that he would end it with her—all those memories had crowded him, making him toss uncomfortably, robbing him of the sleep he'd needed. Of the peace he'd needed.

And here he was now, thinking about her again.

Becoming obsessed with her again.

He forced his attention to his work, to scheduling next month's shifts, to vehicle logs and maintenance reports, to squeezing enough money from next month's budget to send Harvey to a child abuse seminar sponsored by a Butte hospital. But the whole time, she remained in his mind—not Laura, but Carly. The new and improved Laura.

Who might, without warning, turn back into the Laura he despised.

What was she doing over at the hotel this morning? Sleeping in late? The last time he'd seen her, she had looked as if she could use eighteen or twenty hours of restful sleep. Or maybe she was enjoying a late breakfast in the restaurant or visiting with Maureen again or doing something more typically Laura—shopping for new clothes, getting her hair done or indulging in a manicure at Lenore's.

At lunchtime he gave up wondering and went outside to his truck. A glance down the street showed that the blue Chevy was no longer parked in front of the hotel. A quick swing past the Phelps place was futile; no one was home. It was none of his business where she went, he knew that, but it still nagged at him as he drove to his own house. He would eat lunch, he decided, then stop by the hotel and make certain she hadn't checked out.

His question about her activities was answered as soon as he turned off the highway onto the winding dirt lane that led to his cabin. The blue sedan was parked where he normally parked the Bronco; on the other side of it was his own pickup, old and battered, driven only occasionally for personal use.

He parked next to her car and shut off the engine, then simply sat there for a moment, gripping the steering wheel tightly. She was here.

Waiting for him.

So the doctors in Seattle believed her amnesia was real. Interesting the things she had managed to ''remember''— that they had made love at the lake. That on more days than he could count, they had met here on his lunch break for a quick snack and some long, slow sex.

He had believed her, damn it. He had believed her act was genuine, that her confusion and fear were real.

And damn her, she had suckered him.

Again.

Damn her to hell.

There was no sign of her. Of course, back then she'd had a key to his house, and he had usually found her soaking in the tub or stretched out on the sofa, naked except for her high heels. But she couldn't be there now. He hadn't gotten the key back before she had disappeared, but he *had* changed the locks on the doors.

He climbed out of the truck, then started around the cabin. There was a wide deck across the back with a couple of lawn chairs and a hammock. Maybe that was where she was. Maybe she still liked doing it outside. That had always turned her on up at the lake—being in the open, feeling the sunshine on her naked skin, taking the risk of getting caught.

When he rounded the corner, full of righteous anger, he came to a sudden stop, and nausea swept through him, forcing the anger to recede. He had been right. She was reclining in the chaise, her legs stretched out in front of her, looking every bit as smug and self-satisfied as he'd ever seen her.

She was waiting for him.

At least she still had her clothes on. That was something new.

But they wouldn't stay on for long. The dark emotion curling and growing in his belly ensured that. Desire in its basest, rawest form. The kind that had nothing to do with tenderness, nothing at all to do with love, and everything to do with need. With taking and satisfying and using and hating.

Just like old times.

He came around the back and started up the steps. She pretended to be startled into awareness when his boot hit the first step, and then she pretended to be embarrassed at being discovered there. "Sheriff," she said, using that old familiar husky voice again. "I didn't realize—"

She started to sit up, to swing her legs to the floor, but he moved too quickly, blocking her. "Didn't you?" he asked, his voice low and dangerous. "You knew that I would come home about now. I almost always do."

She scrambled out of the chair on the other side, then for a moment she simply looked at him, her eyes wide and innocent and more than a little disturbed. What a hell of an actress she had become, he thought with bitter admiration. If he weren't fed up with her game, if he didn't know her so well, he could almost buy the innocence. *Almost.*

"I fell for your act—you know that, don't you? I be-

lieved poor, pathetic Carly who couldn't remember a thing.
You made a fool of me again." He shook his head in disgust. "*Again*. But not anymore, Laura. I won't believe anymore."

"I don't under—"

"How do you want it today?" he interrupted. He removed his gun belt and dropped it on the empty chair between them, then tugged his shirt free from his trousers.
"Hard and fast? Slow and easy?" Pulling each button free,
first on the cuffs, then down the shirtfront, he grinned
slowly, malevolently. "Or wild and wicked?"

She pretended to be insulted and just a little frightened—
but that wasn't fear he recognized in her eyes when he
shrugged out of his shirt. It didn't even come close. There
wasn't any fear in her voice, either. It was throaty and
husky and eloquent in its arousal. "Obviously there's been
some misunderstanding, Sheriff. I didn't come here to—"

Her voice trailed away as her gaze followed his hands
down to the waistband of his trousers. He wasn't hard yet—
not enough for her to notice—but that was all right. He
would get there. *She* would get him there.

So much for protest, he thought, disappointed in Carly,
in Laura, most of all in himself. So much for innocence.
The games were over. She had come here for this, for him,
and by God, she would get him. Every inch of him.

And he would get—

Bleakly he broke off. He didn't want to think yet what
he would get, besides the dubious pleasure of her body. He
didn't want to consider how easily he was giving in this
time, how little strength he had left to fight her. He didn't
want to remember his arrogance of the last three years without her, his certainty that finally he could feel hatred and
only hatred for her, that finally he could resist her. He
didn't want to acknowledge how quickly that resistance had
given way to this. How quickly…and how shamefully.

Carly tried to speak, but her voice didn't want to work. Nothing in her entire body wanted to work except the muscles that were trembling uncontrollably and the nerves that were sending little shudders along her spine, shudders of fear, of distaste, of... Arousal?

She didn't want to feel that, not now. Not for this man. Not under these circumstances. But God help her, he was such a fascinating man, and it had been so long—at least three years, maybe forever.

Then he leaned across the chair and grabbed her hand, pulling her around, dragging her when she tried to resist, and he drew her hard against his body, and all thought of arousal disappeared right out of her. He wasn't hurting her, but he could—he was angry enough to—and he damn sure was scaring her.

"You want to play it rough, Laura?" he murmured, his face inches above hers, his breath hot on her skin. "You want to pretend that this isn't what you want, what you came for? You want to be forced?"

"Sheriff, please—"

He cut off her plea with a kiss, hard and deep, his tongue forcing its way into her mouth. Physically he held her prisoner, but inside she recoiled in disgust. She had never felt such anger, such bitter cold fury, in her life. It passed from him into her, wrapping around her, drawing tighter until she couldn't breathe, couldn't think, couldn't—God, she couldn't stand it any longer!

She twisted her head away from his, avoiding his mouth when he would have trapped her again, and shoved against him with strength born of revulsion. "Leave me alone, damn it!" she cried, struggling free. "I don't want this, I don't want you to touch me, I don't want *you*! I came here because it felt comfortable, because I thought I might remember something. I didn't know you would be here, I didn't know..." The anger drained from her voice, breaking it into a million tearful, pleading pieces. "Oh, God, please don't do this, Sheriff. Please…don't…"

She didn't know what finally penetrated—her panic, her pushing against him or her words—but he released her so quickly that she stumbled back against the wall. She backed further away, putting more distance between them—the chaise, another chair, a small round table. She didn't stop until she felt the railing against her back, until she knew that if he came toward her again, she could climb the rail and drop the few feet to the ground and run like hell.

But he wasn't going to come after her. He was simply standing there, his hands at his sides, staring at her as if he'd never seen her before. She could identify some of the emotions crossing his face—shock, disgust, revulsion—because she was feeling them, too. Others were foreign to her—such bleakness. Such bitterness. Such emptiness.

After a moment he covered his face with both hands, and she saw a shudder ripple through him, tightening the powerful muscles in his arms and chest. Who was it he loathed now? Her? Or himself?

He *had* hated her. She knew that. For a moment there in his arms she had known that he hated her, that he despised her, with every considerable ounce of feeling he possessed. And yet he had wanted her—had wanted *Laura,* a soft little voice whispered. She had seen his arousal, had felt it when he'd held her so tightly.

Dear God, what kind of woman *was* Laura?

What kind of woman was *she*?

Buck sighed, a lost, achy, hurting-all-the-way-down-in-his-soul kind of sigh, and simply, quietly said, "I'm sorry."

I'm sorry. It wasn't much of an apology, but what else could he have said? How could he apologize for frightening her, for damn near raping her? The most eloquent apology in the world wouldn't have been enough.

Shivering, she hugged herself. "I thought it would be

okay," she whispered. "I thought you were at work. You wouldn't know.... I just wanted to look around...to see if any of this was familiar."

He reached for his shirt, and she turned away. She didn't want to watch him put it on, didn't want to see him button it or tuck it in. She didn't want to think about how he had held her or how he had kissed her.

She sure as hell didn't want to think about how he had hated her, and what she—or Laura—had done to deserve it.

The clunking of his boots made her turn back swiftly. He must have seen the panic in her eyes, because he stopped abruptly ten feet away and showed no intentions of coming closer. "We used to meet here for lunch and..." Underneath that sick look he wore, he flushed. So did Carly. He had already made it quite clear what he and Laura had usually done on his lunch hour.

"So because it was noon and I was here, you assumed..." As he had done, she broke off. Then, with great weariness, she said, "You don't believe anything I've said, do you? You think I'm lying about the amnesia. You think I'm lying about not knowing you."

Somehow he grew stiffer, even more uncomfortable. "If you knew yourself the way I do—"

"You don't know me," she interrupted. "I'm not Laura."

"Of course you aren't. You just have her face, her body and her memories."

"Maybe I used to be her," she acknowledged, "but I'm not anymore. I'm not the same woman I was before the accident. I'm not the woman you knew. I'm not the woman you used to meet in the middle of the day for sex."

She expected him to argue, but he just gave her a long sad look, then bleakly agreed, "No, you're not."

They stood in awkward silence for a time, then she began inching toward the steps. "I—I'd like to go now."

He made no move to stop her. He simply watched until she was at the bottom of the steps. Then he spoke her name—not Laura's, but hers, in a miserably soft voice. She looked up, anxious to go but waiting to hear whatever he had to say.

He struggled with the words, with his feelings, even with his voice. When he did finally speak, it was in a taut, tortured tone. "Carly...I would never have hurt you."

The vow seemed to hang in the air between them, heavy and tense. After a moment she turned away from it, away from him, and continued around the cabin to her car. Clinging tightly to her self-control, she fastened her seat belt, started the engine and carefully backed out from between the two trucks. She was halfway down the dirt lane before she let herself take a deep breath, before she let herself even think about what had happened.

I would never have hurt you, he'd said, willing her to believe him.

But she wasn't sure she did.

That night Carly got a tray from the restaurant downstairs and ate dinner alone in her room. By eight o'clock she had returned the tray to the kitchen and was settled cross-legged on the bed with the television on for company. A typical Friday night, she thought with a humorless smile. For her married friends at home, this was a time reserved for husbands. For single friends, it was date night, or looking-for-a-date night. Because she had never wanted more than the occasional dates she'd had, she had usually spent them alone, watching television.

Tonight, though, she had something a little more serious than TV or weekend plans on her mind. She couldn't forget the incident at Buck's house. It had taken a long time this afternoon for her nerves to settle, and her thoughts never had.

Buck had frightened her, there was no denying that. But there was another, even more disturbing aspect to his actions. He had known Laura Phelps better than anyone else around, and he had believed, had truly believed, that she would enjoy what he was doing. *How do you want it?* he had asked. *Hard and fast? Wild and wicked? You want to play it rough? You want to be forced?*

And how had he described Laura yesterday? Kinky. Unconventional.

Good heavens, what kind of woman had he been involved with? One whose primary interest was herself. One whose sexual appetites were a bit out of the ordinary. One who had a taste for rough sex. One who inspired hatred in the man who should have loved her.

And if she was Laura Phelps, *she* was that kind of woman.

Shifting on the bed, she caught her reflection in the dresser mirror. For a moment, she simply stared, searching the finally familiar face for answers. She saw no signs of depravity there, no immorality. She saw no selfishness, no cruelty, nothing to explain the way the sheriff had acted this afternoon, nothing to account for the venom Trina had displayed yesterday.

All she saw was a woman who cared about other people, who tried to be nice to everyone, who said please and thank you and helped out her friends when she could. A woman who *had* friends, people who missed her, who had visited her in the hospital and had helped her make the adjustment to being home and on her own again. People who had helped her deal with the trauma of the accident and the shock of the amnesia, people who cared about her as much as she cared for them.

Could a blow to the head cause such a drastic personality

change? she wondered, idly fingering the scar that crossed her forehead before disappearing into her hair. Immediately following her return to consciousness from the coma, she had experienced some changes that the doctors had attributed in part to the head trauma—the headaches and dizziness that still plagued her, insomnia and irritability, difficulty concentrating, restlessness and depression. Posttraumatic syndrome, they had called it, and they had assured her that she would get better. For the most part she had. Even the headaches and their accompanying dizziness were gradually going away.

But to change from the woman Laura had been into the woman Carly knew she was now... Was that possible?

A knock at the door interrupted her musings. For a time she sat motionless on the bed, wondering whether he would go away if she ignored him. Because she knew it was Sheriff Logan. The tightening of the muscles in her neck told her, and the sick churning in her stomach confirmed it.

He knocked again, harder this time, and she knew that ignoring him was pointless. If he wanted to come in, he would simply get a key from the clerk and let himself in. If she was going to face him, she would rather do it on her terms.

Rising from the bed, she padded barefoot to the door. There were two locks on the door—an inexpensive dead bolt and a chain lock. She unfastened both, but opened the door only a few inches, blocking it firmly with her foot.

He wasn't in uniform this time. He wore faded jeans, a T-shirt and an old high-school letter jacket, but the casual dress didn't diminish his authority any. It didn't make him look any more approachable. It didn't make him look any less dark, or any less threatening.

"Can we talk?" he asked, his manner subdued, his movements nervous.

Carly's first impulse was to tell him no. The nosy clerk

would overhear everything they said if they went to the lobby downstairs, and there was no way she was inviting him inside her room. Not after what had happened this afternoon.

But he looked so ill at ease, so genuinely regretful. And there were some things she would like to know, things that only he could tell her.

"Go for a walk with me," he suggested. "We'll stay on Main Street."

She hesitated a moment, then another, before silently nodding. Closing the door once more, she put on socks and loafers, got her room key and tugged on her jacket as she crossed the room. She locked the door while he waited silently, and then she followed him down the stairs and outside.

It was cold tonight—typical, she thought, of a September night in the mountains. She zipped her jacket, then shoved her hands into her pockets as they began walking, the width of the sidewalk between them, in the direction opposite the sheriff's department.

For a few minutes Buck was content to do nothing but walk. Finally, though, he spoke. "I'm sorry about today, Carly. I thought... I assumed..." In the display-window lights of a furniture store, she saw him grimace. "I was wrong."

"Laura wouldn't have been offended by it, would she?"

He avoided looking at her as they passed an insurance office, a drugstore and a video rental store. When they reached the corner, he stopped and gazed down at her under the slightly yellow glow of a streetlamp. "No," he said grimly. "She wouldn't have."

It was Carly who broke the contact. She started walking again, across the street and up a broken curb to the next block. "She liked it rough."

A step behind her, the sheriff amended that. "She liked it dangerous."

"And you?" Some rational part of her mind drew back, astonished that she was walking along a quiet dark street asking a man she'd met only two days ago about his sexual preferences. But she might have—probably had—known him in another life, she reminded herself. Somewhere in her mind, in some isolated corner that she couldn't reach, she probably already knew the answer.

How did he like his sex? Buck's smile was bleak. Any way except the way it had been with Laura. Gentle would be nice. And meaningful—that was something else he'd missed in his years with Laura.

Loving. That summed it all up. He didn't want wild, fiery-hot explosions of passion and craving and relief. He didn't want to need a woman as if his life depended on her, and as soon as it was over wish to God that he would never see her again. He wanted to feel wanted, not used. He wanted tenderness and sharing and giving. He wanted to care about the woman in his bed, not just during the act but afterward, too.

He wanted to make love. Not have sex or any of the other cruder euphemisms. *To make love.*

For Carly he settled on the least-telling reply. "Normal. I like it normal."

"This afternoon—that was normal?" she asked.

"This afternoon was madness. I thought..." He had thought she had lied to him again. He had thought she was using him again. He had thought she was mocking him again. "I was angry, but I would have stopped. If you hadn't, I would have. I would never force any woman to—" Breaking off, he shrugged.

"Not even Laura, who liked it that way?" she asked softly.

"When she wanted it rough, she went elsewhere." He

stared stonily ahead. "I'm not into force or pain or anything like that."

Businesses gave way to houses around them, then the lamplight faded and the sidewalk turned into a dirt trail. They had reached the edge of town. Still keeping their distance, they turned and began their return trip in silence.

What was she thinking? Was she wondering about what kind of woman she had once been? Was she dismayed, repulsed, simply curious...or fascinated? Was she tempted to try to be that woman again?

God, he hoped not. For his sake, and for her own, he hoped she was happy the way she was.

Soon they were back on the block where the hotel was located. It was the oldest part of an old town. The sidewalk along the front was elevated four wide steps above street level, and the unpainted wood slats were gritty with pebbles and dirt. Periodically the merchants wanted to modernize a bit, but so far the city fathers had refused. These few old-fashioned blocks were Nowhere's only attraction for the occasional tourists and their money. They were a symbol of what Nowhere had once been.

What it was now was a quiet, unassuming little town. A pleasant place to live.

Until *she* came to town.

Buck expected Carly to tell him good-night and turn into the old hotel, but she passed it. Stopping at the end of the block, she looked around, then took a seat on the top step. "Didn't it make you angry when she went to other men?"

Back to that, he thought grimly. But then, she had never left the subject. Through all those long silent moments she had been thinking about just that.

He sat down on the retaining wall that supported the sidewalk. With his back to her, he answered with a shrug. "We argued about it."

"But?"

"But Laura did what she wanted. I didn't own her. I didn't control her." No, she had taken great pleasure in reminding him that it was the other way around. She was the one in charge.

"But you stayed with her. You loved her...didn't you?"

He looked at her over his shoulder, his brows raised. "What makes you think that?"

"You want her back badly enough to believe that I'm her."

He left the wall to crouch in front of her. For a moment he had forgotten about this afternoon, but when she warily inched away from him, it came back with painful clarity, with guilt and regret so great that he had no words for it, and with an ache that he had lost something he might never get back: Carly's trust.

"If she's back," he said quietly, "I want to know. I need to know." He needed to prepare himself—to protect himself. He needed to make certain that she didn't finish what she'd started with him. He needed to make certain he could survive her this time. "But you're right—I *do* believe you're Laura. You may be a different person...but I believe you're the same woman."

His words didn't please her—it was written clearly on her face as she huddled deeper in her jacket. And he couldn't blame her. All the times she must have dreamed of discovering who she really was, she had never imagined someone like Laura. Who wanted to find out that the past she had forgotten was shameful, filled with deceit and selfishness, with greed and evil and cold, cold hate? How could anyone deal with that?

"Come on," he said, getting to his feet. "Let's go back to the hotel and get warm. I'll buy you a cup of coffee."

For a long time she sat there as if she hadn't heard him. Finally, though, she got to her feet and returned to the hotel with him.

In the restaurant she deliberately avoided the back booth that had been Laura's favorite, choosing the opposite corner instead. When the waitress approached, Buck ordered two coffees and two pieces of coconut cream pie. With a scowl, Carly changed hers to hot chocolate and warm cherry pie with vanilla ice cream. A bid for independence?

"What did you letter in?" she asked, folding her cold hands on the tabletop between them.

He glanced down at his old jacket. "Football, wrestling and baseball."

"How did you go from being a jock to a cop?"

"By way of the operating room." She didn't speak, but merely waited for an explanation, and with a shrug he gave it. "I went to college at the University of Nebraska on a football scholarship. I did pretty well—had the interest of three or four pro teams. But in the first game of my junior year, I got hit hard and tore up my left knee. End of college, end of career."

"And the end of your dreams," she said softly. "That must have hurt."

He looked away, remembering just how badly it had hurt. Not many people had understood his disappointment. They had slapped him on the back and said, "Tough break, kid." They had reminded him that he was young, that he still had his life ahead of him, that football was, after all, only a game.

On the other hand, the guys on the team had understood all too well. They'd had the same dreams and had faced the same risks. When it had become clear that he wasn't going to fully recover from the injury, when they had watched him hobbling around on crutches, struggling through physical therapy and enduring more pain than they could have imagined, they had distanced themselves from him. Instead of their teammate, their buddy, he had become a reminder of what could happen to them. They had understood, and they had sympathized, but every one of them had been damned glad it was him, and not them.

"Yeah, it hurt," he agreed quietly. "Playing pro ball was all I had ever wanted. If I hadn't had a chance, if I hadn't been good enough, I could have dealt with that. But to lose it because some guy hit me wrong..." He shrugged, then settled back so the waitress could serve them. When she left, he continued. "I was twenty-one, in about as good shape as a three-legged dog, had no plans, no money, no future."

"Why didn't you finish college?"

"The coach had to cut me loose, and without the scholarship, I couldn't stay. So I came home and got a job with the sheriff's department. I was the hometown boy who made good—almost—so they didn't care that a ten-month-old in a walker could outrun me. And eventually my knee healed enough to be normal."

"But not enough to play football again."

He shook his head.

"And you like being a cop."

"Yeah, I like it."

"And Laura didn't mind your job?"

He sweetened his coffee, then laced his fingers around the heavy mug, letting the heat seep into them. "Laura liked power," he said flatly. "She preferred to have it herself, but the next best thing was surrounding herself with people who had it." But that wasn't quite true. What she had really preferred was wielding her own special brand of power over people in positions of authority—a teacher, the high school principal, the mayor, the sheriff. Granted, there had also been other men—mechanics, cowboys, students and bums. Anyone who could give her what she wanted at that moment was fair game.

"Did she work?"

He tried to tamp down his annoyance with the conversation. Carly had questions, and more than anyone else, she deserved answers. But he didn't want to talk about Laura anymore. He didn't want to say anything that might upset her, anything else that might deepen the disappointed, disturbed look in her blue eyes. He didn't want to help her understand exactly what kind of woman she had once been.

"No, she never held a job. When her mother died, Laura received a large insurance settlement. The money was invested, and she lived off that." And her aunt Maureen. And her men. She'd had a knack for finding men who generously rewarded every sweet act.

"And after her mother's death, she went to live with Maureen. How old was she then?"

"Fourteen, fifteen. I'm not sure."

"What about her father?"

"She never knew him. Rumor is that her mother was never sure exactly who Laura's father was." Briefly he wondered if that had something to do with the photo in Carly's wallet. Had never having a father bothered her enough that she had created one along with her new identity? Or, more likely, had the picture simply added a nice touch to her lies?

"What about your family?" Carly knew she was being unforgivably nosy, but Buck would have to forgive her. She had a right to know the things she had forgotten...*if* she was Laura. And since he was the one who had raised the question in the first place...

"We had a small ranch south of town. My father worked hard, played hard and drank hard, and he died hard about ten years ago. My mother sold the place, married a businessman from Wyoming and moved down there. I have one younger sister—the one in the photograph—who's married, has four kids and lives in Missoula."

"And your grandmother?"

"She's in a nursing home there. I try to see her a couple of times a month."

"Is that all of your family?"

"Hell, no. I've got aunts, uncles and cousins coming out of the woodwork. Pete Wilson, who owns the barbecue place, is my uncle Paul's youngest boy, and Cheryl, the girl who waited on us there, is a cousin a few times removed. Harvey—the deputy who printed you—is married to my aunt's oldest daughter."

Dropping her gaze, Carly used her fork to flake what was left of the pie crust on her plate. In the absence of concrete memories, she had often consoled herself with the fact that Carly Johnson must have an extended family, that while she had been an only child, surely her parents hadn't been; surely her grandparents hadn't been lonely onlies. Even if she hadn't known these relatives that she'd dreamed about, she had been convinced that they existed, that they were out there somewhere, that occasionally they must wonder about what had happened to Mark and Helene's girl.

Instead, most likely all she had was a sweet old aunt and a cousin who hated her. And instead of the happy, loving family she had imagined, she had come from a mother who had been promiscuous and a father she had never known. And she had been promiscuous herself. Vain, unprincipled, unlikable, selfish, deceitful—and let's not forget kinky, she morosely reminded herself.

She wanted to ask Buck more. She wanted to know why he had stayed with Laura. She wanted to know what it was about the woman that had attracted him. She wanted to dissect every tiny emotion he had ever felt for her. She wanted to understand what Laura had meant to him. She wanted to hear that in spite of his anger, he had liked her, that he had cared for her.

But she didn't ask. Because she was respecting his privacy, she told herself. Because she couldn't bear to hear anything else negative, she knew.

"How long will it take to get an answer from the FBI on my prints?" she asked, pushing the thoughts of Laura from her mind.

"A couple of weeks. How long can you stay?"

She had promised him a few days, until the end of her vacation. That would mean leaving Monday at the very latest, in order to get home in time to return to work Tuesday. She could give him two more days.

Or she could request a leave of absence from her boss. Janice was understanding. She had stood by Carly through her recovery, had kept a place open for her even though she'd been such a new employee at the time of the accident. She had helped her find her way around again, had retrained her on the tasks Carly had forgotten learning. If there was any way Janice could do it, she would give her the extra time off.

And if there wasn't? What was more important—finding out if she really was Laura Phelps or holding on to her job?

She smiled thinly. It should be an easy question. Of course she should care more about learning her real identity than about keeping a secretarial job. She was good at her work; if Janice threatened her with the loss of her job, she could find another one.

But that job was important to her. Although she had probably held others, it was the only one she remembered. The people there had known her before the accident, making it a link—albeit weak—to her missing past.

And what if she wasn't Laura? What if this was all some incredible coincidence? Was she willing to upset the balance of her life in Seattle for something that might not even be true?

Even if she was Laura, the sheriff might not be able to

prove it. She might not remember anything. She could spend twenty years here and still not know for sure.

But how could she go home without trying? Could she be content back in Seattle with all these questions and co-incidences and uncertainties in her head? Could she pick up being Carly Johnson again and be happy again, or would this town and this man haunt her?

Would Laura haunt her?

"It's not such a difficult question," Buck said quietly. When she looked up, he was smiling, not the arrogant grin or the cold smirk that she'd seen before, but a genuine, although halfhearted, smile.

"Monday is my last day of vacation," she replied. She saw the dismay on his face and continued. "I'll call my boss tomorrow and ask her for a two-week extension. If you don't know something by then…" She broke off and shrugged. "I can't stay away forever. I have bills, respon-sibilities."

"When you talk to her, will you ask her to send me a copy of your job application?"

She started to ask why, then realized the answer: he was hoping to use the information a nonamnesiac Carly had given to disprove her identity. They weren't exactly on the same side here, a fact that she had momentarily forgotten. He wanted to prove that she was Laura. She wanted to remain Carly. The more she learned about the other woman, the more she didn't want to be her.

With a sigh, she asked for the sheriff department's ad-dress. Borrowing a pen from the waitress, he scribbled it on the back of a napkin. "I'll ask," she said, tucking the napkin into her jacket pocket. She slid from the bench then and stood beside the table for a moment. "Thanks for the hot chocolate and the pie."

He stood up, too, dropping some money on the table. "I'll walk upstairs with you."

Upstairs. But not into her room. She wasn't going to invite him there.

But once they were in the hallway outside room 3, he didn't seem to expect an invitation. Instead, he offered one of his own. "Would you like to look around tomorrow? See some of the places where Laura went?"

And maybe remember something in the process? She didn't know if it would work, but it would beat sitting alone in the hotel room all day. It would have to be better than going out alone and getting stared at by everyone she met. "All right."

"Then I'll pick you up at nine." Buck watched her turn the key in the lock, then enter the room. With a tight little smile, she closed the door again, and an instant later he heard the lock click, the chain rattle. For a long time he simply stood there, staring at the door. Thinking, wondering, regretting.

Same face, different name.

Same person, different woman.

Ever since Carly's arrival in town, the contradictions had been driving him nuts. Now he could add one more.

Same man.

Different feelings.

Chapter 5

"Do you believe in psychics?"

Buck stopped at one of Nowhere's three stoplights and looked across the seat at Carly. She was watching the traffic as if she hadn't just asked a question so transparent that he could see right through it. "I've never known one myself," he admitted, "but frankly, I'm a bit skeptical."

"But there have been documented instances when a person with psychic abilities has known something that he or she couldn't possibly have known."

"And knowing these things without a logical explanation doesn't change who the psychic is," he finished for her. "So...is Carly Johnson psychic? Is that how you found out these things about Laura? You just picked them up out of the blue?" Grinning, he shook his head. "Tell me what I'm thinking right now."

"I don't have to be psychic for that," she retorted with a scowl that faded as quickly as it came, taking his grin with it. Damn, but she was beautiful enough to make his eyes hurt, like looking at a sun too bright or a star too distant.

She was beautiful enough to make his heart ache.

The light changed, and the driver behind him tapped the horn. Pulling his gaze from Carly, he crossed the intersection, then turned onto the next block.

"There doesn't have to be a rational explanation for everything," she was saying, unaware of the moment he had stared. "There are mysteries in life that were never intended to be solved."

"And who you are is one of them?"

"I still have an identity, Sheriff," she reminded him gently.

"And you're not going to give it up without a fight, are you?" *He* was convinced that she was Laura. The doctor, Maureen, Trina and everyone else who had gotten close enough, who had talked to her—everyone who had known Laura well was convinced. Carly was the only holdout. She was the only one yet to be convinced.

And she was the most important one to convince. With this morning's phone call to her supervisor in Seattle, he'd been given two weeks to do it.

The job application her boss was putting in today's mail should prove something. If his theory was correct and Laura had created a new identity for herself before the accident had claimed her memory, then Carly Johnson shouldn't exist. Fake documentation wasn't difficult to obtain—the birth certificate, the driver's license and social security card. All he needed was a place to start. If she really was Carly Johnson, his search would bear it out. If she wasn't, the fabricated identity wouldn't be too hard to unravel.

Then she would have to believe him.

"Where are we going?"

They were driving down Nowhere's shabbiest street. The

pavement had run out a block off Main, and the houses were getting progressively poorer. Finally he stopped in front of one, a small house with shingled sides and a sagging porch. It had stood empty for years, the boards rotting, the windows broken by kids out looking for trouble. Even when it was occupied, it had never been a source of pride. But it had been the best Nora Phelps could afford.

He shut off the engine, then glanced at Carly. She was staring past him out the window. Her face was a few shades paler, and her hand, when she reached to open the door, was trembling. "Oh, God," she whispered. "This was Laura's house."

An unexplained mystery? A memory? Or another bit of knowledge that she possessed without knowing where it came from? Buck didn't know. He just knew it was eerie, seeing recognition and total bewilderment on her face. He knew it was uncomfortable seeing the fear in her eyes.

He stared at her as she climbed out of the truck. For a moment she simply stood at the edge of the road, studying the house in much the same way she had studied Maureen's place. There was a look of intense concentration on her face—her forehead was wrinkled, her eyes narrowed, her lower lip caught between her teeth. Maybe if she didn't try so hard, he thought, something else might come back to her. Maybe if she wasn't so intense. Maybe if she relaxed a little.

Relax. Hell, under the circumstances, even he couldn't relax. How did he expect her to when she was staring in the face the ugly fact that all the awful things she'd heard about Laura Phelps just might be about *her*?

He got out of the truck after a moment and stood beside her. "Nora Phelps wasn't a bad woman," he said, repeating what he'd heard from his mother years ago. "She wasn't too bright, but she was damned pretty. She loved men, and she loved to party. As wild as she was, everyone was shocked when she had Laura and kept her. Thirty-four years ago in a small town like Nowhere, that just wasn't done.''

''It must have been hard on her—and Laura.''

''I guess so. Laura hated growing up poor, especially after Nora's only brother died and left everything—all his money, his property and that big house outside town—to Maureen. He didn't even mention Nora in his will. Laura was grateful to Maureen for taking her in after Nora died, she really was, but on some level she felt it was no less than she deserved. She believed the old man had owed her and her mother something while he was alive, so she took it after he died. She lived in his house. She let Maureen support her with his money.''

A stone path led to the porch. Over the years grass had slowly crept out across it, sinking its roots in the cracks, leaving irregular borders around each stone. Buck followed Carly as she made her way to the steps. She stopped there. He wondered if she didn't trust the rotting steps, or if she could see all she wanted through the open door and the broken windows.

It was a depressing place. Ghostly. Empty. There was an air of sadness about it because the only two people who had lived here were gone—Nora was dead, and in a spiritual sense, so was Laura. Dead and reborn into Carly.

''This is the kind of place that looks awful in person,'' she said softly, hugging her arms to her chest, ''but makes wonderfully dramatic black-and-white pictures—all stark and desolate and haunting.''

Pictures again, he thought with compassion. Photographs were her memories.

She made her way carefully through an overgrown tangle of weeds and vines to the back of the house. It was little different from the front—decaying wood, shattered glass, emptiness. A rusted clothesline, fallen at one end, swayed in the light breeze. A lawn chair sat at an angle nearby, its bright green paint faded to a dull, practically colorless hue.

"Which room was hers?"

"I don't know."

He watched her look at the house, and he saw her sudden shudder. "I don't like it here," she murmured, turning back toward the front, quickly retracing her steps to the Bronco. He followed more slowly, thinking as he walked about the time Laura had shown him this house. She hadn't liked it then, either.

It had given her chills then, too.

They returned to the main part of town, driving up and down the streets. There weren't that many places significant to Laura, Buck realized, and Carly had already seen most of them. Laura had never worked, she had never gone to church, and she had never had friends whose homes she had visited. He drove by the high school they had both attended, but he didn't point out the second-floor room where a tenth-grade Laura had seduced the drama teacher to gain the starring role in the school play—the role that, up until that time, had belonged to Trina. He didn't mention the office on the first floor where she had often met with the principal, and he didn't show her the shady spot behind the football stadium where she had amused herself with whichever eager young jocks were around.

"So this is where the hotshot football player got his start," Carly remarked as he turned into the stadium parking lot. "What position did you play?"

"Quarterback."

"Of course. And you were the captain of the team."

He nodded.

"And all the girls were in love with you."

He didn't respond.

"But you had eyes for only the head cheerleader."

Stopping at the exit, he gave her a long look that finally

made her laugh. "I'm not remembering anything. It's just so clichéd," she said. "It's a law of nature, I think, that the captains of all high school football teams have to be handsome and charming and date the head cheerleaders."

Handsome and charming. Not a bad compliment from a woman who only yesterday had looked at him with fear in her eyes.

The heat of shame filled him at the reminder of yesterday afternoon. He wished there was some way to erase it from Carly's memory. She had forgotten all the rest of the bad stuff; too bad he couldn't wipe away that, too.

"My neighbor Hilary says that the high school years are the best. If that's true, I've already lived the best years of my life, and I don't remember a thing about them. It's kind of depressing."

"She's wrong." He pulled onto the road and headed back toward Main Street. "High school kids don't know enough about life to appreciate it."

"What were your best years?"

The years without you.

The answer came so quickly, so naturally, that he had to clench his jaw to keep from saying it aloud. The last three years hadn't been easy, but compared to the hell of the preceding two, they had seemed that way. "My best years are going to be the next fifty or so ahead of me."

Approving of his answer—if not of the stiff way he'd given it—she smiled. "Mine, too."

Downtown again, he turned to the right. The road led past the sheriff's department and out of town to the old York place, to the McLane ranch and to his own cabin.

It also led to the lake. The most significant place in this entire area for Laura and him.

Trying to sound normal, to pretend that he wasn't dreading this, he said, "We'll drive up to the lake, then—"

"No."

She sounded cold, harsh, like Laura in a temper. When he glanced at her, she looked that way, too. Frozen. Unyielding.

And afraid.

Of what? he wondered, taking his foot from the accelerator and letting the Bronco coast to a stop on the shoulder. Of remembering?

Of not remembering?

Or of *him*?

Shifting into park, he looked at her, searching for an answer in her profile. Finally he asked, "Why not?"

"I don't want to go to the lake."

"Laura always liked it there."

She glared at him. "But I'm *not* Laura," she said vehemently, then her voice softened and saddened. "At least, not *that* Laura."

He watched as one of his deputies approached, then passed, lifting his hand in a desultory wave. He suspected why she was balking, suspected why she didn't want to go to that one particular place with him. Twisting in his seat to face her, he offered a promise in a low, strained voice. "I won't touch you, Carly. I swear, I won't come near you."

She didn't look at him, didn't seem to even hear him. "I don't want to go to the lake."

"But that's one of the things you remembered—"

"It's one of the things I *knew*," she corrected. "But I won't go there. Not now. Not yet." Turning her head, she stared out the window to the side, registering the trees and the rusted barbed wire fence without really seeing them. She wasn't afraid of the sheriff coming on to her again— she remembered his regret and disgust all too well—but she didn't want to go to the lake. She couldn't even explain why. She just had this feeling that the lake wasn't a place she wanted to be.

''Then will you come to the house with me?'' he asked quietly. ''We can get some lunch and…talk.''

To his cabin. Where he had once taken Laura. Where, until he'd found her there yesterday afternoon, *she* had felt a comforting sense of home. Where he had grabbed her, kissed and frightened her.

Her head said no, go back to town. But her instincts argued that she would be safe at the cabin. Buck Logan was a man of his word—she believed that. He wouldn't hurt her.

When she said nothing, he shifted into gear and pulled back onto the road, taking the first turn on the left and following the lane to his house. She liked his cabin—liked the way it blended into its wooded setting, the way the logs used to build it had weathered, the way it felt comfortable, well-cared-for and loved.

''How long have you lived here?'' she asked as they climbed the steps.

He glanced at her as he sorted through his keys for the one to the front door. ''Since my mom sold the ranch.''

''About ten years.'' He had told her that last night. ''How old were you?''

''Twenty-six.''

''And working for the sheriff's department and eager to have a place of your own.''

''Working for the sheriff's department, and with a grandmother who couldn't live by herself any longer but wasn't yet ready for a nursing home.'' He opened the door, then stepped back for her to enter.

So the ex-jock, the big football star, the macho cop had moved in here to help take care of his elderly grandmother. There was something incredibly touching about that. ''Didn't you want the family ranch?''

''I couldn't work it.'' He followed her into the living room, tossing his keys on the coffee table as he sat down in the rocker. "This job doesn't require much physical activity—an occasional foot pursuit or scuffle is about the extent of it. Ranching is damned physical. It's hard. Most days my knee is fine. Sometimes I favor it a bit. Once in a while it stiffens up and I favor it a lot. I couldn't work the way my dad did." He fell silent, his gaze straying to the photo of the old lady on the shelf. "I'd rather have my grandparents' place, anyway. I was closer to them than to my own folks."

"When did she go to the nursing home?"

"Two years after I moved in. She fell one day and broke her hip, and…" Looking uncomfortable, he shrugged. "I couldn't handle caring for her anymore. I had just become the sheriff, so I was working longer hours, and I couldn't find anyone who could stay with her full-time. But it was her choice. I didn't put her away. She decided that it was time."

"Grandparents are one of the things I miss most. I know I must have had them, but—" She saw the way he was looking at her and broke off. He was thinking that of course she'd had grandparents, at least one set—Nora Phelps's parents. And that she'd never known about paternal grandparents, not even before the accident, because she had never known who her father was. She wanted to argue with him. She wanted to pull the family picture out of her wallet and show it to him again, to make him admit that the baby was her, that the people holding her had to be her parents.

But what good would it do? She would never convince him.

After the last few days, she wasn't even sure she could convince herself.

"Are sandwiches okay for lunch?" he asked, rising from the rocker quickly enough to set it in motion.

Sighing forlornly, she followed him into the kitchen. "That's fine." She rested her elbows on the counter and watched as he removed the food from the refrigerator. She liked watching him, especially in the tight jeans that looked like a favorite, oft-worn pair, and the University of Nebraska T-shirt that fit as snugly as the jeans. He didn't look like an officer of the law in that outfit. No, he merely looked like an attractive man.

A *very* attractive man.

Who may or may not have been in love with the woman she may or may not have once been.

Who definitely had been lovers with the woman she might have been.

Who had, for a few brief moments yesterday, absolutely hated the woman she didn't want to be.

Turning away from him, she saw the answering machine on the counter near the kitchen phone. "You have a message on your machine," she remarked, watching the red light blink on and off.

"Hit the play button, would you?"

She did, and the motherly sweet tones of Maureen Phelps filled the room. "Buck, this is Maureen. Hazel told me that Laura…" A soft sigh. "I mean Carly. I can't quite get used to calling her that. Anyway, Hazel said she left the hotel with you this morning. I was hoping I could get the two of you to come over here for dinner this evening. Give me a call, dear, will you?"

The machine beeped to signal the end of the message. Carly knew without looking that Buck's gaze was on her. He was leaving it up to her. If she wanted to go, he would go with her. If she didn't, he wouldn't make her.

She didn't mind a return visit to that monstrously ugly house. She didn't object to sharing a meal with Laura's aunt. She didn't fear being overwhelmed by Maureen.

But she was afraid of Trina.

Looking up, she met his gaze. His dark eyes were somber, flat. There wasn't even a hint there of what he wanted her to do.

"She scares me," she said softly.

He knew immediately which "she" Carly was referring to. "Trina's harmless."

"Easy for you to say. She's sweet on you. She *despises* me. What did I—" She caught her slip, but saw that he had, too. "What did Laura ever do to deserve that?"

"She was prettier. Smarter. More popular with the boys." He carried two plates to the small round table by the window, then returned to the refrigerator for ice and canned sodas. "Hell, she was even more popular with Maureen, although I doubt Maureen was ever aware of it. But Laura was more…alive. When she was around, you knew it. You noticed her. Trina…she always had a tendency to fade into the woodwork. Living half her life with Laura just made it worse."

He was halfway across the room when he stopped and looked at the cans he carried. "I don't have any diet."

"That's okay. I don't drink it." She slipped her shoes off and sat down, drawing her feet onto the seat, then hesitantly said, "I know you believe that I *am* Laura. Does it bother you, talking about us as if we're two separate people?"

He took a long time to answer, long enough for Carly to eat half her sandwich and drink nearly half her soda. When he finally did reply, it was slowly, thoughtfully. "Laura would never have drunk regular pop. She wouldn't have eaten a piece of cherry pie or a sandwich with mayonnaise."

Carly glanced down at her sandwich, at the thick creamy spread on it.

"She would never have seen anyone without completely hiding that scar under makeup. She would never have let Trina order her around without ripping her to shreds. She wouldn't have asked all those questions about me or anyone else, and she wouldn't have listened to the answers.'' He paused and stared out the window, watching the wind rustle through the trees, then directed a troubled look her way. "Laura wouldn't have been waiting for me with her clothes on yesterday, and she never would have pushed me away."

Her lunch forgotten, Carly simply looked at him. One of these days she was going to learn to quit asking questions of this man. All too often his answers weren't what she wanted to hear.

But occasionally they were.

"No, it's not hard for me to think of you as two people. The more time I spend with you, the better I get to know you, the more I understand that you and Laura *are* different people—kind of a before and after. Bad and good. Dark and light."

If she was the after, did that also make her the good and the light? She hoped so. She didn't want to be bad. She didn't want to bring dark misery to the people around her.

She didn't want to be Laura. But if she was, she didn't want to be the Laura Buck hated.

God help her, she really didn't want that.

"You think you've got everyone fooled, don't you?"

Trina's voice, low and icy, came from directly behind Carly, and it made her skin crawl. It wasn't simply that the other woman had startled her by entering the room and crossing to the window where Carly stood without making a sound. No, the shiver that ran through her was caused by something more subtle, more insidious, more threatening, than a mere surprise.

Trina's harmless, Buck had said, and at first glance, she looked it. She was tall, almost shapeless, straight up and down. Her hair was brown, shoulder-length and straight, and her eyes were also brown, flat and washed-out. She wasn't unattractive, but simply plain. Pinched-looking. Harmless.

But one look in her eyes, and Carly knew Buck was wrong. She saw the venom there. She heard the hatred in Trina's voice, felt the evil emanating from her very pores.

Turning from the darkness outside, she faced Trina, forcing a smile, pretending that she wasn't the least bit disturbed by her. "I'm not trying to fool anyone, Trina," she said, wishing she felt one tenth as calm as she sounded.

"Mother, Buck, everyone in town—they all believe your lies. But not me. I know better than to believe you. I know you. I know what you're capable of."

Still smiling, Carly tightened her grip around the glass she held in both hands and wished desperately for Buck and Maureen to return from the kitchen. Why had the old lady mentioned the broken garbage disposal just as they were finishing dinner? And why had Buck volunteered to look at it for her? Why had they left her alone long enough for Trina to get close?

As if drawn by that last thought, Trina moved closer still, and she lowered her voice until it was little more than a whisper. "Whatever you want this time, Laura, you're not getting it. Do you understand? You can't come back here. You can't take my place with Mother again. You can't have Buck again."

Carly responded instinctively, without thought, without hesitation. "Why? Because you want him for yourself?"

Trina drew back sharply. For a moment she looked stunned, as if she had nurtured a great secret, only to discover that it was common knowledge. Was her attraction for the sheriff supposed to be private? Carly wondered. The woman looked at him as if he'd hung the moon and the stars, too, she hung on to every word he said, she didn't miss a chance to draw his attention her way, yet she thought her feelings for him were her own little secret?

"The sheriff's a big boy," Carly added quietly. "He can make his own decisions."

"When did you ever let him decide anything? He never wanted you. He never wanted to sleep with you or spend time with you. But you forced your way into his life, the same way you did here. You ignored his protests, his needs and desires, but you made damn sure *yours* were met. You made him miserable." Her smile was cruel and sly. "But he finally learned to tell you no, didn't he? When you insisted that he marry you, he turned you down cold. He finally saw you for what you were, and he told you to go to hell. And he'll do it again. He won't fall for this sweet little act of yours. He knows how wicked you are."

Wicked. The word made Carly shudder with revulsion. *Had* she been a wicked person? Had she somehow manipulated Buck into a relationship that he hadn't wanted? Had she taken everything she'd wanted and given back nothing in return? Had she made him miserable?

The questions haunted her the rest of the evening, through Trina's triumphant silence and Buck and Maureen's return. She sat on the sofa beside the old lady, but she didn't take part in the conversation. She didn't hear the talk around her. She simply sat there, cold and dazed, and wished she could leave. She wished she could go home— back to Seattle where she would be safe and comfortable.

After three years of wishing she could remember, now she wished she could forget.

Finally they said good-night, and she and Buck left the Victorian house. They were halfway to the bottom of the steps when he finally spoke. "What's wrong?"

She stopped beside his truck, but didn't reach out to open the door. Instead, tilting her head back, she stared up at the sky. "Did you know that amnesia isn't always caused by

physical trauma?'' she asked softly, but she didn't wait for
an answer. ''Sometimes it's psychological. A person witnesses something too horrible to remember, or the stress in
her life is so overwhelming that she needs to escape, so the
brain shuts off the memory, and, voilà, no more horror. No
more stress.'' After a moment's silence, she sighed. ''I
wonder...''

Buck knew exactly what she wondered—if her own amnesia was, at least in part, psychological. There was no
denying the injuries she'd suffered in the accident, but who
could say for sure that they were the sole cause of her
amnesia? It was entirely possible that, someplace deep inside, Laura had been unhappy, that she had tired of the
selfishness and cruelty, that she had no longer wanted to
face what her life had become, what *she* had become. The
accident had provided the intricate workings of her brain
with a second chance—a chance to give up the selfishness,
the evil and the greed. A chance to become someone else,
someone sweet and decent and good. A chance to care
about somebody, to be cared about in return.

And all she'd had to do to get that chance was forget.

He waited for Carly to voice her thoughts aloud, but she
merely sighed again and climbed inside the truck without
saying anything. He circled around in the darkness, then
slid behind the wheel and started the engine, letting it idle
for a moment before shifting into reverse.

''Did you go out with Trina?''

As he followed the gravel road to the highway, he wondered what had prompted her question. Jealousy? Laura's
jealousy had been hot and ugly, born of her unwavering
need to be in absolute control, absolute possession. Like
everything else, that had softened and gentled in the last
three years. It only mildly flavored Carly's question.
''Yeah, a couple of times.''

The answer seemed to explain something to her. She made a soft sound of understanding and nodded her head.

"If you think that explains why Trina's so hostile, you're wrong," he informed her.

"It explains part of it."

"I've probably gone out with every unmarried woman within fifty miles of Nowhere. They don't all hate you."

"But they aren't all in love with you. Trina is."

That made twice that Carly had said something of the sort about the other woman. He had ignored it in favor of another issue at lunch. Now, with more displeasure than he liked, he asked, "What makes you think that?"

He felt rather than saw the look she gave him. It made him uncomfortable. "The poor woman makes a fool of herself over you, and you don't even notice," she said, her tone sympathetic.

Laura feeling sorry for anyone, especially Trina, was as laughable as anyone feeling sorry for her, Buck thought. Then he reminded himself that this was Carly, not Laura. Not exactly.

"Maybe your dates with Trina weren't important to you, but they mattered to her."

"She couldn't have thought they meant anything. They weren't even real dates. We were doing some work together, and I took her to dinner a couple of times, that's all."

"Did you invite her? Did you pick her up at the house? Did you pay the tab? Did you take her home and kiss her good-night?"

"*No.*" They were in town now, where the streetlamps allowed him to see her expression. She was smiling in a way that made it clear she knew which of her questions had prompted his too-vehement reply, and he scowled in response.

"They were real dates," she said softly. "To Trina they

must have been dreams come true. It must have been hard on her to see you with Laura, knowing what kind of person her cousin was, knowing that in spite of that, she couldn't compete against her.''

Buck pulled into an empty parking space across from the hotel, then faced her. ''What kind of person Laura was doesn't matter much now.''

She looked back at him with such sadness. ''It matters to me.''

The desire to protect wasn't new to Buck—he had often tried like hell to protect himself from Laura. But this was the first time in his life that *she* was the one he wanted to protect. He wanted to wipe away all the dark memories, all the fear and uncertainties, all the sorrow and shame and revulsion. He wanted to protect her from the truth, wanted to restore her faith in herself. He wanted to save her from any further hurt or disappointment.

He wanted to save her from herself.

And maybe, just maybe, he wanted to save her *for* himself.

''Everyone's done things they aren't proud of,'' he said grimly, looking away from her as he spoke. ''You just have to learn to leave it in the past.''

''Maybe that's what I did. And after I got rid of all the bad, there was nothing left. I had to start all over again.''

Maybe she was right, he thought. Maybe being Laura had been too painful, too shameful. She could have lived happily the rest of her life without knowing the truth, but luck, chance or some perverse twist of fate had brought her back to Nowhere. Back to the one place where she couldn't escape who or what she had been.

''What have you done,'' she asked, ''that you aren't proud of?''

His biggest shame, his biggest regret, was his relationship with her. His weakness for her. His obsession with her. She had made him hate himself, and that had made him hate her. But he couldn't say that. For her sake, but mostly for his own, he wouldn't.

"Nothing," he replied at last, giving her a grin made up of sheer will. "I'm the exception to the rule. Come on, it's getting cold out here. Let's get a cup of coffee at the restaurant." But before he could get his door open, she was asking another question.

"Trina said that you didn't want to be involved with Laura, that she forced her way into your life. Is that true?"

That he didn't want to be involved with her. God, that was a major understatement. He would have given anything—his life, *her* life—to avoid the trap she had set for him.

"What did she do?"

He opened the door, then looked at her in the faint glow of the overhead light. "You don't want to know," he said flatly. With that, he climbed out, walked to the back of the truck and waited there for her. He didn't feel the cold that penetrated his leather jacket or notice the puffs of frost that his breath formed when he sighed. He was too numb. Too weary.

Too empty.

After a moment Carly appeared on the other side. "I do want to know."

"No."

"I have a right—"

His bitter laugh interrupted her. "You've changed so much that sometimes, in spite of the face, I forget that you *are* the same woman I knew. But, God, just now you sounded exactly the way you used to—selfish and demanding. You think you have a *right* to my memories, to my past? Well, believe me, if they were that easy to get rid of, I'd give them to you, because I sure as hell don't want them for myself. I don't want to remember having an affair with you. I don't want to remember hating you. I don't want to remember you at all.''

Resting her arms on the side of the truck bed, she laced her fingers tightly together. "I know she wasn't a particularly nice person—"

"Say *I*, damn it," Buck interrupted again. "Quit hiding behind all those *she*'s and *Laura*'s and say *I*. '*I* wasn't a particularly nice person.'"

She grew stiffer and paler in the lamplight, but stubbornly she continued. "I know this isn't easy for you, having to deal with me after three years of peace from her—"

He slammed his fist down, rattling the fender, shaking the truck from side to side and silencing Carly. "You want to know what you did?" he asked softly, dangerously. "You decided that we were going to have an affair. No matter that I wasn't interested. That I didn't even like you. No matter that I was involved with someone else, and so were you. You wanted somebody new, and I was the poor bastard who caught your eye."

He slowly moved toward her. "Everywhere I went, you were there. You came to my office, to my house. If I went to the restaurant for coffee, you were there. When I stopped at the store for groceries, you were there, too. *Everywhere*. And you teased and taunted and played your little games, and you sucked me in. I was a fool. I thought I could handle you. I didn't realize how dangerous you were. I didn't realize how evil you were."

His last words made her wince, but he didn't care. She had demanded to hear this, and, by God, she was going to listen. "I tried to keep you away. I told you no a thousand times in a thousand ways, but you just laughed every time and reminded me that you—" He transformed his voice into a deeper, masculine version of her sexy, throaty purr. "You *always* got what you wanted."

He was in front of her now, only inches away, but she

didn't back up. She just stood there, watching him with an awful fascination, and listened.

"And you got it then, too," he whispered, raising his hand as he spoke and slowly, lightly, brushing his fingers across her cheek. "The more you played, the more I hated you and…God help me, the more I wanted you. I despised you. I loathed everything about you…but I needed you. You were like a sickness that had spread into my very soul."

Slowly she shook her head in denial, dislodging his hand. He let it fall back to his side; then he clenched his fingers into a tight ball. "You almost destroyed me."

"Not me," she murmured, still shaking her head. "Laura."

"You *are* Laura," he insisted.

"No. I wouldn't do that. I wouldn't hurt anyone. I wouldn't hurt *you*."

"You never brought anything but pain to me or anyone else." He knew the words were cruel, but he wouldn't call them back even if he could. "You used people. You took everything and left me with nothing. Not even pride. Not even self-respect."

She walked a few feet away, then stopped, her head bowed, her shoulders rounded. Buck's bitter anger faded, and guilt, painful in its strength, took its place. Not long ago he had wanted to protect her from the negative discoveries she was making about herself. Now he had only added to her burden, and he had done it deliberately.

Maliciously?

"Why did you ask me to stay here? Why didn't you let me go home to Seattle?"

"Because I had to know."

"You haven't proven anything yet."

"No." He waited until she slowly faced him again. "But *you* have."

She stared at him for a moment, then shook her head. "I won't be her. Do you understand? I will not be that woman!"

Feeling suddenly weary and emotionally sore, Buck closed his eyes for a minute, shutting out her challenging stance, her stubborn insistence and the hopelessly forlorn look in her eyes. He wanted to tell her to go back to Seattle, to pack her bags and leave tonight. He wanted to beg her, please, God, to never come back here again. He wanted to apologize for the things he'd told her, to come up with some plausible story that would convince her he had lied. He wanted to erase that anguish and despair from her expression.

He wanted, he realized with dismay, to hold her. To touch her. To draw her close and shelter her, soothe her, heal her.

God help him.

Smiling bitterly, he opened his eyes again and found her watching him, still stubborn, still challenging and still utterly forlorn. "Do you want me to leave now?" she asked in a tiny voice.

That was the one thing he wanted most...and the one thing he couldn't face. Not yet. "I wouldn't blame you if you did." His smile slipped. "You said this wasn't easy for me. I can't even imagine how hard it must be for you."

"Some part of me wants to know the truth," she admitted. "Some other part is praying for another blow to the head to erase the last four days from my memory."

They were both silent for another moment; then, with a sudden shiver, she asked again, "Do you want me to leave?"

He had no right to ask her to stay. After everything he had said, everything he had put her through, the least he owed her was the chance to return home with a clear conscience.

But he couldn't give her even that.

"No," he replied quietly. Then he dragged in a deep breath and said the words that just might cost him dearly.

"I don't want you to go."

The nightmares returned with a vengeance.

Carly awoke late Sunday night to the sound of her own voice, harsh in her ears. For a moment she couldn't remember where she was, couldn't remember anything but the terror, but slowly the comforting familiarity of the hotel room returned, wrapping around her. She lay in bed, her heart thudding, her skin sticky and damp, her breathing labored, and stared wide-eyed at the ceiling.

When did a dream stop being a dream and become a memory? Because this time, for the first time in three years, there had been more to the dream than fear. There had been screams—not the ones that had awakened her, but screams within the dream. There had been horror, paralyzing, life-sapping horror. And tearful entreaties: *Please, God, please, God, please...*

Please what? Don't let me die? Had she dreamed about the accident? Surely she had been terrified when she had seen the other car barreling through the intersection. Surely there had been a moment when she had known there was no escape, when she had screamed in horror. Surely there had been an instant when she had thought she was going to die, when she had prayed.

Had she bargained, as some people did? *Please, God, if You let me live, I'll never be bad again. I'll never use anybody, never hurt anybody, never degrade anybody again.*

And when she survived, had she kept her end of the bargain by becoming someone else? By thankfully forgetting who she had been?

Slowly she pushed the covers back and swung her feet

to the floor. As usual, her nightgown was soaked with perspiration. Shivering, she reached for her robe, pulling it on as she stood up. She had just tied the belt when a knock sounded at the door.

"Laura? I mean, Carly?"

It was Hazel, the desk clerk and, Carly had recently discovered, owner of the hotel. The room she shared with her husband was across and down the hall from Carly's—but not far enough to spare them her dream.

She opened the door, then ran her fingers through her hair. "I'm sorry. I didn't mean to disturb you."

"Are you all right? What's going on?"

"Just a bad dream. I have them sometimes."

The older woman studied her for a moment. "Are you sure you're okay?"

"I will be. I'm sorry."

Hazel reached out and touched her thumb to one of the shadows beneath Carly's eyes. "Try to get some more sleep. You sure could use it."

"I will." Carly closed the door and locked it again. After taking another gown from the dresser, she went into the bathroom and stripped off her robe and the damp gown. Catching sight of herself in the mirror, she paused in the act of pulling her gown on and for a moment simply looked. She was slender and a little taller than average. Her breasts weren't too small or too large, her waist wasn't too narrow, and her hips were a little too rounded, but she had nice legs. It wasn't a bad body, but it wasn't a knockout, either.

It certainly wasn't a body that would entice a man—any man—into an affair against his will.

Certainly not Buck Logan.

What would it be like to have that sort of knock-him-off-his-feet effect on a man? she wondered as she tugged her gown on and smoothed it over her hips.

Exhilarating.

Stimulating.

Powerful.

She had speculated occasionally what her love life had been like before the accident. Had she had more than her share of dates? Had there been anyone special? Had men liked her, been drawn to her? Or had she been a wallflower, shy and gawky or for some reason unable to connect with the opposite sex?

She had never considered that she could have been the kind of woman Buck had described. Bewitching. Seductive. Irresistible. That was pretty heady stuff for a woman who had once forgotten how to kiss, who still remembered nothing about making love.

Then the memory of something he'd said Saturday night came back to her, erasing whatever small pleasure she had found in her thoughts.

You were like a sickness that had spread into my very soul.

Sinking to the handwoven rug in front of the tub, she felt sick, too. Desperately, deathly sick. Covering her face with her hands, she considered the nightmare once more. Maybe she had misinterpreted it. Maybe she *had* dreamed about the accident, but maybe her screams hadn't been born of fear of dying, but of living, instead. Maybe her prayers hadn't been a plea to survive, but a pleading instead for death. And maybe because God had punished her by making her live, she had responded by erasing all memory of herself from her mind.

With a bitter, choking laugh, she wiped a tear from her eye. Everyone—the doctors, the nurses and her friends—had considered her survival and recovery as nothing less than a miracle. Wouldn't it be a hoot if it had all been for this—so she could come back to Nowhere a different woman, a happy, contented, peaceful woman, and face the terrible truth about the person she'd been. So she could live without happiness, without contentment ever again. So she could give up any hope of ever finding peace.

So she could face Buck again. She had made his life miserable. She had brought him nothing but pain. She had almost destroyed him, and he would never, ever forgive her. But here she was back in his life, a changed woman. A woman who was attracted to him. A woman who liked him. A woman who would find it easy to care for him, too damned easy to love him.

That, she acknowledged, would be the cruelest punishment of all.

Chapter 6

Buck was sitting at his desk Monday afternoon when Harvey brought the mail in. On top was a large flat envelope with an express-delivery label pasted across the front. It was from Seattle. Ignoring the rest of the stack, he tore the envelope open and removed a photostat of Carly's job application. It was two pages, stapled in the upper left corner and headed across the top with the name of the insurance company.

Leaning back in his chair, he swiveled from side to side as he began reading. There was a notice near the top that the company reserved the right to dismiss any employee who supplied false information. Underneath that was the interesting stuff.

Some of it he had already come across—the name, address and social security number. She had listed her previous address as an apartment in Dallas, and her birth date was shown as April 4. The lines provided for job history were blank, and there was a penciled note below stating that the applicant's only jobs had been unpaid positions with charitable groups.

Volunteer work. That was a nice touch on Carly's part— and a sign of how thoroughly she had planned her disappearance. She must have realized that an employer wouldn't look kindly on a thirty-something applicant who had never held a job.

Had her claim raised questions in anyone's mind about how she had supported herself all those years holding only unpaid positions? he wondered. Naturally she would have had some answer prepared—the truth, possibly, about her trust fund. Maybe a half-truth about a wealthy family. Or an out-and-out lie about an ex-husband whose financial success made possible the luxury of charity work.

On the second page of the form was a block for education, where she had listed a high school and college in Texas. Under that were lines for three references, but she had filled in only one, a lawyer in Houston. Buck wondered if the lady lawyer really existed and if she did, if Carly had actually somehow known her or if she had simply chosen the name from a Houston phone book.

The final section of the application requested the name and number of a person to be contacted in case of emergency. She had listed Hilary White, her next-door neighbor. The lady who believed that the high school years had been the best of her life. Had somebody called Hilary after the accident? Had they told her that her neighbor had nearly died?

Had she given a damn?

There was a brief statement at the bottom, a declaration that all the information was accurate, then Carly's signature. The signature itself was generic. There was nothing unique about it. Just neatly-formed letters, graceful curves, spiky points. He couldn't say it was Laura's. He couldn't say it wasn't.

Had she felt even a twinge of guilt as she'd signed it? Had her conscience bothered her at all?

Probably not. The form had been filled out and signed before the accident. When Carly was still Laura. Deceitful, unethical, dishonorable Laura.

He was impressed by her thoroughness. She had been relatively honest about the important stuff—job history— and had limited the lies to the things the company wasn't likely to check. Who would waste time and money checking the former address and nearly fifteen-year-old education background on a clerical applicant?

How had she known that? Carly had asked him last week if Laura had known how to create a fake identity for herself. The application in front of him was proof that she had. Unless...

Unless Carly wasn't Laura.

He didn't want to consider the possibility—after spending four of the last five days with her, he *knew* she was Laura, knew it as surely as he knew his own name—but he forced himself to, anyway. What if Carly wasn't lying? What if he checked out the information on this application and it all bore out? What if she really was Carly Johnson of Dallas, Texas?

Then he owed her one hell of an apology.

With a sigh, he reached for the phone book in his desk drawer. Finding the area code for Dallas, he called information and requested the number for the public library. There he was transferred to the reference desk, where a friendly woman with a lazy Texas drawl put him on hold long enough to look up the apartment address in the city directory.

"Are you sure that's the right address?" she asked when she came back on the line.

He read it to her again, knowing as he did so what her response would be.

"I'm sorry, but I can't find a record of such a street anywhere in the city. Are you sure it's in Dallas?"

"It's supposed to be. Listen, could you go back a couple of years—three or four—and check a name for me?"

That search was also futile. She offered to check the phone book, but he declined. In a city the size of Dallas, there would be pages of Johnsons, probably quite a few C. Johnsons and maybe even a Carly or two. But since the address was nonexistent, there was no reason to check further. Dallas was just a part of her story.

One lie down. How many to go?

By the time he quit for the day, he'd disproven a few more of her claims on the application. Neither the high school nor the college had any record of her attendance. There was no listing for the lady lawyer in Houston, and according to the state bar, there had never been an attorney by that name practicing anywhere in Texas. Tomorrow he would start with a call to the Social Security Administration.

Tonight he would talk to Carly.

The prospect made the muscles in his stomach tighten. He hadn't seen her since Saturday night. Standing there by his truck, he had asked her to stay and she had said she would. Then she had walked away, across the street and up the steps into the hotel. He had wanted to go with her as far as her room, but she hadn't invited him so he hadn't offered. Instead he had stood there in the cold, too numb to feel it, and watched until she was safely inside. He had stood there until the light in room 3 came on, until he'd seen her shadow fall across the shade, then disappear again, and finally he'd gotten into his truck and driven home.

Sunday he had stayed as far away from her as he could. He had driven to Missoula, intending to visit his grandmother and his sister's family, but once he'd gotten there, he had decided he was in no mood to socialize with anyone.

His grandmother would have known right away that something was wrong—her health might be failing, but her mind was still sharp—and she wouldn't have given him any peace until he'd told her everything. So instead he had sat through a movie he couldn't remember, eaten a dinner he'd barely tasted and driven around until exhaustion had forced him home.

He reached for the phone to make one last call to Carly at the hotel, then slowly replaced the receiver without dialing. There was no reason to call on the phone when it would take only a couple minutes more to walk over there. When instead of merely hearing her voice, he could look into her face.

On his way out, he told the dispatcher that he could be reached at the hotel, on the radio or at home. It was rare that they had to contact him after hours, but there were possibilities. He was routinely called on all fatalities, whether the cause of death was traffic-related, accidental, suicide or the occasional murder. Anything involving the family of their local senator, who lived fifteen miles out of Nowhere, always required his presence, along with any incidents involving one of his deputies. Sometimes, when he had been with Laura, he had prayed that he would be called away, and later he had always felt guilty for wishing harm on someone else just so he could escape an evening with her.

Tonight he didn't want any interruptions.

When he reached the hotel, he found Carly settled comfortably on the bench across from the desk, cradling a scrawny little red-haired girl on her lap. The baby, Buck knew, belonged to Hazel's oldest daughter and looked just like her mother—pale skin, carroty hair and faded blue eyes. He wasn't surprised to find the kid here—Hazel often baby-sat for her children—but he was surprised to find Carly holding her. Laura had hated all kids, but especially babies for their unfortunate tendencies to spit up, fill their diapers and generally smell bad.

She was smiling at the baby as he approached, and when she saw him, she turned the smile on him. It was lovely, gentle and just plain happy. It made her look as if her troubles were over. It made him feel as if his were just starting.

She had always been beautiful, but it had in some way been tarnished by her nature. Her beauty had always seemed sterile, coldly perfect, her smiles practiced, her sexy seductiveness calculated. For all her passion, she had been empty inside, like a beautifully wrapped box that held nothing inside.

She had never been warm. She had never been real. She had never been innocent.

She had never been this beautiful.

"Hello, Sheriff," she greeted him, shifting on the bench so he could join her.

He sat down at the opposite end, leaving plenty of room between them. "How did you get conned into taking care of this stinker?"

"I volunteered. I like babies. Besides, if I had stayed up there in that room for one more hour, I would have gone crazy." The baby began to fuss, and Carly lifted her to her shoulder, bouncing her gently, patting her back. "How can anyone stand doing nothing all day? I can't even watch TV very well. The set in my room only gets one-and-a-half stations."

He reached out, brushing his palm over the baby's hair. The gesture placed him close to Carly—not as close as he would like, but as close as he had the nerve to get right now. "One-and-a-half?"

"One channel comes in fine. On the second, I get audio on channel five and video on channel six." Carly looked down at the baby for a moment. Her eyes were closed, her mouth open, making little sucking motions. "Hazel was going to fix her a bottle," she said softly, "but it looks like she's going to sleep without it. So, Sheriff, how was your day?"

He looked away from both her and the baby then. She knew that look—knew he had found out something that one of them wasn't going to like. Trying to ignore the sudden thud of her heart, she airily said, "Let me guess. The FBI matched my fingerprints to one of their ten most-wanted criminals."

That earned her a scowl. "The FBI probably hasn't even gotten your fingerprints yet." For a moment the scowl intensified, then faded. "I got your job application from Seattle."

So his news was a setback for *her,* she acknowledged. "That fast? What did Janice do—pay an arm and a leg to send it express?"

He nodded.

"She's so efficient that it's kind of scary. Some of the other managers in the company can't function without their secretaries guiding them by the hand, but Janice is as capable as I am." Realizing that she was rambling, she abruptly broke off, took a deep breath, then asked, "And what did you find out from the application?"

"The Dallas address you gave doesn't exist, the high school and college have never heard of you, and the state bar has never heard of the lawyer whose name you gave as a personal reference."

"But the company hired me, anyway." She smiled a tight little smile. "I must have a real talent for lying."

"Laura was a great liar," he said flatly. "I'm not sure *you* could lie to save your life."

So he was back to making distinctions between them again. After Saturday night she had wondered if he would give up the pretense and insist on calling her by her rightful name. Alone in her room yesterday, she had tried to do what he had demanded—to put herself in Laura's place, to admit that she was Laura and therefore she had done all these terrible things. *I* seduced Buck. *I* was the woman he hated. *I* was the woman who hurt him. *I* was the disease that made him sick.

But the statements hadn't *felt* right. She couldn't imagine doing the things Laura had done. She wouldn't believe she was capable of them. She wouldn't believe she would use and hurt him that way.

Maybe she had once been Laura Phelps, but as she'd told him Saturday night, she wouldn't be her again. Even if he gave her incontrovertible proof, she wouldn't quit being Carly Johnson.

She couldn't.

"So what's next?"

"I'm calling social security tomorrow. I want to find out when your number was issued and where. What about your birth certificate?"

"What about it?"

"Do you have a copy?"

She nodded.

"It's from Texas?"

She nodded again, more slowly this time. If all the information pertaining to Texas on her job application had been fake, what were the chances, she wondered, that the birth certificate was also false? And if it was, that meant her identity—her entire life—was made up. It meant that she certainly was one hell of a liar.

It meant that she was Laura.

"I'd like to get a copy of it," Buck was saying. "I'll contact the state tomorrow and see—"

She interrupted him with the shake of her head. "I—I have a copy. It's in the car."

He gave her a puzzled look. "You keep a copy of your birth certificate in your car?"

"Only on trips." It was an odd habit, she knew, and one that she had given up trying to explain. Most people couldn't begin to understand what it was like to wake up one day and realize that your past was missing. To find a blank in your memory so tremendous that it was as if you had never existed before that day. To look in a mirror at your own face and find a stranger looking back. They couldn't understand the shock, the fear or the terrible sense of loss, of abandonment. They couldn't understand the hopelessness.

"What form of identification," she began softly, looking at the baby instead of at Buck, "is more basic than a birth certificate? It documents your existence, your parents' existence. It proves that you were here a week ago, ten years ago, thirty years ago. It proves that you're somebody, and not just an oddity. A medical miracle. A freak."

Before he could respond, Hazel returned from the kitchen. "Sorry it took so long. I had to check on dinner. Hi, Buck." Pausing for breath, she looked at her granddaughter. "I shouldn't even have bothered with this bottle. Let me have her, Carly, and I'll put her in the playpen."

Carly stood up and handed the baby over. For a moment she savored the warmth where the small body had snuggled against her and the powder-soft scents that clung to her sweater. Then, recalling the conversation Hazel had interrupted, she reached into her pocket for her keys. "I'll get it for you now."

He followed her outside and down the steps to her car. She slid into the passenger seat and, opening the glove compartment, began sorting through the papers there. She had just found the certificate when suddenly Buck leaned past her and pulled a gold chain from the glove box. Wrapped around his fingers so that the medallion it held rested in his palm, the chain looked delicate, and the gold, even though it needed to be cleaned, seemed to glisten against the darker shades of his skin.

She stared at it. She wished she could believe that her sudden difficulty in swallowing and the prickly sense of awareness that snaked through her were normal responses because of Buck's proximity, but she knew they weren't. She knew that if she looked up at him, she would see recognition in his eyes.

She knew this necklace—or one just like it—had belonged to Laura.

"There's something wrong with the clasp," she said at last, her voice soft and strained. "It kept snagging on my clothing, so one day I just tossed it in there and forgot about it."

She did finally look at him, and she saw that she was right. He did recognize the necklace. He seemed to be searching for the right words, but when he'd found them, she abruptly stopped him. "No," she whispered. Grasping his hand in both of hers, she folded his fingers over the medallion, hiding it from sight, then squeezed them tightly. "It's just coincidence. The necklace was a gift. Someone gave it to me."

"You remember...?"

She lowered her gaze. "No. But it's not my style. I never liked it, not from the first time I saw it. I never would have bought it."

He started to say something else, but she continued in a pleading voice, "I don't want to hear it. Whatever you're going to say about it, about *her,* I don't want to know. Please, Buck..."

It was the last that convinced him to oblige her, that soft little *"Please, Buck."* It was the first time she had called him by his name, the first time she hadn't relied on the more formal, more distancing title of Sheriff.

He crouched beside the car, his dark eyes troubled. She could tell he wanted to argue with her, wanted to tell her about this necklace, wanted to tell her things that she didn't want to hear. But he didn't say anything until the urge passed, and then, his voice thick and hoarse, he merely said, "I'll put it back."

But she didn't release his hand. "No. You keep it." She had never cared for the necklace—the medallion was heavy and ugly, an abstract form that felt like a stone around her neck—and knowing that it might be Laura's didn't make it any more appealing.

After a moment he pulled his hand free and slid the necklace into his pocket. Then, touching her again, lightly brushing his fingers over hers, he said, "Come out to the house and have dinner with me."

She considered his invitation for a moment, although she knew immediately what her answer would be. Yes, she would like to have dinner with him. She would like to have his company this evening. She would like to sit in his cozy living room and talk to him, and even more than that she would to like to listen to him. To look at him. "All right. I'll follow you there."

Standing up, he pulled her from the car. "You can come with me. You don't need to be driving back by yourself."

Carly locked the car, pocketed her keys, then presented the birth certificate to him. To her relief he didn't unfold it and study it right there but merely slid it into the inside pocket of his jacket. It was nice that he cared more about something else—going home, getting dinner—than about proving her a liar.

But what further proof did he need? she thought with a bitter smile as they started toward the sheriff's department where he'd left the Bronco. They both already knew that she lied—that Laura had lied, he had specified—as easily as she breathed. Although she appreciated his distinction, it was quibbling. Laura was a liar, and, God help her, it looked like she was Laura.

"When she disappeared, did she take much with her?" she asked as they approached his truck. She caught his sidelong look and shrugged. "The clothes in her closet at Maureen's house all looked very expensive, very dramatic. I didn't own anything like that before the accident. I wore simple dresses for work and jeans, sweaters and T-shirts the rest of the time."

"According to Maureen, she took a couple of suitcases and all her jewelry."

"Including..." She broke off and got into the truck. She didn't want to ask, but she had to know. "Including that necklace?"

Buck closed her door, circled around and got in before answering shortly. "Yes."

"It's hardly unique. There must be dozens, maybe even hundreds, of them around."

"Probably."

He looked so grim, and he sounded that way, too. Carly knew what he was thinking: that she was grabbing at straws. As far as he was concerned, the necklace was just one more piece of evidence, one more bit of proof that she was who he said she was. That she wasn't Carly Johnson. That she was the woman who had taught him so much about hate.

"It's not proof," she said stubbornly, staring straight ahead as he pulled out of the parking lot.

"Not by itself. But taken with everything else..."

Taken with everything else, it was damning. It damned *her*.

After a few miles of silence, he looked across the truck at her. "When are you going to give up? When are you going to accept it?"

She smiled bleakly. "Maybe never, Sheriff."

"Don't do that, damn it!" His words were edged with a savage anger that made her shiver. "Don't call me by my name when you want something, then go back to 'Sheriff' the rest of the time."

In other words, Carly thought shamefully, don't use him. Don't play with him that way. The way Laura had. "I'm sorry, Buck."

He turned off the highway, then parked in front of his house, but for a minute he made no move to leave the truck. "Tell me something, Carly. You remembered Laura's house. You remembered about the lake and about Maureen's house. Why not me? Why don't you remember anything about me?"

She looked at him, smiling faintly. "Good question. And the only answer I have is one you're not going to like." She paused, and he gestured for her to go on. "Maybe I don't remember anything about you because I never knew anything about you."

He responded impatiently. "No more games, please."

"I'm not playing games, Buck. I don't have any other answers. How could I remember places and things and not remember you? How could I forget you so completely unless maybe I never knew you?"

"Forget I asked. I was just curious. Your powers of recall seem to be a little on the odd side."

"That's me, all right," she said flippantly. "Odd." She got out of the truck and closed the door hard, then made her way to the porch without waiting for him.

She was hurt, Buck thought with a sigh as he watched her. All the nonchalance in the world couldn't hide it. The last three years obviously hadn't been easy for her, and in the last few days difficult had gone to damned near impossible. She was upset by the curiosity directed her way, reminding her of all the times in the hospital when she'd been treated as an interesting case, a fascinating history, rather

than a person. She was torn between wanting to know the
truth about her past and wanting to cling to the nice, sweet,
safe identity she had created for herself. She was frightened
by the idea of losing that identity once again, and terrified
by what he might give her to replace it.

She was terrified by the idea of being Laura.

And he didn't blame her.

She stood there on the porch, tracing a line back and
forth with the toe of her tennis shoe, waiting for him to
join her. He wanted nothing more than to do just that—to
take her inside his house, to spend a long, peaceful evening
with no doubts, no fears, no denials. He wanted to see her
smile, to hear her laugh. He wanted to make that look of
distress leave her eyes, wanted to ease the lines of worry
from her face.

God, he wanted too much.

He got out and slowly followed the walk to the porch.
Carly didn't look up as he approached, but she was aware
of his presence. He stopped beside her, close enough to
hear her uneven breathing, to see the sorrow in her eyes.
He just stood there for a long time until finally she raised
her head and lifted her gaze to his. There was none of
Laura's cunning, no deceit, no guile in her face. This
woman didn't know how to lie, how to create an entire new
life for herself. She didn't know how to seduce, how to
take and poison and destroy.

As surely as he knew she was Laura, he was just as
certain that she wasn't. The outside had remained the same,
but there was an entirely different woman inside. A woman
worth caring for. A woman worth wanting.

A woman worth loving?

Buck wasn't certain how long they stood there, long
enough for the sun to complete its slow descent on the other
side of the valley. Long enough for the night chill to settle.

Long enough to find a little of that peace they were both searching for.

He reached for her hand, wrapping his fingers around it, and pulled her across the porch and, as soon as the door was open, inside the house. He didn't release her until they were standing in the center of the living room. He didn't want to release her even then, but he had to either let go or do something more. Draw her close? Kiss her? Hold her?

"Let me change clothes, then I'll build a fire and start dinner."

She nodded and her fingers around his went slack. Even so he had trouble pulling away.

He left her standing there and went down the hall to his room. This time he didn't worry about her coming in uninvited. While that was exactly Laura's style, Carly wouldn't do it.

Not that she would be unwelcome if she did.

He placed his gun belt on a shelf in the closet, then emptied his pockets on the dresser. The necklace landed with a pile of change, his office keys and a paper clip. Fingering the medal, he wished he hadn't seen it in Carly's car, wished he hadn't drawn her attention to it. He wished he hadn't kept it when she had insisted. He didn't want anything of Laura's in his house, and especially not this necklace that had been a gift from another of her men, this necklace that she had worn to remind him that he wasn't the only one.

Picking it up, he started to toss it into the wastebasket. On second thought he opened a dresser drawer and dropped it in there instead. Carly didn't want it right now, but maybe later she would. If she ever remembered.

What would that mean for him—if she remembered? Would she feel sorry and guilty for the things she had done? Would she stay the way she was now? Would she be fascinated by the kind of power she had once wielded? Would she be tempted to use it again?

He wasn't going to think about that. Stripping off his uniform, he dressed in black sweatpants, thick socks and a T-shirt. Then he returned to the living room. To Carly.

She was kneeling in front of the fireplace, coaxing a flame from a small pile of kindling. She looked so earnest, so absorbed in her task. Laura had never found simple things absorbing. Hell, Laura had never found anything absorbing except herself. She had been well and truly in love with herself.

Carly hardly seemed to even notice herself. She certainly wasn't conscious of her effect on others. She attributed all the interest shown her to the question of her identity. She didn't realize that she was so damned beautiful people would look even if they hadn't known Laura.

She didn't seem at all aware of her effect on *him*.

"You like building fires?" he asked as he came further into the room.

"I don't know if I've ever done it. My apartment doesn't have a fireplace. What am I doing wrong?"

He wadded up a page from the newspaper on the coffee table, then tossed it to her. "Slide that in under the grate and light it."

She followed his instructions, smiling as the smaller sticks sent up puffs of smoke, then caught fire.

"You take care of the fire. I'll start dinner."

"I can help," she offered.

"You can cook?"

"I've been doing it all—" She broke off, and her smile faded. "For three years."

She'd been about to say all her life, but it wasn't true. Buck knew that, and she suspected it. "That's okay. I can manage. If you want to watch TV, go ahead. I get more than one-and-a-half channels. And the stereo is over there if you prefer music.''

He went on into the kitchen. A moment later she appeared in the doorway with two cassettes. ''Which do you prefer?'' she asked, holding them up so he could choose.

Having a choice—that was a novel experience. In their two years together, the game had been played by her rules. Where they went, what they did, when they ate, what music they listened to—she had dictated all of it.

With the knife he held, he indicated the one in her left hand, and she disappeared again. Almost immediately music filled the air, soft and relaxing.

Relaxing. He had never relaxed around her before, had never trusted her enough for that. He had never carried on an easy, natural conversation with her. He had never looked forward to seeing her, to spending time with her. He had never felt the same sort of desire for her that he was feeling now—not wild, not passionate, not almost violent in intensity. It was hunger with just enough of an edge to keep it from being too gentle. Yearning for the peace he believed he could find inside her. Lust for the pleasure of making love to a beautiful woman.

It was normal.

Normal.

God help him, he had wondered if he would ever have normal feelings for a woman, any woman, again.

Finishing with the onions he was chopping, he mixed together two small meat loaves and stuck them in the oven, then added two baking potatos. He set the timer on the stove, then joined Carly in the living room.

''That smells good,'' she said with a lazy smile. ''I admire a man who can cook.''

She was sitting in front of the fireplace again, occasionally adding larger pieces to the fire. He lowered himself to the carpet a few feet away. ''When I left for college, I knew how to make sandwiches and open cans. My mother never taught me anything else because she figured I would get married pretty quickly and would have a wife to take care of it for me. I always figured I was going to make it big in football and would live in a house so big that I wouldn't even know where the kitchen was. But when I moved in with my grandmother, she insisted on teaching me while she still could.''

Gesturing above his head, she asked, ''Is that trophy for football?''

He didn't need to look at it. It was only one of many trophies he'd earned, but it was the only one he displayed. ''We were state champs three years running.''

''It must have been hard coming back here and starting over again.''

''I didn't come home until six months after I got hurt. It took me that long to admit that everything wasn't going to be all right, that I wasn't going to be able to play the next season or even the season after that.'' Even after so many years, he knew his smile was bitter. ''I left Nowhere as the hometown hero with one hell of a future, and I came back wearing a brace, barely able to walk and suffering through physical therapy three times a week. I was angry as hell.''

''I know it couldn't have been much consolation, but your family must have been glad to have you home again.''

''My mother was. My father...'' He shook his head. ''My father and I never got along very well. He'd wanted me to stay on the ranch, to work for him until he got old and then to take it over for myself. He thought football was a waste of time. Even when I got the scholarship to Nebraska, he never believed I had the talent to make it. He was angry and disappointed when I came home. Not only had I failed at football, which he had expected, but I had gotten myself so damn hurt in the process that I couldn't work the ranch, either. We lived in the same house for the last five years of his life and hardly ever spoke. The sicker he got, the less work he was able to do, the more he resented me.''

"Did you settle anything with him before he died?''

"No.'' That was one of his regrets. He had tried. He had tried to talk to his father, had tried to explain why he had made his choices, why he hadn't sacrificed his dream to make his father's come true. But by then the old man had been too sick, too bitter. He had known that the ranch he'd worked all his life, the place that his father had treasured, that his grandfather had settled, would be sold following his death. He had known it would still be called the Logan place, because it had been that for a hundred years, but there would be no Logans on it. He had known that a piece of their family history would die with him, and he had blamed Buck for it.

With his dying breath, he had damned his son for that.

Carly touched his hand. "I'm sorry. I shouldn't have asked.''

"Ask whatever you want. Right now it's the only way you're going to learn.''

She started to withdraw her hand, but he twisted his, catching hold. For a time he simply looked at her hand, studying the finely shaped bones, the slender ringless fingers, the unpainted short nails. Her skin was soft, but not too soft—either she'd learned to enjoy occasional physical labor or had given up on expensive pampering.

Drawing his fingers higher, he reached her wrist. It was narrow enough that he could easily encircle it, and it had a small bump over the bone. Doc Thomas had told him that she'd broken this wrist in the accident. The bump must have formed as the fracture healed. The injury had been relatively minor compared to the ones that had almost killed her.

She had almost died.

Three years ago he wouldn't have cared. If the Seattle police had notified him of her accident, he wouldn't have been able to muster even the slightest sympathy for her, only relief that he was free, that she would never torment him again. But now he could feel compassion.

How had she looked with her face stitched up, her nose broken, her arm and wrist in casts? She must have seemed so frail lying in that hospital bed, unconscious, battered and bruised, IVs in her arms. The coma must have been a blessing of sorts, protecting her from the fear and the pain. Waking up and discovering that two months of your life were missing and that you had forgotten even the simplest, most basic facts about yourself had certainly been difficult. But at least she hadn't also had to deal with the pain, with all the broken bones, bruises and contusions. At least she hadn't had to face the fear of dying along with the fear of not remembering.

Absently stroking the back of her wrist, he asked, "What kind of car were you driving in the accident?"

Carly watched each brush of his thumb, wondering how so casual a touch could feel so intense, so tingling and at the same time so sweetly relaxing. It required effort to concentrate on his question, to ignore the sensations he was creating long enough to find an answer. "I'm not sure—a small one. I remember one of the agents at work telling me that cars like mine didn't do well in crashes because they were so small. And I know it was red. When I bought the one I have now, my neighbor's little girl was disappointed because it wasn't red like the other one."

For an instant his thumb stilled. Did that mean the car Laura had driven away from Nowhere three years ago was small and red?

She didn't want to know.

"If it's important, you can ask Janice. When I started working there, I transferred my insurance to them."

"That's okay. I can get it off the police report."

"You have a copy of that?"

"I'll call tomorrow and ask for one. I'll have to go by Jerry Devon's office and see if I can have it faxed there."

He was rubbing again, just a soothing back and forth motion that made her want to close her eyes, snuggle closer and literally purr with contentment. But she kept her eyes open, kept her distance. "Who is Jerry Devon?"

"Nowhere's part-time lawyer. He comes here once a week from Missoula."

"Doesn't the sheriff's department have a fax machine?"

"Honey, I can barely squeeze out the money for salaries and gas. We use Devon's fax on occasion, and the sheriff in the next county runs computer checks for us. We're a small county on a tight budget."

Honey. It was a simple endearment that really didn't mean anything, but it made her feel warm inside. She would bet he'd never called Laura honey.

The kitchen timer dinged, and he got to his feet, pulling her with him. "This time you can help," he said, and she obediently followed him into the kitchen. While he removed their dinner from the oven, she located plates and silverware and fixed their drinks. Then, instead of settling at the small kitchen table or the dining table in the next room, they carried everything to the coffee table and ate in front of the fireplace.

It was the most pleasant meal she could remember.

"So what is Carly Johnson's life in Seattle like?" Buck asked when they'd finished.

"Boring." She leaned back against the sofa, resting her head on one hand. It was a lazy, comfortable position— soft cushions behind her, Buck and the crackling fire in front of her. "You were with me when Maureen asked about that. You heard my answers."

"Not all of them. You didn't answer the last one because Trina interrupted."

Wrinkling her forehead, she tried to remember which one he meant. They had talked about her job, her friends, her hobbies—and men. *Don't you date?* the old lady had asked. *Aren't there any men in your life?* And before she had found a suitable answer, Maureen's daughter had burst in and things had turned ugly and tense.

"There have been a few men," she admitted. "A neighbor, a friend's brother, a guy I used to work with. But dating was hard. I couldn't remember ever being kissed or making out or making love. I felt incredibly naive. It was like being sixteen all over again—or, at least, what I imagine being sixteen is like. Only my dates were men, not boys, and they expected…more." It was like being a virgin again, one of them had told her, and he was just the man to introduce her to the pleasures of lovemaking. She hadn't even mastered kissing yet, and he'd wanted to go straight to sex.

"So you've given up on men."

She laughed softly. "No, not at all. I don't think any woman ever really loses hope that someday she'll find the right person to share her life with. I think I would like to get married sometime. I know I'd like to have children."

Briefly a shadow darkened his eyes, and he looked away from her to the fire. Too late she remembered her last conversation with Trina. *When you insisted that he marry you, he turned you down cold. He finally saw you for what you were, and he told you to go to hell.* Was that what had led to their breakup and to Laura's disappearance? Had she left Nowhere to punish him for refusing to marry her?

"What Trina said was true," she murmured softly, reaching across the table to stack their dishes. "Laura wanted you to marry her, didn't she?"

He just sighed, gave her a grim look and said nothing at all.

"And you told her no, you argued, and she went away."

He still just looked at her, admitting nothing, denying nothing.

"Why did she want to get married?"

"Because I didn't. Because it would strengthen her hold over me. Because as long as I was married to her, I couldn't get involved with another woman. I couldn't have a family. I couldn't be happy."

"So you told her no."

The grimness in his eyes deepened, and his features hardened. "I told her I would kill her first."

"And she went away to punish you. To make you sorry for turning her down." When he nodded, she gave a sad shake of her head. "I can't think of myself as her," she admitted. "I can't imagine doing the things she did." She couldn't imagine treating Buck the way Laura had.

She absolutely could not see leaving him the way Laura had.

She smiled humorlessly. She couldn't imagine leaving him, period. Not if he asked her to stay. Not if he wanted her.

"So don't," he replied stonily, taking the dishes from her and standing up. "Don't think of yourself as her. The things that happened in the past were done by Laura, and she's gone now. You're Carly."

Was it that simple? she wondered as he left the room. Not for her. She couldn't just disregard all the bad things she'd heard about Laura, couldn't absolve herself of responsibility for them simply because she didn't remember them.

She suspected it wasn't that simple for Buck, either. He had a lot of anger and bitterness that he kept in check—usually—by pretending that Carly was a totally different person. Was that the only way he could bear to be with her?

And would that change if one day she remembered? If he knew that she was aware of everything she had done, if she became Laura again, if he could no longer pretend, would he still spend time with her? Would he still smile and laugh and talk to her? Would he still hold her hand and stroke her skin so gently?

Would he want her?

Or would he hate her?

And if he did hate her—as she would surely hate herself for being Laura—would remembering be worth it?

Chapter 7

Jerry Devon's office was located in the same building as Doc Thomas's. After lunch Tuesday Buck went there to pick up the report the Seattle Police Department had sent. Tired of waiting around the hotel, Carly had come with him. Now she stood quietly at the door while he and Devon exchanged the usual pleasantries. After thanking the young man, Buck folded the report and stuck it in his pocket, along with the birth certificate he hadn't yet examined. He had meant to do that last night, but it had been late when he'd taken Carly back to the hotel. When he'd gotten home again, he'd gone straight to bed.

And slept. He had slept more peacefully than he had in nearly a week.

Ushering her out the door, he turned toward his office. Although the sun was shining, it was chilly today. Summer had, as usual, been too short, and winter was coming. Laura had never liked winter—had complained unceasingly about the cold—but he did. He would bet Carly did.

"I've been thinking," she announced as they crossed the street to the next block.

"Does that happen rarely enough to deserve a proclamation?"

She looked up, smiling at him, and he damned near stopped breathing. Sunglasses hid her eyes, her hair was blowing in tangles around her head, and the scar on her forehead was painfully noticeable in the bright sunlight, but she had never looked more beautiful. More touchable.

She had never looked happier.

"Don't get smart, Sheriff," she warned him good-naturedly before launching into her theory. "It just occurred to me this morning that I could be related to Laura. That would explain why I look so much like her."

A few days ago her suggestion might have exasperated him. This afternoon all he did was shake his head and remind her, "Laura doesn't have any relatives besides Maureen and Trina."

"That you know of. But she did have a father, remember? A father that no one knew. A father who didn't just spring up full-grown from the earth. He had to have family of his own somewhere—parents, maybe brothers or sisters." She smiled triumphantly. "Maybe other daughters."

Buck had to admit that he had never considered the possibility. But it only explained the least of his questions—the physical resemblance. It didn't account for the things Carly knew. "As you just said, she had a father that no one knew—not even Laura. If she had a half sister, she didn't know it. She didn't know *her*."

But she wasn't about to be deterred. "Maybe when she left here, she found her father. Maybe she discovered a whole new family someplace. Maybe—"

He laughed aloud, cutting off her suppositions. "God, you are so damn stubborn."

Pushing her hands deep into her pockets, she scowled at

him. "If *you* had amnesia and all evidence pointed toward you being Jack the Ripper, you would be stubborn, too," she said darkly.

"Laura wasn't a murderer."

"Are you sure of that?" she asked dryly.

Outside the sheriff's department, Buck opened the door for her, then stopped her with a gesture. "Let's forget Laura for a while," he suggested gently. "We won't try to prove that that's who you are. We'll just look and see what we can find out about Carly Johnson. Maybe *she's* got a family someplace. Maybe we can find them."

After a long, searching moment, she nodded, then led the way inside to his office. There he removed the fax and the birth certificate from his jacket before hanging it and Carly's on hooks beside the door. Settling in at his desk, he read the traffic report first.

As Doc Thomas had said, the accident had been a bad one. It had happened in rush-hour traffic, when Carly had presumably been on her way home from work. While she waited at a red light, a drunk driver—the man's third such offense—came through the intersection and hit her. His speed had been estimated by witnesses in excess of fifty miles an hour. The impact had reduced her car to a twisted pile of metal, and removing her had taken the combined resources of the police department, the fire department and the paramedics.

The other driver, he noticed with a silent curse, had been treated for minor injuries and released. He had walked away from it virtually unharmed. Because of the extent of Carly's injuries and his previous arrests, he had been charged with felony DUI—Driving Under the Influence— along with an assortment of minor traffic offenses. There was no indication what had become of the man. Buck should have asked the officer he'd spoken to this morning to check on that, too. He would like to know if the man had received the punishment he deserved, or if, like so many other drunk drivers, he had gotten by with only a slap on the wrist.

After brooding over that for a moment, he looked through the notes for the information on Carly's car. An older red Toyota. Not a fast little Corvette.

Of course, she could have sold the Corvette. A car like that would draw attention to someone who didn't want to be noticed. That might have been how she'd bought the Toyota, how she had lived until she'd found the job with the insurance company. Her last withdrawal from her trust fund had been a few days before she left, and it hadn't been a lot—a thousand or so. Laura could go through a thousand bucks in one day. But selling the Corvette would have brought in a tidy little sum and would have made becoming someone else even easier.

When he set the report aside, Carly, standing at the window behind him, quietly said, "I knew you had plants."

He turned in his chair so he could see her as she rubbed one waxy leaf between her fingers. "Of course you knew. You were in here just last week."

"No. Before then. Last Thursday, before I had ever set foot in this room, I knew what it would look like. I knew it would be neat and organized, and I knew it would have plants."

He didn't say anything. What could he say that would possibly matter? *Of course you knew because you'd been in here before, because, until three years ago, you were in and out of here all the time?* Not when only fifteen minutes ago he'd told her they would forget about proving she was Laura and concentrate on Carly instead.

She turned toward him then. "Maybe it was coincidence," she suggested hopefully. "Maybe it was déjà vu. Maybe the room reminded me of some place I'd been, and *it* had plants. Maybe I—" Stopping abruptly, she bit her lower lip to stop it from trembling. She looked so innocent and vulnerable that Buck ached for her. He played along with her.

"A lot of people are neat and organized," he said casually. "And a lot of offices have plants. I bet you keep one on your desk at work. I bet your boss does, too."

She nodded, and the glistening of unshed tears slowly began to fade from her eyes.

"You want some coffee?"

"No thanks," she whispered.

"Hot chocolate? We have some packets of that powdered stuff with little dehydrated marshmallows. It doesn't compare to Hazel's, but it's not bad."

She cleared her throat, sounding more normal this time. "No thanks. I'm fine."

He tapped one finger on the police report. "You are one lucky lady."

"I used to think so."

Until she had driven into Nowhere last Wednesday and had her life turned upside down for her. He knew the feeling, remembered it all too well from the day the coach and the team doctor had walked into his hospital room and told him that he would never play football again.

Maybe someday she would feel lucky again.

Maybe they both would.

Turning his attention back to the subject at hand, he asked, "Do you know what they did to the other driver?"

She shook her head. "I never bothered to find out."

"You weren't vindictive? Bitter?" He shook his head in dismay tinged with disbelief. "He did this to you—put you in the hospital for more than two months, caused you so much pain, took away your memory—and you weren't even curious about whether he was punished? You never considered suing him, making him pay?"

"His insurance company paid for my car and my medical

expenses. That was all I wanted. Finding out whether he went to jail wouldn't make everything all right. Suing him wouldn't bring my memory back." She shrugged. "I was trying to put things back together, to accept what had happened, trying to find some way to live with this big hole in my life. I didn't have the time or the energy to deal with him."

Shaking his head again, Buck repeated, "You are one lucky lady...but that son of a bitch is even luckier. You could have taken him for everything he owned."

"And I still wouldn't have known who I was." She circled his desk and sat down on the other side. "Did I drive the same kind of car as Laura?"

"No."

"Good." She smiled a little crookedly. "It's not much, but I'll take it. Now what?"

"How does Louisiana sound to you?"

"Hot," she answered immediately, then considered it for a moment. "Exotic. I'd love to visit New Orleans someday."

"You've never been there?"

"Not that I'm aware of. Why?"

He probably should have brought this up when he'd first met her for lunch, but the prospect of a pleasant, enjoyable lunch had been too appealing. She had been in a good mood, talkative and laughing, and he'd decided that business, especially bits like this, could wait. "I called social security about your number. They're going to mail me a copy of your application, which we should get in a couple of weeks. I did find out, though, that it was issued in Louisiana."

"They told you that?"

"The prefix did. Each state has its own set of numbers. Yours begins with 4-3-7, which belongs to Louisiana."

She drew her feet onto the seat and hugged her knees to her chest. "Do I sound like I'm from Louisiana?"

"You don't sound like you're from anywhere." But that wasn't so unusual. A person could make a conscious effort to rid himself of an accent, or the loss could happen gradually as he was exposed to other dialects and speech patterns. One thing they did know beyond a doubt was that Carly had moved to Washington three years ago. Whether it had been from Montana as he believed, from Texas as she believed, or possibly from Louisiana as the social security card seemed to suggest, she could have very easily lost whatever accent she'd had.

"Louisiana," she murmured. "I wouldn't mind being from there. I like Cajun food. I'm sure I'd love New Orleans. I'm partial to old Southern mansions. And I like the water." Her smile revealed just a hint of stress. "I could handle being from Louisiana."

"But if you were, why would you tell your friends in Seattle that you were from Texas? Why would you make up a false Texas background for your job application?"

"Maybe I was running away from something."

"Yeah. *Me.*"

Her scowl almost matched his own. "Laura wasn't running away from you, Buck. She was punishing you." After a moment, she suggested, "Maybe I'm an inveterate liar. Maybe I absconded with the company funds from my last job. Maybe I have a split personality."

"Or maybe you once had an incredibly devious mind, and you're having trouble accepting that now."

Carly rested her chin on her knees and studied him gloomily. "What do you want me to do, Buck? Say, 'Okay, I'm Laura'? That you're right and I'm wrong? That I'll be Laura for you?" When he gave her no answer, she shook her head. "What about the birth certificate? It says that I'm

Carly Johnson, firstborn child of Mark and Helene Johnson of Dallas, Texas. How do you explain that?''

"No, it doesn't say that at all." When she started to protest, he raised his hand, stalling her so he could continue. "All the birth certificate says is that *someone* is Carly Johnson, daughter of Mark and Helene Johnson of Dallas. Not *you*. It doesn't have your photograph. It doesn't have your fingerprints. It doesn't have anything to identify *you*."

"You wouldn't accept a photograph as proof, anyway," she mumbled. "I tried that already."

"You showed me two pictures that were between twenty-five and thirty-five years old, pictures that could have been of anyone."

"I hardly know myself, but I can see the resemblance between that little girl and me," she insisted, her voice made sharp by frustration. "Why can't you?"

He looked regretful when he answered. "Maybe you see it because it means so much to you. Because you *want* to be Carly. Because for three years you've clung to those pictures as the only souvenirs of a life you've forgotten and you don't want to admit that you were clinging to someone else's life."

Someone else's life. She carried those two photographs with her everywhere. She had dreamed over them. She had cried over them. She had consoled herself with the facts that she'd had a beautiful mother and a handsome father and that they had probably loved her very much. Even if she was alone now, even if they were gone, if their very existence had been erased from her mind, she still had the photographs and the certain knowledge of their love.

Now Buck was telling her that those were someone else's parents.

That it was someone else's love.

That it was someone else's life.

Oh, God, she couldn't bear this.

Getting clumsily to her feet, she snatched her jacket from the hook and yanked it on. The sheriff—amazing how much easier it was to think of him that way right now— stood up, too, and came around the desk. "Carly, I'm sorry," he murmured, reaching out, taking hold of her arms. "I didn't mean—"

"Leave me alone!" Tears burning her eyes, she tried to pull free, to escape the sheriff and his office before she broke down and cried, but she couldn't break his grip. "I don't want to talk to you, I don't want... Just let me go!"

"Oh, hell, I didn't mean to upset you. Honey..."

She twisted free then and took a step back as the first tears fell. He stood there, looking so uncertain, so angry with himself, so damned distressed, and he made no move toward her again. She was free. She could leave now. But through her own distress, she realized that she didn't want to run away from him—only from what he was saying.

She couldn't endure what he was saying.

She turned to the door, fumbling through her tears for the knob, finally wrapping her fingers tightly around it. The pain was incredible, raw and growing, consuming her. She could run from this man, from this office, from this town and even this state, but she could never run fast enough to escape the hurt, and, dear God, she couldn't stand it alone. She had been alone all her life, all three short years of it.

But she wasn't alone now. Her hesitation at the door was all Buck had needed. Gently he pulled her away, loosening her fingers, drawing her into his arms. He cradled her there, pressing her face against his chest, stroking her hair gently. He didn't tell her not to cry, didn't assure her that everything would be all right. He just held her. Warmed her. Comforted her.

His shirt absorbed her tears as his body, solid and strong, absorbed her shudders. Her fears. Her emptiness. She wanted him to go on holding her like this forever. She wanted to feel this safe, this protected, forever. She wanted...

With a different kind of ache, she realized exactly what she wanted. This man. All of him. For always.

This man who, once he'd proven that she was Laura, wouldn't want her at all.

Her tears dried, her ragged breathing slowed, and the occasional shivers disappeared, and still he held her. Finally, though, he tilted her head back so he could look at her, and with the pad of his thumb he dried the last of her tears away. Once she had thought he lacked tenderness, that he was dangerous, dark and hard. Although the rest was still true, she'd been wrong about the tenderness. No one—not the doctors or nurses in the hospital, not even Hilary's six-year-old daughter who had been so afraid of hurting her and had given her the tentative feathery touches reserved for precious breakables—had ever been this gentle with her.

"I'm sorry," he whispered.

Before she could add her own apology, he lowered his mouth to hers, trapping her words inside. It was a sweet kiss, lacking in passion, in demand, in hunger, but it was exactly what she needed. Friendly. Warm. Soothing.

Maybe, once he'd reassured himself that she really was all right, it would have become something more, but they weren't given the chance to find out. With only an instant's warning tap, the door opened and the deputy named Harvey came inside. "Buck, there's been—"

The sheriff released her quickly, and she moved aside, not stopping until she reached the desk. The glimpse she'd caught of Harvey's face as she moved told her that he was embarrassed. Probably no more than Buck was, she thought a little sadly. Getting caught with her—getting caught *by* her?—must be the last thing in the world he wanted.

"What do you need, Harve?" he asked, his voice just a shade too husky.

"Janssen just called in. He, uh, had a little accident."

Carly quit trying to pretend that she wasn't there and looked at Buck. It was hard to say whether the flush warming his cheeks was from embarrassment or anger. His next words, though, made it clearer. "*Again?* Was anyone hurt?"

"No." Expecting his boss's next question, Harvey continued. "It was his fault. He wasn't paying attention, and he drove right into the back of Tim Martini's truck. Over on Council Street."

"Oh, hell, Martini's truck is built like a battering ram. It probably crumpled that car like a tin can." Running his fingers through his hair, he glanced at Carly. "Tell Janssen I'm on my way."

As the deputy left, she picked up her purse. "I'll let you get to work."

But when she would have followed Harvey out, he stopped her. "Are you all right?" he asked softly.

"I'm fine."

"I wish…"

She waited. She would like to know exactly what he wished. That he hadn't said what he did? That she hadn't cried and he hadn't held her? That he hadn't kissed her?

Or that they hadn't been interrupted?

He pulled on his jacket, then took the Stetson from its place on the shelf. "I wish I could get rid of Janssen. He's absolutely worthless as a deputy, and this is the third cruiser he's wrecked. His girlfriend works over on Council Street. I'll bet you anything he was either looking for her or talking to her when he hit Martini's truck."

"So fire him."

"I can't. He's the—"

"Mayor's nephew," she finished for him. Buck didn't even look surprised that she knew that, she noticed, and she didn't exactly feel it. She didn't even offer herself the usual excuses. Even claiming to have heard Mayor Janssen's name mentioned in the restaurant wouldn't explain how she'd known that the deputy was his nephew and not his son.

She walked outside with him, stopping beside his Bronco. He studied her face for just a moment, then softly asked again, "Are you sure you're all right?"

It was a lie, but she told him yes, anyway.

"Want a ride back to the hotel? It's on my way."

"No thanks. I'll walk."

He seemed reluctant to let her go—as reluctant as she was to be going. Hesitantly she laid her hand on his arm, squeezing through the sleeve of his jacket. "You'd better go now."

"Have dinner with me tonight. We'll drive into Missoula, find someplace new."

She smiled. "I'd like that. I'll be at the hotel whenever you're ready." Releasing him, she stepped back and watched him climb inside. He backed out, then lifted one hand in a wave as he drove away. She waved, too, then slowly lowered her hand to her lips. Her smile became softer, more serene, more satisfied, as she set off for the hotel.

The damage to the deputy's car was as bad as Buck had expected, and so was the reason. Janssen insisted he simply hadn't noticed Martini's truck—hadn't noticed that monster of a truck with its flashers blinking? Buck thought derisively. But a young boy standing nearby called in a mocking, singsong voice, "He was drivin' along talkin' to Georgina, and, *bam,* he ran right into the truck."

Buck looked from the kid to Janssen. The deputy didn't have the nerve to continue his lie, not under his boss's steely gaze. "I was driving real slow," he insisted. "I wasn't being careless. Besides, I'm not totally to blame. Why the hell was he parked in the middle of the street?"

"Wait in the Bronco." Buck approached the boy on the sidewalk. His name was Davey, and somehow, through connections that had become blurred a few generations back, he was related to Buck. "Why aren't you in school, Davey?"

The boy affected a sudden, hacking cough. "I have a cold."

"Then why aren't you home in bed?"

He squirmed, then, just as the deputy had done, gave up his pretense. "Aw, come on, Sheriff. It's just one day of school. We wasn't even doin' anything important. You aren't gonna tell my mom, are you?"

"You wasn't even doin' anything important?" Buck echoed. "Maybe if you were in school, you would be learning how to speak properly. You'd better get home, Davey. And I suggest you come clean with your mom before she finds out from somebody else."

"See you, Buck."

He talked to Tim Martini, then watched as the wrecker from the garage towed the cruiser away. They barely had enough money in the department budget to cover even the essentials, and now this. Besides a full salary paid to a man who didn't earn even half of it, how much had Janssen cost the department in insurance and repairs? he wondered. Maybe he ought to put the young man on a bicycle or a horse. He couldn't be any less effective, and he'd be a whole lot less dangerous—and less expensive.

As he returned to the Bronco, he saw the deputy was watching someone across the street. The lovely Georgina. Nineteen, black-haired and pretty enough to stop traffic in the street. Literally.

But not pretty enough to compare to the woman this incident had pulled him away from. Not pretty enough to make driving away and leaving Carly in the parking lot worthwhile. Sure as hell not pretty enough to merit interrupting their kiss.

"I'm sorry, Buck," the deputy said as soon as he got in.

He didn't say anything, just drove back to the department, escorted Janssen to Harvey and instructed the older deputy to deal with him. Then he shut himself into his office, where he imagined he could still feel Carly's presence. Where he was sure he could still smell her fragrance. Where he wished like hell he had found her waiting.

Going through long-distance information, he got the number for the Department of Vital Statistics in Texas and placed the call. The clerk he spoke to agreed to fax him a copy of Carly's birth certificate. The copy she'd given him seemed authentic, but there was always the possibility that some of the information on it had been changed. Next he called Jerry Devon and told him that another fax was coming to his office, then left to pick it up.

"You know, the sheriff's department could buy a fax machine for a couple hundred dollars," the lawyer said good-naturedly as he removed the copy from the machine.

"The department doesn't have a couple hundred dollars."

"And for the time being, they also don't have one patrol unit." Devon gestured toward the plate-glass window. "I saw the wrecker go by. Let me guess. It was Chris Janssen."

"You got it. Why don't you do this town a favor and take him to Missoula with you when you go?"

"Uncle's not the mayor there. Our sheriff would take one look at him, then send him back." The lawyer sat down on the edge of his desk. "So, Sheriff, answer the mystery of the week—hell, of the year. Is it Laura or just a freak coincidence?"

His use of the word freak made Buck wince. He knew

Devon didn't mean anything by it, but he knew, too, how much Carly hated it. "Don't know yet," he replied evenly, his expression bland.

"Wouldn't that be something if it's not? I never knew Laura—just saw her around occasionally—but I heard she had the face of an angel and the soul of Satan. But this new one… She seems to have not only the face of an angel, but the heart of one, too. She seems sweet. Sort of innocent."

The lawyer was a better judge of character than Buck had given him credit for. After less than five minutes in Carly's presence, he'd described her to a T. "What do you think? What are the odds that this is—or isn't—Laura?"

"Hell, I'm not a gambling man, Sheriff. I can see how the kind of accident she had would leave her a changed woman. On the other hand, maybe she's different because she really is Carly Johnson. Stranger things have happened."

"So she keeps reminding me," Buck said with a scowl.

Devon laughed. "She's none too eager to step into Laura's life, is she? If half of what I've heard is true, I can't say as I blame her." He rose from his desk as Buck started for the door. "Listen, if you need any more faxes while I'm in Missoula, Doc Thomas has a key to the office. He can let you in."

After thanking him, Buck returned to his office to compare the copy with the facsimile. His suspicions hadn't panned out. The two documents were identical.

So now what?

One-and-a-half weeks of the two weeks Carly had promised him were left. He might get a response from the FBI on the fingerprints by then, but it wasn't likely he would hear from social security before she had to leave.

It wasn't likely he would prove anything before she left.

And, damn it to hell, it wasn't at all likely that he would be ready to let her go.

There was a knock at his door. This time Harvey waited a respectable thirty seconds before coming inside. "I put Chris on the desk for a couple of weeks," he announced. "And this time, mayor's kin or not, he's got to pay at least a portion of the damages. If his uncle doesn't want to come up with the money, we can dock it from Chris's pay."

"Sounds fine." Buck set the birth certificates aside and gestured toward the chair. "Have a seat."

"How's it going with Miss Johnson?"

Buck wasn't sure if the older deputy's courtesy was a result of upbringing or his thirty-some years with the sheriff's department. He was always unfailingly polite, even to the folks he arrested, and he was a good deputy. He had no interest in ever becoming sheriff because he wasn't an administrator, or so he claimed, but that wasn't true. He could handle internal problems—like Janssen—as well as Buck.

Sighing, he gave Harvey a rundown of what he'd learned so far. When he was finished, the deputy asked, "What are you going to do now?"

"I was just asking myself that when you came in. You have any suggestions?"

"Have you considered going to Seattle, talking to the people who knew her before the accident?"

Buck shook his head. "You think she hasn't already done that?"

Harvey wasn't at all perturbed by his skepticism. "I'm sure she has, but she's not a cop. Maybe she didn't ask the right questions. Maybe she didn't hear their answers."

That was a definite possibility. Hadn't she refused to listen to things he said that she didn't like? Maybe he could learn something she hadn't. He could take a couple days' vacation, fly to Seattle, do a little poking around. If Carly agreed, while he was there, he could see her apartment, see if there were things there, like the necklace he'd found in her car, that had definitely belonged to Laura.

"Exactly what is it you're trying to do right now?" Harvey asked. "Prove that she is Laura or that she isn't?"

"No matter what I do, she's not going to accept that she's Laura Phelps unless I can prove first that she isn't Carly Johnson. As long as the possibility exists that she is Carly..." He shook his head. "She'll never accept being Laura."

"What about family?"

"She says she doesn't have any, that her parents are dead and she's an only child." Buck rubbed his thumb across the seal, verifying Carly's birth certificate as a true copy. "We know the birth certificate is real, that there really was a baby named Carly Johnson born thirty-two years ago in Dallas. That means the parents are real, too. Maybe they aren't dead. Maybe that was just part of the story she made up to explain why she was so all alone. Maybe Mark and Helene Johnson are still living in Texas."

"And if they are, they can tell you whether or not Carly is their daughter."

"So all we have to do is find them." That wasn't as daunting a task as it seemed. The birth certificate gave the Johnsons' full names, dates and places of birth. All he had to do was contact Sheriff Crowder over in the next county and ask him to run that data through the computer. If either Mark or Helene was still living and had a driver's license issued anywhere in the U.S., it would show up on the computer.

He didn't need to explain that to Harvey. The older man rose from his seat. "Give me the information, and I'll call Crowder."

Buck handed over the facsimile, then sat back to wait. To brood.

What are you trying to prove? Harvey had asked. Buck hadn't liked his answer at all. He knew how desperately Carly valued what little past she had. He knew it would hurt her deeply to have to give that up. He knew she would resent him for making her do it, for proving that she wasn't who she fiercely insisted she was.

But finding out that she was Laura didn't mean she had to *be* Laura. She could remain the same gentle, sweet, caring person she'd been for three years. She could even continue to use the name she'd chosen for herself if it mattered so much to her. He had no problem with that, and he didn't think Maureen would, either. As long as Carly accepted the truth. As long as she accepted the place they and this town held in her life.

As long as she accepted *him* in her life? Was that what he wanted?

He wanted *her*.

The way she was now.

Not, God help him, the way she used to be.

Harvey stuck his head in the door, giving his answer with a grim shake. "No match anywhere."

Which meant the Johnsons were probably dead. The next step, then, was another long-distance call to Texas, only this time he wouldn't be checking birth certificates. He would be asking about death certificates.

A clerk answered the call, asking immediately if she could place him on hold, leaving the line before he had a chance to answer. He was still waiting when Harvey came to his office one more time. "Hazel's on the other line. She wants you to come over to the hotel—says something's wrong with Carly."

His heart thudding irregularly, Buck hung up, grabbed his jacket and started out the door. Behind him he heard Harvey tell Hazel that he was on his way.

Déjà vu. That was how Carly explained a few of the

happenings of the past week. He suspected she thought it much more than she actually voiced it. He was experiencing a bit of it himself now. It had been only a week ago when he'd received an excited call from Hazel about the hotel's latest guest, when she had met him in the lobby with concerns about the woman upstairs. A week ago he'd cared only in a sick, God-don't-let-this-be-her sort of way. He had thought only to protect himself, only to save himself.

How quickly things had changed.

Hazel was waiting in the hall outside Carly's room. "She looks awful, Buck," she said, practically wringing her hands. "I tried to get her to see Doc Thomas, but she said it's just a headache and that I should call you instead. Just a headache, my foot. I've never seen anyone get so sick so fast. Why, I had to help her up the stairs. She could barely—"

He touched her arm, quieting her. "I'll check on her, all right?"

Carly's door stood open a few inches. The shade was pulled, and the lights were off, giving the room a feel of gloom. She lay on her side on the bed, fully dressed just like last time, but awake. Miserably, painfully awake. Her smile when she saw him was more of a grimace. "Do you have it?" she whispered.

"Have what?" he asked softly, crouching beside the bed.

"My medicine. The pills." Her voice sounded thin and thready, matching the frail, insubstantial air about her. "You took them last time...didn't you? You had them when we went downstairs, and I forgot..."

Frowning, Buck swore softly, savagely. He *had* taken the bottle of pain pills last week. He had pried it from her fingers while she slept and had asked Doc Thomas about them. Later, when she awoke, she'd demanded he return them, and instead of giving the bottle to her, he had insisted on joining her in the restaurant downstairs. Then there had been the scene with Maureen, and Carly had fainted, and he...

He had no idea in hell what he had done with the bottle. Was it in the pocket of one of his uniforms at home? Had he dropped it somewhere? Had he lost it?

"Damn, Carly, I'm sorry," he muttered. "I don't know... I'll call Doc Thomas and see if he can give you something, okay?"

He recognized the alarm that briefly flashed through her eyes. She had been caught unprepared by these headaches before. She knew what it was like to ride it out, to endure the pain until it was gone, and the idea frightened her.

As he reached for the bedside phone with one hand, he cupped the other against her cheek, drying the perspiration there, gently caressing her soft skin. "It'll be all right, honey," he assured her. "The doc will have something."

And, of course, the doctor did. He locked up his office and came straight over, bringing a syringe and a small vial. "You'll be just fine," he said, nudging Buck out of the way and giving Carly a fatherly pat. "We're going to get you comfortable, and then I'll give you something to help you sleep." Not changing the low, soothing tone of his voice, he said, "Buck, you go on outside and send Hazel in here."

He wanted to protest but didn't. He'd learned back when Doc Thomas took over his care from the surgeons in Lincoln that when it came to his patients, there was no arguing with the old man. So he waited outside in the hall, silently cursing himself for taking the medication that he'd known Carly needed. If not for him, she would have taken the pills as soon as this headache started. If not for him, it wouldn't have gotten this bad. She would have been asleep already. She would have been beyond the reach of the pain.

Finally the door opened again, and Hazel and the doctor

came out. "You can go in now. She knows what to do when she wakes up. She's been through this before," the doctor said. "And get this prescription filled for her, will you? Just in case it happens again."

Buck accepted the prescription and thanked the old man, then went into the room. Carly was asleep now, the pain-filled lines of her face starting to ease. She lay on her back, snuggled underneath the covers, with just a bit of a pale green nightgown showing at her neck. She looked more peaceful. The grayness was leaving her face, and her breathing seemed less labored.

He felt like a bastard for making her pain worse. Hadn't he already hurt her enough emotionally? Did he have to add physical pain to it, too?

For a long time he stood beside the bed and watched her—just watched the steady rise and fall of her chest with each breath, the occasional stirring, the infrequent whisper of a sigh. The longer she slept, the stronger she seemed to look...or was that wishful thinking?

He wished he had asked the doctor about the headaches. Were they a lingering symptom from the head injuries she'd suffered in the accident? What caused them to still appear after three years? Could the emotional scene in his office this afternoon have brought this one on?

Finally he tired of standing there, but not of watching. Tossing his jacket on the dresser, he moved the rocker from the corner to the side of the bed and settled comfortably in it. The last time she had slept for hours. If rest was what she needed, he hoped she would get it this time, too.

He could wait. He could watch over her all night if necessary.

If she let him, if she stayed, he could watch over her always.

There was something pleasurable, something almost sensual, in awakening slowly, with no alarms, no rude intrusions, just the comfort of her body telling her that she had slept long enough, that it was time now to get up. Carly rarely got that pleasure. On weekdays, there was work; on weekends, errands.

But this morning she came awake a little at a time, becoming aware of contentment first, then of sound—traffic outside her window, deep even breathing nearby. She knew before she opened her eyes that the breathing was coming from Buck, that she would find him, just as she had once before, sprawled in the rocker. He had felt badly yesterday afternoon, had blamed himself for losing her medication. The blame was hers, though. She had known she should keep it with her, yet had never thought to ask him to return it.

Not that it mattered now. She had slept all afternoon and through the night, and she felt strong and hungry, without even a trace of the weakness or pain that had plagued her yesterday.

Finally opening her eyes, she saw that she was right about the sheriff; he was slouched in the rocker. This time, though, he had moved it close to the bed—in case she'd needed him?—and, unlike a week ago, when he had stared at her so darkly, so warily, this morning he was asleep. He hadn't slept long or comfortably, she thought with sympathy. There were lines of weariness etched into his face.

Moving quietly so she wouldn't wake him, she pushed the covers back, then slid from the bed on the opposite side. Then she carefully raised the shade, letting the morning light into the room. She stood there gazing out until he spoke behind her.

"I can damn near see through that nightgown."

Still facing the window, she smiled slightly. Was that a pointless comment, a compliment or a complaint? Based on the hoarseness of his voice, she preferred to accept it as a compliment of sorts, although she felt relatively certain that it was meant as a simple statement of fact.

What would he think if she asked if he liked what he saw? she wondered. Probably that Laura had once again taken control. That seemed like the sort of question she would ask. Unless, of course, she chose to skip asking and went straight to removing the gown so he could see better. Laura would have had him undressed and in bed in a matter of minutes.

If she were here.

But Carly was just Carly, and she had no idea how to go about seducing a man, especially a man who might not *want* to be seduced. Kissing would be a nice start, but she was more comfortable with being kissed than with initiating it herself.

And after that?

She smiled again faintly. She was just too incredibly naive for a thirty-two-year-old woman.

"How do you feel?"

She turned around to face him and saw that he was scowling. But it wasn't the same chilling, hateful look he'd often given her in the beginning. This scowl was less threatening, less intimidating, more what she would expect from a man who had spent the night in a wooden chair. "I'm fine. How do *you* feel?"

"Ragged." He pushed himself from the chair, bracing his hands on the curved arms, then stretched. When he started toward her, she noticed that he was limping just a bit. It probably wouldn't be noticeable to anyone who wasn't watching him closely.

"Is your knee sore?"

"Just a little stiff." He didn't come any closer than the other side of the window. There he leaned his shoulder against the jamb, shifting most of his weight to his right leg. Off the bad one.

"I'm sorry about dinner last night," she said softly, taking up a similar stance.

"Why do you get these headaches?" He sounded perplexed. He looked guilty.

"They're a part of posttraumatic syndrome, which often affects people who suffer head injuries. The symptoms include headaches and dizziness, insomnia, inability to concentrate, depression and a few others." She was speaking calmly, reciting facts that doctor after doctor had explained to her, that she had repeated to concerned friends. "It may last a few weeks or a few years. It's believed to be both physiological and psychological in nature—caused by the actual physical trauma and exacerbated by the emotional trauma. In the beginning I had almost all of the symptoms. Now I have the headaches and occasionally a little dizziness. But it's getting better. It'll go away soon."

"It's getting better?" he echoed. "You mean, it used to be worse than what I've seen?"

She smiled gently. "Much worse."

For a moment they were both silent while he critically studied her. Reaching out, she laid her hand over his. "Don't look at me that way."

Immediately the intensity disappeared from his eyes. "What way?" he practically growled.

"Like an exhibit. A specimen."

"How do you want me to look at you?"

She opened her mouth, took a deep breath, then replied, "As a woman." What she had intended as a normal, unimportant answer came out too breathy, far too important.

Buck's smile was as bleak as it was endearing. "I've been aware of you as a woman from the moment I saw you."

And he wasn't happy about it, she acknowledged, feeling just as bleak as he looked. Just like before, he was being drawn into something he didn't want. But was it Carly he wanted, Carly he was aware of, Carly he needed? Or were his memories of Laura controlling him?

Was his passion for Laura?

Feeling suddenly uncomfortable, she edged toward the bed. Claiming the robe folded there, she slipped it on, belting it tightly. Thus fortified, she forced a vaguely pleasant smile into place and asked, "What's on your agenda for today, Sheriff?"

"*Our* agenda. We're both taking the day off."

She liked that idea, liked it much more than was safe. "To do what?"

"Whatever we want. Any suggestions?"

"I'd like to see the ranch where you grew up," she decided impulsively. "And if it's warm enough and it won't hurt your knee, I'd like to hike into the hills behind your house and have a picnic."

The look he gave her was unsettling. Resignation coloring her voice, she sighed. "I know what you're thinking. Laura wasn't much of an outdoors person. Except for a little exhibitionism at the lake, she didn't care for insects, dirt, wind that could muss her hair or sun that could age her skin. But you asked what *I* wanted to do. Not her."

Buck came a few steps toward her, and she backed away—but only because she knew she would soon reach the wall. Only because she knew *he* would soon reach *her*.

"You're wrong," he said quietly.

"About Laura?" He was so close now that she had to tilt her head back to see his face. He was in need of a shave and about eight hours of sound sleep, and he was scowling again, and his eyes were smoky and enigmatic. He was dangerous and dark and appealing, and he was handsome— God help her—too handsome for words.

"About what I'm thinking." When she finally reached the wall, he braced one hand above her head, the other at her side, and slowly, a bit at a time, leaned toward her.

"Then tell me."

"I was thinking that I'd like to see you at the ranch where I grew up. And that I'd like to share something as normal as a picnic with you. And how much I'd like..." A mere inch or two from her mouth, he stopped both his movement and his words.

Carly couldn't force even one small breath into her lungs, couldn't look at anything except his mouth and the sexy dark stubble that shadowed it, couldn't feel anything except tension and need. Anticipation. Hunger.

But in one instant the certainty that he was going to kiss her—*really* kiss her—gave way to the equal certainty that he wasn't. It was in the sudden distance he placed between them, even though he didn't move at all. It was in the regret that touched his mouth and in the sudden veiling of arousal in his eyes.

Slowly he backed away, putting a few feet, then half the room, between them. Avoiding her gaze, he returned the rocker to its place in the corner and picked up his jacket from the dresser. "I'll wait for you in the restaurant."

He left without telling her what it was he would like so much, but it was just as well, Carly thought, alone in the room with its still-simmering tension. She might be naive, but she could recognize desire.

She could *feel* his desire, could feel it hot and tingly and powerful deep inside herself. And she could feel her own, less focused, less experienced but no less powerful.

There was only one problem. There was no question who *her* desire was for. In the short three-year history of her life, Buck Logan was the only man she had ever wanted this way.

But who did *he* want? she wondered morosely. Her? Or Laura?

Chapter 8

Buck wasn't sure exactly what he had expected when he'd suggested a day off together. A pleasant time, he supposed. Nice conversation. Companionship that he was beginning to rely on.

What he got was a lazy, sweet, uncomplicated, nothing-special sort of day.

And he was enjoying it more than he could have imagined. The conversation, the quiet, the laughter, the discovering. Even the arousal that seemed to have settled permanently deep in his belly was more pleasure than demand. More gentle, less insistent. More natural. Normal.

After a quick trip to his house for a shower and a change of clothes, they had driven out to the ranch, empty now and unused, bought by some distant Billings businessman and forgotten. He had shown her the small, two-story house, once painted pale blue to please his mother but now faded and peeling, its uncurtained windows giving it a look of surprise at its abandonment. The buildings and corrals were in sorry shape, slowly wearing down under the constant assault of wind, rain and snow, heat and neglect.

They had walked and talked—rather, *he* had talked, and Carly had listened. She had gently prodded him for stories, details, long-forgotten memories, and had listened to—had absorbed—all of it. In his life he had gotten more than his share of female attention—star quarterbacks were lucky that way—but he couldn't remember any other woman who had displayed as much interest, as much innocent pleasure, in him as Carly did.

And he couldn't remember any other woman he had wanted more than Carly.

He had wanted but never needed the high school cheerleader, the college girls, the single women he'd dated when he had returned to Nowhere.

He had needed but never wanted Laura.

But his need and desire for Carly had become so entwined that he couldn't tell where one stopped and the other began. He didn't know where physical gave way to emotional.

He just knew he liked the feeling.

Now they were back on his own property, following what had once been a path but had long since returned to nature. Carly walked beside him when possible, skipping ahead or dropping behind when the trail narrowed. She wore a thin quilt around her shoulders like an ancient shawl, faded colors, neat piecing, uneven stitches. It was a sin to quilt with perfectly even stitches, his grandmother had taught him years ago, because only God could create perfection.

Maybe He had failed terribly on his first try, Buck thought with a grin as he watched Carly, but this second time around, He just might have achieved perfection. She was achingly beautiful, honey-sweet, bright and kind and gentle. Except for the beauty, she was the complete opposite of Laura.

She was everything he wanted.

And, because of Laura, she was everything he was afraid to take.

This morning in her room he had wanted to kiss her, had wanted it with a hunger in his soul. And she had wanted it, too. He had seen her eyes go soft, her lips part, had heard her breathing grow shallow and uneven.

But he couldn't do it. He had looked at her—at Laura's face—and he just couldn't kiss her. Even if she didn't remember, *he* did. He remembered the manipulation, the tormenting, the mockery. He remembered the pain of losing his control, his pride, his very self to her. To Laura. And no matter how she had changed, Carly *was* Laura. She had Laura's face and Laura's body, and it stood to reason that somewhere down inside, she had Laura's heart and Laura's beyond-redemption black soul.

And that scared the hell out of him.

He still wanted her, but with a soft, gentle kind of wanting that didn't make him ache too badly at night to sleep. It didn't send its own little brand of torture slicing through him. It didn't leave him feeling raw and hopelessly lost, damned if he took her and equally damned if he didn't.

It didn't threaten him. If he made love to Carly, it would be sweet and gently satisfying. If he didn't, he wouldn't experience anything more than a mild discomfort. A tender loss. A lifetime's regret.

Wanting her couldn't destroy him.

Unless he took her.

And Laura returned.

The trail wound steadily higher, dipping through shallow hollows, skirting trees and boulders, until finally they reached their destination. The valley spread out before them, with Nowhere straight ahead, the interstate curving in and out to the right, the mountains forming the other side a few miles distant.

And to the left a narrow strip of gray appeared, then disappeared. The highway that led to the lake.

Earlier Carly had called Laura an exhibitionist for her penchant for having sex at the lake. And what did that make him? Buck wondered grimly as he unwrapped the quilt from her shoulders and spread it on the ground.

A fool.

No, he disagreed, settling onto the quilt. Turning away from Carly because of Laura—*that* was foolish. That was letting her continue to run his life, to make his decisions, to control him. For all practical purposes, Laura no longer existed, but he was still giving her power over him. His memories of her were still frightening him.

"This place is beautiful," Carly said, joining him on the quilt. "Did you miss it when you lived in Nebraska?"

"Yes, I did." Abruptly, without stopping to consider his reason, he asked, "Will you miss it when you return to Seattle?"

She looked at him, so lovely and thoughtful and just a little bit sad; then she answered as simply as he had. "Yes, I will."

"I wish…" This time he did consider it and bit off the words. There were so many ways he could have finished. *I wish you were different. I wish you weren't blond and blue-eyed and beautiful. I wish I didn't look at you and see Laura. I wish you really were Carly. I wish I could be sure Laura was gone forever.* And most of all…. *I wish you could stay.*

With me.

Forever.

When he didn't go on, she reached across his grandmother's quilt, laying her hand gently on his knee. "Let me guess," she said, a smile on her lips that didn't quite touch her eyes. "You wish I hadn't stopped in Nowhere. You wish you had never come back from Nebraska. You wish the government had built their interstate someplace else and let this town shrivel up and die away. You wish this corner of Montana had never been settled. You wish for whatever it would have taken to protect you and your town and your memories from me."

Her touch was feathery light, but he felt it in every nerve ending in his body. He felt the heat, the weight, the pleasure and the longing for more, so much more.

A damned fool. If he turned away from her, from this, that was exactly what he would be.

Slowly he claimed her hand, lacing his fingers with hers, and just as slowly he pulled her to him. "Wrong again, honey," he murmured, then lied, "I was wishing I could do this."

He kissed her, the slow and easy possession that he'd been hungering for ever since he'd awakened and seen her standing in that thin cotton gown in front of that sunlit window. And he realized that he hadn't lied at all. This was exactly what he'd been wishing for. Nice. Not hot. Not wild. Just a gradually growing awareness. A mild stirring deep in his belly that was lazily curling, growing, ebbing, strengthening.

Reaching blindly, he found her shoulders and drew her closer. Dipping his head, he slid his tongue inside her mouth. She tasted warm and sweet and innocent, God help him, so innocent. He wanted to take that from her, to take and take until the ache in his soul had been eased. Until the hunger in his heart had been satisfied. Until the wounds she'd inflicted had been healed.

He wanted to take it all.

She would give him anything, Carly thought dazedly as he tasted and probed and filled. Anything to make this moment, this feeling, last. Her kisses, if that was all he would take. Her body if he wanted it. Her heart if he believed in it.

She had been kissed more than a few times, but never like this. Not so greedily. So tenderly. So gently. Never so right.

Raising her hands, she allowed herself the luxury for the first time of touching a man with intimate caresses. She brushed her fingers across his chest, over soft, worn cotton that covered broad shoulders, powerful muscles, a flat stomach. He tensed as she stroked him, and through her hands she felt a shiver ripple through him. She wanted more, wanted to touch his skin, wanted to look at him, wanted so much to kiss him that she trembled with it.

Her exploring hands reached the waistband of his jeans, and Buck stiffened, alarm displacing some portion of his desire, fear staking its claim dead center in his hunger. Dating had been difficult for Carly because the men she'd chosen had wanted things from her that she couldn't remember. She probably hadn't been to bed with a man in the last three years. He had counted on that, had relied on her sweet innocence to help erase his memories of Laura. She was supposed to be naive. Inexperienced. Not bold. Not aggressive.

Her hands remained at his waist, toying with his belt buckle, a moment longer. Then she slid them up, over his stomach and his chest to his shoulders. Ending the kiss with a sigh of relief, Buck held her for a moment, then slowly let her go.

They sat there on the quilt, staring at each other. She looked a little surprised, a lot aroused and the slightest bit frightened. He looked aroused, too. Pleased. Satisfied.

"That was nice," he said after a moment of soft, shivery silence.

Carly smiled. *Nice* was such a bland word. Not many women would take such a remark as a compliment—certainly Laura wouldn't—but she appreciated it. Everything she had learned about Buck and Laura had shown that he'd had very few nice times with her. Angry ones, yes, and bitter and dark and hate-filled, but never nice. And that was what he wanted most. Nice and normal.

Lucky for her, that was exactly what she was.

Now, at least.

Pulling her gaze from him, she opened the backpack he had carried from the cabin and began removing their lunch. He had suggested sandwiches and chips; she had voted for fried chicken and potato salad. They had compromised on ribs, cole slaw and baked beans from Pete's, with two pieces of pecan pie from Hazel's kitchen for dessert.

"Is kissing me the same as kissing her?" she asked nonchalantly as she spooned cole slaw and beans onto his plate. When she leaned across to hand it to him, he was looking both annoyed and offended. It made her laugh. "Oh, please, Sheriff, don't pretend that you're not constantly comparing us. She was hateful and I'm not. She was perfect and I'm not. She was a bitch and I'm not. She was sexy and I'm not." Her voice grew a bit wistful on that last one, and she quickly hid it. "So...do we kiss alike?"

He accepted the plate, adding a couple of ribs to it from the foil-wrapped packet, and avoided her question. "She wasn't perfect, not by a long shot."

"She was beautiful," Carly reminded him. That was the one thing everyone, regardless of their feelings for Laura, seemed to agree on.

"Not as beautiful as you are."

"Yes, I'm sure with this nose and this scar that I totally outshine her."

"There's nothing wrong with your nose or the scar," he said chidingly. Then, grimness stealing his voice, he said, "Laura's beauty was flawed because *she* was flawed. Her personality was warped. She lacked compassion. And she wasn't sexy. She was a very sexual person, always aware of her sexuality and its effect on others. It was intense, overwhelming and not always pleasant. Being with her was kind of like being in an elevator with someone who reeks of perfume. In small doses the fragrance might be all right, but too much of it will make you sick.''

And Laura had made *him* sick—sick of her and sick of himself. ''Maybe she didn't leave Nowhere to punish you,'' she said thoughtfully. ''Maybe she just wanted to be someone new.''

''She didn't have to go away to accomplish that.''

''Didn't she? Think about the way you acted my first few days here. It had been three years since you'd seen her, yet you weren't willing to accept that she might have changed. It would have been impossible to change right here in Nowhere, where everyone knew her and expected the worst from her.'' She tossed the bone from the rib she'd been eating into a slowly growing pile, then licked barbecue sauce from her fingers. ''But that's all beside the point. You never answered my question. Was kissing me like kissing Laura?''

She expected another evasion, but instead he laughed. ''Not in the slightest. Laura hadn't been that…'' He broke off to find the right word. Watching him, Carly silently supplied a few possibilities. Clumsy. Naive. Inexperienced.

''She hadn't been that innocent since she was thirteen years old,'' he finished.

Innocent. Like nice, it was an odd little word, capable of flattering or giving offense. But as much as she wished it weren't so, like nice and normal, innocent was exactly what she was. She'd had lovers—including Buck—but couldn't remember any of them. She couldn't remember the things they had done, the things she had done. She couldn't remember the feelings or the needs or the desires that had driven her. It was all new to her, new and exciting and scary as hell.

She was reaching for another slab of meat when he touched her. "I do compare you and Laura a lot. I wish I didn't, but under the circumstances, I think it's only normal. Just for the record...*she's* the one coming up short. *She's* the one who can't compete. You're everything that she could never be."

"Nice and innocent," she said, her voice husky, betraying her weak attempt to tease. "Just what every thirty-something woman wants to be."

The food forgotten, Buck leaned over and kissed her again. He tasted like their lunch—rich, smoky, spicy, dark—but the flavors were uniquely his. They tempted and tantalized her, feeding her hunger and making her crave more, more of this, more of everything, more of *him*.

When he ended the kiss, he didn't immediately release her. Instead he drew the pad of his thumb gently across her lips, still parted, and felt the warm puffs of her breath, still uneven. "Nice and innocent," he repeated softly. "It may not be what you want, but, honey..." He sighed gently. "It's exactly what I need."

Friday afternoon Buck tried again on his call to the Texas Department of Vital Statistics. Once again he was placed on hold, but finally he had the information he'd asked for.

Mark and Helene Johnson were dead.

Just as Carly had said.

It didn't prove anything, he explained to her over dinner in Missoula that evening. Just that she had been thorough in creating her new identity.

"Maybe it just means that my parents really are dead," she countered.

"Carly—"

"Hear me out, Sheriff," she interrupted. "You've explained your theory on how Laura came to be Carly. Now just listen to me, please." She took a deep breath, then asked, "Do you truly believe I am Laura?"

"Yes."

"That was too quick. I want you to *think* about it. You were skeptical about the amnesia. You weren't really sure that the injuries from the accident could explain such a total change. You accused me of pretending, remember?"

Grudgingly he nodded.

"What if you were right? What if the head injuries *couldn't* account for the differences between Laura and me?" She gave him only a moment to consider it. "You said yesterday that we don't kiss alike. You've pointed out other differences, too—basic things, things that make up who we are. Laura hated babies. I love them. She was vain. I'm not. She liked getting rough. I couldn't. Our taste in clothes, even in food, is totally different. Can a head injury explain that? If you banged your head tonight and woke up from a coma next month, would you suddenly love brussels sprouts and pickles and hate rocky road ice cream?"

"I don't know what a head injury can do," he replied stiffly. "But if you aren't Laura, how do you know I hate brussels sprouts and pickles? How do you know I like rocky road?"

She looked dejected, disappointed that she'd let the information slip. "Lucky guess," she muttered in a voice that sounded anything but lucky.

"Carly..." He sighed, feeling disappointed himself.

"Do I *feel* like her?" she asked sharply. "You've spent a lot of time with me. You've kissed me. You've had your arms around me. Do I feel like Laura? When you're with me, do you have the same feelings you had with her?"

Buck wanted to end the conversation right here, but he forced himself to give serious consideration to her question. Did he feel the same things for Carly that he had for Laura?

No way. All the emotions he had invested in Laura had been negative, draining, destructive. When he had kissed Carly, when his eyes had been closed and he'd held her, had it been like kissing Laura? No. She could have been any other woman in the world *but* Laura.

When he was with her, did she *feel* like Laura? In an intangible sense, an almost spiritual sense, the answer was no. Physical resemblance aside, there was nothing about her to remind him of Laura. No familiarity. No connection.

"No," he said gently. "You don't feel like Laura. But that doesn't prove that you aren't. It just proves that you have changed a great deal in the last three years."

She sat back in her chair, her appetite gone, her spirits dampened. She remained that way until they were in his pickup and on the way back to Nowhere. "I really don't want to be her," she said softly as she gazed out the side window.

"I know. But finding out the truth doesn't change anything, Carly. Just because you *used* to be Laura Phelps doesn't mean you have to be again. You can stay Carly forever."

She heard the oddly hopeful note in his voice and gave him a wry smile. "Is that what you're hoping for? That I stay Carly forever? That Laura never comes back?"

Buck reached across the seat, searching in the darkness until he found her hand. "Yeah," he admitted. "I guess it is."

"Me, too," she whispered, wrapping her fingers tightly around his.

The silence this time was comfortable, peaceful, the sort of silence any couple returning home from an evening out would share. For just a moment Buck let himself believe that was all they were—just any couple. Not a sheriff whose job was proving that the woman beside him was someone he couldn't love. Not a woman who might any day now remember who she was, what she was, and become that person again. For the next few miles they could be just a man and a woman who had shared a pleasant dinner and were on their way home where they would share a few pleasant kisses before saying good-night.

It was nearly ten o'clock when he parked across the street from the hotel. He shut off the engine, then looked at her.

"Thank you for dinner," Carly said. She removed her seat belt and faced him, but made no move to get out of the truck. "I enjoyed it."

"Tomorrow..." Breaking off, he pressed a kiss to the back of her hand.

"Yes? What about tomorrow?"

"I'll pick you up at ten."

"For what?"

For a visit to the one place significant to Laura that she hadn't yet seen. For a trip out of the valley to the lake above. For an attempt to jog loose some memory, some feeling, something.

But he didn't tell her that. The last time he had suggested taking her to the lake, she had refused. He wasn't going to argue with her now. They would simply go.

"I don't know," he lied. "We can decide then."

She cleared her throat uncomfortably. "You don't have to spend all your free time with me, Buck."

"I know." Without the restraint of the seat belt, he could pull her closer, and he did, not stopping until her body was snug against his. "Is that a polite way of saying that you don't want to spend tomorrow with me?" he asked, his voice little more than a murmur in her ear.

Her only response was a soft moan that faded away when he kissed her.

It was the only answer he needed.

* * *

Saturday morning Carly dressed in faded jeans and a sweater she'd bought in Helena nearly two weeks ago, a tweedy navy, maroon and tan sweater knitted of narrow strips of thin leather. The unique weave had caught her eye, and she'd paid out fully half of the money intended to get her home. She didn't regret the purchase, though, especially when she saw the appreciative look in Buck's eyes.

She offered him her last doughnut as they left the restaurant. Along with a breakfast of pancakes and bacon, she had already eaten one caramel-glazed doughnut, and since weeks had passed since she'd gotten any real exercise, she certainly didn't need the other. But when Buck took only half, she had no qualms at all about finishing the rest.

Unlike Laura, who wouldn't have been caught dead with a doughnut.

She took great comfort in pointing out differences between Laura and herself. Maybe she was seeking reassurance that she would never become the other woman again—reassurance that no one else could give her. Buck certainly couldn't, because he wasn't so sure himself.

"Where are we going?" she asked as they headed out of town.

"To one of the prettiest places in the county."

"Your house?" She liked the cabin and the woods that surrounded it. She liked spending time there. She liked knowing that this was where he lived, where he slept.

Where he loved.

"You'll see" was all he would say.

She watched as they passed the turnoff for his house with a pang of disappointment. That quickly gave way to suspicion. To dread. When she looked across the cab at him, his stony, stern expression confirmed her fears. "I don't want to go there," she said in a soft, strained, impatient voice.

"Why not?" he asked. But he didn't slow down. He

didn't pull to the side of the road and stop as he'd done before. He didn't look for a place to turn around.

"I don't want to see it."

"It's just a lake—a pretty one. You'll like it," he replied flatly.

"I won't like it. Take me back to town, Buck. I don't want to go there!"

He glanced across at her. He wasn't as hard and cold as his expression had indicated. There was regret in his eyes, an unspoken apology. But there was also determination. "We won't stay long."

"I don't want..." Taking a deep breath, she let her protest fade away. Without a reason—a damned good one—he wasn't going to listen to her. He wasn't going to turn around and take her away from here. And he wasn't going to accept an excuse like "I don't want to go there."

But she didn't.

She didn't want to see the place where he and Laura had made love. She didn't want to stand beside the lake that had drawn Laura, indoor Laura, didn't-like-nature Laura, to its shores. She didn't want to know that this was where she had tempted fate—and Buck—with her exhibitionist tendencies.

Most of all, she didn't want to risk remembering. Granted, she wanted to know what kind of lover Buck was—the possibilities teased and tantalized her—but she wanted to know how he made love to Carly. Not how he had sex with Laura.

She didn't want to remember *anything* about Buck with Laura.

Sitting stiffly in her seat, feeling as frozen and rigid inside as he looked outside, she stared straight ahead and waited.

The road rounded one last curve and ended in a grassy clearing. There were trees, ancient pines, and overgrown grass that had yellowed after the short summer. The ground was littered with beer cans and food wrappers, and pieces of a broken bottle lay at the base of one tree.

Buck shut off the engine and got out, but Carly didn't move. She couldn't. From here she couldn't see the lake. She knew it must be over the small rise up ahead, but she wasn't going to walk up there and see. She *wasn't*.

He opened her door and waited only a moment, then leaned inside, brushing close, and unfastened her seat belt. He took both her hands in his and drew her from the truck, shutting the door with his foot before forcing her up the hill.

She tried to cooperate. If she did, the quicker they could get this over with, the quicker she could get away from here. But her feet wouldn't obey her brain's orders. It took all her energy and a good deal of Buck's to get her to the top of the slope, and she knew she couldn't possibly go any farther unless he picked her up and carried her.

But he was satisfied with the top of the hill. He let her stand there, his arm around her shoulders, his free hand tightly gripping hers, and let her look around.

He had called it one of the prettiest places in the county, but he was wrong. There was nothing pretty about this place. The lake was small, the water dark and murky, threatening. The air was cold, the sky cloudy while elsewhere the sun still shone. The grass and weeds along the banks were dead and yellow, and the trees were a hundred feet tall, as if they, like her, wanted to get away from here.

It was malevolent.

Evil.

Beside her Buck shifted, then released her hand. "We used to go over there," he said, his voice flat and emotionless, as he pointed in the direction of a small cove on the distant shore. "We only came in the after—"

"No," she whispered. "*No.* I don't want to hear this! I

don't want to know!" Jerking away from him, she spun around and started down the hill again. If she walked fast enough, she could escape this place, could escape this fear, this sickness. She heard Buck call her name, but she didn't stop. She heard his footsteps behind her, but she only walked faster and faster. By the time she reached his truck, she was running, out of breath, desperately cold, trembling, unable to grasp the handle enough to open the damned door.

She had just managed the latch when he wrapped his arms around her, pulling her against him, holding her tight. "It's okay," he whispered. "Honey, it's okay."

She might have believed him, might have let go of the fear and the distaste, might have sunk into his arms and let him calm her. She might have...

If he hadn't kissed her.

It was no different from his other kisses, sweet and gentle and searching, but she couldn't bear it, not here, not in this place where he'd brought Laura, not in this place where it would be so easy for him to believe she *was* Laura. *His* Laura. The Laura he claimed to have hated, but had never walked away from. Not even when *she* had walked away from *him*.

Shoving him away required every ounce of strength she could find, but she did it, and did it hard. "Don't do that, don't touch me, don't..." She dragged in a shuddering breath. "Oh, God, I've got to get away from here. Please..."

He was looking at her with a wounded look that made her flinch. Hurt because she had pushed him away? Because she hadn't remembered anything about their love-making here? Because she so obviously didn't *want* to remember anything?

She didn't care. All she cared about was leaving.

He didn't say anything, but opened the door for her.

When she stumbled—her muscles were too taut, her nerves too jerky, for grace—he caught her, and he didn't release her until she was inside the pickup. A moment later he climbed in beside her, started the engine and headed back down into the valley.

Carly was shivering. She had never seen any other place that had had that strong an effect on her. It was an awful place...but more than three years ago, she had gone there regularly. She and Buck had gone there to do things on the shore that she couldn't remember doing. What was it about the lake that had appealed to her then? Its nature that was as dark and forboding as her own? Had that been part of the turn-on, along with the sun and the open space, the risk of being seen, of getting caught with the sheriff? Had making love in such a menacing place appealed to her sense of perversity?

The sheriff. Hesitantly she glanced across at him. He was clutching the steering wheel with both hands, his knuckles pale. His jaw was taut, his mouth a thin line, and there was thunder in his eyes. There was no denying his anger, but was it for her? For Laura? For himself? She couldn't guess, and she couldn't ask. She couldn't say anything at all.

He turned off the road into his driveway. Maybe he had to pick up something before he returned her to the hotel, Carly thought unhappily. Surely he would take her back. Surely he wouldn't want to spend the rest of the day with her now when he couldn't even bear to look at her or speak to her.

But almost immediately he broke his silence, commanding her to come into the house. And he wasn't there on any errand. He jerked his jacket off and tossed it in a chair, threw his keys on the coffee table with enough force to send them skittering off the other side, and dropped into the rocker hard enough to set it in motion. Picking up the remote control, he turned on the television, switched channels until he found a football game and directed his attention to it.

She stood near the door a long time, unwilling to come in and sit down or to walk out by herself. She had to know that if she left, he would come after her, Buck thought. He would never let her go wandering off alone.

He didn't understand her reaction to the lake. Laura had never feared the place. She had liked it, had dragged him up there a hundred times too many. She had felt comfortable there.

But Carly wasn't exactly Laura.

Or was she?

Never shifting his gaze from the television, he rubbed the scratch she had left on his throat when she'd pushed him away. The action made it sting, but he didn't stop. The little tingle of pain distracted him, kept his defenses in place, kept him from leaving the rocker and approaching her again, trying to comfort her again.

Pushing him away had been one of Laura's games. Manipulating, teasing, playing, arousing, then walking away. Purring in that throaty voice, "Sorry, lover, I've changed my mind." It had served as a demonstration of her power over him, one that she hadn't used often, but enough to make him despise it. Enough to make him despise her.

But he didn't despise Carly.

She hadn't meant to hurt him—he knew that as surely as he knew his own name. She had been upset, almost panicked, and it was his fault because he had forced her to go to a place that she couldn't bear seeing.

He gave her a sidelong glance, and the last of his anger and fear drained away. She looked lost and so damned confused. Laying the remote on the table, he left the rocker and slowly approached her, stopping a dozen feet away. She looked at him, sniffled, then looked away again, and still he just stood there. He wouldn't go to her. He wouldn't give her another chance to reject him. But if she wanted him…

After another sniffle, she looked at him again, and he offered her a hesitant smile. He opened his arms, and that decided the issue for her. Hiccuping softly, she walked right into his embrace, wrapping her arms tightly around his waist, hiding her face against his shirt.

Buck closed his eyes, his expression a mix of peace, regret and acceptance. If Laura returned, if the real Laura found her way out of the memories Carly had buried, he would be well and truly damned, because there was no way he could protect himself. There was no way he could stop wanting Carly even if she no longer existed.

And knowing that, knowing how much he stood to lose, there was no way he could walk away from her now.

"That place scared me," she whispered, his shirt muffling her voice.

"It's all right. You won't have to go there again."

For a long time he held her, feeling the shivers that made her tremble. In spite of the sniffles, he didn't think she was crying, but the tears had been close. Slowly her chill faded, and the shudders did, too, and still he held her, listening to her breathe, feeling her relax.

Finally, when she looked up at him, he tentatively kissed her, giving her plenty of chances to draw away. When she didn't, when instead she held him tighter and welcomed him into her mouth, he unleashed the need building inside him, just a little, not enough to frighten her.

She wasn't frightened, but she was sad, and the tears made a sudden appearance. When he tasted the first one, he lifted his head. "Honey, what's wrong?" he whispered.

"I'm not Laura," she replied in a voice that quavered and cracked. "I'm not your Laura. I can't be her for you."

And that was cause for tears? He preferred celebration

himself. "I don't want the Laura I used to know. I want *you*."

"Are you sure? When you kissed me at the lake…"

"I was kissing *you*."

"Were you? If I had another face, another body, if I didn't look anything like Laura, if you knew beyond a doubt that I was someone else…would you still want me instead of her?"

He brushed her hair from her face, then dried the tear that was sliding down her cheek. "Listen to me. I don't want Laura. I'm not looking at your face and pretending that she's inside. God, that's been more of a deterrent than an incentive. It's been hard as hell to look at you and accept that you're different. I don't care how you look. I don't care what name you call yourself." His next words were nearly lost in his kiss. "I want *you*. Just you."

Carly believed him. Maybe because she wanted to, maybe because, heaven help her, she *needed* to, but she believed him, and believing brought the sweetest pleasure she had ever known. Maybe this was why Laura had gone away, why fate had brought Carly back: so she and Buck could share this moment. This pleasure. This loving.

Their kisses went on forever, warm, hungry, fever-building kisses that made her ache with a need long forgotten, that made her breasts swell and her nipples harden. When he cupped her breasts in his palms, the pleasure was so exquisite that it made her groan, and when he pulled his hands away to draw her close, she almost groaned at that, too.

"I want to make love to you, Carly," he murmured, his breath hot and tickling her ear. "I know you haven't…that you don't remember…"

She silenced him with her fingers over his mouth. "Yes."

"What?" Sounding surprised, he brushed her hand away, then brought it back for a kiss.

"Please."

Still holding her hand, Buck studied her for a long moment. She looked like an innocent young girl—her cheeks were flushed, her lips slightly swollen, her eyes dazed—and yet she was a woman, a beautiful woman. A woman, for all intents and purposes, as virginal as any teenage girl. A woman who remembered nothing about making love, about seducing and satisfying. A woman who had been unwilling to let any of the men she'd dated refresh her memory.

A woman who trusted *him* enough to let him.

Suddenly he felt young, too, and naive and clumsy. It wasn't a memory lapse or inexperience that haunted him. It was simply the difference between seducing a woman he was fond of, surrendering to a woman he disliked, and making love to a woman that he was too damned close to loving.

"I've never done this before," he murmured.

For an instant her blue eyes widened, then she laughed softly. "Yeah, right."

"Not like this. Not with someone special."

Her eyes widened again, but this time she didn't laugh. This time she pulled his head down to hers and kissed him sweetly, passionately, gently.

He took her down the hall and into his bedroom. She followed him willingly, watched him trustingly as he closed the drapes, shutting out the midday sun. God, she looked so damned trusting. What if he disappointed her? What if he hurt her? What if…

His capacity for thought, for questions and doubts, disappeared in about ten seconds—the time it took Carly to catch the hem of her sweater and draw it agonizingly slowly over her head. Underneath she wore a bra that was pale and thin, lavished with lace. While he watched, his throat dry, his voice lost, she unfastened it and slid the narrow straps down her arms, letting it fall to the floor with her sweater.

Her movements were purely seductive…but the uneasy, am-I-doing-this-right? look in her eyes was pure innocence. He went to her, pulling her close, and she came eagerly, pressing against him so all he could see was the smooth skin of her shoulders and the soft curves of her breasts.

He kissed her slowly, lazily, taking his own sweet time. He had never made love to a woman so totally without experience, but he was going to make sure she enjoyed every second of it. He was going to kiss her until she burned, stroke her until she was weak, arouse her until she couldn't bear anymore, and then he was going to give her such satisfaction that she would weep.

He was going to teach her how to love.

Hell, he was also going to teach himself a thing or two.

Like how it felt to make love.

How it felt to be normal.

How it felt to be in control.

So far, it felt pretty damned good. Their kisses were making her tremble, but he was all right. He was aroused—so much that it was almost painful—but not unbearably so. He wanted her, but not wildly, passionately, not as if he would die if he didn't have her. He was hot, but it wasn't the kind of heat that threatened to consume him, not a heat of hellish proportions.

He was normal.

This was normal.

He stroked her skin, so soft and smooth, and left a trail of kisses all the way down to her breast. Drawing her nipple between his teeth, he sucked gently, and felt a surprising tug deep in his belly. He bathed the small peak with his tongue, making it harden, and felt a corresponding swelling of his own. Damn, it had been so long. He had forgotten what it was like to make love to someone he cared for, had forgotten that in arousing her, he would arouse himself. But that was all right. That was normal. He could control it.

Carly wasn't sure what she had expected. A slick, practiced seduction from a man who knew all the right things to do and all the right ways to do them? Gentle passion? Fiery need?

But she hadn't expected to feel so special. So treasured. She hadn't expected the weakness or the raw need. She hadn't expected his soft groan when she tentatively slid her hand beneath his shirt, or the quivering in his muscles as she stroked him. She hadn't expected the intensity, the trembling, the soft greedy sounds that were hers, the softer helpless sounds that were his.

She hadn't expected the love. Not his—she didn't expect him to love her, but she felt too much too strongly to regret that now—but her own. Heaven help her, she loved him.

Clumsily pulling at the fabric, she tugged his shirt over his head, then stroked his chest, following smooth skin and taut muscles downward to the barrier of his jeans. Suddenly timid, she would have withdrawn then, but he caught her hand in his and guided it lower, pressing her palm against his arousal, gently folding her fingers around him. He was so hot and thick, so hard. She wanted to snatch her hand away, yet at the same time she wanted to open his jeans and boldly stroke him, flesh to throbbing, heated flesh.

Buck sucked in his breath at her hesitant, shy caress. The control he craved was slipping, and everything she did— every kiss, every brush, every caress—was further eroding it. His eyes shut tight, he stiffened as she pressed an open kiss to his nipple.

Not like this. He didn't want it this way, didn't want to feel so intensely that he shuddered with it, didn't want his body to betray him this way. He summoned his strength to push her away, to give himself time to regain control, to slow his heart rate and ease this fierceness, but then she cupped his face in her palms and kissed him so gently, so inexpertly, so trustingly, that he knew he couldn't stop. He could never stop.

He removed the rest of their clothing, his first, then hers, and lowered her to the bed, joining her there, stroking, playing, teasing. He noticed the small scars, thin white lines against smooth tanned skin, souvenirs from the accident that had almost killed her, and he kissed, then forgot, them. Scars included, she was beautiful, more perfectly beautiful than any woman had a right to be.

Her breathing had become shallow, her body sensitive to his slightest touch, and he was on the edge himself, ready to plead for completion, for relief. Moving between her legs, he braced his weight on his arms and, biting his lip against the sheer pleasure, he eased inside her little by little, pushing until she gloved him, tight and hot, hot enough to sear. Hot enough to destroy.

This was all too much, more than he had wanted, more than he had bargained for. This need—this joining—wasn't pleasing and gentle, mild and tender. It was passionate. Savage. Powerful. It wasn't simple cravings that were part lust, part affection. It wasn't innocent.

But it was the most exquisite thing he had ever experienced.

It was the sweetest.

It was the fiercest.

Practiced. Experienced. He was definitely that, Carly thought, a drowsy, hazy smile curving her mouth. He knew exactly how to touch her, where to kiss her, exactly how to move inside her to create such incredible sensations. With his hands beneath her, he showed her how to move, how to match the rhythm of his deep, filling thrusts, how to sharpen the hunger, ease a little, then increase it again.

And with his voice, his rich dark voice, hoarse and guttural, he encouraged her, soothed her, whispered sweet, soft pleas to her.

When the release he'd promised her came, it surprised her with its intensity, with the weakness and the longing and the pain and the visceral pleasure. It overwhelmed her, drained her, tearing a helpless whimper from deep inside her. It would have frightened her except that Buck was sharing it with her, holding her, murmuring soft comfort.

And after the shudders had subsided, after the frantic beat of her heart had slowed, after the ragged gasps of her breathing had deepened, he still held her. He moved to lie beside her, to gather her close, and he rubbed her with soft little touches and kissed her with soft little kisses.

She had never felt as safe as she did in his arms.

She had never felt so special.

She had never, not in three whole years, felt so alive.

Buck lay next to Carly, watching her sleep, listening to the slow, steady sound of her breathing. Where their lovemaking had stimulated him, leaving him edgy and alert, it had drained every last bit of tension from her. Her body was limp, her sleep deep.

After a moment, he slipped from the bed and located his jeans on the other side. He stepped into them, zipping them, then bent to pull the covers over her. For a moment, he just stood there, stroking her hair gently; then abruptly he turned and left the room.

Everything had changed in the last hour. *Everything.* This morning at the hotel, at the lake, hell, right here in this house, he had been absolutely positive that the woman calling herself Carly was really Laura Phelps. In spite of her arguments and her desperate need to believe otherwise, he had been certain beyond a doubt. He had walked into the bedroom fully believing that he was going to make love—to *make love,* damn it—to Carly. Who was really Laura.

And he'd just walked out equally positive that she wasn't.

Do I feel like Laura? she had asked last night. No, he had told her. No, but... No, followed by an excuse. A reasonable, rational excuse.

The last hour had blown reason and rationale all to hell.

He didn't understand it. All the evidence supported just the opposite—the resemblance, the memories, the medallion. But all the evidence was wrong. He didn't know how to explain it beyond instinct. Emotion. Gut feelings. But, damn it, he knew it was so.

Carly Johnson, the woman he had just made love to, the woman asleep in his bed, the woman he had fallen in love with...

Carly Johnson was not Laura Phelps.

Chapter 9

Did it matter? Buck wondered. Other than the surprise, the disorientation of finding out that something he'd believed one hundred percent was wrong, did it matter that Carly wasn't Laura? Did it make a difference in the way he felt?

Did it make him love her any less?

No.

Nothing could do that.

But it did add weight to a few questions he'd brushed off earlier as unimportant. Such as why she had made up a false former address on her job application. Why she had lied about the schools she'd attended. Why she had created a fictitious lawyer as a reference. Why she had needed new identification three years ago.

Maybe, as she had once suggested, she was wanted on legal charges somewhere. If so, her fingerprints were most likely on file with the FBI and they would notify him....

He let the thought trail away as he considered the absurdity of the idea. Carly a fugitive? No way. He would stake his reputation on it.

He was staking his future on it.

Maybe she had run away from someone—an estranged husband, a possessive boyfriend. Maybe she'd found herself in a desperate situation and had been forced to flee for her own safety. Or maybe she had simply wanted a new start for herself in Seattle, a new life with no reminders of the old one.

Or maybe she really was Laura. Maybe he simply wanted so badly not to be in love with Laura that he was fooling himself into believing it.

Maybe.

But he didn't think so.

So what should he do now? Continue looking into her background? Keep trying to prove that she was Laura? Start trying to prove that she wasn't? Or stop searching altogether? He'd told her that she could be Carly forever. If he stopped looking for the truth, she could do just that. After all, it was just a name. Proving that she was Laura wasn't going to change the woman she was now. Proving that she was Carly wouldn't change it, either. No matter what she called herself, she would remain the same sweet, gentle, loving woman.

Her life would remain a mystery, even to her.

There was only one thing he should do right now, Buck decided with a weary sigh as he rose from the hearth. Only one place he needed to be. Only one person to focus his attention on. He would deal with everything else later.

They would deal with it together.

Carly felt absurdly shy when she joined Buck in the kitchen a few hours later. She was dressed again, and her hair was neatly combed, and surely no one could tell by looking just how thoroughly he had made love to her. Still, she felt awkward. She had no practice at waking up in a man's arms, no practice at all at making slow, lazy love—twice—in the middle of the day. No practice at the after-the-lovemaking times.

He was wearing jeans and nothing else, and he was singing along with the radio in a nice baritone as he fixed their lunch. When he saw her, he interrupted the song and sent such a smug, self-satisfied grin her way that she laughed and her nervousness disappeared. "You think you're a real hotshot, don't you?" she asked as she walked around the counter to help him.

His grin grew even bigger. "I *know* I am."

She shook her head in mock dismay. "Men and their egos."

"Tell me that wasn't the best time you ever had." Before she could speak, he wagged his finger warningly. "And remember. *You* were the one in there moaning, *'Please.'*"

Taking two glasses from the cabinet, she disagreed. "That was *you*, Sheriff. *I* was the one who couldn't speak at all."

His grin faded as he looked down at her. "So tell me," he said quietly.

"It was the best time I ever had," she sincerely replied, then added, "at least in recent memory." She waited for his smile, but it didn't come. "That was kind of a joke—you know, recent memories are the only kind I have?"

But he wasn't amused. In a matter of seconds, he had become downright grim. "Will it bother you if that never changes? If you never remember? If you never know whether you're Carly or Laura?"

She busied herself with filling the glasses and setting out plates and silverware, all too aware of his unwavering gaze. Finally she looked up at him. "You and I are a lot alike, Buck. We've both had to give up dreams. We've both had to face the fact that we couldn't have the lives we wanted.

You had to give up your football career and create a new future for yourself. I lost my past. Maybe someday it will come back. Maybe someday I'll remember what it was like to be Laura. If it does, fine. But I'm not going to live on maybes. If I can't have a past, at least I can have the present. At least I can look forward to the future.''

He dished the grilled cheese sandwiches onto the plates, then carried them to the table. When she joined him there, he somberly asked, ''Do you want me to quit?''

Quit trying to prove that she was Laura. Quit trying to take away the identity she had clung to for three years. Quit trying to get to the truth. Why? she wondered. Why was he willing to do it now? Because after making love to her he was more certain than ever that she was Laura? Because he knew how desperately she didn't *want* to be Laura? Or because he didn't want to face the fact that, no matter how the idea appalled him, he was having an affair—again— with Laura?

''I would like to know,'' she said quietly.

''I don't care who you are.''

She smiled gently. ''Thank you. But I do care. Even if I can't have the rest of my life back, I would like to know who lived that life.''

''Even if you don't like what I find out?'' he asked skeptically.

''I can handle that.'' But what she couldn't handle, she admitted silently, was if *he* didn't like what he learned. If he turned away from her. If he no longer wanted her. But that was a risk she had to face regardless of whether he uncovered her true identity. He hadn't given any indication that he wanted her to stay when her leave from work was up. He hadn't hinted that he wanted her in his life next week, much less next month or next year. He hadn't given her any reason to believe that he cared about her any more than he had cared about all the other women in his life before Laura.

Yes, he had. He had called her special. *Someone special.* He had made love to her as if she were very special indeed.

But the compliment, sweet as it was, wasn't a vow of love or a promise of forever. And a few hours of incredible lovemaking, as sweet as they had been, wasn't anything he hadn't treated other women to.

So which would be worse? she wondered bleakly. To live without him?

Or to live without him and without her past, without even the simple knowledge of her real name?

Buck was sitting in front of a blazing fire Sunday morning, a cup of coffee in hand, waiting for Carly to wake up, and thinking. He couldn't seem to escape thinking about her these days—about wanting her. About loving her. About needing her.

He had been arrogant yesterday when he'd led her into his bedroom, intending to teach her about making love. Instead, *she* had done the teaching. She had shown him that passion could be positive, that hot and needy and wild could be good. She had shown him intensity underlaid with tenderness. Powerful desire built upon love.

She had shown him how natural and right and normal it could be.

She had taught him what loving was about.

Late last night, in the darkness of his room, she had asked the question he'd dreaded, the question he had sworn to himself he wouldn't answer. *Do I make love like Laura?*

But he had answered, and he had told her the truth— although not the whole truth. "No. You make love like Carly."

And it had satisfied her—had even, he'd thought as she had snuggled in closer, pleased her.

But this morning she might ask again. What would he tell her if she did? That making love with her wasn't even remotely similar to having sex with Laura? That she didn't make love like Laura because she *wasn't* Laura?

He wouldn't say anything without proof. For her sake, he had to prove one or the other. Either she was Laura or she was Carly. And since he didn't know how to prove she was Laura, he would prove that she was Carly instead. He would track down whatever information he could find on her.

He was putting another log on the fire when a knock sounded at the door. Brushing his hands on his sweatpants, he skirted the rocker and went to the door, opening it just as his guest started to knock again.

Trina smiled her odd little smile. "Buck. I thought maybe I'd come too early."

"I've been up a while." He glanced down the hall, wishing he had left the bedroom door open so Carly could hear their voices if she awoke. The last thing she needed early this morning was to face Trina. "What can I do for you?"

"Can I come in?"

He stepped back to allow her to pass, then followed her into the living room. She laid her purse down, then removed her coat. Great, he thought, keeping his uneven smile pasted in place through sheer will. Whatever she was here for was going to take a while. Long enough for Carly to wake up? Long enough for Trina to discover her here?

She sat down in the rocker and gestured for him to be seated, too. He chose the easy chair at the opposite end of the coffee table. "I wanted to talk to you while Mother's in church," she began. "I wanted to see what you've learned about Laura."

"I haven't learned anything about Carly except that her birth certificate is real and that her parents are dead, just as she said." And that she was as gentle with him as she'd been with Hazel's grandbaby. That she was lovely and fragile and inherently good. That she was passionate and sensitive, that she could arouse him with no more than a look, that she could make him beg if she wanted, but she never would.

"Why do you humor her by using that name?"

"Because it's the only name she knows, Trina," he said patiently.

"You're not falling for her again, are you? You're not accepting her lies? You, of all people, should know better. You know how evil she is. You know she doesn't deserve to be in this town with good people like my mother."

"What does Maureen think?" he asked quickly when she paused for breath. "Does she believe this is Laura?"

Trina gave a put-upon sigh. "Mother is a good Christian woman. She doesn't have an ounce of meanness in her, and she can't see it in someone else even when it's staring her in the face. She feels sorry for Laura. Can you believe that?" Her laugh was short and sharp. "The bitch took such pleasure in ruining people's lives. She lived off Daddy's money rather than get a job. She fed on other people's misery, and then she disappeared without so much as a goodbye, and now my mother feels sorry for her. 'Poor Laura must have had such a hard time these last three years,'" she mimicked. "Poor Laura should have died in that wreck. She should have *died*."

"But she didn't."

Buck's gaze jerked sharply to the hallway where Carly was standing. Even if she'd been completely dressed instead of wearing only one of his old football jerseys, there would have been no disguising the fact that she had just come from his bed. Her hair was mussed, the lines of her face soft, the look in her eyes one of pure sexual satisfaction.

She looked well and truly loved.

Trina, on the other hand, looked shocked. Disgusted. Dangerous. The gaze she turned on him was filled with loathing, making him understand for the first time what Carly had recognized immediately. Trina's hatred for Laura ran deep.

"You're a fool, Buck. She never cared about you. She never wanted you. She just wanted to break you. You were so big and strong, the football hero, the macho sheriff. She wanted to prove her power. She wanted to destroy you. And here you're giving her another chance to do it. You invite the bitch right back into your life. You couldn't wait to get her into your bed again, could you?" Scorn turned her voice sharp and cold. "You're a fool, Buck Logan. A damn idiotic fool."

Snatching up her purse and coat, she turned toward the door. Halfway there, she faced him again. "This time you'll have to pay for your stupidity. This time you'll be punished, too." Then, with a slam of the door, she was gone, leaving an air of malevolence in her wake.

Carly turned wide eyes on him. "She threatened you."

He stared at the empty entry until the sound of Trina's car faded away. Then he glanced at Carly. Her face was pale, her lips parted. She was afraid of Trina, he remembered. She sensed something about the woman that frightened her. Was it intuition? Or Laura's memories? "She was just talking," he said absently. "She would never do anything to me. I'm the sheriff, remember? I'd lock her up if she tried."

He had hoped to coax a smile, even a faint one, from her, but she wasn't giving up the apprehension so easily.

"Honey, I've known Trina all my life. She's not going to hurt me." And he believed that. Still… "Just to be on the safe side, keep your distance, will you? Don't go around her without Maureen or me."

"I shouldn't have come out here. I'm sorry. I didn't think...."

"She would have found out about us anyway when we check you out of the hotel this morning."

Slowly the shock faded, and it was replaced by a purely stubborn streak. Folding her arms across her chest, she regarded him evenly. "And why would we do that, Sheriff?"

"Because you're going to be spending your nights here with me." He slowly approached her. "Because there's no sense in you spending all that money for a room that you're not sleeping in."

"Are those the only reasons you can come up with?"

He filled his hands with the soft knit fabric of the jersey and pulled. "Oh, honey, I can come up with a really good one if you'll just give me a hand," he murmured, smiling wickedly.

Groaning, she let her head fall back, giving him access to her throat. "That's *bad*, Sheriff," she chided him.

"But we can make it so damn good." He was kissing his way down her throat, one bit of satiny skin at a time, when she sobered again and nudged him away.

"What if she wasn't just talking, Buck?" she asked worriedly. "Jealousy can be a powerful motivator. What if—"

He silenced her with a kiss. "Trust me, Carly. I know Trina. I know what she's capable of. I'm a good judge of character."

She relented grudgingly and with a challenge. "Prove it."

Sliding his hands beneath the jersey, he discovered that she was naked. The swift intensity of the arousal that knowledge created would have frightened him yesterday. This morning he found it perfectly natural. Perfectly normal. "All right," he murmured, gently pressing between her thighs, stroking beneath the soft curls there, seeking out her heat. "Your character must be stronger than mine because I certainly can't resist you any longer. If I don't get inside you, if I don't fill you here—'' he slid his finger inside and felt her moan vibrate through her ''—I'm going to die right now.''

She gave a soft sigh of surrender. ''We mustn't have that. How would I ever explain it to Deputy Harvey?''

He stroked her again for the sheer pleasure of watching her response, of seeing her eyes flutter shut, of hearing her breath catch, of feeling desire steal over her. Then, needing closer contact, he lifted her off the floor, surprising a startled laugh from her. ''Wrap your legs around me,'' he demanded hoarsely, and she did so, bringing her hips achingly tight against his.

He carried her to the bedroom and the rumpled bed, taking her down with him, wriggling free of his clothes, reaching for hers. There she stopped him, rolling away. When he would have protested, she hushed him with a kiss. ''I'm a quick student,'' she murmured with a sweet smile. ''Let me show you what I've learned.''

Her suggestion cleared the haze of desire and allowed the past—memory, with all its fear and loathing—to intrude. Carly saw the uneasiness in his eyes, the uncertainty, the distaste, and she realized what she had asked of him. *Let me seduce you. Give me control. Let me manipulate you, tease and arouse you.* The way Laura always had.

Settling on her knees beside him, she folded her hands in her lap. ''I would never hurt you.''

He moistened his lips. ''I know.''

''I would never do the things she did. I just want...'' She smiled unevenly. ''I just want to love you.'' Then, quickly, before he could realize exactly how she meant that, she went on. ''But that's all right. It was a bad idea. I understand.''

He held her gaze a long time, the wary look slowly disappearing from his eyes. ''Go ahead,'' he invited with a lazy, smug, taunting smile. "Show me what you've learned."

If it hadn't been for that smile, she would have refused. She would have silently cursed herself for bringing Laura into their bed, and she would have lain there passively and let him take the lead. But his smile was so smug, because he knew that everything she'd learned, she had learned from him. So taunting, because he knew she wouldn't back down from his challenge. He knew she would overlook that momentary discomfort and proceed exactly as she had originally planned.

And she couldn't even be annoyed because, damn it, he was right.

She kissed him, a slow and easy exploration of his mouth that wiped his smile away. This time *she* was the one probing and tasting. This time he welcomed her tongue. Before he could take too much pleasure in it, though, she pulled away and left a line of kisses along his stubbly jaw and down to his chest.

"When you first told me that you had played football," she murmured, her breath hot and moist on his nipple, "I thought you were too small. You're nothing like those muscle-bound giants I see on television."

"Quarterbacks don't need muscles," he replied, his voice husky and thick. "They need a good arm."

She murmured in agreement as she kissed his nipple, making it hard. Her gentle nibble drew a pleasured sigh from him, and he reached for her, but she pushed his hand away. This was for him. She would get her pleasure soon enough.

His skin was so warm, so smooth and flawless. His muscles were lean and taut, his stomach hard and flat. His skin rippled as she caressed across his belly, and he caught his breath in a wordless that-feels-good sort of way. It all felt good to her—looking at him, touching him, kissing him. It made her ache all over, made the familiar, shivery heat settle between her thighs, made her feel empty and hungry and sore, as if she'd been that way far too long.

Reaching his hips, she transferred her caresses to his arousal, long, thick and powerful. There was no disguising his need, no disguising the pleasure she had brought him. She cradled him, hot and strong and smooth as satin, in her hands, and she stroked him, making his muscles clench, making him moan. After a moment's dreamy play, she kissed him, only briefly, only for a taste, then shyly she withdrew and moved to take him inside her where she wanted him. Where she needed him.

She gloved him so hot and tight that Buck knew he could finish right now with no more than a thrust of his hips. Biting his lower lip, he closed his eyes on the sight of her, hair mussed, face pale, lips parted, and concentrated on lasting, on waiting, on enduring. Hers wasn't the most skillful seduction he had ever experienced, but it was by far the best. Her gentle caresses, her innocent pleasure in touching him and her shy, hesitant kiss had aroused him far more than the most practiced lover could have.

For the first minute or two she simply sat still, adjusting to his intrusion. Then she moved, and sensation rocketed through him. "Wait," he whispered, or at least tried to, but his voice sounded strangled.

When he opened his eyes, she was smiling at him, a smug, purely feminine smile of triumph. "Wait?" she echoed. "Aren't you ready?"

Sliding his hands beneath the jersey, he gripped her thighs, holding her still when she would have moved again. "Unless you want this to end before we've really started, you'll be still," he growled.

"I don't think so."

This time he smiled, too. The torment was slowly easing, the intensity fading enough to grant him a small reprieve.

It wouldn't last long, he knew—one stroke, one long, deep thrust could send him over the edge—but it would be long enough. "Power goes to your head, lady," he murmured, sliding his hands higher beneath the jersey, over soft skin, his fingertips brushing across what felt like yet another scar, then finally reaching her hips and the soft damp curls between her thighs. Her flesh was hot enough to burn, hot and tender and exquisitely sensitive to his touch. His first caress sent a jolt through her entire body. The next drew her eyes shut and brought a heavy whispering sigh from deep inside her.

"Oh, Buck… Oh, please…" She was trembling now, her muscles weak, her body tightening around his where he filled her.

"Now," he commanded, his teeth gritted. "Now you can move."

And she did. She didn't need his guidance or assistance. She gave herself mindlessly to the demands of her body, of his body, riding, thrusting, taking him deep in a frantic rhythm that created a firestorm of need. He was racing against it, his entire body throbbing, straining for completion, and with a helpless, shuddering groan he found it deep inside her, filling her, sparking her own release, her own cry, her own draining.

She lay against him, her skin slick, her body still sheltering him. Weak as she was, though, she lifted her head and fixed her solemn gaze on him. "I don't want power over you or anyone else."

His earlier words had been teasingly spoken, but under the circumstances, it wasn't surprising that she'd taken them seriously. "I know, but you're stuck with it, so you may as well learn to enjoy it." He gave her another smug smile. "I certainly do."

When they finally got dressed, they drove into town to the hotel. Buck offered to help her pack, but Carly politely refused. He could wait in the restaurant, she suggested, and order lunch for them instead. That was where he ran into Harvey when he and his wife came in after church.

"How's it going?" the deputy asked, stopping beside the table while his wife went on to the back.

"Okay." Then he sighed. "You think Sally can spare you for a few minutes?"

"We're meeting my sister here. They won't even miss me." He sat down on the empty bench and waited patiently for Buck to begin.

Buck fiddled with his coffee cup. Ordinarily he wouldn't give so much as a hint to anyone about what had happened this weekend with Carly, but Harvey wasn't just anyone. He was a friend, father figure and the best damn deputy Buck had, all in one. Besides, since he would hear the gossip, anyway, Buck preferred to tell him himself. "Carly's upstairs. She'll be down when she's finished packing. She's moving in with me."

Harvey didn't comment.

"I don't think she's Laura," Buck continued. "I know it sounds crazy. It sounds like I'm making excuses. I know there are plenty of reasons to believe she is and not a damn one to believe she isn't. But I really don't think she is."

The older man accepted a cup of coffee from the waitress, added cream and stirred in sugar before looking at Buck. "You remember that old hound dog I used to have?"

The question seemed to come out of left field, but Buck wasn't surprised. Somehow, Harvey's lazy old dog was going to make perfect sense in this conversation.

"My brother over in Kalispell has twin sons—identical twins. From the time they were born, nobody could tell them apart just by looking at them, not even their parents. One of them's a good kid—smart, makes good grades, works hard, polite. The other one is as mean as Satan himself.'' Harvey paused to test his coffee, then added more sugar. ''They used to come and stay with Sally and me when they were young. That old hound loved the one. The other used to devil him night and day. Those kids could be sitting on the couch, looking exactly alike, dressed exactly alike and not doing a thing, and Sally and I couldn't tell which was which. But the dog could. There wasn't any logical way to explain it. Just instinct.''

Buck chuckled softly. The dog story applied, all right— only in this situation, *he* was the dog.

''You've been a cop a long time, Buck. You've got good instincts. Sometimes logic doesn't mean a damn. Sometimes you've got to trust in faith.'' Harvey smiled faintly as he watched Carly cross the dining room. ''And sometimes, son,'' he said as he stood up, ''being crazy ain't a half-bad way to be.''

That night Carly stretched out in bed, waiting for Buck to finish with a call from the dispatcher and join her. Her presence had brought a subtle change to his room. Her clothes hung in the closet beside his. Her shoes were pushed beneath a chair in the corner. Her jacket hung on a doorknob. Her watch was on the dresser next to his.

She had never shared living quarters with a man. It gave her a sense of homeyness. Of belonging. For the next week or so, at least. She was due back at work a week from Tuesday. That meant she had to leave here a week from tomorrow. Seven more days.

Unless, of course, Buck asked her to stay.

Would she?

Maybe. It was a big decision. She hadn't known Buck long—although how long was long enough? She knew him well enough to want him. She knew him well enough to start an affair with him. She knew him well enough to fall in love with him. How long did she need to know him before deciding that she wanted to spend the rest of her life with him?

But her life, such as it was, was in Seattle. Her job was there. Her friends were there. Of course, she could find another job, although maybe not in Nowhere. Maybe she would have to commute to Missoula. Commute on winter highways in western Montana. Right.

And she would miss her friends, but she could make new friends anywhere, because regardless of what kind of person she had once been, she was nice now. People liked her now.

At least, she thought with a scowl as Trina came to mind, *most* people liked her.

Oh, hell, she thought with a frown, who was she trying to kid? If Buck asked her to give up her job and her home and stay here with him, she would say yes before he even got the question out.

Buck hung up and lay down beside her, leaning on his elbows down close to her hips. She was wearing his jersey again. It was perfectly modest attire—much too big and falling almost to her knees—but a person wouldn't think so by the way he was looking at her. Plumping the pillow beneath her head, she watched as he used one finger to slide the hem up, and she shivered as he left a trail of kisses along her thigh.

"How did you get this scar?" he asked when the kisses stopped, sounding so casual that she knew immediately he wasn't.

She was familiar with the mark he was referring to, a small, thickened pad of tissue that formed an irregular circle high on her left thigh. She didn't bother to look at it, but simply gave him a chiding look. "Like I remember? In the accident, I suppose."

"Hmm." That was supposed to sound noncommittal, but as with his attempt to be casual, he failed.

"You don't think so?"

"Do you have any others like it?"

She wasn't supposed to notice, she guessed, that he hadn't answered her question. That was okay. She could pretend. "One. A couple of inches above that one."

He pushed the jersey higher, revealing the plain white panties she wore underneath. Tugging the waistband down, he found the second scar and rubbed his finger over it.

"What's so interesting about them?"

"Nothing."

Carly waited, wondering. Was he going to tell her that Laura had scars exactly like those in exactly the same places? If so, she didn't want to hear it. She didn't want to know. "Well, if you have a thing for scars, Sheriff," she said, forcing a lightness she didn't feel, "you certainly came to the right woman. I've got enough of them."

He moved up the bed to join her on the pillow. "We all have them, honey. Some are just more visible than others." He brushed her hair from her face and kissed her forehead, then settled beside her. "Will you be all right by yourself for a couple of days?"

Her throat suddenly went dry. Why did those particular scars, of all the ones on her body, interest him? And why was he trying to pretend that all these questions were meaningless when obviously they weren't? And was this connected to his sudden decision to go away? "I've been by myself for the better part of three years," she replied uneasily. "Where are you planning to go?"

He looked at her for a long time, then sat up and leaned against the headboard. She had to turn onto her side to see him. "Seattle."

Ah. So he was going off to snoop through her life, looking for clues to her identity. "I'll go with—"

"No. I won't be gone long—a couple of days at most. Stay here. Let me handle this my way."

"But you don't know your way around."

"I can read a map."

"I can introduce you to the people you need to see."

"When I'm conducting an interview, honey, I prefer to introduce myself. If you're with me, the only answers these people are going to give me are the ones they think you want me to hear." He smiled, but she didn't find it reassuring. "I may be small-time, Carly, but I'm good at what I do."

"I know you are," she said grudgingly. "I just…" Just didn't want to be there in Nowhere when he wasn't. She didn't want to move into his house—temporarily—only to have him take off for *her* house in Seattle. She didn't want to give up a few of their days together. She didn't want to give up even one of their precious nights. "When did you decide to do this?"

"Tonight. We both want answers, and there's not much I can do here to get them."

"When are you leaving?"

"Probably first thing Tuesday morning, and come back Thursday evening. That'll give me about forty-eight hours. That should be enough."

She sat up, tugging the jersey down to cover her legs. "I could stay out of the way. I wouldn't distract you."

His grin came slow and sly, and it drew a similar response from her. "Yeah," he said, giving her a long, lazy appraisal. "Right."

"I suppose you'll be wanting the key to my apartment."

He simply nodded.

With a sigh, she less than gracefully gave in. "All right. I'll wait here."

"Thank you." Business completed, he reached for her, drawing her slowly along the length of his body. "Now…" His grin returned. "Let me give you a proper welcome to my house."

* * *

It was early afternoon Monday when Buck called Harvey in off patrol for a conference in his office. His airline reservations had been made; now he needed to brief the deputy who would be in charge while he was gone.

"So you're taking me up on my suggestion."

"I'm sure not learning anything here. I don't suppose we've heard back from the FBI on her fingerprints?"

Harvey, whose job included opening the mail, gave him a dry look. "You know you would be the second one after me to find out."

"There's got to be something I'm missing. If she is Laura, there's got to be some way to prove it. And if she's not, hell, she's thirty-some years old. She has to have a background somewhere—relatives, friends, whatever." He drummed his fingers on the desk, listening to the rhythmic crackle of paper underneath them. When he looked down, he saw it was Carly's birth certificate. The one she had turned over to him last week. The one that she had brought on this trip with her because it documented her existence, because it proved that she had family. She had parents.

Who were dead.

"All I asked the clerk for on her parents' death certificates was the date of death," he said thoughtfully. "I didn't ask about the next of kin."

"But if Carly was their only child, naturally she would be listed as the next of kin."

"Probably. But what if the hospital made a mistake and listed someone else—an aunt or uncle? Maybe the paperwork was incomplete. Maybe Carly wasn't there when either of her parents died, and some relative who was got listed instead." It was a long shot—he knew that—but all it would take to find out was one more phone call to Texas.

Mark Johnson had died three years before Helene, and his death certificate, according to the records clerk, said exactly what Buck had expected: his wife Helene was listed as next of kin.

Helene's was the surprise.

Buck sat motionless, the clerk's answer echoing in his mind. *None.* Helene Johnson's death certificate showed her as having no family.

But that wasn't possible. She'd had a daughter—the birth certificate proved that. Maybe an estranged daughter? So estranged that she had refused to go to the hospital to see her dying mother? So estranged that no one involved with the woman was aware of her existence?

Not Carly. There was no way she would have stayed away from her mother's deathbed.

But there was no other explanation. No other way he could think of to explain how a woman who was born in Dallas, who lived and died there, could die so alone that no one knew about her daughter. Surely she'd had friends. Surely her physician's patient record had listed Carly as the person to contact in case of an emergency.

But her doctor apparently hadn't known about a daughter.

The hospital hadn't.

Her friends, assuming she'd had some, hadn't known.

Or maybe…

Maybe there hadn't been a daughter to know about.

He closed his eyes, rubbing the space between them to ease the sudden ache. He didn't want to think about this. He didn't want to pursue it any further. He wanted to just hang up the phone, cancel his airline reservations, go home and tell Carly that if she wanted a name, she could marry him and have his.

But he couldn't.

"Sheriff?" The clerk's voice was loud in his ear. "Are you still there, Sheriff Logan?"

"Yeah. I'm here."

"Is there anything else I can do for you today?"

Sighing heavily, he said, "Yes, there is. Could you look up one more name for me?" He gave her the name, last, first and middle, then waited. Across the desk from him, Harvey waited, too.

"Here it is, Sheriff," the clerk said when she returned. She read the information to him slowly, presumably so he could make notes. But he didn't pick up a pen. He didn't move at all except to hang up the phone after quietly thanking her.

Feeling numb, he swiveled his chair around to stare out the window. So much for intangibles, for feelings and instincts. So much for convincing himself that it was all right to love Carly because she absolutely was not Laura Phelps.

When he finally spoke, his voice was empty and flat.

"Carly Ann Johnson, the only child of Mark and Helene Johnson, died twenty years ago last June. She was twelve years old."

Chapter 10

She wasn't going to cry. Carly swore that every time her throat got tight or tears burned her eyes, and so far she had managed. She sat stiffly on the sofa in Buck's living room, her hands pressed tightly between her knees, and he was in front of her, seated on the coffee table, talking. His words were sweet—it doesn't make any difference, it doesn't change who you are, it doesn't matter—but she felt deep inside that that was all they were. Words. Sweet talk.

Maybe it really didn't matter to him. Maybe it didn't change things. Of course, he had been convinced from the beginning that she wasn't who she believed.

But it mattered to her.

It mattered a hell of a lot to her.

All she'd had, *all* she had been left with, after the accident had been a name, a birth certificate and a few pictures. And now he was telling her that the name wasn't hers.

The birth certificate wasn't hers.

The loving parents in that picture weren't hers.

She had been clinging to someone else's life.

Realizing that Buck had finished talking and was watching her apprehensively, she smiled wanly. "You needn't look so wary, Sheriff. I'm not going to fall apart. You've been preparing me for this ever since I came to town."

"I'm sorry, Carly. I know you wanted—"

Wanted. Oh, she certainly had done that. But she had never been greedy. She had wanted to know who she was. She had wanted to remember growing up. She had wanted the simple, easily forgotten memories that she had never realized were so important until she lost them. She had wanted to know that somebody had loved her, that she had been worthy of loving.

She had wanted her life back. Her life as Carly Johnson. Her life that had never existed.

She smiled again. "Don't be sorry. It's all right."

"I can cancel this trip tomorrow. I can stay here—"

Again she interrupted him. "No, go ahead. I'd like to know the rest. Anything else you can find out…" Suddenly she shivered, and he moved from the table to sit beside her, wrapping his arms around her.

"I'm sorry, honey. I should have dropped it. I should have let you believe… Damn, I'm sorry."

"You offered to," she reminded him, resting her head on his shoulder. "*I* was the one who wanted to know. *I* was the one who said go ahead and find the answers. Now I just have to deal with them."

"At least now you know you're not alone. You know you have relatives," he said, his voice softened by the hope that a family would make this news easier to bear.

Maybe in time it would. Maybe when she got to know Maureen better, she would be happy to have an aunt who loved her. Maybe someday she could even settle things with her cousin. Maybe she could make right all the things Laura—all the things *she* had done wrong.

"How did she..." She paused, then hesitantly rephrased it. "How did I do it? How did I find out about the real Carly Johnson?"

"Go ahead and say 'she,'" he suggested, pressing a gentle kiss to the top of her head. "It's easier."

She nodded a silent thanks. Maybe she had to be Laura Phelps, but he wasn't going to make her accept responsibility for everything she'd done as Laura.

While he considered her question, he stroked her hair gently. She could stay here like this forever, safe and comfortable and cared for, she thought, letting her eyes close. His arm was warm around her shoulders, and his body was solid against hers. His shirt was soft against her cheek, his heartbeat strong and steady beneath her hand on his chest. The gun would have to go, though, she decided with a smile as she shifted her hip away from it.

"If I were going to create a new identity for myself," Buck said at last, "I would go to a large city in another state. I would visit a cemetery there and find the grave of a child who had been born about the same time I was. Then I would rent a post office box using that person's name, and I would write to the state requesting a certified copy of that birth certificate. I would use that to get a driver's license and a social security number, and then I would be in business."

"Why a child?"

"You want to keep it simple. You don't want someone with an extensive background—schools, jobs, a family of her own. Plus, if you choose someone who was old enough to have held a job before she died, then she would have had a social security number, too. And if you apply for a new one using her name, her birth date, her background, the computer is going to show that that person died however many years ago."

"How did this girl die? Did they tell you that?"

He held her tighter. "It doesn't matter."

"It *does*," she said fiercely. "I borrowed her life for three years, Buck. I want to know how she died."

"She drowned."

How sad, she thought, feeling the tears sting her eyes once more. The real Carly had been a little girl, only twelve years old. She'd had her whole life ahead of her, and suddenly it had ended. She had never known what it was like to grow up and date and fall in love. She'd never had a chance to marry or have children of her own. She'd never had a chance to experience life. Only twelve short years.

And her poor parents, losing their only daughter, their only child. They must have had such dreams for her. They must have looked forward to watching her grow up. They must have counted on the happiness she would bring them, the grandchildren, the future, the joy.

Instead, Mark Johnson had died with only the comfort of his wife at his side, and Helene had died alone.

"What about the pictures I have?" she asked, surreptitiously drying a tear from her eye. "Who are those people?"

"I have no idea. If you don't object, when I get back from Seattle, I'll show them to Maureen. Maybe she'll recognize them. Maybe they're relatives or friends of Nora's."

Or maybe they were total strangers, Carly acknowledged. Maybe she had come across the photographs somewhere and had simply taken them because they had suited her needs. The swooping, pointed handwriting on the back that identified the girl as her, the adults as her parents, was probably her own, disguised as part of her charade.

When she didn't speak for a while, Buck gently pushed her away and met her gaze. "I meant what I said earlier, Carly. This doesn't change anything. The things that happened before, the things involving Laura—they have nothing to do with you and me. It's not going to affect us now. Do you understand?''

He was saying that he still wanted her. In spite of all the awful things she had done, in spite of the hatred and loathing she had created in him, he still wanted her.

Maybe she would cry, after all, she thought with a teary smile.

Just a little.

Seattle was a busy city, a world away from his little town of Nowhere. Buck rented a car at the airport, then studied the map the rental agent had given him, marking the locations of Carly's apartment, the building where she worked and the nearby offices of two close friends. Those interviews would take care of what was left of the afternoon.

He was going to stay at her apartment—she had given him the key and permission to look for whatever he could find there—and tomorrow he had an appointment with Dr. Parker, which he would follow with a visit to the hospital. The release she had signed allowing him access to her medical records was in the manila envelope he carried, along with the one item that she didn't know he had brought: the photograph of Laura that he'd kept in his office drawer. Hospitals were busy places. Hundreds, maybe thousands, of patients had passed through there since her discharge nearly three years ago. Names and injuries could be forgotten—although probably not a bona fide case of amnesia, he thought—but faces were a different matter. A strikingly beautiful face like Carly's was damned near impossible to forget.

God knew, he'd done his share of trying.

Then Thursday morning he was going home.

He was going to tell Carly that he loved her no matter who she was.

He was going to ask her to marry him.

Funny how things had worked out. Three years ago Laura had wanted to marry him, and he had sworn that he would die first. She had disappeared in a temper, had come back a changed woman, and now *he* was the one wanting marriage. He was the one thinking about forever.

The insurance company where Carly worked was located in a large square building that was purely functional. There was nothing inspired about its design, nothing decorative about its construction. A plain brick building filled with plain functional offices. A receptionist in the lobby directed him to Janice Graham, Carly's boss, whose office was on the second floor.

She was an attractive woman, maybe forty or so, who barely glanced at his credentials but gave him a long, measuring look. "Have a seat, Sheriff," she invited. "When she asked for a leave of absence, Carly said that she might have discovered something about her past. Did she once live in your town?"

He withdrew the photo from the envelope and handed it across the desk to her. "This is a woman named Laura Phelps. She lived in Nowhere until three years ago."

"And Carly came to Seattle three years ago." She accepted the picture but didn't look at it until she'd located her glasses under a pile of papers and slid them in place. For a long time she was motionless. Then she murmured, "Damn."

"On her job application, she listed a previous address in Dallas, along with schools there and a personal reference in Houston. None of that was checked out either before or after she was hired. Why not? Do you normally hire people without verifying their background?"

Removing the glasses, she gave him a reproving smile. "We were hiring a receptionist, Sheriff. The turnover rate in a position like that can be fairly high. We were more interested in whether Carly could type, answer the phone, take messages that made sense and make decent coffee. She could. She did it so well, in fact, that when she returned to work after the accident, I made her my secretary." Pausing, she returned the photo to him. "I assume *you* checked the background she gave."

He shrugged. No sense in telling her that Carly had lied about all of it. If she decided to return to Seattle, if she refused to stay with him in Nowhere, she was going to need a job. "Could I see her desk?"

She accompanied him to the work space outside her door and politely suggested to the woman working there that she take a break.

"Are these Carly's things?"

"Yes. Phyllis is a temp. She hasn't brought anything of her own."

The desk was similar to any of a number he had passed on his way in, filled with a telephone, a computer and stacks of work. There was a small ivy that was dying from lack of water, a wood carving of a pelican and a glass sculpture of a dolphin. She liked the water, Carly had told Maureen.

But she hadn't liked the lake outside Nowhere.

Fingering the graceful dolphin, he wondered if, in making her plans, Carly had discovered how the twelve-year-old Carly had died, if the girl had perhaps drowned in a lake similar to that one. That knowledge could have remained hidden somewhere in her mind, surfacing only when he'd forced her to go to the lake with him.

Setting the dolphin down again, he picked up the small acrylic frame next to it. It held a snapshot of a small, dark-haired girl, her eyes bright, her smile revealing a missing front tooth, her arms gently cradling a white rabbit. "Who is this?"

"Amelia White. Her mother Hilary is probably Carly's

closest friend. Hilary works in one of the law offices on the fifth floor.''

Hilary, who remembered her high school years too fondly. The single mother who lived next door to Carly, whose daughter, this friendly little girl, Carly sometimes baby-sat.

He returned the frame to its place, then turned to the credenza behind the desk. There was another plant there, a cactus that was flourishing in its neglect, and a sample of the wares she had collected from the craft shows she favored—a ceramic rabbit, a tiny woven basket with a bow on the handle, a miniature clay pot filled with miniature silk flowers and a hand-decorated frame holding another photo of Amelia.

Janice Graham was leaning against the doorjamb, watching him. Slowly he faced her again. ''You knew her before the accident?''

She nodded.

''What kind of changes did you see afterward?''

''She was unsure of herself, of everything. She was shaken. Wary. Frightened, but then she was frightened before.''

Laura frightened. That was an odd image. He couldn't imagine anything that could have put fear into her. Angry lovers, jealous wives, Trina. Nothing had fazed Laura. ''What was she afraid of before?''

''I don't know. She never talked much about her life before she came to Seattle. She told us that she was from Texas and that her parents were dead. I figured she had run away from an unhappy relationship. She was so pretty that men in the office were naturally drawn to her—you know, a little flirting, that sort of thing—but she was skittish around them. I assumed some man had hurt her pretty badly, and that was why she was afraid of them.''

Laura had never been afraid of anyone, and she had been

enticing and, either figuratively or literally, seducing every man she had met since she was thirteen years old. Things just weren't adding up, Buck thought grimly. She had left Nowhere the beginning of October, as brash, bold and aggressive as ever, and two weeks later she had begun working here with a fear of men. What could possibly have happened in those two weeks to explain such a change?

"Was she easier to get along with after the accident?" he asked stiffly. "Nicer? Less selfish?"

Janice Graham laughed. "Sheriff, from the day she walked into this building, we couldn't have found a nicer, sweeter, less selfish or more generous employee—make that *friend*—if we had searched forever. Carly was *never* difficult to get along with. Everyone who worked with her was genuinely fond of her."

Uneasiness joined the stiffness spreading through him. They couldn't possibly be talking about the same woman.

But the only alternative was that they were talking about two different women, and that wasn't possible. He had already proven that Carly Johnson didn't exist. She was Laura.

But a Laura that he'd never known.

A Laura who must have undergone some horrifying experience in the two weeks between leaving Nowhere and coming to work for this company.

"Would you like to talk to some of Carly's friends, Sheriff?" Janice asked. "I can call a few of them in here."

Accepting her offer, he followed her back into her office. Maybe people Carly considered friends could tell him more than her supervisor could. Maybe they could answer a few questions for him.

Or maybe, he thought dismally, they could create a whole lot more.

After a brief search Tuesday afternoon, Carly located the Nowhere phone directory in a drawer in Buck's kitchen and dialed Maureen Phelps's number. He had said he would show Maureen her photographs when he got back from Seattle, but there wasn't any reason to wait. Since Maureen was her aunt, after all, she might as well spend a little time getting reacquainted with her and, while she was doing that, ask about the people in the picture.

The older lady was home, and she would be happy for the company, she said. Her pleasure made Carly feel guilty. Other than her two visits to the Phelps home with the sheriff, she'd made no effort to see the woman. Even though she'd known Maureen would welcome her. Even though she'd suspected that the big ugly house outside town was where she had once belonged.

Now she locked Buck's front door, then climbed into her car. Since arriving in Nowhere she hadn't driven much at all. After her vacation to Mount Rushmore, the Black Hills and the Badlands of South Dakota, along with a side trip to Helena on her way home, it had been kind of a relief to escape the chore of driving for a while. She didn't know, of course, if she had ever enjoyed driving, but since the accident, it had become a necessity rather than a pleasure.

Nowhere was quiet in the middle of the sunny but cool afternoon. It was almost October. Almost three years exactly since Laura had disappeared. Only a few weeks short of three years since she had surfaced in Seattle.

She didn't doubt what Buck had told her—that the real Carly Johnson was dead, that *she,* Laura, had appropriated her name and her life—but she just didn't *feel* like Laura. She didn't feel as if she had grown up in this town with these people. She didn't feel as if she could possibly be the woman she was.

She would adjust. Adapt. Accept. She had done it when she'd awakened in the hospital, had adjusted to a brand new, empty life, and she would do it again.

But where would she do it? she wondered as she pulled into the Phelps driveway. Here in Nowhere, with a family, with Buck?

Or alone in Seattle?

Maureen met her at the top of the steps, her smile warm, her hands outstretched in greeting. She led Carly inside to the parlor and offered her coffee or tea and a piece of warm peach pie. Carly accepted the tea, turned down the rest and waited for the woman to alight somewhere. For the first time she curiously studied this relative, this aunt of hers.

She must have been a pretty girl, and she was a lovely woman with pure white hair and a soft, lined face. She must have a kind heart—she had taken in Laura, hadn't she?— and yet she'd probably had disappointments in her life. She'd been a young woman when her husband had died some twenty years ago, but she had never remarried. She was a loving, giving person, yet she'd had only one child, one mid-thirties, bitter, hate-filled and still single daughter.

Maureen settled onto the couch with a sneeze. "Excuse me. I think I'm finally catching that bug that's been going around. I'll keep my distance, though. I don't want to pass it to anyone else. Is Buck working today?"

"He's gone to Seattle," Carly replied. "He'll be back Thursday evening."

"I understand you've been spending a great deal of time with him. It must be lonely for you over at the hotel with him gone."

"I—I'm staying at his house while he's out of town." Carly silently apologized for the wrong impression she was deliberately creating, but she wasn't about to sit here and tell this nice old lady who had practically raised her that she had moved in with Buck. Of course, Maureen could easily learn the truth from Hazel or Trina, but she would be gracious enough, Carly suspected, not to let on that she knew.

"Mrs. Phelps... May I call you Maureen?"

"Oh, yes, dear, of course."

"The sheriff...Buck found out yesterday that..." She stared for a moment at the glass of tea she held, then took a deep breath. "Carly Johnson isn't my real name. Apparently I chose to use it before I moved to Seattle."

She could literally see Maureen take in the news, could see her eyes brighten at its meaning—that if she knew she wasn't Carly, she must also know that she was Laura.

"Until I came here, I thought I was Carly. When I woke up in the hospital, they gave me my purse with my driver's license, my credit cards, my checkbook, all with that name on it. That's what the people who knew me before the accident called me. I honestly believed it." Setting the tea aside, she opened her purse and pulled out her wallet, then withdrew the two photos. "These pictures were the only real link to my past—or so I thought. According to the back, this one was me, and this one was my parents and me. Everything Buck's learned seems to suggest otherwise. Do you know...?"

Maureen leaned forward to accept the pictures. She studied each one intently, then regretfully shook her head. "I'm sorry, dear. I don't recognize the adults at all. The girl...she looks familiar, but first grade was such a long time ago, and you—Laura didn't live with us then."

So that was that, Carly thought with a surge of disappointment. Her most treasured possessions for three years were fakes. Strangers. People who had never known or given a damn about her.

"You know," Maureen began thoughtfully, "I still have most of Nora's things stored up in the attic. I believe there are some old photographs there. Why don't you come up there with me, and we'll look. We might find something..."

All Carly really wanted to do was go back to Buck's

house, crawl into his bed and pull the covers over her head until he came home again. But rushing off now would be rude, and maybe Maureen was right. Maybe they would find something. Not what she wanted—proof that she couldn't possibly be Laura—but maybe something that would help her remember being Laura.

She was halfway up the stairs, only a few steps behind Maureen, when the skin on the back of her neck began tingling. Looking up sharply, she saw Trina, leaning indolently against her bedroom door. How long had she been standing there? Carly wondered. How much had she heard?

Enough, judging by her smile. It was an eerie thing— not exactly evil, not exactly triumphant, definitely not pleasant. "So..." Trina gave the word a thinly veiled edge of malice. "Cousin Laura has finally come home."

Carly proceeded to the top of the steps one cautious step at a time. "Hello, Trina," she said quietly.

"We're going up to the attic to look through a few of Nora's things," Maureen announced without slowing her steps. "Come along, Carly."

She obediently followed Maureen down the hall to another set of stairs. The essence of Trina's hate trailed along, dogging her every step, reaching out to her, making her inwardly shudder. She had been overly optimistic when she'd thought she might be able to resolve things with the other woman. Trina was too far gone, too deeply immersed in bitterness and anger to ever forgive Laura's sins.

In the attic, Carly joined Maureen on a dusty old bench, where they went through box after box of pictures, souvenirs, mementos. There were pictures of Nora, a pretty, dark-haired woman, and others of Laura—baby portraits, childhood snapshots, school pictures.

And even though there was a resemblance between the young Laura and the little girl in Carly's pictures, it was painfully clear that was all it was. A resemblance.

They weren't the same people.

Depression settling on her shoulders, Carly told Maureen after a while that she needed to be going. She needed a little space. A little privacy.

She needed a little time to grieve for the woman she had believed herself to be, the woman who had existed only in her lies.

She needed time to grieve for the woman she had once been.

The woman she would someday have to be again.

She was outside the house and halfway down the steps to her car when she saw Trina leaning against it. The other woman was smiling with satisfaction, and when Carly slowly joined her beside the car, she saw why.

A scratch extended the length of the car, gouging through the paint and deep into the metal. In itself it was a silly act, a juvenile expression of anger, but it made Carly go all cold inside. The look of pure meanness in Trina's eyes left no doubt that she considered the car a poor target for venting the rage seething inside.

According to Buck, she was harmless, Carly reminded herself, trying to calm her sudden case of nerves. *Harmless.*

"Gee, too bad," Trina remarked, tossing a set of car keys into the air and catching them in her palm. "Looks like somebody didn't like the way you parked."

Carly didn't look at the scratch again. "You have something against my car, Trina?" she asked, her voice even and calm in spite of the fear that made her tremble inside.

"I have something against *you*."

"What?" Her question momentarily stunned Trina, and Carly took advantage of those few seconds to gather her strength. "What did I do to make you hate me so much?"

"You...bitch," the other woman whispered. Her face was white, her eyes dark, her expression filled with impotent rage. "What did you do? You *ruined* my life! You stole everything from me—my mother's love, my friends, my boyfriends! You stole my future!''

''I took Buck, didn't I?'' Carly asked gently. Her fear eased, and sympathy took its place, sympathy for this pathetic, unhappy woman who had never been enough—pretty enough, popular enough, smart enough, sexy enough—to satisfy herself.

''He would have been happy with me if you had left him alone!'' she cried. ''I could give him everything you never could—love, a home, children! He would have loved me! If you hadn't come back, he would have loved *me!*''

''You had three years when Buck was alone—three long years to give him all those things.'' Sighing softly, Carly reached out to comfort her. ''It's not my fault, Trina. You can't blame me.''

The instant she made contact, the other woman jerked away, then burst into tears. ''I hate you!'' she sobbed. ''I wish you were dead!''

Feeling shaken and drained, Carly watched her run away, not up the steps to the house but into the woods at the end of the stone wall. When the sounds of her flight had quieted, Carly got into the car and started down the hill. Buck was right. Trina was sad and dissatisfied, filled with longings that would never be fulfilled, with disappointments that would never ease, with dreams that had shattered years ago. She was all those things and more.

But she wasn't dangerous.

Buck let himself into Carly's apartment, pausing for a moment in the doorway. A young man walking by gave him a curious look, but he ignored it and focused instead on the apartment. On her home.

A tiny hall led into the living room. On the left was a coat closet, on the right, a galley-style kitchen. Closing the door behind him, he set down his suitcase, then opened the closet door. It held a heavy coat, a trench coat, two cardigans and a rubber slicker. The shelf above was filled with a variety of umbrellas and cleaning supplies, and a vacuum cleaner was shoved into one corner.

The kitchen was just as neat and ordinary. The cabinets held pots and pans, plenty of canned food, dishes for four, one set of good glasses, a half-dozen insulated tumblers and a dozen or more plastic tumblers from a local pizza restaurant. The refrigerator shelves were empty but for a bottle of water, a tub of margarine and an open box of baking soda. The racks in the door held the usual condiments—mayonnaise, mustard, catsup and steak sauce—and an entire row of pickles. Hamburger dills, bread and butter, pickled okra, vegetables and onions, and even a jar of pickled peppers. Buck smiled faintly. How had he, who hadn't touched a pickle since his first taste thirty-some years ago, fallen for a pickle connoisseur?

Leaving the kitchen, he walked into the living room. The furniture—sofa, chair, tables, entertainment center—was nice. Nicer than a secretary's salary warranted? Of course, there was the thousand dollars Laura had taken with her from Nowhere, and the little matter of her car. The Corvette could have paid for this.

Or it could be rented.

Or Carly could manage her money very frugally.

In the corner of the living space reserved for the dining room, there was a tiny glass-and-granite table and two chairs. Her neighbor Hilary had been getting her mail, Carly had told him. Apparently she had a key to the apartment, since a pile of letters and newspapers was stacked on the table. He sorted through it, but found nothing personal—mostly junk, a few bills, some outdated sales fliers.

He'd been curious once about what kind of pictures hung on her walls. There were no more mystery family pictures, but beautiful shots of mountains and ocean, of waterfalls and wildflowers and children, of a rodeo and a crooked pine, a wind-eroded cliff and a street fair. There was a charming portrait of Amelia and a small, black-and-white photo of Carly herself, hauntingly beautiful, looking calmly, unflinchingly, into the camera, her eyes inexpressibly sad. He stared at it a long time, wondering whether it had been taken before or after the accident, what she'd been thinking as she had faced the camera, if she realized it had captured her very soul.

Finally tearing his gaze from the portrait, he walked down the short hall to her bedroom. It was funny how a place could become so cold and impersonal when its owner had been gone for a while. The apartment felt utterly empty. These rooms were where Carly had lived for three years, where she laughed and cried and baby-sat her neighbor's daughter. She greeted her dates here, had friends over, watched television and did all the little day-to-day routines of living here.

She had made a life for herself here, and yet it was empty. There was no sign of her. No awareness. No essence.

The bedroom was just a bedroom, nothing special, nothing to suggest what an extraordinary person lived there. The closet was half-empty, and the clothes that hung there were exactly what she had described to him—simple dresses, jeans, sweaters and T-shirts. There wasn't any silk or satin in the lot. No slinky dresses or skirts slit to the hip, no low-cut blouses or three-inch heels.

Returning to the living room, he sat down on the overstuffed couch and reached for the phone. He had been both anticipating and dreading this call. He longed to hear Carly's voice, but at the same time he wasn't looking forward to discussing his day with her. He didn't want to tell her that he was more confused than ever. He didn't want to tell her that, instead of being solved, the mystery seemed to be deepening.

And he sure as hell didn't want to tell her that, in spite of all they knew, in spite of all the evidence, deep down in his gut he didn't believe she was Laura.

"It seems funny," she said when the greetings were out of the way, "that I'm here in your house and you're there in my house. There's something wrong here, Sheriff."

"The something wrong is that your house is five hundred miles away from my house," he replied. "We just may have to do something about that."

She was awfully quiet on the other end. Deciding if she would like that? he wondered. Certain that she wouldn't? Thinking things were just fine the way they were?

Finally she asked, "How was your day? Did you learn anything?"

"Your boss sends her best, along with a reminder that you're due back at work on the sixth." That wasn't all Janice Graham had said, though. *Carly's a good secretary,* she had remarked as she'd walked to the lobby with him. *I found her, and I want to keep her. But you have different ideas about that, don't you? You want her for yourself.*

"Hmm. Are you avoiding my question, Sheriff?"

"If you're asking whether I've learned anything more about your coming to Seattle, the answer is no. I'll tell you every little detail when I get home, all right?"

She laughed then, exactly what he needed to hear. "You make me sound nosy."

"For someone who's not a cop, you *are* nosy. But since it's your life, I guess you're entitled."

"I miss you, Buck."

Her words caught him off guard and set off a wave of homesickness strong enough to hurt. Not for Montana, though. Not for Nowhere, but for *her.* "I miss you, too, honey,'' he murmured.

God help him, how he missed her.

That night he went next door and introduced himself to Hilary White. She was younger than he'd expected, twenty-three, maybe twenty-four. That would make her a far-too-young teenager when she'd given birth to Amelia. She was dark-haired and dark-eyed, like her daughter, not more than an inch or two over five feet, and talkative, friendly, open.

She had met Carly on her third day in Seattle, she told him, the day she'd moved into the next apartment. They had become friends quickly, and Carly had surely needed a friend.

''Why did you think that?''

''She was the most alone person I'd ever met,'' Hilary replied. ''And believe me, I *know* alone. My family disowned me when I got divorced. Amelia and I are all each other has. But Carly didn't even have that much.''

They were sitting at her dining table, drinking cold beers while six-year-old Amelia played on the concrete slab outside the sliding doors. The apartment was just like Carly's, Buck noticed with a look around, although not quite as neat. But, as Hilary had just pointed out, Carly didn't have Amelia, whose toys were everywhere.

''What was she like before the accident?'' he asked, directing his attention back to Hilary.

''Nervous. I thought maybe she'd never lived on her own before, you know? The first thing she did was have new locks put on the doors and windows, and she never went anywhere without making sure everything was all locked up. She wouldn't move in until the telephones had been hooked up, and she wouldn't go out at night. She came straight home from work and wouldn't leave again until the next morning.''

''And you don't have any idea what she was afraid of?''

''I figured it was a man.'' She laughed. ''Of course, being recently divorced at the time, I figured men were at the root of all women's problems.''

''But she never told you, and you never asked.''

Hilary finished her beer, then twisted the bottle in circles. ''Carly wasn't that kind of person, you know? I always had this feeling that certain things were off-limits. I didn't ask about her life in Texas, about who she was running from or what she was afraid of. It wasn't anything she ever said, you know, like mind your own business. It was just the way she was. Private.''

Buck thanked her for her time and rose to leave. Halfway to the door, though, he looked back. ''Did she ever mention the name Laura to you?''

Hilary thought about it, then shook her head.

Thanking her again, he returned to Carly's quiet, empty apartment. There he ate a solitary meal of canned soup at her table, watched her television and showered in her tub, and then he crawled into her bed. Five hundred miles away, *she* was in *his* bed, and here he was alone.

As she'd said earlier, there was something wrong with that.

And as soon as he got back to Nowhere, he intended to right it.

Forever.

Not all doctors were gray-haired, grandfatherly old gentlemen like Doc Thomas. Periodically, Buck needed to be reminded of that, and Dr. Jim Parker did just that. He was in his early thirties, Buck estimated, with shaggy blond hair, blue eyes and a surfer-boy tan. He was charming, six feet tall and muscular, and, if the absence of a ring meant anything, he was single. God's gift to the unmarried women of Seattle.

And after three years as her doctor, Buck acknowledged

with a scowl, he probably knew Carly's body more intimately than Buck himself.

He didn't like that idea.

At all.

Once Parker read the release Carly had signed, he spoke candidly about the accident, the injuries she had suffered and the care she had received. He talked about the two weeks immediately following the wreck when she'd been in intensive care and the next seven weeks she'd spent in the extended-care unit. He didn't sprinkle the conversation with incomprehensible terminology but explained everything clearly, without condescension.

As interesting as it all was—they were talking about Carly, after all—it wasn't of much help.

Until Buck brought up the scars.

He didn't want to. Even mentioning them told the doctor more about his relationship with Carly than he needed to know. But more than that, he didn't want to face what they meant. He didn't want to acknowledge even to himself the ugly suspicions that had been festering in the back of his mind since Sunday night, the suspicions that yesterday's interviews had intensified. He didn't want to even think such a thing about Carly.

But he had to ask.

He had to know.

"She has two scars," he said slowly, reluctantly. "One on her thigh, one on her hip. I don't think they're connected to the accident."

The doctor's gaze was steady, regretful and just a little sad. For a long time he didn't say anything; then he gave a deep sigh. "No, they're not."

"She had them when she came into the hospital."

He nodded.

"Could you make a guess as to how old they were?"

"At that time, they were recent. They weren't even fully healed yet."

"Five, six weeks old? Does that fit?"

Parker nodded again. "You know what caused them, don't you, Sheriff?"

It was Buck's turn to look regretful and sad. "Yes, I do."

"And you know it was deliberate." Settling back in his chair, Parker enumerated the reasons for his conclusion. "Carly didn't smoke. Even if she had, even if she'd been, say, smoking in bed, wearing a T-shirt or nothing at all, and she had dropped the cigarette, it wouldn't have done that kind of damage. It probably would have rolled a bit before she caught it, leaving a longer, thinner, milder burn. Her burns were deep, and the lit end of the cigarette was in direct contact with her skin. It didn't fall—it was held there." He paused, then finished flatly. "Someone forcibly held her down and burned her."

The burns had been small, but Buck knew they must have hurt like hell. Someone had willfully, intentionally, done that to her, probably someone she had known. Probably someone she had trusted.

The knowledge made him flinch, made him feel sick way down inside. It filled him with helpless rage, because there was no way he could find out who had done that to her. He couldn't punish the man. He couldn't make him sorry he'd ever been born.

He was filled, too, with a sort of perverse gratitude for Carly's amnesia. She couldn't remember the fear that must have choked her. She couldn't remember the agonizing pain or the harsh scent of her burning flesh or the cruel pleasure the man had taken in hurting her. To her, the scars were just marks, minor flaws like all the others. They didn't mean anything.

Who could have done it? Only two weeks had passed

between Laura's leaving Nowhere and Carly's arrival in Seattle. Where had she gone? Who had she seen? Which of her men—her *lovers*—had done that to her? Which one deserved to die for hurting her?

"It all fits," he murmured grimly. "Yesterday I talked to her boss and some of her friends. They said that when she first came here, she was afraid. She wouldn't move into her apartment until new locks had been installed, until there were telephones in each room. She wouldn't go out at night. When the men in the office flirted with her, it frightened her."

"That's natural enough under the circumstances," Dr. Parker said. "The burns and the fact that she ran away from wherever prove that she was mistreated. The fact that she feared for her safety when she got here suggests that the person who hurt her might have followed. That she knew him. That he was her boyfriend or her husband or some other man important in her life. That she was afraid he would hurt her again."

Not in this lifetime, Buck thought harshly. If she ever remembered who did this to her, if he ever found the bastard, she would never have cause to fear him again because he would be dead. Buck would kill him.

That was a promise.

Chapter 11

The hospital where Carly had been a patient for so long was a tall, sprawling complex of buildings across the street from Dr. Parker's office. A helpful volunteer in the lobby directed Buck to Patient Administration, where, after talking to a receptionist, two secretaries, an assistant and finally the hospital administrator himself, he was given permission to talk to the staff of the extended-care unit, in the neurology wing. The administrator's assistant took him to the proper floor and introduced him to the charge nurse at the desk, then left him on his own.

"You want to ask about a patient we had three years ago." The nurse's expression wasn't encouraging. "Sheriff...Logan, is it? We've cared for a lot of patients on this floor. What are the chances that we'll remember your particular patient three years later?"

"From what I understand she was considered to be something of a..." An oddity. A freak. Those were Carly's words, but he preferred the less-harmful phrase she had tossed out with them. "Something of a medical miracle. She was in a coma for two months and made a complete recovery when she awoke, except for the amnesia."

Recognition lit her eyes. "If you'd mentioned the amnesia first, I would have remembered right away—not her name and not many of the details, but amnesia…that's pretty unusual. It tends to stick in your mind." Excusing herself, she gathered a small group of nurses at the desk—the only ones, she explained, who had been working this floor at that time.

He identified himself to the three nurses and told them that he was interested in anything they might remember about Carly, anything at all. He knew he was wasting his time and theirs. He knew that after three years, they, like the charge nurse, would remember only the highlights. But it couldn't hurt to ask.

"I don't remember a patient with amnesia," one of the women insisted.

"Maybe you've got it yourself," another retorted.

"That's not amnesia. It's senility," the only man in the group said.

Buck interrupted their banter by laying the photograph of Laura on the counter. There was a moment's silence while each of them studied it, then the first woman murmured, "Oh, yeah, I remember."

"Which one is this?" the supervisor asked.

Buck gave her a perplexed look. "What do you mean, which one?"

"You've really got be more forthcoming, Sheriff," she replied with a chiding look. "Amnesia, I would have remembered. The twins, I would have remembered. Ross here, especially, would have remembered. The one who wasn't a patient made a couple of passes at him."

"Twins," he echoed blankly.

"Not really," a petite Oriental woman replied. "But they

looked so much alike that we called them that. I think they were cousins or something. It was kind of spooky going into the room and seeing—what's her name?—Carly lying in bed unconscious, with the casts and the sutures and the IVs, and then coming back out into the hall and running into her cousin. Weird.''

Looking down, Buck saw that his hands were trembling. He shoved them into his pockets, but the shakes just spread to his arms, down inside to his stomach. He really was going to be sick over this entire mess, he decided, and wondered where the closest men's room was. Then the nausea slowly settled, and fifteen years of being a cop took over. He shut off his emotions and continued asking questions, listening to their answers, committing them to memory.

No one remembered Carly's ''twin's'' name. No, the name Laura Phelps didn't sound familiar. No, she hadn't been at all friendly or talkative the way most family members were.

''Most of our patients are in pretty serious shape,'' one of them explained. ''It's not like having surgery or a heart attack, getting well and going home. These people are in it for the long haul. Their families are usually sick with worry, and they need someone to talk to. They want reassurance. They want to be convinced that their child or spouse or parent is going to be all right.''

''But the cousin didn't want anything from us,'' another one took over. ''Except Ross,'' she added with a grin.

''How often did she come to visit Carly?''

''Every day in the beginning. Sometimes she just stood there by the bed and looked at her, but usually she talked to her the whole time.''

''Talked?'' Buck echoed.

''A lot of people believe that on some level, a comatose patient can hear what goes on around them,'' the charge nurse said. "We talk to our patients a lot. All the families do. It's not unusual."

His throat was too dry to swallow. Keep it professional, he reminded himself. He could deal with the personal later. "And when the patient wakes up, does she ever remember the things you say to her?"

"Sometimes. I think we've all experienced that." Several heads bobbed in agreement.

"You said the cousin came every day in the beginning. Did that change?"

"Yeah." This time it was Ross speaking. "After a while she quit coming. She just disappeared."

She seemed to make a habit of that, Buck thought bitterly. "Was that unusual?"

"Nah. It's hard coming up here and seeing someone you love in the same condition day after day, never changing, never waking up, never knowing you're here," Ross explained. "Some families stay pretty devoted. Sometimes it's only the mother or the wife or the sister who keeps coming back. Sometimes the whole family gives up. For all practical purposes, their child or whatever is gone. They have to get on with their lives."

Buck returned the photograph to the envelope, thanked them, then asked the charge nurse for directions to the nearest pay phone.

"If it's a local call, you can use the phone here." She set it on the counter, then started to turn away. "Oh, Sheriff? How *is* Carly?"

He smiled a little. "She's fine. Beautiful. Doesn't remember a thing."

"Give her our best, will you?" the petite woman asked before walking off.

He called Dr. Parker's office and waited a moment for the doctor to come on the line. "More questions, Sheriff?" he asked.

"A couple. Has it been proven that a comatose patient can later remember things that were said during the coma?"

"Yes, it's been documented. But it's not the kind of recall where you can remember a conversation you overheard three or four months ago. It's certainly not a total recall, but more like bits and pieces. Words. Phrases."

"Descriptions? Actions?"

"Not usually in any great detail, but, yes, that's possible."

"One more. Did you know Carly had a regular visitor the first few weeks she was in the extended-care unit? A woman who looked enough like her to be her twin?"

"No, I didn't. I was only one of a number of doctors seeing Carly at that time. I didn't become her primary doctor until she was transferred out of the unit. It wasn't my responsibility to deal with her family or friends." He paused to murmur to someone in his office, then asked, "Is this person important?"

"I don't know," he lied. "Thanks for your time, Doctor."

Outside the hospital, he breathed deeply, and the nervousness returned, accompanied by a tightness in his chest. His theories regarding Laura had been right as far as they went, but he hadn't counted on the curves. He hadn't counted on the holes.

He hadn't counted on two women.

At his house on Carly's second day in town, he'd wondered why she was so set against the idea of being Laura. She would have a home and a family, he'd argued, and she had simply looked at him. *You can't ask me to give up my only identity on the chance that you might be able to supply me with a new one,* she had said quietly, sadly.

He had been arrogant. He'd been so damned sure that she was Laura, so positive that all he had to do was prove it.

Instead, he had proved that she *wasn't* Carly.

And now it looked as if he'd proved that she wasn't Laura, either.

Changing your name wouldn't change who you are because of those memories. But all I have, Sheriff, is a name. Take that away from me, and I have nothing. Nothing.

And he had done just that. He'd taken her name, her very identity, and he'd left her with nothing.

Nothing but his love.

Under the circumstances, that wasn't much of a consolation prize.

Buck spent the next hour looking for proof that Laura had been in Seattle, that she was the woman who had visited Carly in the hospital. For once, something on this case was ridiculously easy to come by.

It took no more than a drive to the headquarters of the Seattle Police Department, a flash of his credentials and a few minutes with a records clerk and a computer, and he had his proof.

Laura Phelps had never gotten a Washington driver's license.

She had never registered her sleek little Corvette with the state.

But she *had* gotten two parking tickets.

Outside the hospital Buck had just left.

While Carly was a patient there.

Thursday was the first day of October, but it felt more like December, Carly thought, kneeling in front of the fireplace, sliding crumpled newspaper under the kindling as Buck had shown her. It had rained hard last night, and this morning delicately etched ice crystals covered everything outside. If this was autumn, she would like to see what winter was like here. The cabin would be beautiful covered with snow, like a scene on a Christmas card. She could hike through the snow-quiet woods and build a snowman and, best of all, snuggle with Buck beneath his grandmother's quilt in front of a blazing fire.

If she was here this winter.

If he felt like doing anything at all with Laura.

The paper was wadded tightly so that it burned slowly, the flame seeking out each bent and crinkled edge. The kindling on the grate above crackled and burned, sending little curls of smoke into the air, giving out its sweet smoky fragrance. Carly huddled beneath the quilt, drinking a mug of hot chocolate and nursing the fire along, all the while thinking about Buck.

He was due back this evening, and he'd promised to tell her everything. She suspected the news was bad—he'd sounded so reserved when he'd called last night. What had he learned? Had she been the bitch Laura was known to be before the accident? Had her friends been too nice to tell her so? Had Buck recognized more jewelry in the box that sat on her dresser? Had he found clothing, shoes, mementos, anything at all that he knew was Laura's?

She should have told him that it didn't matter. She could handle being Laura. It was a name, after all, a name that belonged to *her*. It was better than nothing. It might not even be so bad. He and Maureen could fill in some of the blanks in her memory. It wasn't the same as remembering, but in twenty, thirty or forty years, she might even come to believe that those remembrances really were memories, and not secondhand retellings.

The fire was burning nicely when the doorbell rang. Carly let the quilt fall to the floor as she stood. Other than her brief visit to the Phelps home yesterday, she hadn't seen anyone else since Buck had left. She hadn't missed the company, though. The only person she really wanted to see was Buck.

Trina was standing on the porch, looking cold and angry. Carly invited her in, but she refused to cross the threshold. "Mother would like to see you," she said stiffly.

"She could have called."

"I had to go to the drugstore to pick up her medicine, so I told her I would come by. Besides, last night's rain washed out the driveway. You'd never get that car up to the house."

Resting one foot on top of the other, Carly hesitated. She could feel sorry for Trina. She could understand why her cousin hated her the way she did. She could even apologize.

But she didn't want to go out with her.

It must have shown in her expression, because Trina muttered a curse. "I told her you wouldn't come. I told her you wouldn't give a damn that she was sick and wanted your company. I told her you'd be too damn selfish to spend an hour or two with her while I run her errands, but she insisted that you had *changed*." She swore again. "You *changed* just enough to worm your way back into her and Buck's lives, didn't you? And now that you're there—"

"I'll get my shoes and jacket," Carly interrupted. Turning away from the door, she went down the hall to Buck's room, shoving her feet into shoes, grabbing a jacket off the doorknob. Back in the living room, she closed the protective mesh screen over the fireplace, picked up her purse and the house keys and met Trina back at the door.

Outside they climbed into the Blazer that was parked behind Carly's car. "Put on your seat belt," Trina instructed as she started the engine. "With your tendency toward having traffic accidents, you should never get into a car without one." Then she gave Carly a long, judging look. "But then, you've been pretty damned lucky. You survived both of them none the worse for wear, didn't you?"

"Both?" Laura had been in an accident? Funny that

Buck had never mentioned it. But maybe it had been a minor one. Maybe he hadn't felt it wasn't important, considering how serious the last one had been.

"You do have the most incredible luck." Trina backed out, then started along the lane. The ruts seemed a little deeper than before, and puddles splashed the underside of the Blazer every few yards. At the end, she looked left and right, then turned onto the highway. Then she glanced at Carly, her expression almost friendly. "But then, everyone's luck runs out eventually."

Carly felt a shiver of unease. It hadn't been a threat, even though it had sounded, had felt, like one. Trina was harmless, remember? She was just a sad, unhappy person with a great deal of frustration.

"Of course, you've been luckier than most," Trina continued. "If your mama had had any sense, she never would have let you be born. Since you were, you should have starved to death, growing up so poor. You should have frozen in that little shack that Nora called home. You should have died with her. You should have been killed a dozen times over by the men you used." She sighed heavily, a long-suffering sound. "You really should have died at the lake."

Another creepy, starting-to-feel-scared shiver trembled through Carly. The lake was evil. It was a cold, dead, awful place. And she should have died there? Was that jealousy speaking? Had Trina ever seen her and Buck at the lake? Had she known why they went there?

"What…" She cleared her throat. "What do you know about the lake?"

"Oh, please, Laura, no more games, all right? I am so damned tired of your games! You've fooled everyone else, but you're not fooling me, damn it! I *know* you! I *know* you, remember! I know the truth!" Her voice rose with each word until she was shouting, making Carly flinch, making her shrink back from the hatred, the malice.

Looking away, Carly saw that they were on Council Street, Nowhere's main north-south street. She'd driven down it a time or two before with Buck, but not when they were going to Maureen's house. She lived on the western edge of town, not the north. As far as Carly knew, there was no way to get to the Phelps house from the north, none at all.

Across from her, Trina was smiling and humming tunelessly to herself. She looked happier, more peaceful, than Carly had ever seen her. She looked more capable. Stronger.

Less stable.

"Where are we going, Trina?" she asked, forcing her voice to remain calm. "Your house isn't this way."

"No," she pleasantly agreed. "It isn't. I've given this a lot of thought, you know. I'm not impulsive, like you. I wouldn't lose my temper and decide to leave town on a whim. I wouldn't get tired of living in Seattle and come rushing back home on a moment's notice. I plan things. I'm very careful. I pay attention to detail."

"I'm sure you do. Listen, Trina, your mother is waiting for us. We don't want to worry her, do we? Especially if she's feeling bad."

Trina took her attention from the road to give Carly an annoyed look. "You haven't heard a thing I've said, have you? After the medication she took this morning, she's sound asleep. Nothing will wake her until this afternoon, and I'll be all through with you by this afternoon. It won't even be hard. I'll finish up here, then go back to Buck's house and pack your clothes in your car and drive it off someplace—I already have the place picked out. It'll never be found there. He'll think you just ran off—*again*. He'll think he was a fool to trust you again. He'll think he should have listened to me, because obviously I'm so much better suited to him.''

"It won't work, Trina," Carly said, hearing the quaver in her voice as her fear grew. "Buck is due back soon. He'll be back before you can pack everything. He'll know—''

"Another of your lies, Laura. Buck is coming back this evening. You said so yourself, and I called his office and double-checked. He won't be in town before six o'clock. That's *hours* away.''

Carly's hands were trembling. Her chest ached, and her lungs felt as if they would burst without fresh air. *Harmless?* She had persuaded herself that this woman was *harmless?* She was planning to kill her! To make it look as if she had simply disappeared again, as if she had run out on Buck again.

Oh, God, she wasn't ready to die. She couldn't, not yet. She had finally discovered what it was like to love someone. She couldn't give that up, couldn't give Buck up. *Please, God,* she prayed. *Please don't let this happen.*

Buck sat at the intersection long after the light had turned green, long after the driver behind him had impatiently honked. The yellow Blazer that had turned onto Council had been Trina's—he was familiar enough with it to recognize it a block away—and that had been Trina behind the wheel.

And sitting across from her had been Carly.

Why? He'd told Carly to keep her distance from Trina. He'd warned her to stay away from her unless either he or Maureen was also present.

He had also told her that Trina was harmless.

A tap at the window startled him. Rolling it down, he found himself facing one of his deputies. "Oh, sorry, Sheriff," the young man said. "I didn't realize—''

"Let me have your hand-held," he demanded. "And your gun."

"What—? But, Sheriff—" Even as he protested, the deputy removed the two-way radio from his gun belt and handed it over, then followed it with his pistol. "Where are you going? What's going on? Do you want me to—?"

Before he finished, Buck was gone, making a sharp turn in front of his cousin Pete. Up ahead he saw Trina's Blazer on a distant curve. Heading where? he wondered, taking a mental inventory of the homes located on that side of town. There wasn't much out there—a couple of ranches, some abandoned houses, a section of national forest that extended into the next county. Where the hell could Trina be headed?

And why the hell was Carly with her?

He should have called her when he'd changed his airline reservations this morning. He should have told her that he was catching an earlier flight, that he had learned all he could in Seattle and was coming home. But it had been early when he'd left her apartment—not even 6:00 a.m.— and he hadn't wanted to disturb her sleep. He'd thought he would surprise her, that he might even catch her still in bed, and, if not, that he could entice her back there.

The hell with surprises.

He kept a safe distance between his truck and Trina's. Periodically they disappeared around a curve in the winding road, making his heart beat a little faster until he rounded the curve himself and saw them again. Driving with one hand, he picked up the radio with the other and contacted the dispatcher. The deputy had already arrived at the office complaining about his strange behavior, and Harvey was standing by.

Quickly he explained where he was and why, and he asked the older deputy to follow. "I can go," he heard one of the men volunteer, and he keyed the mike and ordered everyone but Harvey to stay away. Maybe he was overreacting. Maybe Carly and Trina were on an innocent out-ing—but his instincts said no. And if Carly was in danger, the only backup he wanted, the only one he truly trusted not to get excited and make matters worse, was Harvey.

He had just gotten off the radio when he rounded yet another curve and saw Trina's Blazer parked at the side of the road. The shoulder was wide there, providing parking and a jump-off for a series of seldom-used trails into the woods. Three went off to the right, one to the left. Buck simply stood there for a moment, his mouth dry. He couldn't hear anything but the irregular thud of his heart— no voices, no sounds of passage. How far would he have to follow each trail only to find out that it was the wrong one? They already had a good head start; one false lead would increase that significantly.

He walked to the trailhead on the right. For twenty feet it was one path, overgrown but passable; then it divided into three. One went due north, following the road a ways before disappearing into the trees. The second angled off to the east, and the third traveled southeast. He had hiked all of them himself, knew where they ended, how long they were, how easy they were. He knew the single trail across the road was the longest, the hardest, the least-used because of its difficulty.

And that was the way they had gone.

It was the only choice. If Trina wanted to hurt Carly— and what other reason would she have for bringing her out here?—naturally she would choose some isolated place where no one ever went. This trail started deceptively sim-ple, an easy climb across a sloping hillside, but at the top of the hill, the going got tough. Thick undergrowth, boul-ders, unstable hillsides and steep ravines made the hike arduous, and there was little payoff to make it worthwhile. The views weren't spectacular, the trees weren't impres-sive, and the wildlife hid in the undergrowth.

He raised Harvey on the radio, told him where he was and where he was going and advised his deputy to check the trails on the other side of the road. Harvey, who'd grown up hunting, would have an easier time of it than he would. The deputy could spot signs of recent passage—scuffed dirt, broken twigs, barely noticeable footprints—that Buck would all too easily overlook.

At the top of the hill, he paused, listening. There was his breathing, uneven and tight, and his heartbeat, fueled by fear or the slight exertion or both, and the soft soughing of the wind in the pines. And somewhere, off in the distance ahead, there was a sliding sound, like rocks on a hillside giving way underneath someone's weight, followed by a soft voice.

Feeling with one hand, Buck made sure the pistol was still tucked in his waistband. The radio was inside his jacket pocket, the antenna sticking out beneath his arm, turned off so there would be no unexpected call or squelch to give away his presence.

They were only about five minutes ahead of him. Maybe Carly hadn't dressed for a strenuous hike in the forest. Maybe she was deliberately slowing Trina down. Maybe she had seen him behind them on the highway and was giving him a chance to catch up.

Maybe, after living through so much, she just wasn't ready to give up yet. She wasn't ready to die.

Damn it all, *he* wasn't ready to let her. He never would be.

He pushed ahead, deep into a ravine, up along a rocky ridge. There he found the place where the earlier noise had come from, where a portion of the hillside had collapsed beneath Carly's slight weight, carrying her on a bumpy ride halfway down. He knew it had been Carly because he recognized the shoe that had bounced on down the hill, a red canvas shoe that had landed beyond reach, providing a splash of color against the autumn-dreary landscape. When he'd left for Seattle two days ago, it had been providing a splash of color to his bedroom.

The canvas slip-ons weren't made for climbing these hills, and now, with only one shoe, Carly was at an even bigger disadvantage. That would slow them even more. It would make it easier for him to find them.

Please, God, let it be easy enough.

Let it be in time.

"Okay. That's far enough."

Carly limped to a stop and leaned against the closest tree. Her right foot was so cold that she was hardly aware of the pain. The place on her hip where she'd fallen, though, was another story. It hurt.

Catching her breath, she looked around at the site Trina had chosen to kill her. She'd said in the Blazer that she had given this a lot of thought, that she'd paid a lot of attention to detail. Apparently so. This place was isolated. The trail, such as it was, looked as if it rarely saw any foot traffic. With winter coming, it was almost guaranteed that no one would use it before spring, when nature had had a chance to erase all signs of their presence.

Off to one side of the clearing was a hole, recently dug, gauging by the appearance of the soil mounded beside it. Carly took one quick glance and felt a spasm of pure terror before forcing her gaze away. But after a moment, her eyes were drawn back to it.

Back to her own grave.

It was a little on the small side—but why should she care? She would be dead. It was maybe four feet long and two feet wide, and more than three feet deep. There would be no reports of a body discovered in a shallow grave here. Piled on one side was the dirt taken from the hole; on the other was pine straw, rocks and small branches. By the time

Trina finished covering the grave—*her* grave—with all that, a person would be able to look right at it and never notice that the ground had been disturbed.

"Why, Trina?" she asked, turning her attention back to the other woman. "Because of Buck? You want to kill me because of him?"

"That's part of the reason. You know, I always hated you. Even when you were small, even when I didn't understand what hatred was, that was all I felt for you. You were nobody, nothing. The illegitimate daughter of the town tramp. Your own mother didn't know who your father was because she'd been with so many men. You were poor, worthless, yet you always got what you wanted. And what you wanted was usually *mine*."

Carly wondered if she could make a break for it, if she could run, then immediately discarded the idea. In this tangled, rocky place with only one shoe, already tired and hurting, she didn't stand a chance against Trina in her sturdy hiking boots, not with her knowledge of these woods.

She didn't stand a chance against the small gun in Trina's pocket.

"I'm sorry you're unhappy," she said, trying to keep the panic from her voice. "I'm sorry things turned out the way they did. I'm sorry I hurt you. But—"

"Why did you come back?" Trina demanded. "You knew after the last time that I would surely kill you. Why did you come? Was it Buck? You couldn't stay away from him? Or did you think what happened at the lake was an accident?"

"I—I don't know what you're talking about." Carly was shivering now. Her jacket wasn't adequate for the chill up here, and the sunlight couldn't penetrate the dense canopy the tall pines formed overhead. She tried to control the chill, to ignore it, to channel her energies elsewhere—into survival—but nothing worked. She was trembling from head to toe, inside and out. "What happened at the lake?"

"Amnesia is such a convenient thing, isn't it? All you have to do is pretend, look innocent and say in that helpless little voice, 'I don't know. I don't remember.'" She smiled a vague, eerie smile. "But your little act doesn't fool me. I know it's just one of your games. I know it's a trick. I know you're lying. I know you remember everything—how you treated Buck. How you cheated on him. How you took him away from me."

She moved a few steps closer and lowered her voice. She sounded almost friendly, intimate. "I know you remember what happened that day at the lake. I didn't plan so well then. I made mistakes. When you called from Seattle and said that you were coming home, I had so little time. I couldn't find a way to get my car up to the lake first, and I knew I couldn't trust you to drive up there alone. You would have stopped off at Buck's office. You would have walked right in there, expecting to be greeted with open arms. You would have forgotten about me and the lake."

"So you...." Carly was beginning to understand, and it frightened her, God, more than anything else. "You went up there with me. In my car."

Trina's smile was smug and condescending. "Ah, so you do remember." As quickly as it had come, the smile disappeared, leaving her troubled and annoyed. "But I had to be home when Mother got there. I had to walk all the way back into town from the lake. You used to laugh at me for jogging—remember that, cousin? You said it was such an unladylike thing to do. You said you would never be caught dressed like that, sweating in public. *You* couldn't have made it home from the lake, not as quickly as I did."

Carly wet her lips, but the chill breeze dried them again. "So we went to the lake in my car. I—I don't remember what happened next. My head..." She touched the scar on her forehead.

"Wrong accident," Trina said flatly. "I wanted to destroy your face. Did you know that? All my life I had heard what a beauty cousin Laura was. I had seen men look right through me when you were around, as if I didn't even exist. I'd heard those nasty old biddies in town talk about poor Trina, who doesn't even begin to compare to Laura. Beautiful Laura. Lovely Laura. Gorgeous Laura. God, I hated that! I wanted to smash your face so badly that no one would *ever* call you beautiful again."

She sighed, the corners of her mouth turning down. "But I couldn't do that. No matter how I hated you, no matter how evil you were, I couldn't touch your face. So I hit you on the back of the head. That was considerate of me, wasn't it, considering that you survived?"

Carly didn't know if she was serious, if she expected an answer. Raising one shaking hand, she gestured for Trina to go on.

"None of this rings a bell yet?" She smiled maliciously. "It's no wonder. I hit you hard, hard enough to knock you down, hard enough to knock you out. And I put you in your car, in your precious little Corvette that you flaunted to everyone, and I pushed the car into the lake. The car was so little, so light. One good hard shove, and it went rolling down the hill as easy as you please. It hit the water with a big splash, and it sunk all the way to the bottom."

"And you stood there and watched it sink. But you didn't have much time, so you had to leave. You had to get back home."

"And you got out. Somehow, some way, you got out. If only I'd had more time," she said with a regretful sigh.

But this time she'd have all the time in the world, Carly thought, trying to swallow over the fear rising in her throat.

This time she'd found an isolated spot, dug a grave, made plans to explain Carly's absence.

This time she was going to shoot her and bury her under three feet of solid earth.

This time she was going to succeed.

"Walk over there, please," Trina requested as she withdrew the revolver from her pocket. It was a small one, barely bigger than the palm of her hand, but it looked deadly enough. It scared Carly enough.

"No."

Trina raised her gaze from the weapon to Carly. "You've made my life hell since the day you were born. Just once let it be easy. Do as I say."

Carly just shook her head. Trina was going to shoot her regardless. She wasn't going to walk over to the waiting grave and politely fall into it when she died.

"You're not going to walk away from here, Laura. I won't make the same mistake again. I'm going to shoot you, and I'm going to watch you die, and I'm going to bury you. You're not going to hurt anyone, most of all *me*, again."

"You want to kill me, go ahead," Carly said, feeling as if her heart was going to stop beating first, as if sheer terror was going to end her life long before Trina's gun could. "But I'm not making anything easy for you. Never, Trina."

The other woman shrugged, a have-it-your-way gesture. "It doesn't matter to me where you die, Laura, as long as you do. I've been using this gun for years—Buck taught me himself—and I'm really very good with it. I've got six shots here—"

"And I've got fifteen here."

When Buck stepped out of the trees, Carly's knees buckled, and she sank to the ground in a small, shivering heap. Keeping his borrowed automatic level with Trina's head, he gave Carly a quick glance to make certain she was all right before turning back to Trina. "Give me the gun, Trina," he commanded, his voice as cold as the air.

Her grip on the revolver didn't loosen. "I can't do that, Buck. Don't you see? She tricked me last time. She let me believe she was dead, and she went away, and she laughed at me. She spent three years laughing at me, taunting me. I have to kill her this time—for you, for Mother, for me, for everyone. She'd be better off dead, you know that. We would *all* be better off with her dead."

"She *is* dead, Trina," he said quietly. "Laura *is* dead. This is Carly."

Trina turned a beseeching look on him. "No! That's part of her lies, Buck! That's part of why she has to die!"

"When did you go to the lake with Laura?"

She had to think about it for a moment, had to clear the hatred and rage from her mind. "December. A few weeks before Christmas. She came home for Christmas."

"Carly was in the hospital in Seattle before Christmas. She was there from the middle of November until the beginning of February. She was in a coma then. Trina, she isn't Laura. She *looks* like her, but she's not." He paused to let that sink in, then requested again, "Give me the gun, Trina. Please."

She moved as if to obey, then suddenly jerked back. "You're lying. You're trying to protect her. You let her get under your skin again, and, just like before, you'll do anything for her."

With a slight gesture, he drew her attention to the gun he held, the barrel only inches from her head. "Don't make me shoot you, Trina. Think about what that would do to your mother. Think about what that would do to me, having to kill a friend."

Behind him there was a rustle of steps—Harvey, he knew—but Buck didn't take his eyes off Trina. There were so many expressions flitting across her face—anger, sorrow, despair, grief. Such grief. After a moment, tears filling her eyes, she lowered her arm and offered the gun to him. Taking it, he lowered his own weapon, then stepped aside so Harvey could handcuff her.

Carly was still sitting in a tiny, shuddering heap on the cold ground. Buck crossed to her, crouching in front of her. Shrugging out of his coat, he wrapped it around her, then drew her into his arms. She didn't cry—she was stronger than he'd imagined—but she trembled and shook long after warmth returned to her body. He held her, stroking her, murmuring soft reassurances to her.

Finally she lifted her head and met his gaze. Her eyes, like Trina's, held such despair. Such grief. "I'm not Carly," she whispered.

Silently he shook his head.

"And I'm not Laura, either, am I?"

Wishing he could have broken the news to her more gently, he shook his head again.

What little strength she'd found drained away. He had to bend close to hear her whisper.

"I guess that means I'm nobody." Her little laugh bordered on hysterical. "Just like Trina said."

It was cold at the lake, colder than any October day should be. Buck stood on the shore, his hands shoved into his pockets, his narrowed gaze locked on the surface of the water, and watched as the divers in their wet suits came out. They gave the signal that the car was hooked up, and Harvey passed it on to the wrecker driver. The winch moved slowly, straining, struggling against the weight of the car and the resistance of the water.

Behind Buck on the hill a murmur went up from the crowd as the rear end of the little red Corvette broke the surface. The winching became easier as more of the car was freed from the lake's hold, and finally, with a smooth whine, the car was deposited on the bank.

For a long moment he simply stood there. He knew what he was going to find inside, and right now, God help him, he wasn't sure he could bear it. He had hated Laura, true. More times than he could remember he had wished her dead, but he hadn't meant it. Damn it, he had never really meant it.

Off to the side of the car were the divers, two husky young men from Missoula who volunteered their skills for searches such as this, and one of his deputies. Harvey was nearby, waiting with his camera to take the crime-scene photos. Next to him stood Doc Thomas, who doubled as the county's coroner, and three men from the local funeral home who would transport the body to the state medical examiner's office for autopsy.

And standing at the top of the hill, her arm around Maureen's shoulders, giving comfort when she needed it herself, was Carly.

Beautiful, innocent Carly.

Carly, whose name, whose identity, whose very sense of self, he had stolen.

Carly, who had said two hours ago with such heartrending despair, "I guess that means I'm nobody."

Slowly he walked toward the car. Water was draining from it, forming small rivulets that raced back to the lake. The shiny red that had never shown so much as a fingerprint was caked with mud and weeds. The windows were up and covered with a milky film from the lake bottom, but he could see through them. When he swallowed hard, when he summoned up his courage, he could see.

She lay twisted in the driver's seat, the belt holding her body in place. He recognized the skirt, black wool with a demure slit, and the blouse, red silk and cut revealingly low.

That was all he could recognize.

She had wanted to destroy Laura's face, Trina had said. She had succeeded. What had once been incredibly beautiful was now grotesque. What had once brought men dreams could now haunt nightmares.

"Buck? You okay, son?"

It was Harvey, standing somewhere close behind him.

"Yeah," he replied, but he didn't sound it. He didn't feel it. "Tell Janssen to get those people out of here. You can take your pictures now."

And *he* could go up the hill and tell Maureen that Laura, lovely, seductive, alluring Laura, was dead.

As he climbed the hill, the deputies at the top ordered everyone back, forcing them over the crest and back down into the parking lot. Everyone except Maureen and Carly. They were allowed to wait.

Maureen looked as if she'd aged twenty years. There was no light in her eyes, no joy, no happiness. Only two people had been truly important to her in the past twenty years— Trina and Laura. And now Trina was locked up in jail, charged with murdering Laura. Maureen was a good woman, he thought compassionately, too good to suffer something like this, and with a surge of anger he damned both Trina and Laura. He damned himself.

He didn't have to speak when he reached them. The old lady looked at him and saw the answer in his eyes. With a soft sob, she turned away, leaving him alone with Carly. She looked as pale and insubstantial as the wispy clouds overhead, this woman who had stood up to a killer with a gun. He longed to hold her tight, to forget his job and his responsibilities, to forget his guilt and sorrow, and simply hold her.

But he couldn't.

"Go home with her, will you?" he asked, sounding harsh and unfeeling and cold. "Stay with her."

Carly nodded. She looked as if she wanted to say something, but couldn't find the words. Instead, she reached up and laid her hand gently against his cheek. That was all— just that little touch—yet it told him plenty.

It told him that she didn't hate him for what he'd done. It was a long way from loving him, but it was a start.

"I'll call you."

With a nod, she withdrew her hand, then started after Maureen. And with a soul-weary sigh, he started back down the hill. Back to the car.

Back, for the last time, to Laura.

I'll call you.

Carly sat on a wicker settee on Maureen's front porch, watching the sky lighten by degrees, and wondered where Buck was. What he was doing. When he would call her.

How he was feeling.

Yesterday must have been hard for him. He'd hated Laura, had on occasion wished that she was dead. But Carly knew those wishes had been born of anger, of frustration, of helplessness. He hadn't really wanted Laura to die. He would have given his own life to protect hers.

But she was dead, and Buck was probably blaming himself. And he blamed himself for what had happened with Trina in the forest yesterday. He blamed himself for proving that Carly was neither Carly nor Laura.

When he called her, she would remind him that he had nothing to do with Laura's death. Wishes weren't magical. His hadn't gathered in the darkness somewhere and joined forces with Trina in order to come true.

And the rest didn't matter. He had warned her against being alone with Trina, and she had disregarded it. She had ignored her own convictions that Trina was dangerous, and she had nearly paid for her foolishness with her life. That wasn't his fault. And the name…well, that didn't matter.

He had offered to stop searching, but she had encouraged him to continue. If she didn't like what he'd found out, she had no one to blame but herself.

And on this chilly Friday morning, as the rising sun cast its soft pink glow over the hills to the east, she was so happy to be alive that she didn't mind not having a name. She didn't feel like blaming anyone for anything.

She shifted on the settee, and it creaked beneath her. Wearing a gown and robe borrowed from Maureen and snuggled underneath a blanket taken from her guest room, she was warm and cozy. She felt peaceful. She felt damned near perfect.

A little puff of dust from down the hill announced the visitor's arrival first. Today, Maureen had told her, they would have plenty of company. All her friends would bring sympathy and food, and all her enemies—Carly couldn't imagine the old lady having any of those—would bring food, too, and a sharp ear and a sharper tongue. But it was too early for friends or guests. Most of the town was still asleep, like Maureen.

The light bar on the Bronco came into view first. Smiling smugly, Carly huddled deeper into the blanket. It was okay if this was business, if he needed an interview or information from her or if he needed to talk to Maureen, as long as he gave her just a moment of his personal time. Just a kiss or a look or a softly murmured ''how are you?''

He parked in the clearing below, then appeared a moment later on the steps. Sometime since she'd last seen him, he had changed into his uniform. It was wrinkled now, and the Stetson shadowed his face. He hadn't gotten any sleep; she could see from the way he was moving. Bone weary. Mind weary.

When he reached the porch, he didn't sit down beside her or in one of the nearby chairs, but chose to lean against the railing instead. "You're up early," he said, his voice hoarse and scratchy.

"I couldn't sleep." She paused, listening to the softness of her own voice. "You're up late."

"I couldn't sleep, either." He drew his hand over his stubbled jaw, then removed his hat and finger combed his hair. "The report came back from the FBI on your fingerprints. They had no match. Your social security card was issued in Monroe, Louisiana. If we start there—"

Carly gently interrupted him. "Are you all right?"

For a moment he stared blankly at her, then the shadows slipped from his eyes, revealing pain, confusion, sorrow, guilt. "I'm sorry," he whispered. "Oh, God, honey, I'm sorry."

Untangling herself from her cover, she got to her feet and went to him, wrapping her arms around him, resting her head on his shoulder. She didn't say anything. She just held him and comforted him. She felt the shudders ripple through him, felt the clenching and unclenching of his muscles, heard the pain-sharp breaths he dragged in.

"I went to Helena last night to identify her body," he said at last, his voice unsteady, his breathing ragged. "The remains... The only things I could identify were her clothes, her jewelry, her purse that was in the car."

"I'm sorry you had to see her that way," Carly whispered. "I'm sorry you had to know."

With a steadying breath, he raised his head and touched her, brushing his fingers lightly through her hair. "She went to Seattle when she left here. Somehow she met you there. Maybe you had mutual acquaintances, or maybe she ran into you accidentally. None of your friends knew about her, which suggests that she was somewhat secretive about the friendship. After your accident, once you were moved out of the intensive care unit, she visited you in the hospital.

She talked to you—and, knowing Laura, what she talked about was herself."

"And that's how I learned so much about her."

He nodded. "Dr. Parker and the nurses I talked to all say that comatose patients can sometimes remember things they hear while in the coma."

"Why was she interested in me? She wasn't the type of woman to have female friends. Why me?"

He gently drew his fingertip down her face from her forehead to her chin. "Because you looked exactly like her. You could pass for her. I doubt there was any real friendship involved on Laura's part. Beautiful women put her on the offensive. A beautiful woman who looked just like her would make her feel threatened and, at the same time, intrigued. She probably had plans for you—maybe nothing definite, maybe just the idea that you might come in handy sometime in the future."

She had been a part of Laura's games, Carly thought. No doubt, whatever Laura had intended for her would have hurt someone—probably Carly, maybe Buck, possibly even Maureen and Trina.

Hugging her tightly again, he pressed his face against her hair. "God, I've ruined everything, haven't I? Because of me, you almost died. You've lost the only thing you had left. I knew how important your name was to you, and I took it, anyway. I took everything."

She smiled bittersweetly. "A name is just a name," she whispered. "*You're* the important thing, Buck. Not knowing my name doesn't matter. You've given me gifts far more valuable than that. You've given me yourself. Your body. Your tenderness. Your caring." She smiled again, a haze of tears blurring her vision. "I always wanted to know how it felt to love someone, and you've given me that, too."

Buck stared down at her, the look in his dark eyes intense. "Stay with me, Carly. I know it's not Seattle. I know you'll have to give up your job and your friends. I know this place holds some bad memories for you. But you can probably find a new job, and you'll make new friends, and I'll do my damnedest to give you better memories. Please. Stay with me."

Her smile was so lovely that it made his heart break. "Is that a proposition, Sheriff?"

"It's anything you want it to be," he replied, then added with a fierce scowl, "As long as it includes marrying me and having babies and living the rest of your life with me."

For a moment the light faded from her eyes, and she bowed her head. "You know I'm not Laura."

"You know I've never wanted you to be."

"I don't even have a name of my own."

"Carly is a beautiful first name, and I'll give you my last name." Gently he tilted her head back again. "Will you marry me?" he asked, his voice hoarse, dark, just this side of pleading.

"Will you love me?" she whispered.

He gazed down at her. Didn't she know he already did, that he always would? Didn't she know she was the only woman he would ever want or need? Then he saw the certainty in her eyes. She knew. She just wanted to hear it. "I do love you, Carly."

"Then I'll marry you."

She rose onto her toes to kiss him, but he gently pushed her back. "Is that all you have to say?"

"I've waited all my life for this. For you." She smiled once more, that lovely smile that hurt his eyes, that trapped his breath deep in his chest, that touched his heart with its innocence. "I love you, Sheriff. I will always love you."

Then he let her kiss him.

Epilogue

Whistling softly to himself, Buck sat down at his desk and picked up the mail there. Usually Harvey opened and sorted it for him, but the older man was out of the office today, so the dispatcher had just tossed it all there together. It was the usual stuff—information for upcoming seminars in Butte, catalogs from a couple of supply houses, a batch of missing-person fliers, a job application from a young woman in Kellogg. He left everything on the desk except the fliers, swiveled his chair around and thumbed through them.

A six-year-old boy believed kidnapped by his noncustodial father.

A fifteen-year-old girl who disappeared on her way home from school.

A seventy-three-year-old Alzheimer's patient who wandered away from a Billings nursing home.

And a thirty-three-year-old woman who disappeared from New Orleans.

Four years ago last month.

Putting the flier down without even a glance at the photo on it, Buck stared out the window and listened to the soft whisper of a voice in his mind.

Louisiana. I wouldn't mind being from there. I like Cajun food. I'm sure I'd love New Orleans. I'm partial to old Southern mansions.

He had wanted to look for answers in the last year, but Carly had said no. Whatever was in the past didn't matter. Her life was here with him. Her future was with him. And, less than reluctantly, he had given in. In his own way he had been as afraid of what he might find as Carly was. What if there was a family who wanted her back? What if there was a husband?

God forbid, what if she had children?

She didn't mind not knowing, and he preferred it over knowing something unpleasant. They'd both been hiding.

Now they might not be able to hide any longer.

Slowly he picked up the flier again and forced himself to look at the picture. It was grainy, black and white, poor quality. It was a snapshot of a beautiful woman with blond hair and haunting eyes, a woman who wore her unhappiness like a veil.

It was a snapshot of his wife.

The text, including a physical description, was brief. Ellen Manning disappeared from New Orleans October 2, four years and nearly five weeks ago. She sold her car and pawned several pieces of jewelry before she left. It was believed she had left voluntarily. The contact at the bottom was a private investigations agency in New Orleans.

Buck forced himself to turn around, to reach for the phone, to punch in the eleven numbers. When a woman answered the phone, he almost hung up; instead, in a voice that wasn't his own, he requested to speak to the person listed on the flier.

"This is Sheriff Buck Logan in Nowhere, Montana," he said stiffly. "I received a flier from your office on a woman named Ellen Manning." He faltered then, had to close his eyes and force the next words out. "I may have some information on her."

Ellen Manning had been the only child of wealthy parents. She had lived all her life in New Orleans, had grown up there, gone to college there, buried her parents there and married there.

She had also run away from there four years ago.

Carly stared out the car window, watching the city go by, seeing none of it. She and Buck had been in New Orleans for three days now, and it had been everything she'd expected—exotic, exciting and hot. She loved the city, loved the food and the dialects and the people. She loved the French Quarter and the lazy wide river. But she'd seen all that she wanted.

She had heard more than she wanted.

She wanted to go home now.

Because of the family money, Ellen had never needed to work, but she had given freely of her time. She had been on the boards of several local charities. She'd had a particular interest in charities involving children. What hadn't interested her was the day-to-day details of running the company she had inherited upon her parents' death. When her husband—Carly shied away from the idea of having any husband besides Buck. When the man Ellen had married suggested that she turn everything over to him, she had done so.

Had she known that he was methodically destroying everything her grandfather and father had built? Had she known that he was spending company money—*her* money—on other women, supporting them in style, treating them like queens? Had that started the trouble between them?

Men like Curt Manning rarely needed an excuse, Buck had told her last night in bed. They were bullies, afraid of those who could defend themselves, cruel with those who couldn't. *She* would have shot him, Carly decided. The first time he had hit her, the first time he'd slapped her, she would have put an end to it. She wouldn't have stayed around long enough to suffer. She sure as hell wouldn't have given him a chance to leave those last two scars.

Buck had told her about those last night, too, about what had caused them. She hadn't been too surprised. Maybe she had known all along that they hadn't come from the accident. Maybe she had known that their source had been darker, deliberate, more brutal.

But Ellen had stayed around. She'd begun making her plans when her hus—the man had threatened to kill her. With her best friend's help—Lydia Benoit, the lawyer sitting in the front seat of the car—she had traveled to Texas and found Carly Johnson's grave. She had gotten Carly's birth certificate and had gone to Monroe to apply for a social security card. She had sold her car, all the jewelry Curt had given her—paid for with her own money, of course—and had taken all the money she could from the bank. Then she had bought a bus ticket to someplace away from Louisiana. She wouldn't tell Lydia where or under what name. She had been terrified that Curt would follow her, that he would use whatever weapons he could—including Lydia—against her.

He had been angry and made an attempt to find her; then he had put her out of his mind. He had continued to live in her house and run her company and spend her money, and once the money ran out, he had filed for divorce and skipped town.

But the company had been merely crippled by his management, not destroyed. The board of directors took over and saved the business and the family home, and then they had begun searching for Ellen. State by state in an ever-growing radius, they had sent fliers to every police and sheriff's department. Montana, Idaho and Washington had been their last hope.

The car glided to a stop in front of a house—a mansion, really. *I'm partial to old Southern mansions,* she had once told Buck, and this place certainly was. It looked like something out of a Civil War movie—three stories tall, huge white columns, galleries and balconies, tall windows and green shutters. The front lawn could hold most of the football fields Buck had played on in his career, she thought with a smile and a faint wish that she had seen him play, that she had known him then.

The grass was green even in November, and planted all along the winding brick drive were hundreds of azaleas. Massive live oaks dotted the grounds with their eerie hangings of Spanish moss.

A beautiful old Southern mansion.

And, according to Lydia Benoit, it belonged to her.

She sighed softly. What in the world would she do with a Southern mansion in Montana?

Glancing around the car, she saw that everyone was watching her. Even the driver, a solemn tight-lipped man who hadn't spoken a word, was watching her in the rear-view mirror. She looked from Lydia, her one-time best friend, the woman who had helped her escape the nightmare her marriage had become, to Buck, the man who had made all her dreams come true. He looked a little wary. Unsure. When he'd married her a year ago, he had married a woman who had nothing, not even a name. Now his wife was rich. Did he think it would make a difference? Foolish man, she thought with a gentle smile. He thought it might.

Reaching into her purse, she withdrew her wallet, then

the two small photographs. She handed them to Lydia in the front seat. ''Do you know those people?''

Lydia's smile was genuine and warm. ''This is you— first grade at St. Francis—and this is you with your parents. Richard and Melanie Hamilton.''

Buck saw Carly's tiny satisfied smile as she accepted the pictures and returned them to her wallet. Then she climbed out of the car, closed the door and simply stood there looking at the house.

''None of this means anything to her, does it?'' Lydia asked.

''No. She doesn't remember.''

''We were best friends from first grade on. She convinced her father to give me a job when I finished law school. She used to say that someday I could run the company for her.'' Her expression grew troubled. ''Until she married Curt.''

''Did she love him?''

The woman sighed. ''I don't know. Her parents had just died. She had a load of responsibility dumped into her lap. She was grieving and confused and lonely. I think mostly she felt gratitude for him. He paid attention to her. He made her feel less alone.''

''He used her.'' Like Laura had used him. It was no wonder he and Carly had been drawn together. They shared more in common than either of them had guessed.

Excusing himself, he got out and walked around the car. Joining Carly on the grass, he wrapped his arms around her from behind. ''Nice place.''

She responded with a murmur that he felt rather than heard.

''You could fit the entire town of Nowhere on the grounds.'' He sighed softly, tickling her ear, making her wriggle. ''You're a rich woman.''

Turning in his arms, Carly filled her hands with his shirt. "It's snowing in Montana."

"And eighty degrees in New Orleans."

"Let's go home, Buck. They're not expecting us until next week. We won't tell anyone we're back. We'll sneak out to the cabin, turn off the lights, lock the doors, snuggle under the covers and make love until spring. Can we do that?" she asked wistfully.

"Honey, with money like this, I imagine you can do whatever you want," he said with a chuckle. Then he grew serious. "But what about this? What about Ellen? What about the company?"

"I've been giving that some thought." She looked up at him, reminding him of that long-ago day in Nowhere. *I've been thinking,* she had announced and given him a smile that had damn near destroyed him right then and there. Now he saw it often. He lived with it. He lived *for* it.

"The board has proven that they're more than capable of running the place without my interference. I'd like to leave it in their hands and maybe set up some sort of charitable foundation. The money could be used to help children. And—" She grinned endearingly. "I know a certain sheriff's department that could use a little help into the computer age."

As quickly as the grin came, it faded, leaving her soft and serious and sad. "And maybe some of it could go to help women whose husbands hurt them."

He gazed down at her, loving her more in that instant than ever before. "I think Ellen would like that. But are you sure…? That's a lot of money you'll be giving away— more than I'll ever make in a lifetime. Are you—"

Before he could finish, she laid her fingers over his mouth. "Ellen Manning was a sad woman who found joy in nothing but her charities. Her parents were gone, her marriage a nightmare, her husband abusive." Then she smiled. "But I have a husband I love dearly, a husband who loves me, and a home I wouldn't trade for ten places like this. And in about seven months or so, I'm going to have a beautiful, healthy, happy baby. *We're* going to have a baby."

Before he could respond to her surprise, before he could lift her in his arms and twirl her around on the fancy green lawn, before he could kiss her and hold her and get down on his knees to thank her and God, she continued.

"Ellen Manning was a rich woman, Buck. But I..." Removing her fingers, she gently kissed him. "I'm one lucky lady."

*   *   *   *   *

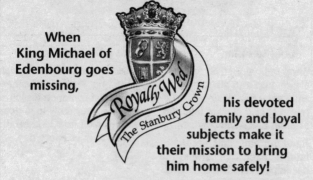

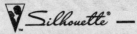

If you enjoyed what you just read,
then we've got an offer you can't resist!

Take 2
bestselling novels FREE!
Plus get a FREE surprise gift!

Clip this page and mail it to The Best of the Best™

IN U.S.A.
3010 Walden Ave.
P.O. Box 1867
Buffalo, N.Y. 14240-1867

IN CANADA
P.O. Box 609
Fort Erie, Ontario
L2A 5X3

YES! Please send me 2 free Best of the Best™ novels and my free surprise gift. Then send me 4 brand-new novels every month, which I will receive before they're available in stores. In the U.S.A., bill me at the bargain price of $4.24 plus 25¢ delivery per book and applicable sales tax, if any*. In Canada, bill me at the bargain price of $4.74 plus 25¢ delivery per book and applicable taxes**. That's the complete price and a savings of over 15% off the cover prices—what a great deal! I understand that accepting the 2 free books and gift places me under no obligation ever to buy any books. I can always return a shipment and cancel at any time. Even if I never buy another book from The Best of the Best™, the 2 free books and gift are mine to keep forever. So why not take us up on our invitation. You'll be glad you did!

185 MEN C229
385 MEN C23A

Name	(PLEASE PRINT)	
Address	Apt.#	
City	State/Prov.	Zip/Postal Code

* Terms and prices subject to change without notice. Sales tax applicable in N.Y.
** Canadian residents will be charged applicable provincial taxes and GST.
   All orders subject to approval. Offer limited to one per household.
   ® are registered trademarks of Harlequin Enterprises Limited.

BOB00   ©1998 Harlequin Enterprises Limited

January 2001
TALL, DARK & WESTERN
#1339 by Anne Marie Winston

February 2001
THE WAY TO A RANCHER'S HEART
#1345 by Peggy Moreland

March 2001
MILLIONAIRE HUSBAND
#1352 by Leanne Banks
Million-Dollar Men

April 2001
GABRIEL'S GIFT
#1357 by Cait London
Freedom Valley

May 2001
THE TEMPTATION OF
RORY MONAHAN
#1363 by Elizabeth Bevarly

June 2001
A LADY FOR LINCOLN CADE
#1369 by BJ James
Men of Belle Terre

MAN OF THE MONTH

For twenty years Silhouette has been giving
you the ultimate in romantic reads. Come join
the celebration as some of your favorite authors
help celebrate our anniversary with the most
sensual, emotional love stories ever!

Available at your favorite retail outlet.

Silhouette®
Where love comes alive™